"Gina Holder has The Puzzle With through the pages recommended!"

...g. Highly

— MARY ALFORD, *USA TODAY* BEST-SELLING
AUTHOR

"A heart-pounding, fast-paced, wonderfully twisty new series opener! In this gripping romantic suspense, professional stakes turn personal as two experts are thrust into what seems to be a straightforward assignment —but nothing in this story is simple, and complexity builds by the minute. As everything unravels, both characters find the healing they never knew they needed. I couldn't wait to see how it all connected, and Holder brought all the moving parts full circle with a breathtaking climax."

— JOANNA DAVIDSON POLITANO, CAROL
AWARD-WINNING AUTHOR

"Fasten your seat belts--The Puzzle Within will take you on a spin with hairpin twists and turns you won't see coming."

— PATRICIA BRADLEY, *USA TODAY*
BESTSELLING AUTHOR OF ROMANTIC
SUSPENSE

Published by Scrivenings Press LLC
15 Lucky Lane
Morrilton, Arkansas 72110
https://ScriveningsPress.com

Printed in the United States of America

Paperback ISBN 978-1-64917-472-7

eBook ISBN 978-1-64917-473-4

Editor: Erin R. Howard

Cover by Hannah Linder Designs.

All characters are fictional, and any resemblance to real people, either factual or historical, is purely coincidental.

THE PUZZLE WITHIN

THE GAME MASTERS | BOOK ONE

GINA HOLDER

Scrivenings
PRESS
Quench your thirst for story.
www.ScriveningsPress.com

To my grandma, Elaine Allison.
I wish you were here to see this.
Thank you for always believing in me.

Gina L. Holden

Ps. 45:1
Prov. 25:11

"For my thoughts are not your thoughts, neither are your ways my ways, saith the LORD. For as the heavens are higher than the earth, so are my ways higher than your ways, and my thoughts than your thoughts" (Isaiah 55:8-9 KJV).

CHAPTER 1

Friday, 02 February
1700 Hours

Ari planted her palms flat against the desktop and locked gazes with Senior Special Agent Matt Updike. *I didn't become a federal agent to babysit a diplomat's spoiled daughter.*

"Come on, Matt. Don't do this to me. I deserve a second chance."

"This is your second chance."

"I can't do this assignment."

Matt thrust the chair backward, rounded the desk, then closed the distance between them in two steps. "You don't have a choice."

His stale coffee breath blasted her in the face.

She wrinkled her nose, crossed her arms, and refused to back down. "I'll take it to the top."

A muscle twitched in his cheek. "Assignment came from the top. Director Carlton's orders. Shrink doesn't think you're ready." His expression softened. "Not yet."

"Not ready? How am I not ready? It's been six months."

Six months since her life spiraled out of control.

Matt raised his hands, palms out. "I know that, but there's nothing I can do."

She tried another angle. "Why isn't the Bureau of Diplomatic Security handling the situation? That's their jurisdiction, isn't it?"

He cleared his throat and returned to his seat.

"Matt?" A knot formed in her stomach.

"DSS is handling it." His gaze darted to a manila folder on the desk. "They're borrowing you." He air quoted the word *borrowing*.

"What am I, a library book? Why me?"

"Ambassador Nathan Van Sloan personally requested you. That's the only reason the director hasn't placed you on permanent leave. Carlton is not convinced you're fit for active duty." He jutted his chin toward the folder. "Don't make this any more difficult than necessary."

With a sigh, Ari perched on the desk and flipped through the contents of the file. A two-page report outlined the threats Ambassador Van Sloan had received of late. The most recent threat targeted his daughter, Bridgette.

Ari read the photographed note.

Daughters are life's greatest gift. Time with yours has ended.
-Enigma

She raised her head. "What do we know about this Enigma person?"

"Very little. That's the third threat Van Sloan has received signed that way, but no one's seen the perpetrator. No fingerprints. Nothing."

"Where was this message located?"

"Miss Van Sloan's bedroom. On her pillow."

Ari ran her finger over the 8x10 glossy of Bridgette Van Sloan, the ambassador's only child. The girl had been adorable as a toddler, but now at nineteen, she was stunning. Long blonde hair fell in soft curls over the shoulders of a blue prom dress. Her arched eyebrows and duck lips matched the flirty persona she gave off to the world, but a smidgen of sadness reflected in her round brown eyes. Ari hadn't seen Bridgette in fifteen years. If half of what the media reported was true—the young woman hadn't changed a bit.

Ari closed the folder. "I still don't understand why it has to be me. I'm not Secret Service. I investigate child abductions."

"Look." Matt reclined. "Consider it a trial period. You keep Bridgette Van Sloan safe, and I'll speak to the director about getting you reassigned to CARD."

CARD—the Child Abduction Rapid Deployment team. Her dream job ever since her high school teacher had violated her trust and somehow skirted punishment. But what if the shrink was right? What if she wasn't ready to return to the field?

She shook off her insecurities. "When do I start?"

"Report to the Diplomatic Security Service's resident office here in Platte City first thing Monday morning. Ask for Nicholas Trueheart."

Ari coughed. "Trueheart? Seriously?"

Her boss arched an eyebrow. "You're in no position to judge. *Arizona Powers*. I put my neck on the line to get you this assignment. Don't make me regret it."

"I won't." She turned to leave.

"Hey, Ari?"

"Yeah?"

"For what it's worth, you're a good agent. Don't forget that."

"Thanks." She resisted the urge to slam the door behind her.

I can handle this. Keep the coddled coed safe until Enigma is apprehended. How hard could it be?

———

The Colorado sky blazed brilliant hues of pink and orange over Platte City as Ari maneuvered her teal MINI Cooper Convertible onto the quiet residential street. She signaled, slowed, then made a left turn into the driveway of her two-story townhouse.

Barren rosebushes followed the concrete walk between the drive and her fiery-red front door. Two empty terracotta pots decorated the covered porch. The xeriscaped lawn required minimal attention, a necessity in her line of work.

Ari left the car in the driveway and entered the house through the well-organized garage. She carried her purse and takeout bag inside, then rapped the button on the mudroom wall. The garage door descended, blocking out the rest of the world. Inhaling, she closed the interior door and tried not to flinch when the lock clicked in place. Uneasy goosebumps raised on her arms. Would she ever feel safe enough to park inside the garage?

After setting her purse and dinner on the kitchen counter, she followed her normal routine, moving throughout the house, firearm in hand, checking exits and turning on lights, pausing only to adjust the thermostat, knowing it wasn't the chill in the air that made her shiver. Maybe if the nightmares went away, she could have trusted that nothing would harm her, but until then, she checked and rechecked.

Satisfied that everything was in order, she entered the home office, placed her weapon in the desk drawer, and pressed the on button for her whole-house audio system, starting her playlist.

Elvis's *Love Me Tender* vocalized over the speakers.

She changed into an oversized sweatshirt and leggings, then jogged downstairs to the kitchen, opened the takeout, and took a whiff of the Pad Thai she'd picked up on the way home. Her stomach growled.

The song changed to *Are You Lonesome Tonight?*

She shoved the plastic container into the microwave, set the timer, and pressed the start button. Even the soulful vocalizing of "The King" couldn't drown out the profound silence of living alone. She had gone on a few dates, but her demanding career always drove them away.

At least, that's what she told herself.

The microwave beeped.

Ari's cell phone rang.

Holding the electronic device in place with her shoulder, she retrieved her dinner. "Hey, what's up?"

"How went the meeting with Updike?" Aunt Sheila's voice carried over the line.

The background music morphed into *Hound Dog*.

As Deputy Secretary of Threat Investigations for the Bureau of Diplomatic Security, Aunt Sheila had the necessary security clearance to be informed of the assignment.

"Matt isn't giving me my job back. I'm being loaned out to DSS to protect Bridgette Van Sloan." Ari trudged into the living room, turned on the TV, muted the evening news, and settled onto the couch, tucking one leg under her.

"I know it's not what you wanted, but it's better than being let go, right?"

Ari slurped noodles. "That's one way to look at it."

"What's the problem? Is security detail beneath your pay grade?"

Ari jabbed at a sliver of red bell pepper. "No, it's not that. It's just not … you know … it's not what I do." She stabbed the vegetable with the fork tines.

"Which is what?"

Her head formed one answer, but her heart gave another. Unfortunately, her head and lips were on better speaking terms. "I track down the bad guys and throw them in jail."

Aunt Sheila coughed. "I thought you rescued missing children."

"That, too."

Ari's thoughts shot to all her open case files that had been reassigned to other agents after she had been admitted to the mental facility. Were any of them still active? Her mind wandered back to that last investigation—the one where everything went wrong.

"You there?"

Ari blinked. "I'm here. What were you saying?"

"I said it sounds like you're focusing on the wrong thing. Be patient. God isn't finished with you."

"I don't think He's paying much attention to us down here."

A heavy sigh carried over the phone. They'd had this argument before. "We have to believe He knows what He's doing, even when we don't understand."

Ari bit her lip and tasted blood. "A good God would never allow wicked men to get away with their crimes."

If I don't stop the bad guys, who will?

There was a long pause, then Aunt Sheila's voice broke the silence. "He will punish evil. Someday."

"Not soon enough for me."

A mortifying thought entered Ari's mind. "You didn't have anything to do with me getting this assignment, did you?"

Her aunt cleared her throat. "I might have made a recommendation."

"But Matt said Van Sloan requested me."

"He did. At my suggestion."

Ari groaned. "Aunt Sheila!"

"I was just trying to help."

"What happens when people find out? You'll be accused of nepotism."

"I can live with that."

Ari stuffed her mouth full of noodles, chewed, then swallowed. "Want me to stop by your office on my way in?"

"I won't be there. I'm out of town for the next couple of weeks. My office knows how to get in touch with me, if needed."

"What can you tell me about this agent, Nicholas Trueheart?"

Might as well get the four-one-one while she was at it.

"He's—hold on."

Voices chattered in the background. Aunt Sheila's voice grew soft, then louder again. "Sorry, I have to go. Can we talk later?"

"Sure."

"I'll be praying."

Ari appreciated the sentiment. Even if it was unnecessary. "Love you, Aunt Sheila."

"Love you, too."

The call ended. Ari placed her phone in her lap and turned up the volume on the television. She finished her lukewarm stir fry and set the empty container on the coffee table, then wiped her mouth with a paper napkin.

The Channel Four logo swirled around the screen, and the female newscaster began the evening report. "Local authorities have reopened the investigation into the death of Jayda Roach—wife of Raymond Roach, the CEO of AegisTech Solutions, and the daughter of retired General Cal Burgess.

"Four years ago, Roach was tragically murdered in her home. Local law enforcement identified no viable leads or suspects, leaving the case unresolved. However, new evidence has surfaced, reigniting the hope for justice and holds the potential to uncover the truth and lead to an arrest. When approached for a statement, Chief Wayland had this to say."

Police Chief Wayland's face appeared on the screen, where he stood behind a podium surrounded by microphones.

"We are committed to bringing closure to this tragic incident and ensuring that justice will be served. This discovery has provided us with a renewed sense of determination and a promising lead. We will spare no effort in our pursuit of the truth and will hold those responsible accountable for their actions."

The chief disappeared, and the camera returned to the newscaster.

"As the investigation continues, the community eagerly awaits further updates and remains hopeful that this new evidence will finally shed light on the mysterious circumstances surrounding Jayda Roach's untimely demise. Stay tuned for more developments as this story unfolds."

Ari changed the channel to a mind-numbing sitcom, then

rolled to her side. With her head on a throw pillow, knees bent, and feet tucked against her, she closed her eyes, allowing the droning voices on the television to lull her into a fitful sleep.

The ice-cold, pitch-black cellar stank like urine. Stone walls surrounded her on all four sides. A tiny, darkened window prevented anyone from seeing in or out. The little girl, curled on the stained, thin mattress, wouldn't stop crying. An eerie melody resonated from a wooden music box in her tiny hands.

Ari tried to soothe her. "Shh, it's okay. It'll be okay."

She touched the girl's soft cheek.

Eyes lifted to meet Ari's.

Ari's own face stared back at her.

With a scream, Ari bolted upright. Cold sweat soaked her hair, and her pulse raced. Her lungs demanded oxygen. Her skin crawled, and the scent of mildew burned her nostrils. The texture of sandpaper scratched her throat. Another nightmare.

Would they ever stop?

Hands trembling, she swiped her glass from the coffee table and gulped down the lukewarm water. She clutched the glass to her chest and rocked, her heart pounding against her ribcage. The disturbing dream lingered with an unease she couldn't shake.

Closing her eyes, she drew a deep breath, attempting to block out the depressing scene.

According to the doctor, the weight of her failures and of the horrors she'd witnessed over the years had left a heavy burden on her psyche, generating the hallucinations. Her brain was attempting to resolve the painful circumstances those victims endured.

Only ...

The nightmares had existed long before she'd become an FBI agent.

While the sitcom on the television continued its pointless blather, Ari forced herself to focus. She would face whatever challenges this assignment presented, just like she always had. She couldn't let personal problems or haunting dreams distract her from doing what needed to be done.

With a determined sigh, she set the glass on the table and stood. After stretching her stiff muscles, she shuffled into the kitchen to make a fresh pot of coffee. The night was young, and she had preparations to make and people to research before Monday.

Psychoanalyzing her nightmares would have to wait for another day.

CHAPTER 2

2200 Hours

Nick gulped a mouthful of black coffee and grimaced. Cold. Yuck.

He lowered the cup and raked his fingers through his hair for what felt like the millionth time today, unable to tear his gaze away from the image on his computer screen.

What kind of kook sent a diplomat a jar of sheep's eyeballs?

It was undoubtedly the strangest thing he had ever come across, or at least close to it.

Deciphering whether something was a genuine threat or simply odd fell under his jurisdiction, and often, it turned out to be the latter.

Like the eyeballs.

Some nut's idea of a practical joke.

He chuckled and powered off the computer. Stretching his back with his arms over his head, he let out a sigh, then rolled down his shirt sleeves and rebuttoned the cuffs.

The other cubicles had emptied hours ago.

He stood, grabbed his suit jacket from his office chair and slipped it on, then straightened the collar. With a quick motion, he transferred his belongings—keys, phone, and wallet—from the desk drawer to his pockets.

Aiming the disposable cup at the trashcan, Nick mimicked an NBA All-Star. To his dismay, the lid popped off upon impact, splashing trace amounts of liquid onto the commercial carpet. What a mess. He'd thought it was empty.

He strolled down the dark hallway to the break room and snatched a wad of paper towels from the counter. On his way back, movement at the end of the hall caught his eye. "Who's there? This office is closed."

He quickened his pace and jogged into the open space, finding nothing but an empty bullpen. Had he only imagined it? Maybe he was losing his mind.

"I've got news, and you're not going to like it." His superior's gruff voice carried from his right.

Nick whirled, facing his boss, approaching from the corner office. A rising moon observed them through bulletproof windows. Silver light slanted across empty desks and cubicle dividers. "I didn't realize you were still here."

Special Agent in Charge Luke Santiago dripped with perspiration, his necktie unknotted, and his shirtsleeves rolled to his elbows. He extracted a handkerchief from his pocket, dabbed his brow, mustache, and sideburns, then stashed it away.

"What's with the sweat? It's got to be twenty degrees outside, and the heat's been off for hours."

"Ambassador Van Sloan received another threat."

"That makes three, right?"

Santiago nodded. "He's requested you for a special assignment. Security detail."

Nick swallowed. "Protect the ambassador? I'm a risk analyst, not a field agent."

"He's aware. He wants you because of your ability to quickly analyze a situation and make sound judgments. Besides, you won't be providing security for Van Sloan."

"Not the ambassador?" Nick's brow furrowed. "Then who?"

"His daughter, Bridgette."

Nick coughed and ran his finger between his collar and neck. "I'm not sure I'm comfortable handling her on my own."

"You won't be. FBI is transferring someone."

"Who?"

"Special Agent Powers."

Nick raised an eyebrow. "Agent Powers? As in *Arizona* Powers, the one who flipped out after that Mitchell kid was murdered?"

"You've got the gist. She'll be here first thing Monday morning."

Nick had never met Powers in person, but he'd read enough news articles and heard enough scuttlebutt to know that working with her would not be without its challenges. According to the media, the woman had a personal vendetta against kidnappers, and her nervous breakdown and subsequent stint in therapy had been widely publicized.

"Is she stable enough to return to work?"

"Director Carlton assured me Powers is fit enough for this task. Take it easy on her, Trueheart. If it weren't for this assignment, she'd be collecting unemployment. I'll see you Monday." Santiago turned to leave.

"Have you seen anyone else on this floor tonight?" Nick hollered after the retreating SAC.

Santiago paused midstride and looked back over his shoulder. "No. Seems we're the only ones who don't know when to call it a day. Not like we have anyone waiting for us." He jabbed his hands into his pockets and dragged his feet toward the elevator as if the weight of the world hung on his shoulders.

The down arrow blinked. The doors opened, and Santiago disappeared behind the metal panels.

Nick would have had someone waiting for him—if life were fair. His gaze lowered to his empty ring finger. Had it really been two years? He crushed the crumpled paper towels in his fist. No amount of self-pity could bring back his wife.

The coffee spill had seeped into the carpet fibers, blending with the multi-colored pattern. Discarding the useless towels, he turned to leave. Out of the corner of his eye, he caught a glimpse of the fire escape.

With a soft creak, the door crept shut on its own.

Nick steadied his nerves, refusing to let his imagination get carried away. He pressed the downward arrow to call the elevator, took it to the ground floor, then waved at the security guard on his way out. His black Honda Accord waited in the parking garage to take him home to his lonely, empty apartment. A drizzle whispered against the pavement, mingling with his own melancholy thoughts.

Wet blacktop shimmered beneath the streetlights as Nick parked under the carport at the south-side apartment complex.

His downstairs neighbors were engaged in a heated argument on their tiny ground-floor patio. Between vile insults and angry retorts, cigarette smoke swirled around them. Ashes fell like snow to the concrete slab surface.

Nick turned off the ignition, then exited the vehicle, waving politely as he passed. He wrinkled his nose at the acrid smell. A thick haze burned his eyes, and his throat tickled. Masking a cough, he jogged up the exterior stairs to his one-bedroom apartment on the upper floor.

He'd forgotten the porch light again. Stumbling over the welcome mat, he fumbled for the lock. Once the door was opened, he flipped on the light and straightened the rumpled mat. A small package leaned against the vinyl siding. Had he ordered something? Not that he remembered.

He shrugged, picked up the package and carried it inside, then placed his belongings on the dining room table, hung his coat on the back of a chair, and ambled into the kitchen to fix his dinner.

Adjusting the *paella* recipe to accommodate for his green pea allergy, he omitted the vegetable and opted for extra broth instead of white wine. As he cooked, a robust aroma filled the small apartment.

Once the *soccarat*, a caramelized crust, formed on the bottom of the pan, he removed the skillet from the range and covered it with the lid and a towel while he changed into sweatpants and a T-shirt from his college days at MIT.

Returning to the kitchen, he garnished the finished dish with chopped parsley and lemon slices, then balanced a full plate, along with a fork, napkin, and a glass of unsweetened tea, and carried them to his desk. As he lowered into the ergonomic chair, his gaze landed on the framed photo of his wife.

A knot formed in his throat. *I still miss you.*

Rachel's brunette waves cascaded to her shoulders. Her brown eyes twinkled with *joie de vivre*. She wore a navy pinstripe suit and the owl brooch that he'd given her on their first wedding anniversary—a brooch that had never been recovered after the fire.

Emotions choked him as he wrestled with memories, both good and bad. He would figure out who took her from him, and they would face the consequences of their actions.

His gaze shifted from the photo to a wooden easel nearby and the corkboard overflowing with photos, news articles, maps, crime scene diagrams, forensic reports, witness statements, and a meticulously crafted timeline connected with red string like the ones in a TV police drama.

Nick stood, plate in hand, and approached the board, pondering the giant figurative question mark at its center. Who killed Rachel Reynolds Trueheart?

The perpetrator had eluded law enforcements' every attempt to uncover their identity.

I just need a name, Lord. I know You know who did this. Tell me, please.

He ate while staring at the murder board, then carried the

empty plate to the kitchen, adding it to the collection of dishes encrusted with crumbs and dried sauces.

Returning to the desk, he checked his email and found two more responses to his social media plea for video footage or snapshots from that fateful day. After downloading the files, he watched the videos, straining until his eyes blurred and making note of the smallest details that might point him in the right direction.

As fatigue weighted his eyelids, he yawned and glimpsed the clock in the corner of the screen. Zero three hundred hours.

Closing the laptop lid, he stood. A weekend at his sister's house with his precious nieces was just what he needed to clear his mind before the long week ahead. He paused at the bedroom door and glanced once more at the corkboard. The questions that had haunted him for two long years would not elude his grasp forever.

Whoever you are. Wherever you are. I promise. I will find you.

CHAPTER 3

Ari strode through the revolving door of the massive brick office building on East Preston Street and entered the lobby, head high, carrying two steaming cups from Beans of Insanity on 5th Street.

A thoughtful offering of caffeine couldn't hurt to set things off on the right foot with Agent Trueheart.

That was the theory, anyway.

A security guard met Ari with a curt greeting. "State your business."

"Special Agent Arizona Powers to see Nicholas Trueheart."

The guard's hawklike glare landed on her full hands, and without uttering a word, he gestured toward a nearby metal table.

Understanding the nonverbal cue, Ari set down the coffee cups then emptied her pockets, placing her keys and cell phone into a plastic container. She unholstered her Glock and laid it beside the other items. Lastly, she retrieved her badge case from her back pocket and handed her identification and credentials to the guard.

He scrutinized her documents before motioning for her to pass through a metal detector.

"The firearm stays here. You can secure it in one of those lockers."

Ari froze. "Excuse me." She buried her trembling hands in her jacket pockets. Her pulse spiked.

"Until you have the proper security clearance, you can't carry that in here. FBI or not. It's protocol."

Ari passed through the metal detector, then reclaimed her belongings, minus the Glock. She straightened her shoulders and tightened security against her paranoia. As a professional, she could follow protocol, even when it clashed with her instincts.

The guard returned her papers, then pressed his lips to the radio on his shoulder. "Special Agent Arizona Powers to see Nick Trueheart."

After a brief pause, a female voice responded through the receiver. "Cleared for access."

"You can go up now. Suite three eleven."

"Thank you."

Ari's apprehension grew as she bypassed the elevator and climbed the stairs to the third floor. Her shoes squeaked on the polished tile. Two intersecting corridors stretched out before her. Polished brass plates displayed the suite numbers. She took the hallway to the right, passing canvas paintings of the Platte City skyline and local mountain range.

At the designated office, she balanced the two cups in one hand and turned the doorknob with the other. A handful of plastic, stackable chairs lined the walls of the reception area. A large picture window offered a view of Sanford's Peak, the region's tallest mountain.

A second security guard sat behind the curved reception desk. He raised his head, made eye contact, and promptly stood. "Special Agent Powers?"

"That's me."

"May I see your identification, please?"

Smiling at the guard's pleasant demeanor, Ari set the coffee cups on the counter, then took her badge case from her pocket again.

The guard reviewed her papers. "If you could sign in here, I'll let Mr. Trueheart know you're waiting."

He held out a clipboard.

Ari scribbled down her name, phone number, the current time, and the name of the person she was meeting. When she finished, she returned the clipboard to the counter, stuck her badge case in her back pocket, and picked up the coffee.

The guard dialed the phone, holding the receiver to his ear. "Nick, Agent Powers is here to see you."

After a brief conversation, he hung up. "He'll be right out."

"Thank you."

Her weekend internet search had yielded results for "Nicholas Trueheart," an escape artist who performed in Las Vegas as "Nick of Time." Two years ago, he disappeared from showbiz after a tragic accident took the life of his wife. Speculation about his disappearance ranged from theories that his wife's death wasn't accidental and he'd fled the country, to bizarre claims that he'd pulled off a magical vanishing act and could reappear at any moment.

The oddest theory she'd encountered was that "Nick of Time" had opened a portal to another dimension and been sucked into the swirling vortex.

Just imagine—an escape artist working for the DSS. Inconceivable. Obviously, the internet had misled her.

After a few more minutes, the interior office door swung open, and "Nick of Time" entered the room.

Her mouth dropped a little, and she clamped her jaw shut before she embarrassed herself. The only difference between the entertainer and the man before her was his attire—business casual instead of a twinkly skin-tight costume.

"Special Agent Trueheart?"

Trueheart sported a quiff in his short, dirty blond hair. Bushy eyebrows hovered over hooded eyes that carried a touch of grief within their inky depths. The sharp angle of his chin and high cheekbones conveyed strength and bravery. A mustache capped his full lips, and his slightly protruding ears finished off his distinctive features. Only inches taller than Ari, his short stature and chiseled physique had likely aided him in navigating tight spaces during his performances.

He's good-looking. There's no doubt about that.

He smiled and offered his hand. "I'm not an agent. I'm a security specialist. Welcome to the DSS, Special Agent Powers."

Not an agent? Ari was taken aback by his revelation. After awkwardly shifting the cups to her left hand, she clasped his extended hand with her right. His calluses scratched her palm.

He looked her over from her Plain Jane nut brown hair drawn into a ponytail to her practical black ankle boots. She wore a leather bomber jacket, a green turtleneck, and black slacks. No makeup or jewelry.

Her cheeks warmed under the intensity of his gaze. Did she pass his inspection?

Ari exhaled, glued on a smile, and held out the aromatic peace offering. "I brought this for you."

"Um, thank you." Trueheart accepted the beverage and sniffed. "I appreciate the gesture. Follow me."

"Lead the way."

They entered an open floor plan divided by cubicles. The corner office's door hung ajar, while others were closed and marked with signs—Meeting Room, Interview Room, Evidence Locker, and Restricted Access. Security cameras captured the entirety of the bullpen from their positions on the ceiling.

"My desk is here." Nick stopped beside an enclosed workspace.

Stacks of papers nearly buried the computer monitor and keyboard, while a half-eaten pastry lay on a napkin alongside a generic disposable coffee cup.

The chaos brought out Ari's inner urge to organize the mess, but she refrained.

He set the coffee she'd brought onto the desktop without drinking it. "Down that hall, you'll find the break room, kitchenette, restrooms, and storage. We'll get you a security pass and a parking pass so you can come and go on your own as needed. We have a briefing with Luke Santiago, the SAC, before we begin."

Trueheart led the way into the private corner office, and Ari followed.

A Black man, in his late thirties, stood from behind the desk when they entered. Dressed in a navy sports coat, white dress shirt, and navy slacks, he introduced himself and extended his hand. His teeth glimmered when he smiled.

"Glad to have you on board, Agent Powers. Won't you have a seat?"

They settled into the vinyl chairs facing the SAC.

Ari sipped her coffee and crossed her legs. "Ambassador Van Sloan employs a private security firm. Why does he need us?"

Santiago walked to the window and leaned against the pane, hands in his pockets. "The ambassador believes someone may have infiltrated the security company. That's why the two of you have specifically been chosen for this assignment. You're the only ones he trusts with his daughter's life."

Doubt crept in. Her previous assignment had ended in failure —what if she messed up again? She chewed her lip until Trueheart glanced her way. Did he know of her breakdown?

Of course he did. Everyone did.

Santiago lifted an evidence bag from the desk and passed it to her. "Another threat arrived this morning. That brings the total to four."

Ari read the red ink on the torn sheet of printer paper.

For crimes done in times gone by. For every hurt and every lie.
Unless you admit the pain you caused, everyone will see your flaws.

-Enigma

"But it doesn't mention Bridgette by name?" Ari passed the note to Trueheart, who examined the threatening message, then handed it back to the agent in charge.

"No, it doesn't, but combined with the others, we still believe Miss Van Sloan is the target."

"Where did they find this one?" Trueheart asked.

"Pinned to a ceramic bust of Mozart in the music room."

Someone had entered the house undetected and bypassed the security guards and alarms. No wonder the ambassador questioned the reliability of the security company.

"Has the staff been interviewed? Is there anyone else who might have had access to the house?" she asked.

"None of the staff observed anything out of the ordinary," Santiago replied. "The security footage has been analyzed, both outdoor and indoor recordings. All persons of interest have been identified and questioned. Still no leads."

Trueheart's right leg tremored. "Are you sure I'm the best choice for this assignment? I'm a risk analyst, not a field agent. I've never even fired a gun."

Ari raised her eyebrows. How effective would he be in a high-pressure situation?

"Powers will be your muscle. She knows her way around a firearm."

She frowned and narrowed her eyes. Was that an insensitive jab at her mental stability? She took a deep breath and relaxed her shoulders. It was likely just an observation. No need to take it personally.

And he wasn't wrong. A bullet had left her barrel a time or two … or three. As FBI, it wasn't uncommon for firepower to be necessary to resolve a conflict. Or prevent one.

She relaxed her face and cleared her throat.

Both men looked her direction.

"Is this undercover? Strictly need to know?" she asked.

The SAC perched on the front of the desk. "Miss Van Sloan has been made aware of the situation—not that she was happy about it. The ambassador has requested that you keep as close to a normal schedule as possible. He doesn't want this to upset her any more than necessary, but you two are to stick as close as possible to her side. Don't let her out of your sight. Tail her into the bathroom if necessary, Powers. Otherwise, keep your identities under wraps and try not to draw attention to yourselves."

Ari shifted. "Is it possible Bridgette wrote the notes herself? She has the reputation for seeking publicity."

While spoiled in other ways, the girl had been raised in boarding schools and had had minimal parental involvement in her life. Did she fabricate the danger to garner attention from her father?

Santiago shook his head. "A graphologist has analyzed the handwriting. It doesn't match Miss Van Sloan's. No fingerprints were found on the note."

Trueheart interjected. "Maybe she bribed an employee to write the note for her, and they wore gloves."

He'd read her thoughts.

"It's possible," Santiago agreed. "You're expected at the Van Sloan residence at zero nine hundred hours. I'll be your point of contact, and I'll expect a full report each evening."

Ari and Trueheart stood.

"And Powers?" A hint of warning tinted Santiago's words.

"Yes." She met his gaze.

"I've been informed that you and Miss Van Sloan have a storied history. I don't care what your personal issues are with the ambassador's daughter, but on this assignment, you will refer to her as Miss Van Sloan. Is that understood?"

"Yes, sir."

Heat climbed Ari's cheeks, and she bit her tongue to refrain from making a sarcastic retort. The unnecessary rebuke stung. Did he think so little of her professionalism?

She might not be well-versed in the art of schmoozing dignitaries, but Bridgette Van Sloan would receive the respect she deserved, whether or not Santiago believed it. Or maybe that was his point—treat *Miss Van Sloan* with respect she didn't deserve.

Ari cast a sideways glance at Trueheart. "Got the address?"

He nodded. "I'll drive."

As they headed for the door, Santiago's voice halted them. "One more thing."

They faced him.

"There's more to this case than meets the eye," the SAC warned. "Trust no one. If something happens to that girl, there will be severe repercussions for all of us."

CHAPTER 4

0900 Hours

A piercing screech resonated from the grand foyer's left staircase.

Nick ducked as an object hurtled across the room and smashed into the door frame just inches from his head, showering the tile floor with glass fragments and cell phone debris.

An opulent chandelier, worth more than his yearly salary, glistened in the morning sunlight and made rainbows on the black and white tile floor.

Agent Powers brushed his shoulder as she stepped into the house, and the butler, wearing a penguin suit and white gloves, closed the door behind them.

A striking young woman, with bleach-blonde hair, pouty lips, and a skimpy dress, stamped an ankle boot on the carpeted stairs. A small handbag with a long strap swayed from her shoulder and a set of keys dangled from her manicured fingertips.

A harried male scrambled after the young woman. His salt-and-pepper hair—more salt than pepper—stood on end as if he'd run his fingers through it one too many times. A crooked tie and swinging earbuds gave him an air of frenzied disarray.

"Please Miss Bridgette, it's for your own good. Your father—"

Bridgette Van Sloan interrupted the man with another foot stamp. "I don't need a babysitter. Especially not two government morons. If my father is so concerned about my safety, he should come home from Washington and protect me himself."

That last statement supported Powers's theory. Was this nothing more than a cry for attention? According to their file, the Van Sloans had had less than stellar involvement in their daughter's life.

Miss Van Sloan marched down the staircase. Reaching the foyer, she picked up a decorative antique vase and hoisted it over her head. "I don't want a babysitter."

Nick lunged and snatched the vase before the girl hurled it to its death.

Surprise widened her eyes, and she lowered her arms. "Who are you?"

"We're the government morons, Miss Van Sloan." He set the vase on the floor. "Agent Powers and I have been assigned to your security detail."

The young woman gave him a flirtatious head-to-toe appraisal, and her icy demeanor melted. With a simpering smile, she held out her hand as if expecting a kiss.

He clasped the outstretched appendage in a professional handshake.

Miss Van Sloan's smile vanished, then, as she faced Agent Powers, it morphed into a scowl.

The two women shook hands.

The younger woman scrutinized the agent with an upturned nose.

Recognition flickered in both their eyes.

The frantic male skidded to a stop at the base of the staircase, his dress shoes squeaking on the tiles and interrupting the stare down. He stepped forward, extending his hand. "I'm Banks Kinsley, Miss Van Sloan's personal aid. Thank you for …" His focus drifted to the spoiled debutante, and he sighed. "… coming to our rescue."

Miss Van Sloan stiffened and tossed her hair. "Why are they so old? Don't they have any younger agents?"

"Old?" Agent Powers scoffed. "I'll have you know I'm the youngest FBI agent in the state. I graduated from Quantico in—"

"Agent Powers and I are at your service." Nick intervened before Powers could stick her foot in her mouth. According to his teenage nieces, anyone over the age of twenty-five was considered old. "Please know that we will do everything in our power to ensure your safety—"

"Yeah, yeah, yeah." The girl waved her hand dismissively. "I have things to do. See you around." She headed for the exit without permission.

Agent Powers blocked the door, arms akimbo. "I'm sorry, Miss Van Sloan, but you can't leave. We're required to discuss your schedule, evaluate the current security measures, and create a safety plan before anyone goes anywhere."

The young woman nailed the agent with a sour expression. "Look here, Agent Power Outage. I don't care what you all need to do. Just stay out of my way. My friends are none of your business. I'll see whomever I want, go wherever I want, do whatever I want, whenever I want. Got it?"

Miss Van Sloan appeared remarkably unfazed by the current danger threatening her life.

The hypothesis that this was a fabricated threat grew in probability by the nanosecond.

Agent Powers's face reddened. "Your safety, not your social life, is our highest priority. If you continue—"

Nick interrupted. "We understand that you have had no say in this arrangement, so Agent Powers and I will aim to make this process as smooth as possible and minimize the disruptions to your schedule."

Nick felt Agent Powers's eyes on him as the girl's shoulders relaxed, her posture softening. He'd refereed more than one fight between his nieces. All they needed was a gentle hand and a reassuring—

Miss Van Sloan fluttered her eyelashes and walked her fingertips up Nick's forearm. Her body pressed against him. "Why don't we ditch the old lady, and you can be my personal bodyguard?"

Agent Powers scoffed and muttered something under her breath.

Heat rushed Nick's face. "I am a professional, Miss Van Sloan. You are a client. Anything more than that would be inappropriate."

The teenager pouted and withdrew her hand. "My friends and I are going to an escape room. We have a reservation at ten."

"Which escape room?" he asked.

Platte City was the escape room hub of the West—it could be any of a hundred different businesses.

Miss Van Sloan retrieved a printed flyer from her purse and released it into his outstretched palm.

He scanned the marketing information.

Wanderlust Escape
A pop-up escape room
1721 River Road
Open 2/4 - 2/5 only! 9 am - 11 pm
Escape While You Can!

Questions bombarded Nick's brain. How long had the company been in business? What was their BBB rating? His instincts demanded they run a background check on the owner and scout the location beforehand. However, judging by Miss Van Sloan's determined expression, that wouldn't happen.

Bridgette Van Sloan was used to getting her own way.

They could confine her to the house, but what good would it

do? Playing along was their best bet at keeping her safe. They didn't want to be scouring the city for her because she snuck out the minute their backs were turned.

Agent Powers peered around his arm. "What's a pop-up escape room?"

Nick hadn't heard of them either.

Miss Van Sloan crossed her arms and remained silent.

"It's a temporary setup. They usually appear at random in vacant buildings, like a rave," Kinsley answered. "They stay for a short time, then close up and move on."

Nick's stomach knotted. Abandoned buildings offered countless shadowy corners for ambushers to lurk in. "Where did you get this flyer?"

"Everyone in the neighborhood got one. I'm going whether you like it or not."

"Miss Van Sloan," Agent Powers began, her tone gentler than it had been. "How are we supposed to protect you if you won't listen to us?" She lowered her arms from her hips and moved away from the door.

"It's simple. You're my bodyguards. Guard my body."

"We're not body—" the agent protested. "We need time to run background checks on your friends and verify the validity of the business before—"

"You are not creeping on my friends. They have nothing to do with this. Leave them alone."

"Bridgette, Miss Van Sloan, if you would just—"

Their young charge made a beeline for the fiery-red Corvette parked in the driveway.

Adrenaline surged through Nick. They had no choice but to follow her. He exchanged a quick glance with Agent Powers, silently sharing her frustration before hurtling after the teenager.

He quickly caught up and grabbed her arm, halting her in her tracks. He kept his voice free of alarm but packed with the seriousness the situation demanded. "I understand your desire to maintain a sense of normalcy, but it's imperative that you follow our directions. We are under orders to keep you safe, and I respectfully request that you don't make it difficult."

She released an overly dramatic sigh. "Fine."

"Starting with the fact that we're taking my vehicle."

Miss Van Sloan's eyes widened, then flickered between the flashy Corvette and his sensible Honda. "Why?"

"For starters, the Corvette doesn't have enough seats for all of us. Secondarily, we haven't had the opportunity to check it for damage or …"

He paused. *A bomb.* "We'll try our best not to ruin your fun." He opened the Accord's rear door and bowed low. "Entrer."

"Merci beaucoup." She giggled and slid into the seat. "I guess it'll be all right as long as no one sees me in this."

Agent Powers grasped the passenger side handle. "And please, if anything feels off or you notice something amiss, let us know." Her tone was firm but tinged with frustration and concern.

The girl rolled her eyes. "Whatever. Let's just go before we're late."

He turned the key in the ignition, and the engine roared.

Miss Van Sloan's stubborn nature would only add to the complexity of this assignment. If she refused to listen to reason, she could end up cornered with no escape.

Agent Powers twisted in her seat to face him. "I'll see what I can learn about Wanderlust Escape. If it's legit, it shouldn't be too hard to locate a website and some reviews." She pulled her cell phone from her coat pocket as he put the car in gear. "I'm not comfortable going into this unprepared."

"Me neither." Nick slowed his breathing—a technique he'd mastered years ago.

Clear his mind.

Focus.

No matter what happened, he wouldn't let himself be caught off guard.

Not again.

CHAPTER 5

1000 Hours

Ari appraised the nondescript building as Nick maneuvered his car into the asphalt parking lot. A two-story brick warehouse, lined with steel-framed, blacked-out windows, loomed at the far side of the blacktop.

Five individuals—two girls and three guys—exited the massive front doors, heading for a row of parked cars. They laughed and chattered, gesturing wildly. One guy face-palmed himself while his two companions punched him in the shoulders.

After Nick parked and shut off the ignition, Ari exited the vehicle and scanned their surroundings, noting the other rundown buildings along the street and the remnants of blackened snow in the shadows. The sound of car doors echoed across the parking lot. Engines turned over, and the others drove off, leaving behind a deafening silence.

A plastic bag fluttered down the empty road, and a stray cat leaped from a metal trashcan. Ari flinched. Her limited knowledge of the escape room industry hindered her ability to thoroughly analyze her surroundings, and her unease gained weight.

A quick internet search during the drive had indicated this was a legitimate business. Wanderlust Escape, according to her findings, had been in existence since the start of the escape room boom. They had a professional-grade online presence and only a couple of negative reviews with the usual complaints.

Still, something nagged her instincts. They were too exposed —too many angles to watch, too many directions from which trouble could arise.

If she thought it would work, she'd simply shuttle Bridgette right back home. Too bad the stubborn girl would simply find a way to sneak out again—unless one of them sat on her. If only that were an option—they couldn't fail this assignment.

Car doors opened behind her, and Trueheart and Bridgette stepped out.

"Keep your eyes on Miss Van Sloan while I clear the area. I don't want any surprises."

Without waiting for a reply, Ari headed toward the alley between buildings, moving out of earshot just as Trueheart asked Bridgette about her friends' absence. She'd wondered the same thing. Shouldn't they be there by now?

Ari unsnapped her holster and withdrew her firearm, appreciating the familiar grip in her palm. Treading carefully, she sidestepped suspicious puddles and piles of garbage. At the back corner, she peered around the rear wall.

Nothing.

She circled the building.

A rusty fire escape with a retracted telescopic ladder led from an exterior door about fifty feet above ground. From this corner, she had a decent view of the neighborhood and the entire parking area.

Despite her trepidation, all seemed on the level.

Another set of vehicles pulled into the lot and parked. Two teen guys jumped out and climbed onto the trunk, eyes glued to electronic devices. From the second vehicle, two teenage girls emerged, checked their phones, then spoke to the guys. Their voices carried on the wind.

Ari overheard something about being too early for their time slot and if the boys wanted to freeze their butts off, fine, but they —the girls—were waiting in the warm car. Tugging their winter coats tighter around their slender bodies, they climbed back inside.

Ari crossed to where Trueheart and Bridgette waited.

Bridgette perched on the hood of Trueheart's Honda, her thumbs prancing across an electronic screen like clog dancers. Obviously, the cell phone that had nearly collided with Trueheart's noggin hadn't been *Bridgette's* cell phone.

Ari briefed Trueheart on her findings. "I guess it's all legit. I haven't seen anything out of order. I still don't think we should lower our guard even for a second. Too much room for error if we're not careful."

"Chill, Powers. You're too intense. It's an escape room. Nothing is going to happen."

A loud chime reverberated from Bridgette's cell, and she exhaled dramatically.

"Did they ghost you?" Trueheart asked her.

When did a thirty-year-old single man learn to speak teenagese? Ari hadn't been able to connect with the other teenagers when she was one.

"No," Bridgette groaned. "They're running late because the cops pulled them over for speeding. Eden talked her way out of a ticket, but it took forever. Don't the police have anything better to do?"

Speeding? Talking law enforcement out of a citation? What kind of girls did Bridgette associate with?

The blatant disregard for authority ruffled Ari's feathers. She kept her opinion to herself, though a sarcastic remark about Bridgette's choice of friends made scars on her teeth in their attempt to escape.

Instead, she feigned interest. "What are your friends' names?"

"Ivy Vail and Eden Deetz. Do you have to hold that thing?" Bridgette's gaze dropped to Ari's hand.

The firearm. Ari returned it to the holster and snapped the strap in place, then assumed a relaxed pose, pretending to examine her fingernails. "How did you meet them? School?"

"We're in the same classes."

"What are you studying?"

"I know what you're doing."

Ari met Bridgette's stormy gaze. "What am I doing?"

"You already know everything about me, from what I had for breakfast to the color of my underwear. You're prying into my friends. Just like I told you not to." Bridgette spun on her heel and stalked off across the parking lot.

"You really have a way with her, you know that?" Trueheart smirked. "Have you considered not coming across with the abrasion of a sandblaster?"

Ari opened her mouth to make a sharp comeback.

Tires squealed. A purple Jaguar peeled into the parking lot, heading straight for Bridgette.

Ari drew her weapon and aimed for the tires.

"Hold up." Trueheart's hand gripped her shoulder.

She cringed beneath his touch. "I don't have time to hold up."

The sports car came to an abrupt stop, parking haphazardly in an angled space. The doors flew open, and two teenage girls, clad in leather jackets and sunglasses, despite the overcast sky, burst from the vehicle.

Bridgette squealed, and the three girls embraced.

"See. I told you there was nothing to worry about."

"How did you know?"

"License plate."

He was right—*Prncss1* screamed entitled teenage girl. Why

hadn't she noticed that? She needed to up her game—carelessness was an expense she couldn't afford.

Ari approached the girls, and they fell silent. She offered her knuckles for a fist bump. Do teenagers still engage in such greetings? The girls left her hanging, and she lowered her arm awkwardly. "Good morning, I'm …"

She paused as Santiago's instructions came to mind. Strictly need to know.

One girl slowly raised her sunglasses, revealing cornflower-blue eyes and reddish freckles. "Why does your aunt carry a gun?" She snapped her bubble gum for emphasis.

Bridgette's gaze blazed a path to Ari's hand. "Um, she's from Saint Louis, the most dangerous city in America. A girl's got to protect herself."

So, that's how they were playing this.

Ari holstered her weapon. She had to give Bridgette credit—the girl was quick-witted.

Embracing each girl with zealous enthusiasm, Ari covertly patted their pockets and hoped her voice refrained from using the sarcasm welling inside her chest. "Hello, girls. You must be Eden and Ivy. Bridgette has told me so much about you, I feel like I've known you for as long as she has. I'm pumped to hang with you girls today."

Trueheart stepped forward. His musky cologne flirted with her nostrils.

What identity had Bridgette assigned him?

"And that's my uncle. He's from Saint Louis, too."

Surprise widened his expression, and he tilted his head to make eye contact with Ari, demanding an explanation.

"I'll tell you later," Ari whispered. She raised her voice. "Well, we don't want to be late. Why don't you lead the way Tru —my heart." She coughed to cover her mistake, but nothing would hide the flush that must be spreading to her ears.

My heart? What had possessed her to say that?

Trueheart wagged his head and headed for the warehouse entrance as Bridgette's friends turned to follow.

Ari glanced at Bridgette still standing beside the shiny sports car.

Her eyes reflected a scathing review of Ari's performance. She strode off, ankle boots making a clear statement with each step.

Ari cracked her neck, then scanned the area once more for any signs of potential danger, before joining the others inside.

The sooner this was over, the better.

And she wasn't just talking about the escape room.

CHAPTER 6

Ari stepped over the threshold, and the steel door swung shut behind her. An electronic lock engaged. She whirled and grasped the handle. Air escaped her lungs, refusing to return. "Nick," she squeaked. "We're locked in."

He appeared at her side, eyebrows raised. "That's what makes it an escape room."

She forced air into her lungs as her eyes adjusted.

Paint blacked out the windows, preventing natural light from entering the building. Industrial metal beams crisscrossed with copper pipes and large florescent fixtures. Stained concrete formed the flooring. A PVC pipe dripped, creating a puddle beneath it. Neon graffiti defaced the interior walls, and wooden crates on pallets formed makeshift aisles.

At the top of a rusty metal staircase, thin panel walls enclosed an upstairs loft into an office—according to the faded sign on the damaged wooden door. The air carried a musty scent, a combination of neglect and something she couldn't identify.

Surveillance cameras and audio speakers huddled in the corners of the ceiling.

Were they being watched? Heard?

"Welcome to Wanderlust Escape," a voice, carrying the

youthful timbre of a college-aged female, echoed in the large open space.

Ari's focus snapped to a young woman standing at the top of the staircase. The girl's black hair had been pulled back into a messy bun, and she wore jeans and a company T-shirt.

Bridette and her friends clasped their hands together and squealed, scrunching their faces in excitement.

"Are you ready to embark on a journey that will test your wits and unravel the secrets within these walls? My name is Melody Quinn, and I'll be your game master. Please sign the waivers there on the tablet, and we can begin."

It took several minutes to read through the release of liability form. The list of risks turned Ari's stomach inside out. When she finished signing her name, she stepped back to allow Trueheart access to the tablet mounted on a podium.

Why are we letting Bridgette do this again?

Something brushed her arm, she jerked, instinctively covering her weapon.

It was Miss Quinn.

"You can't have that in here." Her gaze dropped to Ari's holster.

"I have the right to open carry if I'm certified." Stating she was law enforcement might break the "need to know" order.

"Not in here. Owner's policy."

Ari clenched her jaw and ground her teeth. "What do you suggest I do with it?"

"You can put it in there." Miss Quinn motioned toward a small row of metal lockers.

Ari sighed and stored her firearm. As she shut the door and pocketed the key, Miss Quinn addressed the group.

"Your objective is to escape the locked warehouse in sixty minutes. You'll encounter a series of perplexing riddles, hidden clues, and challenging puzzles that will test your teamwork and problem-solving skills. Communication and collaboration are key to your success. Don't hesitate to think outside the box and explore unconventional solutions. And remember, if you need a hint, I'm just a shout away.

"Just a couple of rules before we begin. If it takes more than two fingers of pressure, an object does not move. We mark anything not part of the game with a sticker. Please place all cell phones in the box provided. Now, code breakers, step into the 'Warehouse Escape' and let the mystery unfold!"

Ari exchanged glances with Trueheart.

"Still think it's a trap?" he asked.

"I guess not."

They followed directions, stowing their phones inside the plastic crate beside the main entrance. Ari patted her empty pocket, feeling almost naked without the device. A cramp seized her neck muscles, and she attempted to massage it loose. The no phones policy prevented players from cheating, but it was doubtful anyone could get a cell signal inside the warehouse anyway.

When they finished, a computer recording of a male voice carried from the speakers. "For the past three months, you and your team of secret agents have pursued the deplorable fugitive known as Codex. But a member of your team has deciphered a coded message. Codex has agreed to meet you at an abandoned warehouse across town. After you arrive, the doors lock behind you, and you realize it's a trap. A smoky haze pours from a vent in the corner of the room, and a note is nailed to the exit. You have sixty minutes to escape from the warehouse. Or this will be your last mission."

The recording ended.

Melody spoke again. "Good luck! The clock is ticking, and the adventure awaits." She disappeared inside the upper room.

Giggling and ignoring their chaperones, the three girls dashed out of sight.

Ari took a deep breath, relaxed her shoulders, and crossed her arms.

Were there other exits besides this one that they needed to

worry about? Anyone hidden among the props that may present a danger to Bridgette? Some of these old buildings had housed speakeasies during prohibition, using secret passages and concealed exits to evade arrest during a raid.

"I'm going to have a look around."

Trueheart nodded. "I'll head this way. Meet back here?"

"Yes."

Enthusiastic chatter carried from somewhere among the maze of crates. Three distinct voices. The same feeling surfaced that her therapist had endeavored to extinguish over the past six months—the feeling that if she blinked she might miss something important.

According to the counselor, it was impossible to anticipate every risk, and she shouldn't blame herself every time things went wrong. Situations would occur that were beyond her control, and she just had to accept that as fact.

Easier said than done. The girls were her responsibility—she *had* to anticipate every risk.

Fifteen minutes passed.

Confident the area was secure, Ari parked herself in front of the main door.

To her left, the girls arranged a shelf of paint cans. What were they looking for?

"How about it?" Nick's voice came from her right and made her flinch.

"How about what?"

"You and I could figure this thing out before those teenage girls." He gave her an impish grin.

"Santiago said not to take our eyes off of her."

"They can't get out without going through the front door. As long as we can hear them, I don't see any reason to watch their every move. There's no smoky haze oozing through an air vent either, so I think they're safe."

A smile tugged Ari's lips. He had a point. Maybe. "Have you ever done one of these before?"

"Um, no, but I've escaped several other things in my lifetime. It shouldn't be too difficult. Have you?"

Ari shook her head. "Bridgette seems intent on giving us the slip. You're positive there's no other way out?"

"It wouldn't be a very good escape room if there was a second exit." He rubbed the back of his neck. "Agent Powers, I analyze risks for a living. Do you think I would even suggest it if I thought those girls were in danger?"

Ari skimmed the room once more. "Where do we begin?"

"How about with that?" Nick pointed at a leather briefcase leaning against the wall nearby.

Squatting, she rubbed her finger over the combination lock. "We need a three-digit code."

"That's one thousand possible answers. Unless each number can be used only once, which would mean there are seven hundred and twenty possible answers." Trueheart rotated his neck, peering around the room. "Did you notice that some letters in the graffiti are backward?"

Ari stood. "Backward?"

"Yeah, that E. That S. That—never mind, I've found your code. It's nine, two, three."

"Are you sure?"

Trueheart nodded. "The words are BIR9IE WA2 H3RE. Yeah, I'm pretty sure."

Ari scrolled through the numbers until she entered the correct code.

The lock flipped up, and the case opened.

Inside, she found a metal tin, a locked book, and a note. She handed the tin to Trueheart, then read the note aloud. "First in the first, second in the second, third in the third, and so on." She scrunched her nose. "What's that supposed to mean?"

"I don't know, but this was inside the box." He held up a key. "Does it unlock the book?"

Ari held it out, and he tried the key in the lock.

He shook his head. "Nope, not the right one. Must open something else."

"That could be any number of things."

The girls had finished with the paint cans. Letters across the labels spelled the words, Open Me. The three of them dashed across the end of an aisle, waving a piece of paper, heading for a poster on the wall.

A padlock dangled from an electrical panel across the room.

"Maybe it opens that." Ari started toward the breaker box.

"I don't think we're supposed to mess with that."

Ari rolled her eyes. "Humor me. It doesn't have a 'do not touch' sticker."

He handed Ari the empty tin, then tried the key in the padlock.

The shackle sprang loose.

He removed the lock from the hasp and opened the electrical panel. Only one comically large switch resided inside. A sign above read: Switch Must Remain On.

And it wasn't.

Her fingers itched to pull it. "Do you want to do it? Or shall I?"

"By all means, have at it, my lady."

Trembling with adrenaline, Ari grasped the switch with both hands and flipped it to the on position.

Something exploded from the wall and skittered across the floor.

Trueheart nearly jumped out of his skin.

Ari pressed her fingers to her lips to hide a chuckle. That alone was worth the price of admission. She checked the remaining hollow while he retrieved the object. "There's nothing here."

"That's because it's still attached." Trueheart returned with another key dangling from the plate cover. He took the book from Ari and tried it in the lock.

It opened.

After handing the key and lock to Ari, he opened the book and flipped through the pages. All were empty except for the first.

Your hope will be dashed
If next you can't see
For each clue leads to another
But one more is all you need
Your task remains forever hidden
Unless you riddle me this in deed
For no matter where you look, crate victory is unachievable
So keep on looking until the truth B found
To solve, only one number matters and that's fifty-two

"That's got to be the worst poem I've ever read." Trueheart handed Ari the open book. "Got any ideas?"

Ari rubbed her chin and muttered aloud. "First in the first, second in the second, third in the third, and so on."

Trueheart's eyes flickered over the text. He pointed at the page. "Look here. The first word in the first line is *your*. Second word in the second line is *next*. The third word in the—"

"Clue," Ari interrupted. "Your next clue is hidden in crate B fifty-two."

Trueheart raised his head and scanned the maze of crates. "Let's go."

Ari made a pile on the floor of everything they'd gathered so far, then jogged after him. It took several minutes to locate crate B fifty-two. She ran her fingers over the wood, then tried to lift the lid, but it didn't budge.

"We'll need a crowbar to open this," Ari suggested.

"Unless we're not supposed to open it. Remember, the host said if it takes more than two fingers' worth of pressure, then it's not intended to move."

Ari pinched her lips together. "The poem said our next clue

was hidden *in* crate B fifty-two. Do you see any other markings or maybe a button or a switch?"

"I'll check the other side." He loped down the aisle and rounded the end. Moments later, footsteps approached on the other side of the crates. "It's labeled B fifty-two over here as well, but that's it. I don't see anything else."

"We're missing something. Keep looking."

Ari slid her fingertips along the wood, stopping only to suck her pinkie after a splinter jabbed the soft skin.

Adrenaline raced through her veins, fueled by the energy of the game. What could be inside the crate? What was the next clue?

The PVC pipe dripping on the floor, and the sound of their own breathing were the only noises in the room. Ari's enthusiasm ground to a halt. It was too quiet. She stood on her tiptoes to peer over the crate. "When was the last time you heard the girls?"

Trueheart paled. "Not recent enough."

Ari swallowed. "Me neither." They had to be around there somewhere. "Help me find them."

"On it." He headed down one side of the aisle as she made her way down the current row.

Before her next breath, the fluorescent lights powered down, engulfing them in tomblike darkness. Panic cemented her feet to the floor.

A hair-curdling scream echoed.

Metal scraped metal.

Then came a soft thump and a muffled shriek, then sobs.

Ari's pulse thudded against her ribcage. The darkness pressed around her, making it impossible to see anything. A haunting melody pierced the air. The melancholic tendrils of the lullaby from her nightmares wove through the room, its spectral strains chilling her to the core.

Emptiness suffocated her, clawed at her spirit, dragging her into a feeling of helplessness.

"Is everyone okay?" Trueheart shouted over the music. "Answer me if you can."

Ari's paranoia latched onto his strength. "I'm here."

"We're scared." Either Ivy or Eden responded, the voice brimming with confusion and fear. "What's going on, Nick?"

"I don't know," he answered. "Seems like a power outage. I'll try to make my way back to the entrance and get our phones for flashlights. I'm sure Miss Quinn will be down any minute."

Footsteps retreated on the concrete floor.

Fighting the oppression, Ari inched forward, waving her arms. "Help me find you, girls. Make some noise."

Their voices came from her right. Rotating toward the sound, she slammed her leg into a solid object. "Ouch!" She bent and rubbed her aching kneecap. How could she find them when she could barely move?

The lights flickered, then came back on.

Ivy and Eden clung to each other in the middle of the room, trembling. Their eyes bulged, and their chests heaved. Tears soaked the redhead's cheeks.

Two girls. Not three.

Where's Bridgette?

CHAPTER 7

A s soon as the lights came on, Nick dashed for the plastic crate, grabbed the cell phones, then hurried to where Agent Powers waited with the girls.

They stood together beside a metal column. Ivy and Eden hugged each other, sobbing. Agent Powers looked whiter than fresh snow.

"What's going on?" He furrowed his brow and scanned the surrounding area. No snakes, spiders, ninjas ...

"Bridgette is *missing*." Agent Powers hissed, gawking at him.

Nick's head jerked toward the girls. Only two. "Where's Miss Van Sloan?"

"She's gone." Agent Powers's tone hinted at panic. "I told you this was a bad idea."

How did she get past them?

He raced back to the front entrance and tugged the door handle. It didn't budge. He checked the locking mechanism. It appeared to be a solenoid lock that would have stayed engaged during the power outage. How had she escaped? How did Bridgette even find the door in the dark? He'd barely been able to see his hand in front of his face.

A noise sounded behind him.

The three women had followed him.

"I'm going to check the security footage. You call the police." Nick tossed Agent Powers her cell phone, then took the loft stairs two at a time. An uneasy feeling settled in his gut. Why hadn't Miss Quinn emerged from the office when the power went out?

"Open up! We've got a missing girl." He pounded on the rickety door.

No answer.

"Hey, let me in. This is important."

Still no response.

Nick reared back and kicked.

Wood splintered. The door swung open and bounced off the wall. Screens monitored the lower level from every angle. Melody Quinn sprawled on the floor, motionless, her neck cocked at an awkward angle. Eyes blank.

"Melody? Miss Quinn?"

Nick knelt beside the body and pinched her wrist. No pulse. Nausea gripped his stomach. He rose and surveyed the room, spotting the emergency exit. He tested the handle and shoved the door with his shoulder. It shifted half an inch, but something kept it from opening fully. They couldn't get out that way.

Whirling to face the computers, he bent over the keyboard and brought up the security footage. The last twenty-four hours had been erased. His heart sank.

The metal stairs clanked beneath his shoes as he descended to the ground floor. Agent Powers had disappeared, but Ivy and Eden hadn't moved. He approached them, struggling to keep his cool. They had to know something. They'd been with Bridgette the entire time as far as he knew. "Where's Miss Van Sloan?"

They stared at him, with tear-streaked cheeks and pitiful whimpers.

Nick took a slow breath before he lashed out. "Bridgette. Where's Bridgette?"

"We don't know. She was here when the power went out," Eden answered. "It's like she vanished."

"Did you see anything? Hear anything? Did someone take her?"

Ivy shook her black braids. "We couldn't see anything. It was too dark."

Agent Powers rejoined them, her expression mirroring his own. She'd retrieved her firearm from the locker.

Nick swallowed the bile that rose in his throat. "Melody Quinn is dead. Someone broke her neck. The security footage from the past twenty-four hours has been erased. Bridgette didn't just disappear. Something bad happened here."

They shouldn't have taken their eyes off her.

"Bridgette might be a troublemaker and a flirt, but she isn't a killer. Someone must have taken her." Agent Powers frowned at the security cameras. "How did they get inside the warehouse? The door was locked. How did we not see them?" She paused. "Did you check the fire escape?"

"It's blocked. We can't get out that way. But I'm certain our killer came in through there. Did you call the police?"

Powers shook her head. "I can't get a signal."

There had been no way in or out except the front entrance and the fire escape. He checked his watch—the room had been dark for only two, maybe three minutes. That wasn't time enough for someone to kidnap Miss Van Sloan and murder Miss Quinn. *Whoever did this had an accomplice.*

Agent Powers tightened her fists and turned a circle, hands in the air. "How are we going to get out of here? We've got to find Bridgette."

Nick clenched his jaw. "And how do you suggest we do that?"

"We could finish the room. Solve the final clue that lets us out of here," Ivy suggested.

"There's no time for that. We have to get out now."

It was only an illusion—they weren't truly locked in. As an escape artist, illusions had been a frequent tool in his arsenal. "The builder of the escape room would have installed an automatic emergency release, otherwise, it would violate safety regulations. I'll look in the office. You check down here."

Powers didn't respond, but movement out of the corner of his eye caught his attention.

With her jacket protecting her hands, she wrapped them around a copper pipe section, and with her foot against the cinder blocks, pulled, grunted, and jerked.

The pipe groaned and shuddered.

"Whoa! What are you doing?" He waved his arms.

She gave the pipe a hard yank. "Getting us out of here."

"Didn't you hear me? I just said I could unlock the door."

"Too slow." The pipe broke loose, nearly knocking Powers off her feet.

Steam shot from the gaping hole.

"Now we've got our deadly vapors."

Agent Powers rolled her eyes. "Give me a break. It's not deadly, just hot."

With determined strides, she crossed the room and slammed the pipe into the corner of the windowpane. A small web cracked from the impact point.

"Vandalism is a crime," Eden warned. "We could get into serious trouble. I don't want to go to jail."

"We're ... already ... in ... serious ... trouble." Powers punctuated each word with a jab at the glass.

The window shattered, and fragments showered the concrete.

She scraped the glass clear and tossed the pipe outside, then hoisted herself over and out the window.

Nick raked his fingers through his hair. His temples ached.

"We're wasting time. Help the girls over."

He worked his jaw while assisting Ivy and Eden through the window, then ducked his head, straddled the block wall, and dropped to the ground below.

Agent Powers paced the parking lot, phone to her ear, shouting at someone—most likely the police.

His vehicle was where they'd left it, and the teenagers off to the side hadn't moved, oblivious to the world around them. He loped across the lot, startling the boys still perched on the trunk.

Their heads shot upward. "What's happening, dude?"

"Did you see a blonde girl come out of the warehouse?"

The boys shook their heads.

"Did anyone else show up? Anyone circling the building, acting suspicious?"

"No, man. We didn't see nothing."

Nick glanced at the phones in their hands. They probably hadn't even looked up until he'd startled them. "What about the girls with you? Maybe they saw something."

One guy jumped down, tapped on the window of the second car, and motioned for the girls to join them.

They stepped outside, fussing about the cold.

Nick asked them the same questions and got the same answers. They hadn't seen anything.

One girl twirled bubble gum around her finger. "So, are you guys finished in the escape room? Is it our turn now?"

"Sorry. This is now a crime scene. A girl is missing, and another has been killed. The police are going to need your statements, so don't go anywhere."

The teens exchanged horrified glances.

Was that about the crimes that had taken place or the fact that the police were coming? He walked away, shaking his head.

As he approached, Agent Powers lowered her cell. "The police are on their way. What did *they* say?" She jutted her chin toward the group of teens.

"They didn't see anything."

"Not *anything*? How is that possible? Not a vehicle? Not someone climbing the fire escape?"

A glance in that direction confirmed the ladder had been extended. Nick's gaze followed the stairs to the outer door. A crowbar had been wedged across the handle. No wonder he couldn't open it from the inside.

"I'll be right back." Agent Powers took off toward the alley.

Nick stayed where he was. Poor Ivy and Eden looked ready to faint. "Here, have a seat." He gestured to the curb. "Everything's going to be okay."

Even *he* didn't believe his words, so how could he expect them to?

The girls settled onto the sidewalk slab, clinging to each other.

Agent Powers appeared around the far side of the building, approaching at a rapid pace.

He met her halfway. "Find anything?"

"There are fresh tracks that weren't there earlier. Someone arrived after we did."

Nick glanced at Miss Van Sloan's friends. "What do we do now?"

"We can't do anything until the police arrive and finish their questioning. After that, we'll canvass the neighborhood. See if anyone heard or saw anything."

"And if they didn't?"

"We'll tear this city apart until we find her."

CHAPTER 8

1600 Hours

The clock in the DSS conference room ticked louder than any Ari had ever heard.

Tension, as thick as Platte City's rush hour traffic, packed the air. Bridgette was still missing, and every hour that passed decreased the chances of recovery.

They'd canvassed the entire neighborhood. No one had seen anything. How was that possible? Bridgette couldn't have just disappeared.

Matt sat at one end of the long conference table with his head burrowed in his palms. He had avoided eye contact with anyone over the past ten minutes. He was disappointed in her. Not that she blamed him. He'd believed in her, put his job on the line, and she'd let him down.

Luke Santiago paced the patterned carpet. "Is it possible that this is some kind of publicity stunt or cry for attention?" His hands gripped his hair, nearly pulling it out at the roots. Ten paces to the window and back again. His chest heaved, and a vein in his neck bulged.

Ari shook her head.

The murdered game host blew that theory out of the running.

Bridgette Van Sloan may be a spoiled brat, but she wasn't a killer.

Execution of a plan of this magnitude required significant know-how and an accomplice, but how that second person got inside—Ari had no explanation, and it irritated her like a splinter she couldn't pry loose.

How did the kidnapper get in and out in such a short time? Were they hiding somewhere inside before the game began? Could the UNSUB be Enigma? Had he made good on his threats?

Before the blackout, she and Trueheart had been standing in the aisle. The lights went out. Then came a scream, a muffled shriek, a thump, and scraping metal.

And then something else—a chilling tune that had sent her soul plummeting to the lowest parts of the earth. The lullaby from her nightmares.

She glanced at Trueheart. Had he heard it, too?

The only way to know for sure would be to ask him, but that would risk exposing her insanity. If he hadn't heard it, he'd never believe her, and they'd send her back to the mental health facility. How could a nightmare be connected to a real-life kidnapping? Was it possible she only imagined the music?

Santiago stopped pacing. "Ambassador Van Sloan wants your heads on a silver platter, and Director Carlton over at the FBI isn't too pleased either. How did you lose Miss Van Sloan on your first day?"

Trueheart spoke up. "I take full responsibility, sir. I should never have encouraged Agent Powers to take her eyes off Miss Van Sloan. It was foolish and unprofessional."

He might be trying to shoulder the blame, but she was accountable for her own actions. "That may be true, but I knew better. I let myself get caught up in the game. In our defense, we did our due diligence. We were certain Bridgette wasn't in any danger."

"Too bad you were wrong," Santiago snapped.

The phone rang from the middle of the table, and the SAC picked up the receiver. "Santiago. Yeah, put him on." Silence reigned as he listened.

"Right. Keep me informed." He hung up the phone. "An abandoned vehicle was just located at the river on boat slip fifteen. The uniforms found traces of blood in the trunk. The lab is running it now to see if it's a match. You had better hope it's not." Santiago leaned over the conference table with his palms flat. "You're not fired. Neither one of you."

Nick sighed audibly. "We appreciate that, sir. We'll do our best to locate—"

"However," Santiago interrupted.

Ari swallowed.

"You're both on administrative leave until Miss Van Sloan is recovered. I'm hoping this will satisfy the ambassador for now. If that girl turns up dead, neither one of you will ever work in this business again. You'll be reduced to meter maids or mall security. If you can even get that."

"But sir," Ari leaped from her chair. "You can't suspend me. I should be out there looking for her, leading this investigation."

Santiago shook his head. "Sit down, Powers. We have your statements. Be grateful. Van Sloan wanted the federal government to take disciplinary action against you both. If you know what's good for you, you'll stay away from this investigation and this office."

Ari returned to her seat and looked over at her boss. Why wouldn't he say anything? He'd always come to her defense before. "Matt?"

He raised his head, rubbed his palms on his trousers, and stood. "Special Agent Arizona Powers."

His tone carried the weight of a mother calling you by your full legal name.

Her heart sank. "Yes, sir." Her cheek twitched.

Matt's chest swelled beneath his white dress shirt, then collapsed. "I warned you that not everyone was convinced you were ready to return to the field. This … disaster … has only reinforced their negative assessment."

He paused and cleared his throat. "The Office of Professional Responsibility will conduct an internal investigation. If their evaluation substantiates the allegations against you, your employment with the FBI will be terminated. After that, it will be up to the court to decide what to do with you as the ambassador has threatened to press charges for criminal negligence."

"Criminal negligence? But—"

Matt held up his palm. "Take it up with the review board. I've stuck my neck out for you one too many times."

Trueheart rose. "If I may, sir, Powers and I bear equal responsibility—"

A shake from Matt's head interrupted him. "Powers is an experienced field agent. You, no offense, are support personnel. I informed her of the potential consequences when briefed on this assignment, and she was well aware of what she was risking if she failed. It's gallant of you to take the heat, but she, and she alone, is being held accountable for Miss Van Sloan's disappearance."

Ari's jaw tightened. Why was this all her fault? Trueheart was just as guilty. "Is that everything, sir?"

"Not quite." Matt coughed. "I need you to surrender your credentials and firearm. For public safety. You can have them back when this is all over."

She should have seen that coming. It was standard practice.

Ari removed her badge case from her back pocket and tossed it onto the table, then unholstered the Glock 19, removed the clip, and placed them both beside the leather case, setting them down harder than necessary.

"You're making a huge mistake."

Matt gave her a sympathetic half smile. "You are dismissed."

Kicking the chair out from under her, Ari left the conference room without another word. Without a backward glance. If she made eye contact with anyone, she might cry—or scream—and neither was an acceptable response from a federal agent.

Even for a suspended federal agent.

Guilt cemented Ari's feet to the floor, making it difficult to walk. Waves of questions threatened to drown her in their undertow.

Maybe the rumors were right. She was losing her edge. Losing her mind. No, she couldn't just give up and give in. It wasn't in her nature. Bridgette was her responsibility, and she wouldn't stop until she brought her home. She'd prove she wasn't incompetent. Or unstable.

But what if Bridgette was already dead?

She swallowed the lump in her throat. Her shaky finger pressed the down arrow to call the elevator. She needed a solitary place to release the emotions welling inside her chest.

If Bridgette was dead, Ari would track down the killer and make him wish he'd never crossed paths with Arizona Powers. No one was going to make a fool out of her, not if she could help it.

Running footsteps echoed across the bullpen. "Wait, Agent Powers. We need to talk."

"Just leave me alone."

The elevator dinged, and the doors opened. She stepped inside, but Trueheart caught the door before it closed.

Ari scowled. "What do you want? Ruining my career wasn't enough for you. Want to shove me in front of a bus, too?"

The mechanical gears groaned, and the elevator started moving.

"I want to apologize. I tried to come to your defense and take the blame. This is not your fault."

"You didn't do a compelling job of convincing *them* of that." She folded her arms and angled her body away from him. "I can't believe you're getting off scot-free when playing the game was your idea."

Trueheart scoffed. "I wouldn't say scot-free. I got suspended, too."

"A slap on the wrist. I'm being threatened with criminal charges."

The elevator jerked to a stop on the ground floor, then dinged as the doors opened. Ari exited the office building into the parking garage. Her convertible was parked on the second level. Dusk shrouded the city in semi-darkness. Snowflakes swirled around the streetlights.

"What are you going to do now?" His heels tapped the blacktop as he followed.

Ari shot a look over her shoulder. "I'm going back to that warehouse."

"You heard Santiago, we're off the case. We have to let the authorities handle it. Besides, we've already asked around the neighborhood. No one had any helpful information."

"I'm going to take another look. Too many unanswered questions. I want answers."

His hand grabbed her forearm, jerking her to a stop. "The police have the area cordoned off. We can't get inside. You'll get arrested."

She tugged from his grip. "My career is finished, and I'm facing prosecution. What more do I have to lose?"

He pinched his lips together.

That's what she thought. "I have to do this. I have to find her."

"Then I'm going with you."

"No." Ari stormed toward her vehicle. "You've done enough damage. I don't want your help."

Trueheart kept pace. "I can't let you go back there alone. Either you let me come with you, or I'll march inside and tell my boss what you're up to."

Ari halted. Blackmail. Nice. "Fine. Just stay out of my way."

CHAPTER 9

A gent Powers was going to get him fired ... or killed.
The flurries thickened, making it difficult to see the road. The snow in the headlights reminded Nick of the starfield simulation screen saver of the 90s. Commercial buildings flashed past the windows. She made a sharp turn, and he grabbed the door handle to keep his balance. The speedometer on the dash had frequently clocked fifteen over.

Driving like a maniac would not help them find Bridgette faster. He should have volunteered to take his own sensible vehicle rather than let her drive her coffin on wheels, especially in her state of mind. She hadn't said a word since they'd gotten inside the car. Was she focused on the road or on the missing girl? Probably ... hopefully ... both.

They crossed the Platte River Bridge and entered the industrial district. Powers slowed the convertible. The warehouse loomed on the right, and as expected, a uniformed officer stood guard from inside his patrol unit. Yellow police tape cordoned off the front entrance and the empty parking lot.

"See, I told you we couldn't get in."

She cast him a sideways glance but didn't respond, instead continued to a four-way stop, took a right, then a second right onto a gravel alley half hidden in the shadows.

"Where are we going?"

The MINI Cooper came to a full stop behind a large building. Ari moved the gearshift into park, then cut the ignition. "We'll walk from here."

Nick unbuckled his seatbelt and joined her outside the car. "Agent Powers, what are you doing? Are you going to tell me the plan or what?" His frustration grew. "Why do I get the feeling you're leading me straight into a trap?"

"Can't you just trust me?"

Trust her? He was starting to believe she was as loony as everyone said. "We're supposed to be partners. Don't I deserve a little more respect?"

"You're right. I'm sorry. I'm blaming you for what happened today, but it's not your fault. It's mine. I knew better."

Footsteps crunched gravel, and her silhouette drew closer until he could feel her breath on his neck. "I'm sure the uniforms boarded up the window we exited through earlier, but maybe we can locate another entrance. Someone got Bridgette out of that building without either of us seeing or hearing them. I want to know how. I'd also love to get a look inside the abandoned SUV, but I know that's not going to happen."

Nick kept his voice low. "We could check out the boat slip where the police found the vehicle, if you want."

How could he even be suggesting this? Breaking and entering. Contaminating a crime scene. What next? Destroying evidence?

"That's a good idea." Ari stepped back, leaving a cold gap between them. "Follow me. And stick to the shadows. We don't want Captain America to spot us."

Nick chuckled. Captain America? Maybe Powers did have a sense of humor underneath all that intensity.

The only sound amid the quiet was the crunch of their shoes on gravel, occasionally interrupted by a soft slosh as cars passed on the road.

A streetlight illuminated the entrance to the escape room parking lot, reflecting off the snow accumulating on the ground. A cold breeze cut through his leather jacket, and Nick shivered. Though it likely had more to do with their present circumstances than the winter weather.

Powers pressed her back to the brick wall, peered around the corner, and made a clicking sound.

He halted beside her. "What's wrong?"

"The uniform is not in his car. If he's making rounds, we'll be spotted."

A faint glow materialized on the far side of the warehouse, and the officer's body followed.

Powers took in a sharp breath. "What now?"

"I've got an idea."

It was probably a terrible idea, but it was the first thing that came to mind.

Without warning, Nick scooped Powers into his arms, tipped her backward, and lowered his face until his lips nearly brushed her cheek.

"What are you doing?" She squirmed. "Let go of me."

"Shh, be quiet. Pretend you're into me."

The flashlight beam created a halo around them. "Hey! You two shouldn't be here. This is a crime scene."

Nick didn't move. Powers's warm breath tickled his nose. She smelled of peaches and woman. He'd been right. This was a bad idea, but he had no choice but to follow through.

"I said move along," the officer raised his voice.

Nick straightened, raising Powers, but kept both their faces out of the light. "Sorry, officer. I got caught up in the moment, you know how it is. We'll get out of here."

He put his arm around Powers's shoulder and turned her away from the officer, propelling her back in the direction they'd come.

"Just a minute."

Their steps froze. So close.

"Lady, is this man harassing you? Do you need help?"

She lifted her eyes to Nick's, and he read her thoughts. Her face had been plastered all over the news as the FBI agent with the nervous breakdown. If she turned around, the officer was sure to recognize her. He might call her in.

When she spoke, Nick prayed her voice wouldn't quiver.

"No, officer. Everything's fine. Thank you for asking."

"If you're sure. Have a nice evening. Though I don't know why anyone would be out here when it's colder than Rudolph's hooves."

Quirking the corner of his mouth and feeling the officer's gaze on their retreating backs, Nick led Powers around the corner, out of sight.

She ripped from under his arm. "What was that?"

His little stunt had made her uncomfortable.

"Look, I'm sorry. I know we're practically strangers, but it's all I could think of. If the officer assumed we were—" Nick cleared his throat—"Taking advantage of the darkness, I figured he'd not ask too many questions and just shoo us off. And it worked, I might add."

Silhouetted fingers played with the ends of her hair as she turned a circle, the other fist on her hip. "You're right. It worked, but can you warn me next time before you go sweeping me off my feet?"

Next time? She thought there might be a next time. His face warmed, and he tugged at his collar. "What now?"

"Let's go." She took a few steps toward the warehouse.

"Are you nuts? We almost got caught. You want to try again?"

"Yes."

They were going to end up in a jail cell before this night was over, but he ignored the warning, and against all reason, followed her to where the officer had busted them just moments ago.

Peering around the corner, she nodded. "All clear. He's back inside the patrol unit."

"You know if you can see him, he can see you, right?"

"We'll just have to be more careful."

"He could look this direction, and we wouldn't be able to tell."

"Are you always this negative?"

"I'm a risk analyst. It's literally in my job description."

"Well, Debbie Downer. You can stay here and keep watch. I've got a missing girl to find."

"Powers, wait—"

Before he could finish, she dashed across the opening between buildings and disappeared into the darkness.

He'd heard rumors that Arizona Powers was rash and acted without thinking, but he wasn't sure how he felt about experiencing her brazenness for himself.

He obsessively weighed the pros, cons, risks, and rewards before acting on a decision.

Agent Powers wasn't going to give him that opportunity.

Nick rolled his neck, then followed.

She knelt in the dirt behind the warehouse, running her fingers along the steel panels of the rear wall.

"What are you looking for? A secret exit?"

"Yes."

He raised his eyebrows. He'd been joking. She really thought she'd find some hidden entrance into the escape room. "Why?"

She crawled on her knees, making her way down the length of the building. "Some of these old warehouses housed underground speakeasies during Prohibition and had a secret exit in case the police showed up. I remember hearing metal and a muffled thump when the lights went out earlier. And—"

Powers stopped talking. "Gotcha," she whispered. "Here, help me," she raised her voice again. Her fingers curled around the edge of a panel. She tugged, and the metal sheet detached with a loud clang that echoed in the stillness.

Nick winced, then took it from her and set it aside. Hopefully, the officer on duty hadn't heard that.

A gaping hole appeared where the panel had been.

He pulled out his cell phone and tapped the flashlight app. A ray of light illuminated a dark tunnel with a sharp turn to the left.

"What in the world? How did we miss that?"

"I wonder where it lets out." Powers leaned forward, then jerked back. "It's really dark in there."

"You can use my phone." He held out the electronic device.

She didn't move.

"You okay?" He inched the beam higher, careful not to blind her.

Her wide pupils reflected the light ... and fear.

He furrowed his brow, then squatted and touched her shoulder.

She trembled.

"Arizona?" Was she afraid of the dark? Or small spaces?

Her gaze remained focused on a spot on the asphalt. She twitched, then made eye contact. "You—" she swallowed— "You can go. I'll—I'll stay out here and keep watch."

"Are you sure?"

It was a dumb question, but he'd asked it anyway. He wasn't surprised when she nodded.

He cracked his neck. "Let's see where this thing goes."

She scooted out of his way.

He held his phone in one hand, then climbed inside the metal tube. A snug fit, but he'd squeezed inside smaller spaces. He inched his way forward, sliding along the smooth interior. The tunnel made very little noise while he huffed and grunted. The flashlight beam fell on an obstruction. He smacked the flat metal wall with his palm.

"I can't go any farther. Something's blocking my path." He glanced over his shoulder and shined the light back the way he came in.

Powers's face and shoulders leaned into the tunnel. "There has to be a way in. See if you can find a latch or a switch or something."

Nick sighed, turned the glow on the obstacle, then ran his fingertips along the trim. The light glinted off a bronze latch near the bottom right corner. Shifting to get a better grip, he slid the latch to the left.

It creaked, and the wall sprang open by an inch.

After recovering from his wonderment, he pushed the corner, and the panel swung open, revealing a pitch-black room. Swinging his legs forward to sit on the edge of the wall, he shined the flashlight around the familiar wooden crates, metal beams, and PVC pipes.

The escape room.

"Powers!" he shouted. "You've got to see this." He leaned backward into the tunnel.

Her head appeared. "Did it work?"

"Just like you said. Come see."

"Can you confirm Bridgette was taken out this way?"

"I'll look around."

Nick stood and swept the room. Everything looked exactly as it had that morning, except for the boarded window. He pivoted, shining the flashlight back into the tunnel.

A scrunched piece of paper in the corner caught his attention. He hadn't noticed it before, maybe he'd crushed it when crawling through. He picked it up, revealing a plastic tip cover to a disposable syringe hidden beneath it. He snatched up the cover, then held the note into the light.

Chilling words had been penned across the page, leaving no doubt to the writer's identity and purpose.

> *Sorry for interrupting your game.*
> *I couldn't waste this perfect opportunity.*
> *-Enigma*

His stomach knotted. "Powers."

"Yeah?" Her voice echoed in the distance.

"Enigma took her."

CHAPTER 10

I f words could stop a heart, Ari would have gone into cardiac arrest. She leaned as far as she dared into the dark tunnel. "What did you find?"

Whatever it was, it had made him certain Enigma had abducted Bridgette.

No response.

"Trueheart? Nick?"

"Hold on. I'm coming back."

The tension in her shoulders eased at the sound of his voice. A bright light appeared, blinding Ari. She reeled off balance and blinked away the spots.

Trueheart crawled out of the tunnel and handed her a note and the tip cover to a syringe.

> *Sorry for interrupting your game.*
> *I couldn't waste this perfect opportunity.*
> *-Enigma*

"Where did you find these?"

"Just inside there." He thumbed behind him. "I'm going to take a guess that our UNSUB used a syringe to knock Bridgette unconscious, then dragged her through the tunnel to a vehicle waiting out here."

"Wouldn't we have heard them?"

Dragging all that dead weight would have been a cumbersome process.

"The tunnel's insulated. It made very little noise when I was crawling through. The perp had enough time to get Bridgette out while we were distracted by the power outage."

Or the music had drowned them out. "How did they turn off the lights?"

Trueheart swept the flashlight over the rear of the building. "There."

The beam illuminated an exterior breaker box.

Security cameras used infrared to see in the dark, plus they typically had a battery backup in case of a power outage. If the kidnappers had hacked the feed, they could have known exactly where Bridgette had been standing at any given moment.

"But why bother turning the lights back on? They could have left us in the dark." Her heart sank to her toes. She swallowed the lump that formed in her throat. "They wanted us to know they had her."

Liquid squeezed from the corners of her eyes. She swiped it away before Trueheart noticed. Not that he could see her in the dark. They could only hope the perpetrators contacted Ambassador Van Sloan with their ransom demands, then CARD could move in and recover Bridgette without incident.

Memories resurfaced like monsters rising from the black lagoon. The overwhelming stench of gunpowder, body odor, and rank alcohol filled her nostrils.

Her pulse bombarded her eardrums, drowning out everything else.

"Stand down, Agent Powers," Matt shouted.

Her chest heaved. Sweat soaked her hair and collar. She

aimed her weapon at the heart of the man who'd ended the life of an innocent child.

Scum of the Earth—he deserved to die.

"Powers. This isn't how we do things. Put down your weapon."

Her hands shook.

His hand moved.

With a wild, guttural scream, she squeezed the trigger.

"Powers, you okay?" Trueheart's voice jolted her back to the present.

"Let's go." She pivoted and headed down the alley toward her vehicle.

Trueheart crunched gravel behind her. "What now?"

"I want to get a look at that boat ramp."

Trueheart grabbed her forearm, jerking her to a stop. "Hold up. We need to call this in."

Ari yanked her arm from his grip. Why did he keep doing that? "Do what you want. I'm going. Maybe I'll see something the Evidence Response Team missed."

"You're not going to see anything in the dark. Sleep on it, and if you still want to investigate the area in the morning, I'll go with you."

Heaviness weighed the atmosphere. Feelings of guilt crushed her chest as she glanced at Trueheart out of the corner of her eye. His advice had put them on this trajectory. It wouldn't happen again. She'd check out the boat ramp in the morning without him. He was a liability she couldn't afford.

"I can't sleep. I have a missing girl to recover."

"It's not our job to find her. We're not even supposed to be here." Trueheart's voice softened. He stepped closer, and his enlarged pupils gazed intently into hers.

Ari's pulse launched to rocket speed at his nearness. She folded her arms, stuffing down the flutters in her gut. "Every minute is crucial to recovering her alive. If we delay, the crime scene will become contaminated. We won't know what's important and what's not."

"I know the statistics, Powers. But statistics don't change reality. I doubt ERT has finished in the area. We won't get close enough to see anything. The vehicle's already been towed to the precinct for sweeping and analysis."

Ari pinched her nose and sighed. "Does that ever get tiring?"

"What?"

"Being right."

A chuckle carried in the darkness. "No."

At least he was honest.

Ari stuffed her chilled hands into her jacket pockets. "Can I give you a ride home, or do you need to go back to the office?"

"To the office. My car's there."

"Right."

A half-hour later, she slowed the car and idled along the curb in front of the DSS building. The windows of the third floor still glowed. No one in that office would sleep tonight. She'd been down that road before. Crossing every 't' and dotting every 'i'. Leaving no stone unturned. Waiting in anticipation for the ransom call with adrenaline and caffeine pumping through her veins.

The passenger door opened, and Nick stepped onto the curb. The dropping temperatures sent goosebumps down Ari's arms. Or maybe it wasn't because of the chill in the air. Maybe it was knowing Bridgette was missing, and there was nothing she could do about it. She couldn't go to work tomorrow or the next day or the next … only God knew when that cycle would end.

Brigette might not be her favorite person in the world, but Ari didn't want to see her harmed. Her vision blurred. If she thought God was listening, she'd ask him how to make this right and bring Bridgette home.

"Good night." Trueheart's voice carried from the open doorway. "Here's my card. If you need anything, just call."

She didn't move to take the card, and it landed on the

passenger seat. "Good night," she responded, hoping that would signal she was ready to drive off.

"Tomorrow?"

A thousand questions were presented in that one word.

"I'll—I'll see you around." She put the car in gear. Once the door shut, she drove away without glancing in her rearview. It was better this way. He'd only slow her down. She was better off on her own.

Forty-five minutes later, she arrived home after swinging by the Bao House to grab some dinner. She parked in the driveway, exited the convertible, and approached the garage, slowing her steps the closer she got. Without her gun, she couldn't clear her house, couldn't be sure she was safe. Her hand trembled as she reached for the knob.

What am I going to do?

Call Trueheart.

At least she wouldn't be alone. She didn't have anyone else— Aunt Sheila was out of town.

Ari returned to her vehicle, picked up the business card, and dialed.

"This is Nick."

Just the sound of his voice relieved some of her tension. "It's me. Arizona."

"Agent Powers. What's up?" His surprise to hear from her so soon was apparent.

She swallowed her pride. "I need a favor."

CHAPTER 11

Nick followed the GPS to Ari's address and pulled up in front of the townhouse twenty minutes after he hung up the call. He may have broken a traffic law or two on his way over.

Her vehicle sat in the driveway, lit by the orange glow from the open garage. The snow had stopped, leaving the ground dusted with crystalline particles. Serenity blanketed the middle-class neighborhood, but something had caused Powers to be alarmed, or else she wouldn't have called him.

He killed the ignition and exited his vehicle.

Agent Powers turned from her perch on the hood of her car. Her jaw moved, chewing something. "Hi." She gave him a sheepish grin, pressing her finger to her lips. "Sorry to call."

He rounded the front bumper. An open Styrofoam container sat beside her. "No problem. Did you lock yourself out?" If that was the case, she would have called a locksmith, not him. "How can I help?"

Agent Powers sucked her lip and averted her eyes. "This is really embarrassing."

"Can't be that bad. What's going on?"

"I don't have my gun."

He glanced toward the door of the house. "Is there someone in there? Did you call the police?"

"No. I don't know." She stared at a dark spot on the concrete drive and rubbed her forehead.

"You're not making sense. Did you see signs of a break-in?" He pulled his phone from his pocket. "I'll dial nine-one-one."

"No. Don't do that. There's no one there."

"But you just said—"

"I know what I said." She hopped down, then paced the driveway with a groan. "I have a routine. Every day when I come home, I clear my house, turn on all the lights, and check the windows. I can't do that because I don't have my firearm if … if … this was a mistake. Never mind. You can go."

She faced away from him, arms folded, her chin tucked to her breastbone. Deep shudders shook her torso. Somehow this tougher-than-iron special agent had been traumatized. It was happening again, just like at the tunnel. Afraid, but too embarrassed to admit her fear.

"I'll look around." He headed for the garage.

"Are you sure?"

He looked over his shoulder.

Agent Powers made eye contact, her eyes wide.

"I've got this," he reassured her.

She nodded her appreciation.

Opening the garage door, he stepped over the threshold and flipped on the light switch. Wooden cubes held a perfect lineup of shoes. An FBI-issued jacket and a black cardigan hung on wall hooks beside a washer and dryer. Taking his time, he cleared the well-organized house, checking for intruders. Not a paper clip out of place, as far as he could tell.

When he entered the home office, his gaze landed on a ballerina music box on the desk. Agent Powers didn't seem like the ballerina type. Maybe it was a keepsake from her childhood. Matchbox cars and G.I. Joe soldiers remained buried in the back of his closet.

With a shrug, he returned to the garage, certain the house was free of monsters. "All clear. You can go in now."

"Thanks." Her shoulders relaxed. "Bao bun?" She held out the Styrofoam container.

Nick shook his head and scratched his whiskered chin. Curiosity and propriety arm wrestled in his chest. How did an FBI agent get too paranoid to enter her own house without a firearm? "Look, Powers—"

She set the to-go box on the car hood. "You can call me Arizona, or Ari. You earned it." She pulled her knees to her chest. "After all, you checked my house for the bogeyman."

"Nick." He joined her on the hood. "My friends call me Nick."

"Thanks again for coming over, Nick."

"No problem." He paused. "I'm just curious, and you don't have to answer if you don't want to, but why did you call me? What are you afraid of?"

"It's stupid, really."

"I doubt it." He playfully bumped her shoulder. "Come on. You can tell me."

When she didn't answer, he continued, "What if I tell you about something that scares me?"

She looked at him.

"Chipmunks."

A smile played at the corner of her frown. "But they're so cute. How could anyone be afraid of chipmunks?" A twinkle sparked in her pupils.

He owed her the story.

"One afternoon when I was about ten, my brother, sister, and I were playing in the park, and we fed this chipmunk our leftover chips until we ran out. I got the brilliant idea to hold out my empty hand. That chipmunk bit my finger, then crawled inside my pants."

Nick shivered. "I can still feel its tiny toenails running up and down my skin. I had to get a rabies shot. And …" He held out his right pointer finger. "… I still have a scar."

Ari grabbed his hand and pulled it closer.

Her touch warmed his insides.

Squinting, she leaned forward to get a better look, then scoffed. "That's nothing. You'd need a magnifying glass to see it."

"It's not nothing. It was a very traumatic experience." He feigned offense. "Now, your turn. What are you afraid of?"

Ari picked at her fingernail. "Tell me about your siblings."

Her request caught him off guard. His jaw locked, and he worked it loose. "I have an older sister named Marylin. She lives about an hour away from here with her husband and two daughters."

"What's your brother's name?"

"Tobias. We call him Toby."

"Where does he live?"

"In Rochester, New York, with my mom and dad." Nick cleared his throat. "He's unable to live on his own."

Ari's lips parted, and her eyes widened. "Oh, I'm so sorry."

"Yeah, me, too."

And he meant it. "Look, I don't really like talking about Toby. Can we change the subject?" Like to why she kept avoiding his question.

"What do you want to talk about?" Ari hopped down from the car and tossed her takeout container into the wheeled trash can.

Obviously, she didn't want to talk about her fears. He could respect that. He had personal issues he didn't talk about either—Toby being one of those. "Did you ever take dance lessons?"

He tried to picture Ari in ballet slippers and a tutu.

"No. Why? Did you?" She turned from the trash can. The lid banged as she dropped it.

Now that was a crazy thought. "No." Nick chuckled. "I saw

the music box on your desk. You'd have made a cute ballerina. Playing the part of the Swan Princess or a Sugar Plum—"

Ari's face turned as white as the Styrofoam. "What music box?" she demanded.

Her response pulled his eyebrows together. "A wooden one with ballerinas on it. It was sitting in the middle—"

Without a word, Ari dashed through the garage, flinging the mud room door against the wall, and disappeared into the house.

What was that all about?

CHAPTER 12

A ri skidded on the hardwood floor in the hallway, grabbed the door frame, swung into the office, and froze.

There it was.

On her desk.

The music box from her nightmares.

Her lungs seized, and she lowered into the task chair, legs quivering. It didn't make sense. They were just bad dreams. All the shrinks said so.

"You're experiencing Nightmare Disorder and sleep-related hallucinations. Imagery Rehearsal Therapy can modify the content of these nightmares and create more positive dream scenarios. Practicing good sleep hygiene and relaxation techniques can help, and we can look into medication, if you'd like to go that route."

Hallucinations or not, she was positive nightmares couldn't produce tangible objects.

She stretched out a trembling hand and touched the music box.

No doubt about it. It was real. Nick had seen it, too.

So, how did it get on her desk?

A shiver coiled at the base of her neck. She eased out of the chair and viewed the room with suspicion. Nick had said no one was in the house. But someone had been.

Her muscles twitched.

Dashing across the hall to her bedroom, she grabbed the personal firearm she kept in the small drawer next to her Bible, clipped in the magazine, then returned to the office.

Nick stood at the desk. As he turned, his gaze dropped to the weapon, and he held up his palms. "I'll go. You could have just asked. There's no need to draw a gun on me." A smile played at the corner of his lips.

Ari grew warm, and she set the firearm on the desk. "No. I'm sorry. You don't need to go. I just got spooked."

"What happened? I mentioned the music box, and you took off."

"It's not mine."

His smile faded as he stepped closer. "I swear no one was here. And I didn't see any signs of forced entry."

"Are you sure? I don't mean to question your thoroughness, but how else could it have gotten here?"

"I checked. Everything was locked up tight."

How could a figment of her imagination show up in physical form? Maybe it wasn't the same one. She glanced at the antique brass winding key. Would it produce the same tune? No way to know without giving it a try.

Not wanting to smudge any fingerprints, she grabbed a Kleenex and used it to hold the music box steady, then with a second one, turned the key. It wound tighter and tighter until she released it. Music filled the air—the same haunting melody from her nightmares.

The same one she'd heard in the escape room.

"It's not possible." Black spots flashed in front of her eyes.

The music box slipped from her fingers. The wood cracked upon impact with the floor, fracturing into pieces. Ballerinas scattered. The music grew craggy and warped, until it faded altogether. Then, silence.

How could this be happening? Had she lost complete control of her faculties?

"Hey, what's going on?" Nick's voice was soft, offering a listening ear.

Could she trust him with the truth?

"When we were in the escape room, after the lights went out, did you hear music?"

Nick's forehead wrinkled. "Now that you mention it, I did. That was the same tune, wasn't it?"

Ari nodded. At least she wasn't the only one hearing things.

"That's an odd coincidence." He knelt and picked up one of the pieces. "It seems illogical for them to be the same. Wouldn't that mean—" His words and hand hung midair.

An SD card lay haphazard among the wreckage.

He picked it up, then stood. "Who would put an SD card inside a music box? You might have tossed it out without ever seeing it." Nick pointed at a piece of paper on the desk. "Or we could have read the note."

Hidden among the springs and cogs, I've left you a gift.
Broken dreams. Broken lives. Broken music box.
-Enigma

"It's from Enigma." She glanced at her laptop. "I'm going to look at it."

"No, don't." Nick stayed her hand.

"Why not?"

"It might be a bug."

"Don't you want to find Bridgette? This might give us a clue to her location."

"Of course I do. But shouldn't we turn it over to the police?"

"I am the police."

He arched his eyebrow.

"Sort of." She bit her lower lip. "Give me one good reason we shouldn't look at it."

"This isn't our case. We're interfering with an investigation by withholding evidence. We could go to jail."

"That's three reasons."

Enigma had broken into her house and left a music box, identical to the one in her nightmares, on her desk. And he'd hidden a micro-SD card inside. All of this on the same day Bridgette Van Sloan disappeared through a prohibition tunnel from a locked escape room.

Coincidence?

"I have to do this. It's important."

"Fine."

Ari inserted the SD card into her computer. After a couple of clicks with the mouse, a media player appeared on the screen, and she hit play.

A dark figure sat center screen with a blank wall behind him. Nothing to give them any clues to his whereabouts.

"Good evening, Agent Powers. Mr. Trueheart." A deep, computerized voice emanated from the eerie silhouette. "Looking for something?"

The camera turned to reveal a frightened Bridgette tied in a chair with duct tape around her ankles, wrists, and mouth. Blood stained her hair, cheek, and jacket.

Ari gasped, fighting the urge to yell at the computer. It was a recording—not live. How could anyone treat another human being in such a despicable manner?

"If you thought the escape room was over, you thought wrong. Our little game is just beginning. And if you ever want to see this girl alive again, you'll play by my rules. Which means no police. No FBI. No DSS. If you alert the authorities, Bridgette Van Sloan dies. Is that clear?"

Ari and Nick exchanged glances. What kind of twisted game was this?

"Here's your first clue. 'On an island of pebbles in a sea of black, the highest in the land. Without coast or shore, a house of light will guide your way.' I suggest you write it down because I'll only repeat it once."

Enigma repeated the riddle.

"Remember, no cops. Just to make sure, I coded the video to erase itself in three … two … one."

The screen went black.

Ari grabbed a piece of paper and scribbled down the strange rhyme. "On an island of pebbles in a sea of black, the highest in the land. Without coast or shore, a house of light will guide your way."

The room fell silent.

She lowered into her chair.

Somehow the music box of her nightmares was connected to Bridgette's disappearance. No ifs, ands, or buts about it. What now? If they turned the riddle over to the Bureau, Bridgette could die. If they went along with Enigma's psychotic game, they might have a chance, or she still might die. Either way, she was gambling with Bridgette's life. If they recovered Bridgette, they'd also be guilty of misconduct and impeding an investigation.

Was that a risk she was willing to take?

She lifted her head to make eye contact with Nick. His thoughts were impossible to read. "What do you think we should do?"

His eyes widened. "Now, you want my opinion?"

"Yes."

"We should weigh the pros and cons—"

"There isn't time for that. We need to decide now."

"I can't make a decision without first considering the consequences—"

"We're doing this." She snatched the riddle from her desk and headed for the door. "I'll put on the coffee." She wasn't getting any sleep tonight. Bridgette's wellbeing came first.

Nick glanced at his watch. "I should go. It's getting late."

"Wait, you're leaving?" Ari paused midstride. Her stomach curled in on itself, tight and trembling at the thought of being left alone.

"It's clear you don't need or want my help."

Her shoulders drooped. "I didn't mean to give that impression. Please. I won't be able to figure this out on my own."

"Why not? You seem perfectly capable of taking care of yourself."

She loathed this feeling of helplessness. Hated it with a passion. But far worse was the feeling of being … vulnerable.

"Please, Nick. It's not about the game. It's …" She bared her soul. "Someone broke into my house. It's my worst fear materialized. What if Enigma comes back?" A whimper choked her throat.

"If we're going to do this, I have equal say. Equal partners?"

"Equal partners."

"Grab your stuff. We'll go to my apartment to figure out what we need to do next." He took Enigma's note from her hand and stuffed it into his pocket.

"Got a coffee maker?" she cocked her eyebrow.

"I've got something better."

"What's better than a coffee maker?"

"An espresso machine. There'll be plenty of caffeine to keep us awake."

Determination coursed through her veins as they headed downstairs. Enigma wouldn't get away with this. The bad guy wouldn't win. Not this time.

CHAPTER 13

Tuesday, 06 February
0300 Hours

Nick couldn't concentrate with Ari pacing his living room like a caged leopard. "Would you sit down? You're making me anxious."

"I can't. What do you think it means?" Her sleeve brushed his arm, and her breath tickled his ear as she leaned over his shoulder. "Does any of it make sense to you?" The aroma of espresso wafted from her ceramic mug.

"No."

Her closeness wasn't helping. There was something about her that drew him. She was strong and independent but carried a vulnerability that made him want to be her hero.

He didn't blame her for taking control earlier. She had every right to be worried. But he'd given her grace, and she'd agreed they'd be equal partners.

That was a step in the right direction.

He replayed it all in his head—every mistake he'd made since that morning. He'd weighed the risks. Calculated the consequences. It all should have worked out fine. How was he to know Enigma had been waiting in the wings?

Who was this person? Where did they come from? What was their fascination with Van Sloan's family? Why go to the effort of creating an entire persona for only one kidnapping?

Unless it wasn't the only one. Had Enigma struck before? If Nick had his work laptop, he could ... nothing. He could do nothing. DSS had restricted his access.

Ari drummed her fingers on the desk. "A house of light almost sounds like a lighthouse, but we live in a landlocked state. There are no lighthouses in Colorado."

"Maybe Enigma's referring to the tallest lighthouse in the entire nation."

"Where is that located?" Her phone clicked as if she was typing. "Cape Hatteras Light Station in North Carolina."

She lowered her cell. A photo of a black-and-white structure was visible on the screen.

Nick rubbed his chin. "But it's on the Atlantic coast, and the riddle says without coast or shore."

"But that's the tallest. Is there another one that isn't on the coast?"

"What use is a lighthouse if it's not on a coast? Isn't that the whole point?" A twinge sparked in his temples. "What about the island in a sea of black? The Black Sea?"

"By Turkey?" Her pitch raised. "You think we're supposed to fly to the Middle East? There's a war going on there."

"Just throwing out ideas."

With a loud exhale, he moved to the couch, flopped back on the cushions, and stared at the ceiling tiles. A lighthouse made the most sense, but what lighthouse didn't have a coast or shoreline? Unless it was a small one just for looks.

What if highest referred to its elevation?

After opening the internet browser on his cell phone, he typed the words *highest elevation lighthouse in North America.*

The photo of a white lighthouse with black trim on a small pebble-filled island in the middle of the parking lot at Sapphire Point Marina appeared on the screen. At nine thousand feet above sea level, it was the "highest" lighthouse in America, located at Silver Lake just seventy miles outside of Platte City.

He bolted upright. "I know where we need to go."

"Where?" Ari set her espresso on the coffee table.

"Sapphire Point Marina." He faced his phone in her direction.

Ari's jaw dropped. "How did you figure that out?"

Nick put on his shoes and socks. "It's a matter of elimination. Thinking outside the box."

"Let's go. We'll grab coffee on the way." She grabbed her jacket from the back of an armchair.

"You just finished an espresso."

She paused, hand on the front door handle. "Something tells me it's going to be a long day."

Sunrise wasn't for another four hours. They cat-napped in the car, then grabbed breakfast at a convenience store in Byron, the town nearest Silver Lake. No sense stumbling around in the dark, exhausted and half-starved.

The Sapphire Point Marina parking lot and dock slips stood empty as Nick parked in a marked space. An American flag, at the top of a twenty-foot pole, snapped in the morning breeze. Patches of half-melted snow lay in the shadows. A sliver of sunlight tinged the sky orange and pink over the glassy lake.

The sound of the car doors echoed off the mountains.

Nick zipped up his jacket as they approached the lighthouse.

A twenty-six-foot-tall octagonal wooden tower stood in the center of the lot on a concrete island filled with beige pebbles and dead bushes.

No one was around, but that didn't mean they weren't walking into a trap.

He wouldn't make that mistake again.

"Do you see anything unusual?" He stuffed the final bite of a granola bar into his mouth and pocketed the wrapper.

"We don't even know what we're looking for." Ari tilted backward to study the glass lantern room at the top. "It's not up there, do you think?"

Nick shrugged. He scanned the base. Just rocks, dead leaves, and used cigarettes. He paused at the door, eying the giant padlock and the "Do Not Enter" sign, then glanced back at Ari.

Neither would stop her.

"Can you pick it?"

He didn't even have to guess what she meant. It was a standard Master Lock No. 3, heavily criticized for its vulnerability. Obviously, the town of Byron wasn't too concerned about vandals or trespassers.

Ari tugged at the padlock. "Well?" She arched her eyebrow.

"Are you sure we ought to add breaking and entering to our list of crimes?"

"If it means locating Bridgette."

"I'll be back in a minute." He rubbed the back of his neck and returned to the car, retrieving the lock-picking kit he kept inside for emergencies.

Not that he'd picked a lock in years.

Slamming the trunk closed, he rested against the bumper. Time was of the essence. But he needed a moment to think through the details. He couldn't just rush ahead and open that lock. Who knew who or what waited inside?

The lighthouse only had one door and two small windows— a cramped space with no way of escape. Had Ari yet realized how snug it would be in there? Or maybe she'd planned to be the lookout and send him in on his own again?

If they both went inside, Enigma or a well-meaning security guard could lock them in.

Security guards? He hadn't thought of that. What about cameras? With all the expensive vessels that occupied the slips during the summer, the marina was guaranteed to have security. Was it still active during the off season?

Security lights and a camera were mounted on the boathouse beside a stack of colorful canoes. Another one was bolted to the public restrooms. And a third was affixed to a light pole. None of the cameras looked damaged.

They couldn't break into the lighthouse without getting caught on video.

Which also meant Enigma couldn't have left a clue inside the tower without being seen.

Nick folded his arms, and his line of sight moved past the lighthouse, out to the alpine waters of Silver Lake. Something floated on the horizon. Squinting, he stepped to the right.

Was that an island?

He grabbed a pair of binoculars for his bird-watching excursions from the trunk, focused the lenses, and pointed them toward the strange object.

Pale light shimmered off the surface of Silver Lake, but most of the body of water remained in the shadows. An island stood in the middle of the lake. At the top of a rock formation on the island was a twin lighthouse identical to the one in the parking lot. Could it be that simple?

"What are you looking at?" Ari's giant face filled the lenses. "We're in a bit of a time crunch here."

He lowered the binoculars. "There's an island in the middle of the lake. That's where we need to go."

Ari fitted the binoculars to her face. "What makes you think we'll find our next clue out there?" She moved the binoculars, then raised them again.

"The parking lot is under heavy surveillance. Enigma couldn't have left a clue here without getting caught on video. But out there—" he pointed—"under the cloak of night, it would be a sea of black. Easy place to hide a message."

"How do we get out there? Swim?"

"We'd get hypothermia before reaching the island. We're going to borrow one of those canoes."

"Borrow? You mean steal?"

"No. Borrow. I plan on bringing it back." He'd rather get caught borrowing a boat and bringing it back than for breaking into a lighthouse.

Using a hook pick, he jimmied the padlock, then he and Ari slid a green canoe from its rack and carried it to the water's edge.

Nick held the boat steady while Ari climbed inside.

It rocked, and she grasped the sides with a gasp. "We don't have a paddle."

A long piece of driftwood had washed up on the shore. He grabbed it, then hopped into the back of the canoe. It swayed, then balanced. With efficient, smooth strokes, he propelled the boat through the icy water.

Only God knew what they'd find when they reached their destination.

CHAPTER 14

O ver the horizon, the sun rose higher, while the island in the distance grew larger.

Ari glanced at Nick over her shoulder. She should ask if he needed a break—after all, she'd committed to being equal partners. She hadn't intended to take the lead, it was simply easier to count on herself.

His jacket lay across the bench. Muscles in his chest and arms flexed with each stroke. Right, then left, then back again. Smooth. An experienced, rhythmic cadence. Too perfect for an amateur.

"How did you learn to paddle a canoe?"

Nick's expression widened with surprise. He shifted his weight, and the canoe rocked. Water dripped from the driftwood as he switched sides. A breeze tousled his hair.

"My dad taught me. He's a nuclear physicist. My mom, too. When I was growing up, their work kept them cooped up in the research lab fifty-one weeks out of the year, but for one week, our whole family went on a camping trip in the mountains. We fished, bird-watched, canoed, hiked …" He pinched his lips together. "Sorry, that was probably more than you wanted to know."

"No, it's fine. I think that's great."

Nick used the makeshift paddle to steer around a log. "What about your family?"

Her tongue dried. She licked her lips, then swallowed against the grainy feeling in her throat. "I have an aunt who lives in Platte City."

If she told him the truth about her aunt, he might think she only got the security assignment because of her connections.

If she lied …

Relationships were built on mutual trust.

Then again, he'd lied to the uniform about them when he let the copper think they were in a romantic relationship.

The warmth of his breath on her cheek and the protective strength of his arms around her waist had both irritated her and tipped her off-balance with feelings she had never experienced before.

What would it be like to be in a real relationship with him?

That could never happen. Her job came first. She didn't have time for romance.

"What about your parents?"

Ari faced forward. "They died."

"Oh. I'm sorry."

"Yeah, so am I."

Dad had died before she'd started kindergarten. Sometimes she thought she had a faint glimmer of a memory, but it always faded just as quickly as it appeared.

More like a visceral sense than anything tangible. The sound of his voice—rough, gravely, and deep. The feel of his smooth face beneath her tiny fingers. And he'd smelled of starch and aftershave.

Ari always assumed she had her father's looks. Except for her physical stature, she bore little resemblance to the fragile blonde-haired woman who'd brought her into the world.

She'd never been able to locate a single still shot or video clip of Jamison Powers. Even his military records had vanished. Almost as if he'd never existed.

Mom had been a fearful person, jumping at her own shadow and never letting Ari out of her sight. How anyone had talked Ophelia Powers into the helicopter that took her life was beyond Ari's imagination.

The island drew closer until the canoe scraped bottom and came to an abrupt stop. Evergreens and bare aspens dotted the stony islet. Ari reclined to gaze upward at the lighthouse. Much smaller than the one back at the marina, but its identical twin.

Water splashed as Nick leaped overboard, then dragged the canoe onto the sandbar.

Ari's shoes sank into the soft surface. It was quiet. Too quiet. Wind whispered through the branches and shook the evergreen needles. Large footprints lingered in the off-white sand. Vegetation had been smashed down.

Someone had recently been on the island. Maybe still was.

She filled her lungs with air. "Do you see that?"

"We'll be careful." He moved to the rock formation and tested it with his boot. "Shouldn't be too difficult to climb. Are you up for it?"

"Of course." Fingers gripping crevices, she pulled her body to the first ledge, using her feet against the wall for leverage.

One step at a time, they worked their way to the top.

Nick gave her a hand when they reached the pinnacle.

Her breath caught in her throat as she stood. "It's gorgeous up here."

Silver Lake glistened in the morning sun. A gentle fog cascaded over rows of thick pines surrounding the lake, and in the distance, snow-covered mountain peaks melded with the rising dawn. Cerulean gradually replaced the blazing hues of sunrise.

"Glad you're not afraid of heights. You would have missed this," Nick teased.

Heights was one phobia that hadn't made it onto her ever-growing list. The more she feared, the harder she worked to maintain control—over herself and over her circumstances.

Approaching the "lighthouse," the corner of her mouth lifted. It was no taller than her chest, more like a decorative model than a true beacon. None of the surrounding dirt or vegetation looked disturbed. Did the lighthouse itself hold their next clue?

"Do you see anything?" Nick moved to stand beside her.

"Still looking."

She ran her fingers along the cap and felt a small indent. She tugged, and the entire roof and balcony came off. A small box sealed with clear plastic tape and a crinkled photograph lay inside the faux lantern room.

As she reached for it, Nick stopped her with a hand on her arm.

"Aren't you worried about fingerprints?"

Her eyelid twitched. "Why? We don't have any way to analyze them. What good would they do us?"

Setting the roof aside, she removed the photo from the "lantern room." The snapshot captured the likeness of an aging stone building with a green metal awning and three large windows in the front. A large clock and red letters that spelled Wynkoop Station hung above the decorative molding.

She released the photograph into Nick's outstretched hand, then removed the small box from the lighthouse.

A jigsaw puzzle piece had been hidden underneath.

The pattern wasn't anything identifiable, just a hodgepodge of color. She held it in her palm, then flipped it over. The word *Revenge* had been written in small print on the cardboard backing. "Look at this."

She handed the puzzle piece to Nick, then picked at the edge of the clear plastic tape on the box.

"Whoa. Hold up." Nick grabbed her hand. Again.

Electricity coursed through her palm. "What now?"

"What if it's a bomb?"

Ari eyed the box. "It's not a bomb."

He folded his arms. "Really? How do you know? You have X-ray vision now?"

"No."

What if he was right? Why couldn't Enigma have armed an explosive this early in the game? They had no idea what this criminal was capable of. "What should we do? Throw it in the lake? It might have something important in it."

Neither of them had access to imaging equipment.

"I'm just going to open it." Ari gave the tape a sharp yank.

Nick flinched and covered his head.

When nothing happened, Ari removed the box lid. No wires, counter, or explosives. "It's a key." She held it up.

"To what?"

"Good question."

The rectangular key with a small hole at one end held a plastic identification tag bearing the number twenty-seven. She rubbed her thumb across the notches and grooves in the blade. "It looks like a locker key from a gym."

What did a locker key have to do with a puzzle piece marked *revenge* and a photograph of Wynkoop Station?

She licked her lips. "Don't train stations have lockers for passengers to protect their personal possessions while they eat or explore or whatever?"

"That's a possibility, we should—"

A buzzing sounded in the distance, and Ari swiveled toward the noise. A speedboat sliced across the surface of the lake.

Toward the island.

Toward them.

As it neared, Ari made out the figures of two people, burrowed in heavy winter jackets and stocking caps. The passenger held something against their shoulder. A rifle.

A sharp crack echoed off the mountains.

"Get down," Ari shouted and covered her head. She dropped to the ground, slamming her knees into the solid stone surface, wincing against the pain that shot through the bones.

Two more rounds rang out, then the hum of the motorboat faded, and silence prevailed once again.

Ari moved her arms and raised her head, but the shooters had disappeared. She twisted her neck to evaluate Nick's condition, finding him prostrate beside her, arms over his head.

She rose to her knees and called his name. When he didn't respond, her hand found his shoulder. Blood seeped from a gash just above his right ear.

Oh, dear God. He's been shot!

CHAPTER 15

Ari called his name, but he couldn't answer. Not yet.

A splitting headache tormented his forehead where he'd slammed it into the rock. How could he have been so stupid? Get down, sure, but he could have done it with more finesse. Of course, he had never been targeted before either. Maybe he'd overreacted, but could anyone blame him?

With a groan, he rolled over, rubbing the sore spot above his eye.

What about Ari? Did she get hit?

He squinted, the bright sunlight compounding his discomfort. "Are you okay?"

Hovering over him, she looked whiter than Casper the ghost. "Your ear. It's bleeding."

Nick pressed his fingertips to the warm, sticky spot. "I split my ear on a sharp rock when we were climbing earlier. I said, 'ouch.' Obviously, you weren't paying attention."

A rosy shade of pink replaced her paleness. "You split your ear on a rock?" She shoved his shoulder. "I thought they shot you, you big doof. You scared me."

"No. No bullet holes." He patted his body. "If we were their target, that shooter had terrible aim."

Ari narrowed her eyes and scanned the summit. "I don't see

any damage on the rock or trees, either. It's like they missed us completely."

Nick sat up, then closed his eyes until a wave of nausea passed. "That's odd. I was sure they were shooting at us." Not that he had much experience with firearms, but those pops sounded like gunshots. "I guess I thought wrong."

"No, you were right. Someone was shooting at us. I saw the rifle. Maybe it was intended to scare us off rather than cause any permanent injuries. Or maybe they misjudged the distance. Whatever the reason, it's clear someone is trying to stop us from finding these clues."

"Enigma?" he suggested.

"Maybe. But why? Is he really that psycho?"

It wasn't beyond the scope of possibilities. A machination of this level took years—not merely days or weeks—to formulate. Enigma was in complete control of their every move. He knew it —and they knew it.

"May I see the puzzle piece?" Nick opened his palm.

Ari handed it over.

He mentally indexed the patterned side, then flipped it over to the back. *Revenge.*

Villains are made, not born.

He couldn't remember where he'd heard that phrase, but it couldn't be truer. Empathy for this stranger wrecked Nick's anger. Enigma had been driven to this. But on whom was he exacting revenge?

Ambassador Van Sloan? Bridgette? Ari? The government?

Me?

Nick added the puzzle piece to his coat pocket, along with the photo and the key.

Ari moved toward the edge. "We need to go. They might return, and they might not miss next time." She began her descent.

He held back a moment, then joined her, careful to maintain a firm grip and a steady foothold. If he fell, he'd not only hurt himself, but he could also injure Ari. And that was the last thing he wanted to do.

His breaths grew heavy, and his muscles flamed. He grimaced and shifted to another crevice. Checking that Ari was safely on the ground, he jumped the last few feet. His legs wobbled, and he leaned against the boulder to catch his balance. And his breath. He'd been behind a desk for far too long.

Ari gasped. "We were wrong. They weren't shooting at us."

Three blast holes ripped the side of the plastic canoe. Already the vessel dipped half submerged in the lake.

His heart sank. How were they going to get back to the marina?

"Do you have a signal?" Ari held her cell phone in the air.

He checked. "No. Do you?"

"No." She stuffed the device into her pants pocket, plunked down on the sand, and pulled her knees to her chest, resting her chin on top. "What are we going to do now? Are you sure we can't swim across?"

He moved to the shoreline and stuck his hand in the water, gasping as the icy particles attacked his skin. He jerked his hand back, shook it off, then tucked it inside his coat to warm up.

"That water has to be close to negative fifteen Celsius or colder. We'd become hypothermic before we got across the lake. We're a long way from the marina."

It had taken binoculars to see the lighthouse, and his muscles had been on fire by the time he'd rowed them to the island. Adding to that, the climb to the top of the boulders—he'd honestly been concerned about his ability to paddle them back to the parking lot.

"I might get a signal up top." He faced the rock formation, inhaled, then hesitated. His head pulsed as he reached for the first handhold. This wouldn't be easy.

"You don't have to be so macho."

He paused at the sound of Ari's voice. "Excuse me?"

"You can admit you're tired."

"I'm not tired." He angled toward her and folded his arms.

Ari raised her eyebrow. "Yeah, you are. I can see your muscles twitching from here. Take a break. I'll climb back up and see if I can't get a signal."

She ascended out of sight, and he lowered onto the sand, picked up a smooth rock, and tossed it between his hands.

Ari wasn't completely unprepared to deal with dangerous situations. In fact, she was probably—no, not probably, she *was* far more prepared than he was. Hopefully, she reached help. Otherwise, they could be here a long time before someone came looking. Neither of them was expected at work, and his family didn't care where he was or what he was doing.

He pinched his lips together and attempted to reroute his thoughts. Been down that road too many times before. Working alone ensured he didn't hurt anyone else. That way, the only person paying the price for his mistakes was himself.

But now …

Both Bridgette Van Sloan and Arizona were in danger because of him.

A breeze shook the barren tree branches. Lazy clouds floated in the powdery blue troposphere. A hawk rode a thermal, preying on his next meal.

Nick flung the stone across the lake's surface, and it skipped twice before sinking to the bottom.

He'd help Ari find Bridgette and get her job back, then she'd be out of his life. Even if he had a tiny heart flutter whenever she was near. Better that way. It wasn't worth losing her, too.

He checked the clock on his phone, leaned back, and shouted heavenward. "Everything okay up there?"

Silence.

The hawk dove into the water, then rose, wings swooshing, with a trout clasped in its talons.

Nick stood and brushed the sand from his pants. "Arizona? Agent Powers? How's it going up there?"

Another beat passed.

Ari's head appeared. "Everything's fine," she shouted. "I've given the park service our location. Someone should be here with a boat in ten to fifteen minutes." She swung her legs over the edge and started down.

Halfway, her hand slipped, and the toehold beneath her shoe crumbled. Pebbles and dirt rained on him. Scrambling and dangling from one branch, she reached for another growing out of the rock. Her fingers curled around it, only to have it snap and tumble to the ground.

Nick jumped back. His heart raced. "Ari, hang on!"

She slipped again, and limbs flailing, gravity had its way with her. She let out a scream as her body plummeted toward the ground.

"No!"

It was too far—he'd never be able to catch her.

Springing backward, he threw himself beneath her to cushion her fall, and she crashed into him, the force of the collision jarring his breath from his chest. His back slammed against the ground, and Ari sprawled on top of him, a tangled mass of limbs.

He groaned. "Are you okay?"

Her face hovered less than an inch from his.

Their gazes locked, and a shiver ran through her, reverberating through him. Her warm breath feathered his skin. The weight of her pressed into his chest. Soft. Warm. Lovely. She smelled of coffee and exertion.

His focus dipped to her lips. What would it be like to kiss her?

He closed his eyes. A weight lifted from his chest, and his lungs filled with air.

How could he think this way? He was still very much in love with his wife.

Some said love at first sight didn't exist, but he'd fallen for Rachel the first time he'd laid eyes on her.

Of all the hundreds of people in the audience that night, she had caught his eye. His heart had flipped so hard, he'd nearly forgotten how to escape the antique bean cuffs around his wrists.

As soon as the show had finished, he had located her in the lobby where she waited for a taxi. A thunderstorm drenched the world outside the theater. He signed her program, then held open her cab door. He'd asked her out, and, to his surprise, she'd agreed.

When her taxi pulled away from the curb, he'd stood in the rain like an idiot until his manager had dragged him back indoors.

"Nick?"

Ari's voice pulled him from his reminiscing, and he opened his eyes. She had moved from off him, and her hand hung extended, waiting to help him up.

"Thanks." He shook away the mental cobwebs, grasped her hand, then used her as a counterbalance. He brushed the dirt from his clothes and hair. "Are you sure you're okay? Nothing broken?"

"I'm fine. Did I hurt you?"

Nick shook his head.

A motor whirred in the distance. A patrol boat with an outboard engine headed in their direction. *Park Ranger* was painted on the side in large bold letters.

"Let's go. We've got to find that next clue." Ari headed for the shore, waving her arms.

Nick hung back. He was at risk of losing his heart to her—a heart that wasn't his to give.

The sooner they finished the game, the better. For everyone involved.

CHAPTER 16

The Honda Accord puttered along the winding mountain road toward the interstate.

If Ari had been behind the wheel, they'd be there by now. "Can't you go any faster?"

Nick glanced in her direction. "I'm already going the speed limit. It's not safe to take these turns too fast. We could end up at the bottom of the ravine."

A sheer drop-off ran parallel with the road. It made for stellar views, but it would be a rough way to reach the bottom of the mountain.

"We're running out of time."

"Don't you think I know that?" Frustration colored Nick's tone.

Ari bit her tongue. His knickers had been in knots ever since they left the island. Something was bothering him, no doubt, but she hadn't been able to put her finger on it. Something other than the fact their interaction with the park rangers had taken far longer than desired.

Explaining their presence on the island and the sinking canoe —without revealing their careers, the twisted puzzle hunt, or any connection to Bridgette Van Sloan's kidnapping—had required a feat of verbal gymnastics.

They could have denied any knowledge of how the canoe had ended up on the island, but the security footage from the marina would clearly show them helping themselves to the rental.

In the end, Nick had persuaded the park rangers that after using the canoe for target practice, they had accidentally dropped the firearm into the lake from the top of the rock formation. Ultimately receiving a ticket for destruction and unauthorized use of property for their efforts.

It hadn't hurt that one of the rangers had recognized him as "Nick of Time." Apparently, a signature and selfie with a retired escape artist had considerable influence in avoiding theft charges.

It wasn't the lie that bothered her. Deception was an art form most law enforcement officers had had to employ at one time or another. Undercover agents did it all the time.

But Nick had feigned romantic entanglement between them twice in less than twenty-four hours. Not meaning a word of it—or at least, she hoped not. She wasn't interested in getting involved with a computer geek who still carried a torch for his dead wife. The murder board in his apartment spoke volumes.

She shifted in her seat. "So, Nick of Time, huh?"

"Yeah, I know. It's corny, but it sold tickets." The corner of his mouth twitched. "Don't act like you didn't know. You looked me up."

"How'd you guess?"

"Isn't that what any good agent would do?" He glanced at her before taking the next tight turn.

She put her hand on the dashboard to keep from falling over. "It's an unusual vocation. Why'd you choose it?"

"Don't you mean, why did I quit?"

"I'm actually interested in why you became an escape artist."

They had an hour and a half to kill before they reached the train station, and she certainly wasn't going to use the time to talk about herself.

Nick hesitated. "I mentioned earlier that my parents are nuclear physicists. They celebrated academic success. It seemed it was the only thing that made them proud. I—no brag, just fact —was the smartest person in my elementary school. Too smart for my own good. I didn't have to study or even try—it just came naturally. But our school district didn't believe in advancing kids beyond the grades their chronological ages dictated."

"What is your IQ?"

"One-fifty-five." He peeked at her again. "Are you sure you want to hear this? I already sound like an insufferable blowhard."

"Continue."

"Okay." He cracked his neck. "My brilliance, and subsequent arrogance, rankled my classmates to no end, but I was desperate for friends, so I started entertaining them with sleight of hand … and pranks on the teachers. My actions infuriated my educators, as you can imagine, but it made me popular with the other kids.

"In my boredom, I read books about Harry Houdini and learned his stunts. When I was thirteen" –he swallowed— "there was an accident. My parents blamed me, and I ran away from home and joined the circus."

Ari tried not to chuckle. This was obviously a pivotal moment in his life, but join the circus? He had to be joking. It seemed a little too cliché to be genuine.

"I showed the ring master what I could do, and he hired me. Over the years, I mastered more complex tricks, and when I was twenty-five, I moved to Las Vegas and debuted as an official escape artist. A year later, I was one of the biggest names on the Strip."

The interstate sign winked past the window.

The Honda's turn signal blinked, and after taking the ramp, Nick merged into traffic. In another hour, the Platte City skyline would appear on the horizon, leaving the mountains in their rearview.

Ari faced the window and watched the passing scenery—a rolling landscape of high desert plains, tumbleweeds, and sagebrush. A small herd of Pronghorn fed among the dry vegetation.

She risked a peek at Nick. His eyes kept flickering to the mirrors and front windshield then back to her, like a homing pigeon returning to its base. "What?"

"I spilled my guts. Now it's your turn."

"Not much to tell." He already thought she was crazy, anything more would only add to his diagnosis.

"Really?"

Ari shrugged. "Really."

Nick moved into the fast lane to pass a semi-truck. "Tell me how you know the Van Sloans."

She cocked her eyebrow.

"Santiago said Van Sloan requested you personally for the security detail. He mentioned you had a storied history, and if your behavior toward Bridgette was any indication, I'd say the two of you have engaged in a few altercations before now."

Ari scratched an itch on her nose. "I used to babysit her when we both lived in DC. She often hid from me, but one day, I couldn't find her anywhere—searched the entire house over. Got the staff looking for her, then I called her parents, who, in turn, alerted the police. We honestly thought she'd been kidnapped for ransom. I think she had the entire city out looking for her.

"I finally found her hidden inside the china cabinet. Apparently, she'd fallen asleep. Gave everyone quite the scare. When she went missing yesterday, everything inside of me hoped it was just like that day. That we'd find her" –a sob caught in Ari's throat— "asleep in the china cabinet."

When Matt had told her of the assignment to be Bridgette's bodyguard, all the fear and hysteria of that day came rushing back. She'd failed the Van Sloans once, she couldn't bear to do it again. Would this escapade end as happily as that one had?

The turn signal clicked, and Nick slid the vehicle back into the slow lane, letting an impatient driver pass. "Bridgette used to be a little stinker."

"Used to be?"

He chuckled. "Is that why the ambassador asked for you?"

Ari nodded. Obviously, he hadn't held that day against her. *Maybe he should have.*

Nick glanced at the rearview. "What brought you to Platte City? I mean, if you'd stayed in DC, you could have been working for Hoover himself."

J. Edgar Hoover may have been the longest-serving director in the history of the FBI, but he'd died years before Ari was born.

"Technically, I do work for the head of the Bureau. But you mean, why choose Platte City when I could have been working at national headquarters?"

"Right."

"My mom died when I was fifteen, and I moved to Platte City to live with my aunt. She's the only family I have, so when I graduated from Quantico, I made a request to return to Colorado. Agents weren't exactly clambering to work in the Old West, so my petition was granted."

"What happened to your dad?"

Ari looked out the window again.

A battered pickup truck had been left to rust beside an abandoned windmill.

"My dad died when I was very young. I don't remember him at all, and no one talks about him."

"How did your mom die?"

"In a helicopter crash."

His brow furrowed. "That's ... unusual. What did she do?"

"You mean for a living?"

He nodded.

She shrugged. "I don't know. She was just 'Mom.'"

His head jerked. "I don't know many moms who get to ride in helicopters. Was she on a sightseeing tour?" He swerved to avoid something in the road. Probably a tumbleweed.

"I don't think so. I guess I've never thought about it before."

"Your mother dies in a helicopter crash, and you didn't wonder what she was doing there?"

"I was a grief-stricken teenager. I lost my mother, my home, everything, and moved in with a stranger. Aunt Sheila had never raised children and honestly, didn't have the slightest idea what to do with me. I was pretty much on my own. She loves me, and we have a good relationship now, but"–Ari blinked back tears— "It was hard. I don't know. I guess I just forgot about it."

"I'm sorry. I didn't mean to stir up bad memories. Forgive me for prying."

An awkward emptiness settled over the vehicle. Nick meant well, but talking about the past had never been easy for her. And he was right. Too many unknowns. Too many unanswered questions. Not that she hadn't tried, but Aunt Sheila was sealed tighter than a top-secret security clearance.

"It's fine. You didn't do anything wrong. I'm just a little overly sensitive."

"Passionate."

"What?" Ari wrinkled her forehead.

"You're a passionate person. You obviously emote with your entire being. Sometimes I can't feel anything at all."

How should she respond to that? I'm sorry? That's rough? Those words all sounded painfully lame. "It's not all it's cracked up to be. I wish I could compartmentalize my emotions from what needs to be done. That's what got me in trouble last year."

Nick's chest swelled. "When you shot that perp?"

"He—" Her throat choked up. "How could someone do that to a child? A child."

"I'm sure there was a reason."

"He was a bad guy. That was his reason."

"I don't believe that. There's always a reason. Villains are made, not born."

She recognized the quote from the X-Men comics. The reading material at the mental health facility had been limited.

"Okay, Professor X, don't tell me you believe everyone is inherently good?"

"No, of course not. I'm a Christian, and I believe everyone is born with a sin nature. I'm just saying that people are usually driven to commit such heinous crimes. They're rarely evil for evil's sake. Their circumstances or the actions of others pile on them until they snap. Think about it. You took a life. In the mind of some, that makes you a villain."

His words hit like a hot knife in butter. "I'm not a villain. I was righting a wrong. Exacting justice on an evildoer, for lack of a better word."

"There's your answer."

"I don't understand."

"Take Enigma, for instance, and that puzzle piece we found today. Enigma wants us to know he's avenging a wrong done to him in the past. In his mind, he's the hero."

"Enigma did what he did because he's an evil man."

"So, you think criminals do what they do simply because they're evil? And when they get caught, they should be punished without mercy?"

"Sure." If they were, there'd be a lot less crime in the world. "Honestly, I don't know why God gave us a free will knowing we would choose to do wrong. If I were God, I would have created mankind without a will, so I could control them."

Nick choked. "That's why he's God, and you're not."

The Platte City skyline appeared on the horizon, right on schedule.

Ari tucked her hair behind her ears and crossed her arms.

I'm not a villain. I did what I had to do. And I'll do it again if that's what it takes to bring Bridgette home.

CHAPTER 17

T he ornamental clock struck one as they walked under the metal awning and through the double doors into the great hall of Wynkoop Station. The century-old train station in the heart of downtown Platte City was a vibrant destination for more than just travel. Sculpted with ornate molding, stone arches, and fifty-foot pillars, it housed a five-star restaurant and the oldest hotel in town.

Queues formed at the ticket booths, and occupied benches filled the waiting area. Families and friends embraced before going their separate ways, while others entered and exited through the security gates leading to the outdoor platforms. Rails for both Amtrak and RTD stretched beyond the building. A wide staircase descended to the underground bus concourse beneath their feet.

Ari scanned the massive building, searching for signage. Standing on her tiptoes, she tried to get a better look, then grunted in exasperation. "I can't see. I'm too short."

Nick chuckled. Though shorter than average for a man, he still had a good seven to eight inches on her. "The lockers are this way." He gestured forward and started toward the west wing.

Ari followed, then slowed her steps as the hairs on the back of her neck stood on end.

Someone was watching her.

An Audrey Hepburn-esque woman sat on the bench closest to the wall, wearing sunglasses and a gray scarf over her head. Silver hair peeked from beneath the silk fabric. A gray pantsuit hung on a lanky frame. Pointed-toe shoes peeked from under the hem of her pant legs.

Only the visually impaired or people hiding their identity wore sunglasses indoors.

The woman raised a newspaper to block her face, raising Ari's suspicion. Her actions had been purposeful as if she wanted Ari to notice.

"Nick." Ari tried to get his attention. "Nick."

He didn't turn. Probably couldn't hear her over all the hullabaloo.

She looked back toward the bench, but the woman had vanished, leaving behind the newspaper. Ari's nerves tingled. Jaw clenched, she wove through the waiting area and picked up the discarded *Platte City Gazette*. A handwritten note across the top drew her focus.

Quit now. You'll never rescue Bridgette Van Sloan.

Ari's head snapped up, and she scoured the large room for a glimpse of the mysterious woman.

A gray scarf and pantsuit headed for the rear doors.

Ari dashed after her. "Hey. You. Come back. What do you know about Bridgette? What did you do with her?" She elbowed her way through the tight mass of bodies.

The woman glanced over her shoulder, then ducked out the doors.

"Ari!" Nick's voice reached her over the bedlam, and he grabbed her shoulder.

She whirled and gestured toward the exit. "We have to go after her."

He frowned. "After whom? What are you talking about?"

Strangers came in and out of the doors, but no lady in gray.

Too late. They'd never find her now.

"There was a woman. Watching me." Facing Nick, she couldn't shake the creeping feeling that crawled over her skin. What if that had been Enigma? Or someone close to him?

Nick's brow furrowed. "Where?" He skimmed the crowd.

"She's gone now. But she left this." She handed him the newspaper. "She knows about Bridgette."

His eyes flickered as he read the message. "Enigma?"

"I don't know. Maybe. But the note isn't signed. That breaks his *modus operandi.*"

Was the warning part of the game? Whatever its purpose, it was a distraction they couldn't afford. They proceeded to the locker room, and Nick held the door open. Walls of white metal lockers, four rows deep, ran the length of the rectangular room. Numbered plastic tags dangled from the locks of some, while other keys were missing, indicating that the unit was in use. Black numbers on a white strip labeled each locker, matching the number on the identification tag.

"What number was on our tag?" Ari asked.

"Twenty-seven."

The tile floor squeaked beneath their shoes as they walked between the lockers, searching for their target. They found number twenty-seven in the second row about a quarter of the way down the aisle.

"May I?" She held out her palm.

"Be my guest." He dropped the key into her hand then stepped back, creating space between them.

She inserted it into the lock, paused, then eyed Nick. "Did you give me the key because you're worried there might be a bomb in there?"

"Maybe." His cheeks flushed a distinct rosy red. "You can never be too careful."

Ari rolled her eyes. "Fine. I'll be the brave one."

What if it were a bomb? There was only one way to find out. She turned the key and tugged on the door. It creaked. She held her breath, cringed, and waited, but nothing happened. All was quiet.

No bomb. Her lungs complained, and she exhaled. "Let's see what we've got here."

Nick stepped closer.

A small black flashlight and a rolled-up piece of stained fabric lay next to a second puzzle piece.

Ari took the objects out of the locker and closed the door. She handed the puzzle piece and flashlight to Nick, then unfurled the soiled piece of material.

In the center, an emblem depicted an eagle wearing a crown, grasping a triangular ax in one talon and a skeleton key in the other.

"Ever seen anything like that before?" Nick asked.

"Doesn't look familiar. But it gives me a weird feeling in my stomach." Knots plagued her gut. "Does the puzzle piece have a word on it?"

Nick flipped it over in his palm. "Yep. Look here. The word is *death.*"

Saliva choked Ari, and she coughed. "That's not very promising."

Nick mashed the power button on the flashlight with his thumb. It lit up, but instead of a bright white light, the lens glowed neon blue.

"It's an ultraviolet black light." He waved the flashlight around, the beam invisible under the fluorescent tubes overhead. "I'm guessing we're supposed to use this to read a message."

"Where? Here?"

They didn't have access to the power switches. It was impossible to make the room dark.

Maybe the message wasn't at the station at all. But if so, where were they supposed to go to find their next clue?

A cemetery, perhaps? At night?

Nick's scrunched face studied the UV light, then glanced back at locker twenty-seven. "Hear me out. Open the locker."

She reopened the cabinet. "Now what?"

"Step back."

She moved out of the way, then he stepped forward and shone the flashlight inside the compartment. Moments passed without a word from him.

All this secrecy was trying her patience. She tapped her foot. "See anything? What does it say?"

He leaned back. "Look for yourself." He handed her the flashlight and traded places with her.

The back wall of the locker glowed with blue markings—a series of random letters, invisible to the naked eye without the blue light.

D RUFLC HN CD RDBH.
QAWDSNA HK IA HDMTL.
T MFRA HK IA QALALCDQAE.
T LANKUFEM HN CD FONKSAEM.

She lowered the flashlight. Why couldn't Enigma have left a note? In English.

Nick retrieved his phone from his pocket. "It looks like a Playfair cipher. We'll need a five-letter keyword to help us solve it."

"Think it could be that one?" She pointed at the puzzle piece in Nick's hand. "Death?"

"It's worth a shot. Here. Let me have the flashlight. I'm going to take a photo of the message."

He held up the electronic device and the flashlight, then snapped a photo. "There. Now, we won't lose the cipher." He took a second photo of the emblem. "Let's get out of here and find a quiet place to decipher this."

Ari pivoted toward the exit.

A churlish male, clad in a leather jacket, blocked the doorway. "Going somewhere?"

CHAPTER 18

The man's tone held a dangerous edge. His shoulders filled the door frame, and his bald head nearly brushed the lintel. He wore a white T-shirt, leather jacket, and biker pants. A jagged scar ran from his forehead, across his left eye, to the corner of his downturned mouth.

A muscle in Nick's cheek twitched, and he glanced at Ari.

Her fists clenched and unclenched at her sides. He could see it in her eyes—the quiet, dangerous calm before a storm.

"Can we help you?" Nick's voice quivered. "Are we blocking your locker?"

That probably wasn't the case. But words weren't flowing freely at the moment.

"Andre the giant" blinked, tipped his head, then burst into a belly laugh. "Scared ya."

Nick exhaled and pinched his lips together. He exchanged a look with Ari. What was happening here?

"You going somewhere or coming back?" Andre moved into the locker room and stuck his hand in his pocket.

Nick flinched, his muscles taunt. Did this stranger pose a threat to their safety?

"We're taking part in a scavenger hunt." Ari's voice cut through the awkwardness. "We found a clue in one of the lockers." She maneuvered toward the exit, looking like a sprinter at the start of a race.

Andre faced locker seventeen with his back to them. "Sounds fun."

"That's right. And we need to get going. Nice talking with you." Nick took a step backward. "Enjoy your afternoon."

"Just a minute."

Nick's blood ran cold. "Yes?" Of course, it couldn't be that easy.

Andre withdrew a knife from his jacket. The silver blade glistened. "You're not going anywhere." He lunged at Nick, just missing Nick's shoulder and slamming into the locker behind him.

"Run!" Nick bolted for the door, glancing behind to confirm Ari followed.

Andre was right on her heels. As she passed through the metal door, she swung it hard into his face, drawing a howl from the big man.

They threaded through the crowded station, pushing past startled commuters, and burst through the double doors into the parking lot. Nick hit the unlock button on his car keys. The taillights flashed in response. "Get in," he shouted.

Ari skidded to a stop. "No, Nick, wait. Look!"

"What's wrong?" He slowed his pace.

"The tires."

All four tires had been slashed. They weren't going anywhere in his Honda. Nick glanced over his shoulder. Andre was closing in. Brakes squealed as a car entering the lot narrowly missed the big man.

Across the street, a taxi idled in front of a hotel.

"Follow me." Nick took off toward the cab with Ari right beside him. They darted into traffic—brakes screeched, and horns blared—but they didn't stop until they reached the vehicle.

Nick yanked the rear door open, urged Ari inside, then

slammed the door behind him. "Go. Go. Go." He waved his hand at the driver.

"Where to?" The man behind the wheel made eye contact through the rearview.

"Just drive. Please." Nick struggled to catch his breath.

"I need a destination."

Andre made his way toward them. More brakes. More horns.

Nick pulled out his cell. "I will Venmo you two hundred dollars right now if you'll drive as fast as you can and not ask questions."

"Right-o." The taxi driver put the car into gear and merged as soon as there was a break in traffic.

Nick monitored Andre's progress through the rear window. "Take a right at Keystone Avenue."

"Got it."

Thirty-seconds later, the driver took the turn, clipping the curb as he went, dumping Ari against Nick.

He laid a hand on her shoulder and met her eyes. "Are you okay?"

"I am. How about you?"

"I'm fine. Who *was* that?"

"I've never seen him before."

"Neither have I." Nick checked the rear window once more, then assured that no one was following, relaxed. "At the second light, take a left onto Market Parkway."

"Will do."

"Where are we going?" Ari asked.

"To my apartment. We need to do some research on that emblem, and I need a quiet place to decipher that code."

"You said it's a Playfair cipher. Is that the one from *National Treasure 2*?"

Nick nodded. "It's a manual encryption technique using a five-by-five grid of letters. It can be complicated to work out."

Ari's stomach growled. Her cheeks flushed. "We haven't

eaten anything since early this morning. I'm feeling a little woozy."

"I'll make you something when we get to my house."

At the traffic light, the smell of fried fish wafted through the air vents. Ari took a deep breath, sighed, then pointed at the ocean-themed food truck parked on the shoulder. "Can we stop and grab something to eat? I'm starving."

Nick clenched his jaw. "There's food in my fridge."

"Seriously, the truck is right there. It'll only take a minute."

His frustration grew. Couldn't she just leave it alone. "And just forget about Andre back there?"

"Are we being followed?" Ari whipped around and gawked out the back window. At least four cars waited behind them in the turn lane.

"I don't think so, but we can't take that chance."

Nick breathed a sigh of relief when Ari settled back in her seat. "How do you know his name is 'Andre' if you've never seen him before?" she asked.

"I don't. That's just what I'm calling him."

"But why Andre?"

"Like Andre the Giant. Famous wrestler. Played Fezzik in *The Princess Bride*."

"Oh."

The light changed, and the taxi driver turned. "Which way now, boss?"

"Go three miles, then take a right at Chauncey, get on the interstate until you reach the exit for Glendale Parkway. My apartment complex is roughly four miles down Glendale, off Oak and Pine."

"Got it."

Nick leaned his head back against the seat and closed his eyes. He'd expected this assignment to be difficult, but he hadn't expected this much trouble.

Someone didn't want them to find those clues.

He needed internet access to figure out that strange emblem

and to interpret the peculiar message. The data plan on his cell phone was an option, but after one look at the battery bar, he changed his mind. It was nearly dead, and he still needed to transfer money to the taxi driver.

Pulling up the Venmo App, he filled out the info using the card on the dashboard and added an extra fifty on top of the two hundred he had promised. As soon as the money transfer went through, the phone blinked, then died. He stuffed it into his pocket. It'd need a charge before they left the apartment.

Ari's fingers tapped on the door handle.

Something would need to be done about his car. At some point, he'd call a tow, but it seemed a minor concern in contrast with their current predicament.

The taxi slowed, then stopped along the curb beside the entrance to the apartment complex.

Finally.

Nick opened the door, exited, then helped Ari out of the taxi as the driver rolled down the window. "You're all set. I sent the money and added an extra tip."

"Thanks, boss." The driver stuck his hand out the window.

Nick shook it, then as the taxi drove away, led Ari across the complex to his unit, his hand on the small of her back.

As usual, his neighbors argued on the downstairs balcony, and the air swirled with nicotine. He climbed the stairs, unlocked his door, then held it open.

She stepped inside the foyer. And gasped. Her hands cupped her mouth.

He sprang like a startled jackrabbit through the doorway, swatting at the light switch on his way inside.

His furniture had been overturned, and his belongings dispersed. He stepped over a slashed couch cushion. Kitchen drawers had been yanked out and their contents spilled haphazardly on the tile floor. Broken glass littered the living room carpet from shattered photo frames.

He lifted Rachel's photo, a jagged scar now running across

her face. When a sharp edge sliced the tender flesh on his forefinger, a tiny drop of blood stained Rachel's suit. His sinuses burned as he turned three hundred sixty degrees to take in the carnage. An uneasy feeling turned his stomach to soup. Someone had ransacked the place. What were they looking for?

Ari squeezed his bicep. "I'm so, so sorry. We'll catch whoever did this. Do you think it was Enigma?"

"I don't know, but we don't have time to find out. I don't want to be here if they come back. There're leftovers in the fridge. Help yourself. I'm going to gather a few things, then reserve us a rental car."

He gave the bedroom door a gentle shove. It creaked open, exposing an upended mattress and ripped pillows. All his personal items—clothing, books, and papers—were scattered across the room.

He plugged his phone into the charger, then returned to the living room.

Ari stared at something on the kitchen wall. Her body blocked his view.

"What is it?"

She moved aside.

Memories are like food for the soul
Once consumed, they fuel the mind
Some things can never be forgotten
Not your pain and not mine
-Enigma

Ari looked green. "I've lost my appetite. Enigma knows where I live, where you live. Where can we go? A hotel?"

"I'll think of something."

He scratched his head as he collected a T-shirt from the back of his couch and headed for his bedroom. "We'll go to my granny's house. She doesn't have internet, but if I use my phone for a hotspot, we can look up the information we need on my laptop."

He paused, walked backward, then pivoted toward his desk.

Piles of shredded paper.

Empty cords.

No laptop.

He bit his tongue and slammed his fist on the back of the couch. "He took my laptop."

"Why would he do that?"

"I don't know. Maybe he thought he could access sensitive data or use it to hack into the DSS."

"Is that possible?"

Nick shook his head. "It's my personal laptop—I don't keep government files on it."

He hadn't felt this violated since he learned that someone had sabotaged the fire suppression system that would have prevented Rachel's death.

If Enigma thought he could access confidential files from DSS, he'd be sorely disappointed. And if he was just after the laptop, did he really have to destroy the rest of the apartment in the process?

Nick's gaze shifted to the murder board, but nothing had been moved. Why destroy everything but that? His laptop contained digital files of everything that was on the corkboard. Could that be what Enigma had been after?

Could Rachel and this Enigma person have known each other, or had she crossed paths with the Van Sloans before meeting Nick? Was her death somehow connected to Bridgette's kidnapping and Enigma's twisted game?

The only way to find out was to keep playing.

CHAPTER 19

"Not your pain and not mine."

Nick ground his teeth during the entire two-hour drive east of the city. His jaw ached by the time they passed through Last Chance, the town nearest his grandmother's ranch. He turned north on County Road 71 and headed into the middle of nowhere.

If Enigma had lost someone he loved, then that could be what this was all about—some sort of payback—and that first puzzle piece seemed to indicate as much.

And this second one—*death*.

That had to be the key word to decode the cipher, or at least Nick hoped it was.

Andre, the attacker at the train station, had carried a knife but not a gun. Had they really been in danger or was it just a façade?

Just like with the canoe, no one had been hurt, just inconvenienced.

And what about that strange emblem? All the flags of the world hung in the lobby of the DSS headquarters, but that particular eagle wasn't on any of them. Neither did it resemble any country or regional seals he'd ever encountered.

Could it represent a guerrilla operation in the Middle East?

Ambassador Nathan Van Sloan had been evacuated a month ago from his position in Zahrim when a rebellion overthrew the local government. Could Bridgette's kidnapping be related to his governmental position and the war overseas?

Nick glanced at Ari.

Her eyes were closed, and her lips were parted. Soft snores emanated from her throat. They'd been going for hours. The woman looked dead on her feet.

Now that he thought about it—his eyelids were getting heavy, too. He blinked, then shook off the sleepiness. Bridgette needed them. There would be plenty of time to rest once they recovered her from Enigma's grasp.

He switched on the rental car's headlights as the final rays of sunset slipped behind the mountains to the west, and darkness enveloped the prairie. A mailbox and a driveway materialized along the dirt road. Loose pebbles crunched beneath their tires. The barren grasslands stretched as far as the eye could see. A small herd of Limousin cattle grazed on the scrubs near a water trough. A southward breeze spun a metal windmill's rusty sails.

Ari stirred and opened her eyes. "Are we there yet?"

"We're here."

The house came into view at the end of the driveway, and their headlights landed on a minivan with New York plates parked in front of the Ranch-style dwelling.

Nick swallowed. "I've changed my mind. This is a bad idea."

Ari straightened. "What's wrong?"

"Nothing. This is just a bad idea." He shifted the car into reverse, then twisted to see out the rear window.

"Unless Enigma is sitting on that front porch, we don't have any other options. Our homes have been compromised. I would call my aunt and ask to borrow her place, but that would mean another two-hour drive back into the city. I'm staying here." Ari unbuckled her seatbelt for emphasis.

Nick put the gearshift in park, shut off the ignition, and exited the car.

"What are you so worried about?" Ari asked over the roof of the rental.

"That"—Nick jutted his chin at the van—"It belongs to my parents."

Seventeen years had passed since he last saw them.

They headed for the house, but before they reached the porch, the front door swung open, spilling light onto the concrete foundation and welcome mat, and Granny stood in the doorway, wearing a lounger, slippers, and hair curlers.

"Nicky." She grinned and spread her arms. "It's so good to see you. I wasn't expecting you."

He stepped up onto the porch and bent at the waist, kissing his grandmother on her weathered cheek. "Sorry for not calling. This was a last-minute emergency."

"Never mind. You are always welcome." Granny waved her pale, wrinkled hand toward Ari. "And who is this? Come here and give me a hug."

Nick stepped across the threshold into the cozy foyer as his grandmother greeted Ari, who looked like a basketballer compared to the elderly woman.

"This is Arizona Powers, Granny, a friend of mine."

Ari made eye contact over Granny's white hair and pink curlers.

Somewhere along the way, they had become friends. And if circumstances were different, maybe more.

"It's nice to meet you." Ari hugged his grandmother, then stepped inside the house.

Granny shut the door. "Are you hungry? There are leftovers in the fridge. I just finished putting everything up, but we can reheat it in the microwave."

"Thank you, Granny. We appreciate—"

"Hello, son."

A familiar voice cut him off. A chill raised goosebumps on his arms. "Hello, Dad." Nick faced the man. "I didn't expect to see you here."

"I could say the same about you."

The temperature in the room dropped several degrees. Time had weathered Dad's features. Silver hair. Crow's feet and frown lines. Only a faint resemblance remained of the man he used to be, and he looked older than his sixty-one years.

"What's this about a last-minute emergency?" Dad's eyes shifted from Nick to Ari, then back to Nick.

"Would you mind if we camped out here for a little while?" Nick addressed Granny instead of answering Dad's question.

There'd be time for that later.

Or not.

Granny nodded. "That's fine. Though with your parents and Toby here, the guest rooms are taken."

"We don't plan on sleep—wait. Toby's here?" His eyes misted.

"Yes," Dad answered, folding his arms. "He's in the living room with your mother."

A second later, a man's voice with child-like enthusiasm carried down the hallway, blending with the sound of an electric wheelchair on the wood floor. "Nicky!"

Nick's vision blurred. "Toby," he whispered.

Leaving behind his little brother had been, and still was, his greatest regret in running away from home. "Hey, Toby. It's good to see you."

The two men embraced, and the years melted away.

Toby's tears wet Nick's cheek. Or maybe those were his own. "How've you been?"

Toby released Nick, then used the joystick to change the angle of the chair. "I'm doing good. I have a girlfriend. Her name is Angela. She's really nice." His halted speech nearly brought on another onslaught of tears. "How are you?"

"That's good, little brother." Nick squeezed Toby's shoulder. "I'm good."

A woman appeared in the hall.

"Mom."

"Hello, son."

He crossed the room, then hesitated. His mother had never been affectionate, and he doubted that had changed. "What are you all doing here?"

Rebecca Trueheart's hair had grayed since he last saw her, and her clothes hung loose, but she still had the same cowlick in her bangs, same glasses, and same pearl earrings.

"Your father and I are attending a convention in Platte City. Granny's caregiver kindly offered to monitor Toby in our absence. We didn't expect to see you."

He hadn't expected them either. If fact, he wouldn't have come if he'd known they were in town.

Ari glanced at Toby, then at Nick. "Toby?" she mouthed.

Obviously, she hadn't been expecting the wheelchair. He'd left out that detail when he'd spoken of his brother earlier that morning.

Nick nodded.

"Hi, Toby," she held out her hand and shouted. "It's nice to meet you."

Nick cringed. "Toby has excellent hearing, Ari. There's no need to shout."

"I'm sorry. I didn't realize." Ari's face reddened.

Toby took her hand and planted a kiss on the back. "Are you Nick's girlfriend? I have a girlfriend. Her name is Angela."

Ari's complexion turned a shade brighter.

Nick changed the subject to rescue them both from further embarrassment. "How's Marylin? Will you see her while you're in town?"

"She's well. The twins are keeping her on her toes." Mom spoke of Sandy and Mandy, Marylin's twelve-year-old twin daughters. "We spent last evening with them in Colorado Springs. She mentioned seeing you this past weekend. I'm glad you keep in touch."

He didn't miss the hitch in Mom's voice. How could he keep in contact with Marylin but not the rest of them?

Marilyn hadn't blamed him for Toby's accident. She hadn't made him feel unwelcome in his own home.

The air in the foyer grew hot, crowded, and tenser than two alley cats sizing each other up.

Granny touched her cheek. "Why don't we take a seat in the living room? There's no need for us all to stand around in here."

Once everyone settled, Dad folded his arms and eyed Nick. "Now, what's this about a last-minute emergency?"

Nick and Ari exchange glances. How much should they share? "We've run into a little trouble."

"We've?" Mom raised her eyebrow.

"What kind of trouble?" Dad asked. "Is this woman involved?" His gaze shifted to Ari, and he frowned.

"Yes."

Both of Dad's eyebrows shot up.

Nick's neck warmed when he realized what his father was thinking. "No," he shook his head vigorously. "Nothing like that." He sighed. "It's complicated. Um, family, meet Special Agent Arizona Powers. Agent Powers works for the FBI."

"FBI? You really must be in trouble."

"Not that kind of trouble either, Dad."

They fell silent. They should have had a lot of catching up to do, but he couldn't think of a single thing to converse about. The Bull Elk in the room was too big and too angry to pretend it didn't exist.

Ari's stomach growled audibly. She gave him an embarrassed smile. "Sorry."

Nick chuckled. "We could use those leftovers, Granny. We haven't had much to eat all day."

"Of course." Granny stood. "I'll get them right now."

"I'll help." Mom pushed off the couch.

The two women disappeared into the kitchen.

"What are you really doing here? With an FBI agent?" Dad scooted to the edge of his seat, folding his hands in his lap.

Nick glanced at Toby staring at him in admiration. He didn't want to exclude him from the conversation, but stories of kidnappings, potential murders, and home invasions might be too intense for his emotional and intellectual immaturity.

"Can we talk about it later?"

Dad seemed to read the situation. "Will there be a later?"

Before Nick could respond, Granny and Mom entered the living room carrying bowls of homemade green chili, spoons, and napkins.

"Thank you." Mom handed him a bowl.

Ari took hers from Granny, held it to her nose, and inhaled deeply. "Oh, this smells amazing. Thank you so much." She closed her eyes for a moment then dug in.

Steam rose from the thick liquid. He stirred the chili, releasing the fresh, peppery aroma with a hint of citrus and cilantro. Granny made the best green chili in the state—not that she'd ever won any accolades or recognition for it, but that was his personal appraisal.

"Tell me about this convention."

While he and Ari ate, his parents expounded on the particulars of the *International Symposium on Nuclear Physics and Reactor Technology*. It was likely he was the only one who followed the scientific dictionary spouting from their lips.

When their bowls were empty, Mom asked Ari about her position with the FBI, and with eyes shimmering, Ari spoke of the children she'd reunited with their families, while not divulging confidential or unsettling details. She avoided any mention of the Mitchells or her nervous breakdown.

The grandfather clock in the hall chimed eight times.

Dad squinted at his wristwatch. "It's getting late, Toby. We have a busy day tomorrow. You need to go to bed."

"But Dad," Toby whined.

Nick didn't blame him. He hadn't seen his big brother in

seventeen years, and now he was being sent to bed like a little kid.

"You can visit with Nick in the morning." Dad faced Nick and nailed him with a frown. "You will be here in the morning, won't you? Unless you're planning to disappear in the middle of the night again."

Dad was still hurt. Angry. Bitter.

"Dad, I—"

The paternal hand went up like a stop sign. "Later."

Would later actually come? Would Dad give him a chance to explain? Or would it be like all the other times?

Nick conceded. "Goodnight, Toby. I'll see you in the morning."

"We can't stay here all night." Ari hissed in his ear. "We need to decipher the riddle and keep moving."

He'd think of something—anything that didn't involve running off without an explanation.

With an audible groan from its driver, the motorized wheelchair headed for the guest room adjacent to the kitchen. The door slammed, and Nick winced.

"Does he need assistance?" He rose from his seat. The least he could do was lend a hand if his brother needed it—that would give them a few more minutes together. And a few more to avoid Dad's inquisition.

Dad waved him down. "You're not going anywhere until you tell me what's going on. Your mother will help your brother get ready for bed."

Mom stood. "Goodnight, Nick. Agent Powers. It was nice to meet you."

"Goodnight, Mom."

She leaned down and planted a kiss on his cheek.

Nick's stomach flipped. Had his mother ever shown him affection before? Not that he remembered, but it felt good.

Real good.

Too bad they couldn't hang around for a visit. Bridgette was still in danger, and every hour that passed increased the odds in Enigma's favor. As soon as the bedroom door closed the second time, Dad didn't give him a second to procrastinate. "What's going on, son? No more excuses."

Nick inhaled through his nose. "It's a long story."

"I've got all night."

Dad might, but they didn't. And neither did Bridgette.

CHAPTER 20

The grandfather clock struck twenty-two hundred hours as Nick opened his dad's laptop and connected it to his cell phone's data plan.

Ari had fallen asleep on the sofa, her cheek smushed against the throw pillow. Her hair fell in soft ringlets against her skin. He didn't begrudge her the rest—she needed it.

He covered a yawn, took a bite of his third piece of Granny's homemade apple pie, clicked on the internet browser, then leaned back in the recliner.

The interaction with his family had thrown him. He hadn't realized how much he missed them until he'd laid eyes on his parents and younger brother. Toby was all grown up. Physically. Not mentally, of course. That was never possible.

And it was all Nick's fault.

Because of an accident caused by his negligence, he could never undo or make amends for the fact that his brother was permanently handicapped.

He shouldn't have left his illusion kit out. Shouldn't have left the trunk unlocked. If he'd been responsible, Toby would never have climbed inside. Never would have been without oxygen for so long.

He couldn't let Bridgette die and Ari be incarcerated because of his failings. He wouldn't let another person pay for *his* mistakes.

He shifted and leaned forward, typing the words *emblem, eagle, crown, ax,* and *key* into the search box. Several images of eagles with crowns appeared on the screen. But no ax or key.

He skimmed the text. The eagle and crown symbol was often associated with royal power and authority. But no one had any information on this particular imprint.

"What are you looking for?"

Nick startled. "Dad. I thought you went to bed."

"I forgot my phone." Dad reached across the table and grabbed the cellular device. "Is this it?" He picked up the fabric with his other hand. "The clue you mentioned?"

"I've never seen that emblem before. Have you?"

Dad shook his head. "Sorry, I don't recognize it."

"I didn't think so."

"Is there anything I can do to help?" Dad lowered onto the couch cushion beside Ari.

Nick's eyes widened. Help? "Sure, um, ever solved a Playfair cipher?"

"In college."

Nick switched to the photo storage app on his phone. "I need to know what this says. It should be the directions to our next clue."

"What's the five-letter keyword?"

"We think it's *death*."

Dad left the room, then returned with a pen, a sheet of paper, and a pair of reading glasses. He sat on the couch, leaned forward, and drew a crude table on the paper. Five letters across. Five letters down. Skipping the letter J.

In a Playfair cipher, the letters I and J were treated as the same letter as they were often used interchangeably in early Latin texts.

D	E	A	T	H
B	C	F	G	I
K	L	M	N	O
P	Q	R	S	U
V	W	X	Y	Z

Dad muttered the rules aloud as he worked. "If the letters are in the same row, replace them with the letters to their immediate right, wrapping around to the left if at the end of the row.

"If the letters are in the same column, replace them with the letters immediately below, wrapping around to the top if at the bottom of the column.

"If the letters form a rectangle, replace them with the letters at the corners of the rectangle.

"If the letters are different and not in the same row or column, form a rectangle with the two letters and replace them with the other two corners of the rectangle."

Dad wrote a series of letter pairs along the bottom of the paper:

AP RI CE TO BE PA ID RE VE NG ET OB ET AK EN AN AM ET OB ER EM EM BE RE DA ME MO RI AL TO BE IM MO RT AL.

He rewrote them, separating the letters into comprehensible words.

A price to be paid.
Revenge to be taken.
A name to be remembered.
A memorial to be immortal.

"Any idea what that means?"

Nick shook his head. This one was going to take some deliberation. His brain felt like a bowl of oatmeal. Where did he even begin to unpack this riddle? Maybe Ari would have some ideas when she woke up.

Dad lowered his reading glasses and laid the pen on the table. "Can we talk?"

They'd never talked after the accident.

Maybe if they had, Nick wouldn't have felt like he'd had to escape. Mostly, Dad had yelled, and he had listened. Listened while his dad blamed him. Even if it was his fault—the guilt alone was punishment enough.

"Sure, Dad." Nick closed the laptop. "Does Toby really have a girlfriend?"

"Angela is his new nurse. She's a sweet young lady and enjoys taking care of Toby while Mom and I are at the lab. We've reduced our work hours, so she's only part-time."

Nick frowned. "Does Toby know the truth about her?"

He'd hate to think of some woman deceiving his brother, then breaking his heart when she found someone else.

"He knows. It's just a game they play."

Silence settled over the room, except for the ticking of the grandfather clock and Ari's heavy breathing.

Dad cleared his throat. "Marilyn said you work as a risk analyst for the Diplomatic Security Service. How long have you been doing that?"

"About two years." Ever since his world fell apart. "Putting my big brain to good use instead of wasting it as an entertainer."

"Son—"

"You and Mom were right. I should have listened."

If he had, maybe Toby would still be whole. Rachel would still be alive, and Cosco wouldn't have—

Too many people had paid for his stupidity.

"I know you still blame me for what happened to Toby. I'm

131

so sorry for my irresponsibility. If I could go back and do it over—"

"No, son. We were wrong." Dad made eye contact and held it. "It was fallacious of us to believe we could force you to be someone you weren't. If being an escape artist made you happy, we should have supported it, not tried to mold you into our career choices."

This was not the response he had been expecting. Who was this man, and what had he done with Nick's dad?

"But Toby—"

Dad laid his hand on Nick's knee. "Loved to climb inside of things. He was always getting stuck and needing Mom or I to rescue him. Your mom pulled him out of the dryer at least three or four times."

"But he was emulating my tricks, trying to be like me."

"We were removing Toby from dangerous places long before you had an interest in being an escape artist."

Nick sucked a breath in through his teeth. "Then why did you blame me?"

"We never blamed you. You blamed yourself. We tried to tell you it wasn't your fault, but you wouldn't listen."

"But ... you yelled at me." He hated to sound like a little boy, but this was all so overwhelming.

Dad inhaled until his chest swelled, then exhaled. "We yelled because we were afraid. Toby wasn't breathing, and we were scared out of our minds, and we took it out on you. We are so sorry we made you think you were to blame. Accidents happen. If not your magic trunk, it just as easily could have been something else. Yes, you left your stuff out, but Toby decided to climb inside. You didn't make him. You didn't push him. You didn't refuse to let him out."

Maybe Nick hadn't been directly responsible for Toby's accident, but still his handicap had resulted from Nick's lapse in judgment. Cosco had still died. And Rachel ...

"My wife died because I insisted on demonstrating a trick I had never successfully performed."

"She just as easily could have stepped out in front of a bus. When did you become a deity?"

Nick stood. "Excuse me?"

"Who put life and death in your hands? Who made you the controller of destinies? Bad things happen. Even to good people. You can't blame yourself every time something bad happens. Life is never safe. It's full of risks. If you never take a chance, you'll miss out on life's greatest blessings. I'm not saying we're not held accountable for our actions or that our lives don't influence those around us, but we are not responsible for the decisions of others or the consequences of those decisions."

Nick lowered to the edge of the Lazy Boy.

He heard what Dad said, but it was still his carelessness that had caused Toby's accident. his pride that had killed Cosco, and his foolishness that had taken Rachel's life. And if he hadn't encouraged Ari to play the escape game, they would have been more vigilant. Everything that had happened since that moment had a direct correlation to his poor decisions.

And now, Ari was going to lose her job and probably go to jail if they didn't find Bridgette alive. Ambassador Van Sloan was going to lose his only daughter, and a felon would get away with murder. This was all his fault, and he was going to make it right.

If it was the last thing he did.

CHAPTER 21

Wednesday, 07 February
0700 Hours

Dawn cast a warm glow over the living room. Ari stretched, then bolted upright. *No. No. No. We fell asleep!* She threw off the blanket someone had draped over her legs and sprang to her bare feet.

Nick slept in the recliner, head back and mouth open.

"Nick!" She grabbed his shoulder and shook. "Nick! Wake up!"

He blinked, and his expression morphed into one of shock. "I just meant to close my eyes for a minute."

His hand dropped to the side of the chair, and the footrest plummeted with a bang. He stood, raking his hands through his hair.

"We've got to get going." She scrambled to gather her shoes and socks, then screeched to a halt. "Did you figure out where we're going?"

"Dad deciphered the code, but I can't make heads or tails of where it's telling us to go."

Ari lowered to the couch cushion. "What does it say?"

Nick perched on the armrest. "A price to be paid. Revenge to be taken. A name to be remembered. A memorial to be immortal."

How cryptic. "That's clear as mud."

"Yep."

Ari rubbed the sleep out of her eyes and took a deep breath. An earthy aroma filled her nostrils. Coffee. Someone had made coffee. She'd need that to get through this day. Hopefully, they would locate Bridgette before nightfall, and see Enigma behind bars.

An archway to the east of the living room led to the restroom in the hallway. After making use of the facilities, Ari entered the kitchen in search of caffeination.

Nick's brother, Toby, stared at a toaster. An open package of store-bought bread, a butter knife, and a container of margarine inhabited the countertop.

"Good morning, Toby. How are you today?"

A pot of liquid gold waited in the carafe. Had Toby made the coffee? No one else seemed to be awake.

"Good morning," Toby answered. "I'm making toast. Do you want some?"

Ari poured the coffee into a mug that said, "World's Greatest Grandmother." Hopefully, Mrs. Trueheart wouldn't mind if Ari borrowed it.

"I like toast," Toby remarked with child-like enthusiasm, engaging her in conversation.

Ari took a sip of hot black coffee. It had just the right amount of bitter combined with a nutty, robust flavor. "I like toast, too. Did you fix the coffee?"

Toby's head wagged. "No, Granny made the coffee. I don't like coffee."

Ari set the mug on the counter. Steam rose from the ceramic. "Where's your grandma now?"

"Dad took her to see the doctor."

The toast popped up, redirecting Toby's focus before she could ask about his grandmother's health. Hopefully, it was just a routine visit and not something serious. Granny Trueheart was the kind of grandmother Ari would have loved to have had when she was growing up.

Toby touched the steaming slice of bread. "Ow, it's hot." He stuck his fingers in his mouth.

"Here." Ari crossed the kitchen. "Let me help." She snatched the hot bread and laid it on the plate, then spread butter on each piece. "There you go. It's ready now."

"I can do it. All by myself." Toby picked up the plate, then with one hand guided his chair into the dining room and up to an open space at the table.

"Sorry." Ari grabbed her coffee and joined Toby. "I like jelly on my toast. Sometimes, I put peanut butter."

Toby wrinkled his nose. "I don't like jelly."

"And he's allergic to peanut butter." Nick's mom entered the room, using a towel to dry her hair. "Good morning, Agent Powers."

"Good morning, Mrs. Trueheart."

"Please, call me Rebecca. Mrs. Trueheart is my mother-in-law." Rebecca poured a cup of coffee, added cream and sugar, then joined them at the table.

"Is everything alright with Mrs. Trueheart? Toby said your husband took her to see a doctor."

"Just routine bloodwork. Where did you and Nick meet?"

"Work. We were assigned to a security detail for a diplomat's daughter."

Rebecca glanced around the room as if expecting a third person to materialize. "Where is she now?"

"Someone took her," Nick answered as he entered the room and kissed his mother on the forehead. "Is there more of that coffee for me?"

Rebecca gasped. "That poor girl." Her gaze followed Nick into the kitchen.

"We're trying to find her"—Nick's voice carried from the other room—"but the bad guys have turned our search into a game." He returned with a steaming ceramic mug in hand.

"What kind of game?" Toby asked. He tore off a chunk of buttered toast and stuffed it into his mouth. "Monopoly?"

"Not a nice one, buddy. These are bad people." Nick sat at the table and took a swig.

"A puzzle hunt," Ari added, facing Rebecca. "Yesterday, we found fabric with a strange emblem, two puzzle pieces, and a coded message only visible by black light."

Rebecca hadn't heard them recount the last twenty-four hours to Nick's father.

Nick set the coffee cup on the table, then pulled the clues from his coat pocket and laid them beside the mug. "The last message was written in Playfair cipher. Dad decoded it last night, but I don't know what it means."

"And you're sure you have the correct keyword?" Rebecca turned the paper to read her husband's handwriting. "A name to be remembered? A memorial to be immortal?" She wiped her lips with a napkin. "Like the Washington Memorial? Or the Lincoln Memorial?"

"Maybe." Nick looked at Ari. "You used to live in DC. Could the clue mean we have to go there?"

"I hope not." Crossing state lines would compound the difficulty this game had presented.

"The Toby Memorial," Toby suggested, then laughed.

Nick smiled at his brother. "Thank you for the suggestion, Bro, but I don't think I've ever heard of The Toby Memorial."

Rebecca rubbed her cheek. "Maybe Toby's on to something. What's the name of the missing girl?"

"That's confidential. Sorry," Ari answered. "In respect for the family, we can't share that information. Not until it's public knowledge."

If and when it went public, Ari's name would be smeared from here to Timbuktu for a second time.

Ari raised her eyebrows. "What about the USS Arizona

Memorial? I'm named after the ship. My grandfather was stationed at Pearl Harbor. He didn't survive the attack."

"You think our next clue could be in Hawaii?" Nick asked. "That's a long flight."

"No, no." Rebecca waved her hand. "Not Hawaii. At lunch yesterday, I overheard some of the other scientists discussing a new exhibit at the Platte City Library. A piece of the USS Arizona is on display in honor of a local survivor of the attack on Pearl Harbor."

"No way." Ari looked at Nick. "Do you think that's it?"

"Cheaper than a plane ticket. We shouldn't eliminate it as a possibility until we've checked it out. Thanks, Mom." He stood. "The library should be open by the time we get back into town."

Rebecca carried her empty mug into the kitchen, then began adding ingredients to a large bowl. "At least eat breakfast before you go."

The Saint Andrew's Cathedral's bell struck ten as Ari and Nick entered the foyer of Platte City's downtown library. The rotunda was a blend of mahogany, brass, and antique molding. Sunlight beamed through a series of small windows around the vaulted ceiling.

Ari inhaled the smells of musty paper, leather bindings, and wooden bookshelves.

Mrs. Mayfield, the head librarian, stood behind the circulation desk, scanning a stack of books. She wore her silver hair in a bun and her reading glasses attached to a gold chain around her neck. With ease, she swiped the bar codes, then set the books on a metal cart to be shelved.

The USS Arizona Memorial display was on the second level.

At the top of the stairs, they located the multi-paneled exhibit of photographs, digitized videos about Pearl Harbor, a WWII uniform, memorabilia, and interactive biographies of some of the men who served on the ship.

In the center, encased in glass, sat the one-hundred-and-fifty-pound piece of the USS Arizona superstructure gifted by the US Navy.

Above the display, a red light flashed on a security device.

"Where do you think we'll find the clue?" Ari scanned for anything that stood out or looked suspicious or unusual. "We don't even know what we're looking for."

"We'll just have to keep our eyes peeled and hope we spot something."

"How long do we search before we decide we're at the wrong location?"

Nick snorted. "That's the question of the hour."

"I know. That's why I'm asking it." Ari allowed the corner of her mouth to lift. "I don't want to waste time on a fool's errand."

"Me neither. But I also don't want to miss something because we get impatient."

Easy for him to say—impatient was Arizona's middle name.

Two hours later, she'd read every piece of writing twice—forward and backward.

Nothing.

Ari returned to the center display and sat on the floor; legs crisscrossed. Were they in the wrong place? She hadn't seen anything, and unless it was written in invisible ink again ... but they didn't have time to wait until the library closed and the lights went off. Either they were missing something, or the next clue wasn't here.

She flopped backward onto the carpet at the thought of scouring Pearl Harbor or Washington, DC for a clue.

The security camera's blinking light caught her eye. If anyone was watching the video feed, what would they think of her lying on the floor of the library?

In her boredom, she copied the pattern of the flashes—Dash dot dot dash, dot dot dot, dash dash dot, dot dash—Ari scrambled to her feet. *That's not random. That's Morse code!*

"Nick! Come here."

A passing librarian, with eyes glaring, hushed Ari's outburst.

"Sorry," Ari mouthed as the woman disappeared out of sight. Someone moved behind Ari, and she pivoted. Nick. "Look at the blinking light on the security device. Notice anything?"

He watched for several seconds. "No."

"It's Morse code."

"That's crazy, why—"

"I don't know, but I'm guessing it's our next clue. Can you interpret Morse?"

"No, can you?"

"Yes." She knew something the great "Nick of Time" didn't. If they weren't in such a time crunch, she'd take a moment to relish the discovery. "Dash dot dot dot dash. That's BT, which indicates the beginning of a message."

.... -.. . .---- ..--- ...-- . ....- ..... .- -.... --...

"It's HDE one-two-three E four-five A six-seven," she said aloud.

Nick pulled his eyebrows together. "That's too long to be a license plate number."

"Or a phone number," she added.

She watched the lights a second time and got the same code —HDE one-two-three E four-five A six-seven. "Could that second E be a decimal point like in a library call number?"

Nick waved an invisible fly out of his face. "One-two-three-four-five doesn't exist in the Dewey Decimal System."

"It doesn't?" She wasn't up on her Dewey Decimals. "Would it hurt to look?"

"Fine. We can look, but I'm telling you, one-two-three-four-five isn't a thing."

Ari set off at a quick pace, down the stairs to the stacks, then scanned the signs on the ends of the bookcases. She motored down the 100s aisle, then stopped at the 120s, and ran her finger along the spines until she got to 130.

No 123.45. "It's not here."

Nick stepped forward and stuck his fingers where 123.45 should be. "Of course not. Decimal four-five would correlate to a precise subcategory that doesn't exist."

"Then what are we looking for, genius?"

"The call sign one-two-three stands for determinism and indeterminism. Do you know what that is?"

"No." What normal person would?

"Determinism and indeterminism are philosophies dealing with the question of whether events that happen in the world are all determined by prior decisions or if there is an element of randomness or unpredictability in the world.

"Determinism is the belief that everything that happens in life is caused by an unending chain of cause and effect. If you could determine what all those events were, you would have the ability to predict the future, knowing exactly what would happen next.

"Indeterminism is the belief that some outcomes simply arise by chance. Both concepts have been debated among philosophers and theologians for centuries."

Ari took a moment to process Nick's lengthy explanation. "Determinism implies the future is completely predictable?"

"Yes."

"What if Enigma is telling us the next clue is predictable? As in, we already know what it is."

Nick laid a hand on her forearm. His gaze carried the weight of an inescapable tragedy. "Or maybe, he's saying that no matter what we do, Bridgette Van Sloan is going to die."

CHAPTER 22

N ick couldn't let that happen.

Why would Enigma send them on this wild goose chase if the outcome was set? Wasn't that the point of the game? To give them an opportunity to win. Was there really no chance of recovering Bridgette alive?

Why send them to a section of the DDC that didn't exist? Unless it wasn't a library call sign, but another type of coded message. He tried several ciphers in his head, but all came out just as nonsensical as the original.

He scrubbed his neck. HDE 123 E45 A67. He grouped them in threes, making it easier to remember. Non-fiction didn't use letters in the DDC code. 123.45 could make sense if it existed, but what about the letters HDE and the A67? What could it all mean?

Intelligence carried a heavy price, and Ari expected him to have all the answers. But he didn't. "I'm stumped, Ari. I have no idea where to go from here."

Unless this really was Enigma's way of telling them their search was futile.

Ari's visible agitation grew. "No. It has to be here."

Yanking books from the shelves, she shook them upside down, then tossed them on the floor. A pile formed at her feet.

"Ari. Ari, stop." Nick grabbed her hands.

She struggled against his grip, with a wild look in her eyes. Her breath came in short, shallow spurts. Her nostrils flared, and hives climbed her neck where her veins bulged.

"Calm down. This is getting us nowhere. We're clearly not at the top of our game. Let's go to your house and recharge. Shower, change clothes, and reassess."

Ari's lips parted. She stopped struggling.

"We won't do Bridgette any good if we run around in circles."

A figure cast a shadow across the aisle. When a throat cleared, Nick swiveled toward the sound.

The gray-haired librarian stood, arms folded, a frown tugging on her mouth. Her eyes dropped to the books on the floor, then back to Nick and Ari. "Is this your doing?"

"I apologize. We'll clean it up right now." Nick bent and picked up one of the books.

"No." The librarian spoke harsher and much louder than expected. "Get out of my library. Now. Before I call the authorities." She spun on her heel and stalked off.

"You heard the woman. Let's go." Nick looked back at Ari and stuck his hand in his coat pocket for the car keys, but something didn't feel right. He removed the growing pile of clues. One paper had gone missing—the note from the tunnel. He must have dropped it somewhere in the library. "I'll be right back."

Leaving Ari in the aisle, he jogged upstairs. At the top, he paused and considered the security device where Ari had seen the Morse code.

Flash. Flash. Flash.

He wasn't fluent in Morse, but the blinking looked normal to him. Had Enigma stopped transmitting the message? Or had Ari seen something that was never there? He wanted to give her the benefit of the doubt, but look at where it had gotten them—a brick wall. He shook his head and returned his focus to finding the missing paper.

It lay on the floor halfway through the battleship display. A person in jeans and a dark hoodie bent down and picked up the piece of paper.

"That's mine. It's not trash."

The stranger darted across the room and pushed through the emergency exit.

"Hey, hold up. I need that." Nick chased after him.

Their footfalls echoed in the stairwell. The thief's sneakers scuffed the concrete, while Nick's hard soles tapped down each stair. At the landing, the thief dropped the paper, then shoved through the exit, and the glass door swung shut behind him.

Nick scooped up the discarded paper, then broke through the door and scanned the busy street for the runner. Gone. Disappeared into a sea of people. Nick stuffed the note into his pocket and entered the library on the main floor.

Ari waited in a plush chair beneath a sign that read 500-599. Her eyes stared blankly at an invisible spot on the gray carpet, and her arms were folded over her chest like the sleeves of a straitjacket. A strand of brunette hair dipped into her forehead.

Compassion tugged at his heartstrings. The poor woman looked on the verge of another nervous breakdown. Did she have the stamina for what lie ahead? What would it do to Ari if they couldn't rescue Bridgette in time?

He took the keys from his pocket and jingled them.

She lifted red, swollen eyes, and a knot formed in his stomach.

He'd look into plane tickets to Washington, DC. To be honest, that had made more sense to him than the USS Arizona exhibit. He hadn't wanted to argue with Ari about it, but maybe he should have. This whole diversion had put them behind schedule.

Time was ticking, but chasing ghosts around the city wouldn't help them locate the missing girl any sooner. Seeing clues where there were none was the exact opposite of what they needed right now.

This was ridiculous. She wasn't crazy. That security light *had been* blinking Morse code. Why it had led them to a call number that didn't exist—she had no answer.

Maybe it *was* all a ploy to get them off track.

Nick seemed to think so. She heard it in his voice—saw it in his body language. He didn't believe her.

What about the theory of determinism? It seemed too coincidental that the very call number she'd seen stood for a philosophy that life was predetermined and predictable. She didn't believe that to be an accident. Enigma was telling them something—she was sure of it—even if Nick thought she belonged back at the mental institute.

She unlocked her front door and let Nick inside to clear the house, then she scanned the neighborhood while she walked to her mailbox and removed a small stack of envelopes.

No one seemed to be watching the house. No strange cars were parked along the curb anywhere in the vicinity. All was quiet.

She returned to the porch to wait for Nick's all clear.

He opened the screen door. "It's safe. Come on in."

"Thanks." Ari pushed off the railing and followed Nick inside.

He flopped on her couch and closed his eyes. "Wake me when you're finished, then we'll go to my place, and I'll shower and change, too."

The corner of Ari's mouth tilted. Her knight in shining armor.

She tossed the mail onto the dining room table, went to the office, and powered up the MP3 player, then ordered a pizza from her favorite pizzeria.

The music box still lay in pieces on the floor. The lonely melody played in her head. She shivered and left the office to the sound of Elvis's *Blue Hawaii*.

She undressed, turned on the shower, climbed into the tub, and closed the curtain. Turning her face into the spray, the steaming water swept away sweat, grime, and frustration. Questions swirled like they were caught in a whirlpool.

During the drive to her house, she'd used her phone to browse the news channels for any update on the case but found nothing. No mention of it. DSS must be keeping this one as close to the vest as possible.

She knew the routine. Often kidnappers were looking for attention from the media, and by thwarting that desire, the authorities stayed in control of the situation. Sometimes, though, the plan backfired, and witnesses didn't know to come forward with information.

Unfortunately, in this case, there were no witnesses.

It still baffled Ari that Enigma and his accomplices had abducted Bridgette from the escape room without anyone seeing anything. How had the kidnapper seen her in the dark? Night vision goggles? Anyone could snag a set from Amazon, it wasn't difficult. But what about the syringe? What drug was used on Bridgette? Where, or better yet, *how* did Enigma get his hands on it? The black market?

Why hadn't the Morse code lead them anywhere useful? Where was Enigma hiding Brigette, and what did he want with her? Where did they go from here?

And right now, she had no idea.

Nick couldn't sleep. As soon as the shower came on, he sat up and spread the clues across Ari's coffee table, taking inventory— a vintage photograph of Wynkoop Station, a piece of material with a strange emblem, two puzzle pieces labeled *revenge* and *death,* a black light flashlight, and two paper notes from Enigma. The other two messages were digital—the SD card and the photo on his phone.

He picked up one of the papers. "Have you opened the package?" was written across the page in Enigma's warped handwriting.

Where had that come from? Nick scratched his head. When did the messages get switched?

At the library.

He'd assumed when the thief had dropped the paper, he was releasing the same one he'd pilfered, but he must have exchanged the first note for a new one.

How would he know Nick would drop it?

Obviously, he hadn't, but the stranger had taken advantage of the situation.

What package was it referring to? They'd opened the box hidden inside the lighthouse, the one containing the locker key. Had they received any other packages?

The one from his porch.

He'd never bothered to open it. But whatever was in there had arrived *before* Bridgette's abduction.

Before the music box.

Nick sprang to his feet and glanced up the stairs. Should he tell Ari he was leaving?

He fetched a piece of paper and a pen from the office, then scribbled a note and pinned it to the refrigerator with a Colorado state magnet.

THERE'S SOMETHING I NEED TO DO. I'LL BE BACK SOON. —NICK

CHAPTER 23

A ri sighed and shut off the faucet, only because the water had grown cold.

Nick was right—she needed that.

Feeling calmer and clearer minded, she threw open the shower curtain and reached for a towel. Something caught her eye. Her head snapped up, and her heart leaped into her throat.

Unveiled by the steam, a message had appeared in the mirror over the sink.

Funny how a wayward path leads down a crooked trail.
The direction that you seek can be found within the mail.
-Enigma

"Nick!" Ari's chest heaved.

He'd been there. In her house. Again.

Or had he written it when he'd left the music box on her desk?

She glanced around the small room. Surely she would have heard someone enter the bathroom while she was in the shower.

Her wet hair dripped on the tile floor. "Nick," she shouted a second time, but still he didn't come. Where was he? He should have been right at the bottom of the stairs. Had he fallen asleep?

As the steam cleared, she reread the fading message. The mail? As in her mail? She dressed and ran downstairs, pausing at the foot of the stairs. Her couch was empty. Where had Nick gone? She wouldn't jump to conclusions. He could easily be in the restroom or have stepped outside.

Dashing into the dining room, she searched through the pile of envelopes on the table. An unaddressed yellow coin envelope, complete with string and button, lay beneath the bills and advertisements. She unwound the string, peeled open the flap, and squeezed the sides to create an oval.

Folded-up newspaper clippings had been tucked inside.

She stuck her fingers down inside and withdrew the articles. One glance at the headlines conveyed their primary function. Obituaries. She lowered onto a ladder-back chair and spread the clippings out on the table. Each rectangle had tiny blue numbers written around the border. Her pulse pounded.

Four faces. Four names.

Jayda Roach.

Lila Dominguez.

Tanya Keller.

And Rachel Trueheart. *Nick's wife.*

Ari read the obituary from the *Las Vegas Review-Journal.*

Last Saturday evening, Rachel Jane Trueheart,
wife of legendary escape artist "Nick of Time"
died in a tragic accident at the Luminary Mirage
Theater where her husband was performing.
Trapped beneath the stage, Rachel succumbed
to smoke inhalation, then perished in the fire
caused by a malfunction in her husband's latest trick.
An investigation is ongoing. The police have made
no comment at this time whether Trueheart's death
will be ruled an accident or foul play was involved.

Lila Dominguez's obituary had been published six months

before Rachel's. All available agents, including Ari, had been dispatched to West Texas to aid in the search for the governor's missing daughter. The death of his only child had devastated Governor Dominguez, and in his grief, he resigned the governorship.

After missing for three weeks, Lila Dominguez,
daughter of Texas Governor, Ricardo Dominguez,
was found dead by a hiker on a trail outside the
Irvine Observatory on Mount Kennedy.
According to authorities, Dominguez had been dead
at least 24 hours before the body was discovered.
An investigation is ongoing. Foul play is suspected.
Governor Dominguez had received several violent
threats in the days before the disappearance.

The Bureau never learned who had sent the threats or who had killed Lila, and the case was closed—without answers.

A loud knock nearly jolted Ari from her chair. Nick? She jumped up, used the peephole, then opened the door.

A teenager dressed in a *Bunkhouse Pizza* collared shirt and baseball cap stood on the porch, holding a warming bag. The aroma of tomatoes and melted cheese made her stomach growl and her mouth water. She'd forgotten all about it.

"That'll be twenty-two, ninety-nine."

"Be right back."

Retrieving her wallet, she paid in cash, then took her order and closed the door. Setting the pizza box on the table, she lifted the lid and leaned forward to get a good whiff.

She gave a happy sigh as steam warmed her face, and she licked her lips. Popping back into her seat with one leg tucked under her, she took a slice straight from the box and took a bite.

Where had Nick gone? He couldn't have been in the bathroom this long. Maybe he'd run to the store. Without telling her? She walked to the picture window facing the street and peeked from behind the thick beige curtains. The rental car was gone.

She alligator-wrestled the panic building in her chest.

If something had happened to Nick, there would have been signs of a struggle in her living room. He wouldn't have let Enigma or one of his lackeys take him without a fight. And she doubted they would use the rental car to whisk him away.

Why hadn't he left a note?

She licked her lips. Anxiety had turned her mouth cotton dry. Water would help. She walked into the kitchen and spotted a piece of paper pinned on the fridge.

Enigma?

She lunged forward and snatched the note.

There's something I need to do. I'll be back soon. -Nick

She released the tension in her shoulders, poured a glass of water, then returned to the dining room, picked up the bitten pizza slice, and moved on to the next oldest obituary—published four years ago.

Jayda's case had been on the news just the other night. Something about some additional evidence being brought to light and the cold case reopening.

Monday morning, Jayda Roach, wife of Raymond Roach,
CEO of AegisTech Solutions and daughter of retired General
Cal Burgess was tragically found dead in her home
in San Jose, California. There were no signs of a break-in and
no suicide note has been discovered. Mr. Roach is on record as
stating theirs was a happy marriage, his wife was not suffering
from depression or mental illness. An investigation is ongoing.

A second pizza slice disappeared from the box.

The fourth and oldest obituary told the sad tale of military veteran Tanya Keller.

Captain Tanya Keller (37) died last Friday morning after
entering the lion's exhibit at the National Zoo in DC.
Keller was discovered by a zoo worker during morning rounds.
Keller had a history of mental illness, according to authorities.
Cause of death is ruled as sharp force and blunt force injuries
associated with massive blood loss. Keller was living in a shelter
for homeless military veterans up until the day of her death.
No suicide note was found among Keller's belongings, but the
medical examiner has declared this to be a suicidal act.

What a horrible way to die. Ari reclined in her chair and combed her fingers through her hair. A disconcerting sensation seized her stomach.

Call it intuition.

Call it experience.

Call it indigestion.

But these obituaries weren't just a coincidence—Enigma had chosen them on purpose.

The question was, how were Rachel Trueheart, Lila Dominguez, Jayda Roach, and Tanya Keller connected? And how did Bridgette fit in with the others?

No similarities between their deaths. No obvious *modus operandi* to speak of. The deaths happened in all different parts of the country, no resemblance between their physical appearances, and they all came from very different life backgrounds.

Ari turned her attention to the series of blue numbers around the edge of all four clippings. After retrieving her phone, she did an internet search for cipher examples until she found one that matched. It looked like an Ottendorf cipher.

But the first number couldn't be the page number because it wasn't a book. Maybe the first number was the line, the second in the sequence was the word, and the third was the letter in that word. Uncertainty niggled at her confidence. All she could do was try. Hopefully, if she made a mistake, it would be obvious and not lead them down another dead-end road.

Ari retrieved a scrap of paper from her office, then took her time, carefully counting each row and letter. She scribbled down the letters as she solved them, starting with Tanya Keller's obituary.

1:2:1, 8:1:2, 3:7:1, 7:4:4, 9:2:8
5:5:1, 8:5:3, 1:1:6, 4:6:3, 2:3:5

T-O-W-E-R R-U-I-N-S slowly appeared on her page, one letter at a time.
Ari deciphered Jayda's obituary next.

2:3:1, 3:2:1, 4:11:1, 7:2:9, 6:2:1
2:1:1, 1:1:5, 5:2:1, 7:7:6, 7:5:3, 5:3:4

A-B-B-O-T C-A-S-T-L-E.
She worked her way through the cipher on Lila's obituary.

4:4:1, 3:2:2, 1:7:7, 9:7:11, 6:2:5
8:5:4, 5:3:1, 2:4:1, 7:5:4, 3:3:2

This time, *M-O-U-N-T E-A-G-L-E* emerged as she wrote.
She paused to run a quick internet search. The Abbot family had built a castle at the Summit of Mount Eagle in the late 1800s, but two years after its construction, the building was struck by lightning and burned to the ground. The castle ruins were accessible by a hiking path at an elevation of nine thousand feet above sea level.
Only one more to go.
She rubbed her finger over the black-and-white image of Rachel's beautiful face. Nick must have been devastated when she'd passed away.
With a sigh, Ari worked through the last cipher.

1:5:1, 9:8:3, 6:2:2, 10:5:4, 6:5:5, 9:1:2, 1:3:4

8:6:1, 10:7:2, 2:1:1, 4:1:3, 5:5:1, 2:4:2

J-A-M-I-S-

Her pulse picked up speed as she added the last two letters.

J-A-M-I-S-O-N

That's my dad's name.

Maybe it was a coincidence. Just like with Abbot Castle, the next word would be a noun that belonged to this Jamison or was named after this Jamison. Another building or a part of nature ... maybe a lake?

Her heart in her throat, she finished the rest of the puzzle.

Jamison Powers.

The bottom dropped out of her stomach. Only a fool would think this was an accident.

What did Dad have to do with any of this? He'd been dead since she was a little girl. Why would Enigma use his name as one of the clues? It didn't make sense. Hopefully, the Abbot Castle tower ruins shed some light on the mystery.

They could go as soon as Nick got back.

Glancing at the clock on her cell phone, Ari checked the time. 1330. Nick had been gone a long time. That uneasy feeling settled in her stomach once again. She dialed his number and pressed the phone to her ear. When the voice mailbox answered, she lowered the phone and shot off a quick text.

No response.

Maybe he'd gone home to shower and change clothes. But he should have been back by now. Something must have happened. Had he gotten sidetracked cleaning up his house?

Or had Enigma been waiting for him when he arrived?

She tried not to picture Nick, broken and bleeding, but couldn't shake the image. Stuffing the obituaries into her purse, she retrieved her Glock from upstairs, then grabbed her keys and dashed outside to the convertible.

Please be all right, Nick.

CHAPTER 24

Two ruby eyes winked at him from his palm.

His wife's owl brooch—the one she'd been wearing the night she'd died—was never discovered among the ashes of the theater. It was unknown whether her killer had taken it as a souvenir or if someone else had helped themselves, planning to hock it for a few hundred dollars.

He'd thought it was lost forever. So, how was it here? Now? How did Enigma know anything about it?

The last two years seemed to slip away, and Nick was back on that stage with a wooden crate, a wooden stage, and a flame-retardant device that malfunctioned.

The fire had roared. Larger, brighter, and hotter. He'd stomped repeatedly on the fire suppression switch, but nothing happened. Heat charred his hands and singed his facial hair. The audience's screams echoed as they crawled over each other to get to safety.

The curtains caught fire, and the flames rose to the ceiling. Wires sparked. A track of spotlights broke loose and smashed into the floor. Smoke suffocated his lungs. His manager grabbed his shoulders and dragged him from the theater. Rachel was not among the attendees filing into the street, and the first responders had to hold him down to keep him from running back inside.

Once the fire was put out and the embers had cooled, the charred remains of her body had been located beneath the stage. Just inches from his feet. Her cries for help had been drowned out by the thrill-inducing music thundering from the speakers.

During the investigation, the police had found evidence of rope fiber among the ashes. Someone had tied her up before the fire.

Her death—and the fire—had not been an accident.

His blood pressure rose as he clenched his jaw until his teeth hurt. If Enigma had had possession of the brooch all this time, then it didn't seem a difficult jump to assume Enigma had set the fire and murdered Nick's wife.

But why? What did he have against a med student from Maryland?

A knock sounded on the front door of his apartment, interrupting his thoughts and pulling him back to the present.

"Nick." A female voice called from outside. "Nick, are you in there? It's Arizona."

He blinked and glanced at the clock on his cell phone. Fourteen hundred hours. He'd forgotten all about her.

"Coming." He opened the door, and Ari stepped inside, drenched from head to toe. "It's raining."

"Yes, it is." She shivered and wiped her face. "What happened? Why did you leave?"

Nick closed the door, battling the urge to pull her into his arms and share his body heat. "I had something I had to do." After retrieving the note and brooch from the table, he handed them to Ari. "This arrived a couple of days ago. I didn't open it until today."

Ari's eyes flickered over the note. "Have you opened the package?" She looked up at Nick with questions in her eyes.

He explained what had happened earlier in the library.

"It was at your house that I noticed the clues had been switched. I rushed home to find out what it was."

"I would have done the same thing." She looked at the brooch in her palm. "And this was in the package? What's significant about it?"

Nick rested on a chair arm, hands in his pockets. "My wife was wearing that the night she died. It was never recovered from the rubble—until now."

"It's beautiful."

"An anniversary present. I never thought I'd see it again."

"Do you think Enigma had it all this time?"

"What other conclusion could there be? But why return it now? Or at all? It doesn't make sense."

"That's not the only strange thing that happened this afternoon."

His head shot upward. "What do you mean?"

"Enigma left an invisible message on my bathroom mirror. The steam made it appear. It said, 'Funny how a wayward path leads down a crooked trail. The direction that you seek can be found within the mail.'" She withdrew something from her purse. "Here's what he sent."

Nick took the crinkled newspaper clippings and laid them out on his desk—Rachel's obituary lay among three others.

"Somehow these women are connected to Bridgette's kidnapping."

Nick skimmed the articles. All women. All suspected homicides, except one. All from different states.

"We should get in touch with their families. See what they know. What are these numbers?" He gestured at the blue scribbles on the borders. "Some kind of cipher?"

"That's exactly what it is. The game is afoot."

His mouth twitched, and he chuckled. "Okay, Sherlock Holmes, where do we go from here?"

"According to the ciphers, we need to go to the Abbot Castle ruins on Mount Eagle. It's about an hour outside of town."

Ari bit her lower lip and grew silent. Her eyes turned downward, and she stared at the floor. Something bothered her, something she was reluctant to share.

"What is it? You can tell me."

She lifted her eyes. "Jamison Powers."

Nick frowned. "Who's that?"

"My dad."

"Your dad? I'm not sure I understand."

She tapped her finger on Rachel's obituary. "That's the message I deciphered. *Jamison Powers.*"

"What does your dad have to do with this pseudo-game?"

Ari shrugged. "I don't know. I have zero memories of him. There are no photos ... nothing. It's like he never existed. If you thought my mom's death in a helicopter crash was weird, what do you think about a dad who just disappeared from off the face of the earth?"

He couldn't deny the oddity of the whole situation. "Can you think of any reason your dad would be linked to Enigma?"

Ari sat on the couch, setting her tangled hands in her lap. "The only thing I know is that he served alongside Ambassador Van Sloan in the military before I was born. My mother used to say that Dad risked his life for the ambassador's. Every year, Ambassador Van Sloan still sends us a Christmas card and a check."

Survivor's guilt? "So, your families have been affiliated for longer than you've been alive?"

"Apparently."

Tower Ruins. Abbot Castle. Mount Eagle. Jamison Powers? One of those things was not like the others. What did Ari's parentage have to do with Enigma?

A wild thought rocketed through his brain. Could Ari's father be Enigma? He shook off the ridiculous suggestion. Hopefully, they found the correct answers to their questions before his imagination got out of hand.

Nick cringed as *Jail House Rock* came over the radio in Ari's coffin on wheels. This was the third Elvis song in a row, and while she seemed to enjoy the "King of Rock and Roll," his voice grated on Nick's last nerve.

A brown sign announced their arrival at Abbot Castle Ruins, and Nick sighed in relief.

Once Ari parked in the empty lot and shut off the ignition, the sweet sound of silence filled the car.

He launched from the convertible and drew a deep breath of fresh mountain air. The mountain range peeked between the evergreen trees.

The driver's door opened, and Ari stepped out.

He faced her, stretching his arms over his head. "So, Elvis, huh?"

Ari shut the door, and the sound echoed. "He's a classic. Don't you like Elvis?"

He coughed. "Uh, no."

"Why?"

"The whole hip thing." Nick made Elvis's signature *ah huh huh* and swayed his hips, Elvis-style.

Ari laughed and covered her eyes. "Yeah, don't ever do that again." She pulled a hood over her head, tucking her hair inside. "Ready?"

A breeze rustled the pine branches and sent goosebumps down his arms. A thicker coat would have been a good idea. "Let's do this."

They passed two metal trash drums and headed up the steady incline. Their shoes crunched and shuffled on the dirt path. The aroma of pine intoxicated the atmosphere. A fat squirrel scampered across the trail and disappeared into the trees. The lack of oxygen made him feel heady, and he slowed his pace.

Before they left his apartment, Ari had borrowed his clothes while hers dried. The image of her in his oversized honorary "Engineers" football jersey—he hadn't played on the team, just tutored them—had given him heart palpitations. Rachel had often borrowed the shirt. And seeing Ari in his clothes ...

At the memory of his earlier thoughts, erythema made his neck itch.

"How long have you been a Christian?"

He stumbled over his feet. "What?"

She cleared her throat. "Earlier, you mentioned you were a Christian."

"Oh, right." He lifted his eyes to the cloudless sky, where a large bird of prey soared overhead. "About eighteen months ago, a co-worker invited me to a children's performance at his church. His daughter was singing in the production. I'd never heard about God before that, but I was intrigued. I went back several weeks in a row. The preacher preached on sin and Jesus's death on the cross. It took little to convince me I was a sinner and needed salvation."

A tear formed in the corner of his eye. "Rachel's death would have been a lot easier to deal with if I could have known that we would see each other again."

But they never would. Not in this life. And not in the next.

"She wasn't saved?"

Dirt clung to the black leather of his shoes. "I can't know for sure, but I don't think so. She was a good woman, but she gave no indication she'd ever been born again." He gave Ari a sidelong glance. "What about you? Are you a Christian?"

She stepped over a rock. "Aunt Sheila is a devoted Christian. I started going to church after I moved in with her. I got saved a couple of months later."

"It must be a relief to have missed out on all the baggage that living a life of sin brings."

Ari eyed him with a funny look.

"What?"

"Just because I became a Christian at a young age doesn't mean my life has been a bed of roses."

"Yeah, I know. I just meant that you were spared a lot of regret. Have you ever struggled with alcoholism or fornication or addictions?"

She stared out into the distance. "No, but I've seen them tear plenty of families apart. I've had a lot of Christian friends that have struggled in those areas, too. And it's not like I've never faced temptation."

"Of course not. None of us are perfect. Or immune to temptation. That's what makes grace so wonderful. And so undeserved."

Ari jammed her hands into her pockets. "Some people don't deserve grace." Her jaw clenched.

Nick came to a halt. "You really think so?"

Ari stopped beside him. "Yes, I do. Some things are unforgivable."

For if ye forgive men their trespasses, your heavenly Father will also forgive you: But if ye forgive not men their trespasses, neither will your Father forgive your trespasses.

"The Bible never says it will be easy, just that we're supposed to do it."

"Do what?"

"Forgive."

"I don't think I could." She started up the path once again.

Nick jogged after her. "How bad would someone have to wrong you before you wouldn't forgive them? Why are some hurts forgivable and not others? Who makes that determination?"

Ari's pace quickened, and he struggled to keep up.

The ruins appeared at the top of the hill.

"Ari," he called after her. "Ari, come on." His lungs heaved.

She whirled to face him. Tears wet her cheeks. "If you'd witnessed the horrors I've seen, you would understand why I feel this way. How could God expect us to forgive a pervert who molests a child? Or a psycho who guns down schoolchildren in their classrooms? Or a sociopath who locks girls in a basement? Or a maniac who holds people against their will for money? Or the scammer who robs the elderly of their life savings? Why do those people have any right to be forgiven?"

"Why did I have a right to be forgiven? Why does anyone?"

She sniffled and ran the back of her hand over her face, then onto her pants. "I've asked this question so many times, and no one's been able to give me a satisfying answer."

"I wish I knew what to tell you."

Ari shrugged. "It is what it is." She pivoted and marched up the rest of the hill, a cloud of dirt at her heels.

CHAPTER 25

A ri couldn't have been more relieved to reach the top of that hill.

Her conversation with Nick had gotten a lot heavier and a lot more personal than was comfortable. She didn't want to saddle him with her psychological issues. She had unanswerable questions—who didn't—but from now on, it was probably better she keep them to herself.

The 360-degree view from the top was spectacular—a stunning blend of dark green trees, blue sky, and pristine snow. Like a painting. The stone house lay in a U shape with a barren tree in the center courtyard. Only the outer walls remained. The tower stood out as the tallest point among the ruins.

A sense of loss settled over her as she slowed her steps. A placard shared the story of the Abbot family and the destruction of the castle. It would have been a beautiful home before the fire. A wooden split-rail fence and a sign kept visitors from getting too close.

She rested her hands on the weathered boards.

Castle Ruins Unstable. Delicate Historic Area. Please Keep Out.

Footfalls thumped from behind. Nick stopped beside her. "See anything?"

"We're going to have to get a lot closer."

She ducked under the rail and rounded the outside wall, then approached the remains of the tower and stepped inside an opening. Light filtered in from a hole overhead.

Something brushed her shoulder, and she startled.

Nick's enlarged pupils scanned the masonry. "Any idea what we're looking for?"

"No." Enigma's riddle had specified nothing other than the tower ruins. Where had he hidden the next clue? Was it behind or inside a brick?

Ari touched the crumbling mortar. Bits and dust loosened and tumbled to the concrete slab at her feet. A scratch mark beside her sneaker caught her eye.

She squatted, brushing the dirt away and uncovering the eagle emblem. The same one from the train station locker—a crowned eagle, grasping a key and an ax in its talons.

They were on the right track, but what next? Smash it like Indiana Jones did to the floor in *The Last Crusade*?

Ari leaned back on her haunches. No way could she damage a historical site. She looked upward at Nick.

His lips were pinched tight, and his jaw set. He'd noticed the mark, too.

He squatted beside her. "Do you think this was added later, or does the Abbot family have some connection to Enigma?"

She straightened up, shook her head, and shrugged. The mortar around one of the bricks had crumbled, and from this angle, it looked loose. "Got a knife?"

"No."

What could she use to scrape around the brick? Her car key?

She pulled the set of keys from her pants pocket, then used one to chip away the eroding plaster. The brick wiggled, and with a good yank, came loose from the wall.

She winced, hoping the whole thing wouldn't come tumbling

down on top of them. When nothing happened, her breath came out in a shaky sigh.

Nick exhaled loudly, bringing a smile to her face.

They'd had the same thought.

She stuck her fingers inside the gaping hole, brushing something wedged deep inside. Clawing at it until she got her fingers hooked, she tugged a dusty, dirty collection of paper bound by a leather strap, out of the wall. A wax canvas cover made the book water-resistant, but the pages were weathered, worn, warped, and yellowed with time.

Had Enigma put it there or had he only directed them to find what was already hidden there by someone else?

She blew off a layer of dirt and coughed.

"What is that?" Nick asked. "Some type of field journal?"

"Maybe." She cracked it open to the first page and read the inscription.

Specialist Tyler Keller, Service Number: 423892677
United States Army, Crimson Thunder Division

"It belonged to a soldier named Tyler Keller." Ari angled the journal toward Nick and furrowed her brow. "*Tanya* Keller was a soldier who committed suicide five years ago. Do you think she and Tyler could be related?" She shivered, remembering how Tanya had died. What circumstances would drive someone to choose suicide by wild animals?

"For now, let's assume they are until proven otherwise," Nick stated.

Ari nodded and flipped through the fragile pages. She stopped at the final entry, dated thirty years ago.

22 February
Island of Tyrrhenea, camped on beach

Sarge says we attack at dawn. I don't want to do this anymore, but Sarge said only a coward would back out after the money's been paid. I don't care about the money. I just can't stomach killing a bunch of innocent people. I miss my wife and my daughter. And something in my gut tells me I'm never going to see them again. Even if I survive the assault, we're going to be executed as traitors. Sarge said we'll be fine as long as everyone keeps their mouths shut. To be honest, I don't know if I can carry a secret like this to my grave. I have to put it here, even if no one ever reads it.

The mercenaries are as follows:

Sergeant Jamison Powers
Corporal Ricardo Dominguez
Private First Class Cal Burgess
Private E-2 Nathan Van Sloan
Specialist Elliot Reynolds
Specialist Tyler Keller

Her pulse thundered. Her dad's name was on this list, but it had to be a lie. He wouldn't have done something like this. Or would he? What did she really know of Jamison Powers? And Nathan Van Sloan? As in *Ambassador* Nathan Van Sloan? The ambassador was an honorable man. He'd never involve himself in something so heinous as attacking innocents.

No one would believe these men were traitors. They were all upstanding citizens.

A sharp gasp sounded at her shoulder, and Ari tilted her head to glimpse Nick half-hidden in the lengthening shadows. "What is it? Is something wrong?"

"Elliot Reynolds. That's my father-in-law's name."

Nick's father-in-law. As in, Rachel's dad.

Where was Tyrrhenea? Why had she never heard of the country before? She took her phone from her pocket to research the island. No bars. She'd have to look it up once they got back to the city.

"Is there anything else in there?" His gesture indicated he meant the wall, not the journal.

Ari handed Nick the book, crouched, and shone her cell phone's flashlight into the hole. The beam lit up the small space. It wasn't empty—another puzzle piece lay inside. Her stomach spun like a dryer as she withdrew the cardboard square and flipped it over. *Daughter.*

Revenge. Death. Daughter.

A heady feeling took hold of her. "If what Keller says is true —about these men being mercenaries—what if one of them killed Enigma's daughter during the attack on Tyrrhenea? What if he's taking revenge against them?"

Nick frowned. "By what? Murdering their daughters."

"It's possible. Look at the names. Most of these men have had their daughters killed."

He met her eyes, then lowered them to the journal page. "Ari. Your dad's name is on this list. Which means—"

"I'm next."

Crack!

A blast echoed off the mountains. Something whizzed by her face and slammed the stone wall behind her. Pieces of rock exploded and scattered.

"Take cover," she shouted as she pulled her Glock from her waistband. Fifteen shots. That's all they had. Would it be enough?

Pop! Pop! Two more bullets shattered the bricks. Nick crouched against the wall. This was not what he signed up for.

On the opposite side of the doorway, Ari pressed her back to the wall, holding a gun close to her face. She must have had the weapon hidden under her coat.

"How many rounds do you have?" he asked.

"Fifteen." She tried to peek around the opening but ducked back when another shot just missed them. "Do you see anyone?"

"No, but they've got us pinned down."

"We're going to have to make a run for it."

Nick raised both eyebrows. "We'll be dead."

"It's the only way. I don't have enough bullets to hold them off forever. Our only chance is to bolt for the car. A moving target is harder to hit than a still one."

"That's true, but shouldn't we think about this?"

A bullet slashed the threshold, spitting rocks and dirt.

"You got a better idea?"

"We need a plan. We can't just rush ahead."

"There isn't time. We're sitting ducks right now." Ari fired a shot in the direction the bullets seemed to be coming from. "Don't overthink it. Just run when I tell you to."

His muscles froze. "I can't help it. I overthink everything. It's part of my charm."

Silence fell over the countryside.

"Where are they?" Nick risked a peek out the open doorway. Why had the bullets stopped? Were the ambushers out of ammunition?

"I don't know." Ari leaned forward—gun aimed.

"Are they gone?"

"I doubt it. Probably trying to draw us out. We stick with the plan."

Nick threw his hands in the air, panic raising his voice. "What plan? You haven't told me the plan."

Crack! Whiz!

Ari ducked out of the line of fire. "It's now or never. When I say go, run for the car. I'll be right behind you."

"I don't think—"

"It's the only way." She stepped into the opening and fired. "Go!"

He hesitated.

"I said go." She fired a second time. "Don't wait for me."

He urged his feet forward and left the tower at a full run, kicking up dust as he went. Shots echoed off the mountain range.

Ari's car appeared. It beeped, and the lights flashed.

Dread turned his gut into a tangle of knots. The urge to reach safety drove him forward.

A piece of paper, trapped under the windshield wiper, thrashed about in the mountain gusts. He yanked the note, then grabbed the door handle, threw it open, and jumped inside the car.

A second later, the driver's door opened, and Ari dropped behind the wheel. She slammed the door, put the key in the ignition, threw the car into gear, and mashed down on the accelerator. The car lurched forward and fishtailed onto the gravel and dirt road.

A shot pinged off the metal, and another shattered the rear window. If one of those bullets got their tires, they'd be in big trouble.

His pulse thundered as if he'd been placed inside a cannon and was waiting for it to go off. He twisted in his seat. No one followed. The tension in his jaw eased, and the knot in his stomach untangled.

The dirt road turned to asphalt, and yellow and white painted lines flashed past the windows. He glanced at Ari. White knuckles clutched the steering wheel, and the color from her complexion had drained.

"What's wrong?"

A dark stain had formed on her flannel shirt and was growing larger.

"You're hit."

"I know," she hissed.

"How bad is it?"

"I don't know, but you need to drive."

Her lungs filled with air, held, then exhaled. The stain grew larger. Blood dripped onto the seat buckle. The car jerked sideways, across the rumble strips, to the shoulder. She stomped on the brake, then threw the gearshift in park.

Nick unbuckled and opened his door.

She climbed out of the car, weak and pale. Sweat beaded on her forehead, wetting her hair. Her knees buckled.

He caught her before she hit the ground.

Forearms under her armpits, he dragged her around the vehicle, then carefully helped her into the passenger seat, laying it back, and buckled her in. His chest tightened at the sight of her blood on his hands. Taking off his outer shirt, he pressed it to her wound. Red crept along the threads. As soon as he had cell signal, he'd call for an ambulance to meet them.

Hang on, Ari. Don't you dare die on me.

CHAPTER 26

2000 Hours

"I'm fine. Everyone needs to stop fussing."

Nick paced the hospital recovery room. "You're not fine. They gave you two pints of blood. You have a cracked rib and thirty stitches. You could have died."

The bullet went clean through. That, at least, was something to be thankful for.

Ari shifted and winced. "I would have been fine if you would have run when I said to. Why did you hesitate?"

"I didn't want to act without analyzing the situation and thinking things through. Hasty decisions lead to mistakes."

She folded her arms. "Your mistake was not acting quickly. I didn't have enough shots to keep them down until we got to the car. Why do you have to overthink everything?"

"Why do you rush in without thinking at all?" Nick mirrored her posture.

"I don't understand you. You used to be 'Nick of Time.' You were known for your recklessness and impetuosity. What happened? Is this all because of Rachel?"

Nick lowered into the chair. Ari deserved the truth.

"After I ran away from home, Circo Fratelli employed me as

an escape artist for seven years. People loved my tricks. The crazier the stunt, the more applause I received. When I was twenty, I heard about this trick that involved being locked inside a burning box. I practiced it a couple of times but never successfully completed the stunt.

"One windy night, the ringmaster canceled all acts involving fire. The crowd booed the lack of flame, and I wanted to wow them, so I demanded to do the burning box trick. Cosco the Clown, my friend and mentor, urged me to reconsider. I wouldn't. I even threatened to quit.

"A big gust of wind blasted through the tent in the middle of the trick. Flames soared, catching the canvas on fire. As our customers scattered, Cosco helped me out of the box. Because I was wearing a flame-retardant suit, my injuries were minimal. Cosco wasn't so lucky. He died, and I was fired.

"After I left the circus, I went to college and graduated with a degree in cyber security. I tried it for a while, but I missed the applause. I thought if I was careful, it would all work out okay. I practiced harder, and I never did a stunt without fully testing it first. That night, the night Rachel died, the crowd was going wild. I was hyped up on adrenaline and accolades. I asked Rachel to set up the burning box trick, even though I'd still never successfully performed the stunt. She cautioned me against it, but I wouldn't listen."

Nick exhaled. His vision blurred. "You know the rest. Maybe if I hadn't been in such a rush to prove myself, she'd still be alive. Cosco may still be alive."

"I'm so sorry." Ari's fingers twisted in her bed sheet. Her color drained. She laid her head back on her pillow and closed her eyes.

"Are you in pain? Want me to get the nurse?"

This, too, was his fault. Anyone who got close to him got hurt.

"Please do," she whispered with a strained voice.

Nick jumped from the chair and ran to the doorway. The

nurses' station stood only a few feet away. Nurse Reese, the head nurse, spoke with a middle-aged woman with blonde highlights and wearing a black dress and pumps.

"Nurse! Nurse Reese."

Both women looked his direction.

His eyes widened. "Deputy Secretary, what are you doing here?"

The only reason the head of the Threat Investigations and Analysis Department might be at the hospital at this moment was to fire him.

"Mr. Trueheart." Deputy Powers held out her hand. "Arizona is my niece."

Footfalls urged Ari to peel open her eyes. Nick, Nurse Reese, and Aunt Sheila entered her hospital room. She tried to sit up and smile, but the pain that shot through her side stole her breath away. "Aunt Sheila. What are you doing here?"

"The hospital called me."

Nurse Reese stepped up to the bed, hung a bag on the IV pole, then pressed some buttons. "You're on a morphine drip. If you start hurting, just press this button." She handed Ari a small device. "Need anything else?"

A sense of relaxation washed over Ari, and her eyelids drooped. "No. I'm fine. Thank you."

"Call if you need anything." Nurse Reese paused next to Aunt Sheila. "Nice to meet you, Miss Powers. I wish it was under better circumstances."

Aunt Sheila shook the nurse's outstretched hand. "Me, too. Thank you for taking such good care of my niece."

"You're welcome. She'll rest more comfortably now." Nurse Reese left the room.

Aunt Sheila sat on the bed, picked up Ari's hand, and patted it. "Really, Arizona. How did you get shot when you're not even on assignment?"

Nick coughed and faced the window overlooking the street below.

She hadn't told him the truth about her aunt when he'd asked about her family. Now he knew.

Ari's eyelids grew heavy. They closed, and she opened them again. Her limbs felt light, like she was floating. "We were trying to find Bridgette."

"We?" Aunt Sheila cast a scalding glance at Nick over her shoulder. "Neither of you are supposed to be working on that case."

"We were too invested to give up." Ari's voice grew thick. "Enigma is still out there. The game isn't over."

"What *game*? And I don't want the Reader's Digest version, Arizona. I want the truth. What is this game you're talking about?"

Ari's eyes wouldn't stay open. "Nick had better explain."

She closed her eyes and slowed her breathing. The pain had shrunk to a manageable level, and exhaustion took over.

How would she find Enigma like this? How could she rescue Bridgette now?

Nick's soft voice filtered into her mushy brain. "Deputy Secretary ... she never mentioned ... same agency."

Ari opened her eyes. The track lighting had been turned off, and Aunt Sheila sat nodding off in the chair beside the bed. Nick was nowhere to be seen. "Where's Nick?"

Both her thoughts and voice had cleared.

Aunt Sheila opened her eyes, leaned forward, and took Ari's hand. "I sent him down to the cafeteria to get something to eat. How are you feeling?"

Like she'd been thrown into the FBI fitness test on day one at Quantico—without warning.

"Fine."

A sharp pain in her side reminded her how not fine she really was. She winced and sucked a breath in through her teeth. "Did he get everything explained?"

"More or less. What were you thinking?"

"I wasn't. I just wanted to find Bridgette. I just wanted to stop Enigma."

"By going against protocol? You were suspended. It wasn't your case."

"I know. But I had to do something."

Aunt Sheila shook her head. "Sometimes you remind me so much of your father. He ran headlong into trouble, too."

Ari swallowed. This was her chance. "Speaking of Dad, how did he die?"

It was something they had never talked about. Dad was Aunt Sheila's only brother, and yet, she never even mentioned his name.

"Arizona—"

"What was Mom doing in that helicopter?" The numbers on the heart rate monitor increased. "What happened to my parents?"

"I don't know how my brother died. His death records are sealed. And as for why your mother was in that helicopter that day—I don't know that either. All I know is that your parents worked for the United States government. Some alphabet soup agency, like DSS, FBI, CIA, DEA, FDA … I didn't ask, and they didn't tell me. Probably couldn't."

Aunt Sheila's thumb stroked Ari's knuckles. "Why didn't *you* tell Nick the truth about who I am?"

"I didn't want him to think I got the assignment based on my connections." Ari's tongue felt like it was stuck to the roof of her mouth. "Water, please."

Aunt Sheila picked up the plastic water tracking carafe from the rolling table and handed it to Ari, who took a drink through the flexible straw.

Her tongue loosened, and her throat soothed. She sighed, then wiped a dribble of water from her chin. "Why did you suggest I be assigned to Bridgette Van Sloan's security team?"

"Director Carlton was going to fire you. Transferring you to DSS was the only way to save your job."

Ari's sinuses burned. "I ended up suspended, anyway."

"I know. And I'm so sorry. I never expected things to go so wrong." Aunt Sheila released Ari's hand again, stood, and faced the window. Moonlight slanted through the glass, illuminating her profile. The silence stretched on for several minutes. "The authorities are doing everything they can to locate Bridgette."

But what if it wasn't enough?

A knock rapped on the wall, and the curtain peeled back. A nurse entered the room, pushing a cart with a laptop. "Hi, I'm Nurse Bynum. We just need to update your records. We're missing your parents' medical histories."

Spasms pulsated through Ari's midsection. She shifted, trying to get some relief. "I don't have much to tell you, but I'm sure my aunt can answer your questions."

Aunt Sheila pivoted. "Do you need to know their medical histories?"

The nurse frowned. "It helps us get a complete look at Miss Powers's overall health."

"But do you *need* to know?"

"It's okay, Aunt Sheila, you can tell her."

Aunt Sheila cleared her throat. "I would tell her, but I can't."

Maybe it was all the pain medication, but confusion turned Ari's mind into a jumbled pile of pickup sticks. Why was Aunt Sheila being so evasive? "Why can't you? I don't understand."

Aunt Sheila faced the nurse. "Even if I told you, it wouldn't matter."

"Why is that, Miss Powers?"

Aunt Sheila slowly turned toward Ari. "Because you were adopted."

CHAPTER 27

"I was what?" Aunt Shelia's bombshell sucker-punched the air from Ari's gut.

"You were adopted."

"I'll let you two have a moment alone." The curtain moved, and the wheels on the cart squeaked. The door closed.

"Adopted? How can that be? I've seen my birth certificate. It was issued by the District of Columbia. My parents are Jamison and Ophelia Powers." Ari struggled to grasp her aunt's world-shattering revelation. How could everything she knew about herself be a lie?

"I know. I've seen it, too. I imagine your original certificate was sealed, and a new one created by the courts. Not only were your birth parents' names altered, but also the hospital name and location of birth."

"Are you sure? What proof do you have?"

Why would Aunt Sheila say it, if it wasn't true? What would she have to gain by lying?

"Thirty years ago, Ophelia called and said that she and Jamison had adopted an infant daughter. You were three months old, and your birth mother was a single girl who couldn't afford to keep you."

"Do you know her name—my birth mother?"

"I'm sorry. I don't. I've always assumed it was a closed adoption."

"Why didn't you ever tell me?" Ari's sinus cavities stung as her vision blurred. Hot tears ran down her cheeks, and a heavy weight crushed her lungs. "I could have handled it."

Aunt Sheila squeezed Ari's hand. "What good would it have done to tell you? Your life had already been turned upside down enough. I couldn't destroy the memory of your mother. I thought I was doing the right thing."

Ari turned her face toward the window. The knowledge her parents had worked for the US government had been shocking enough, but nothing was more earth-shattering than learning someone else had brought Ari into this world.

Her brain was bombarded with questions. Two specific ones stood out the most, who were her birth parents, and should she try to contact them?

Her pain increased, and she hit the button to release a dose of morphine. A woozy feeling slammed her forehead like a tsunami. The pain subsided, and her limbs became weightless.

Nick pushed the cold, congealed beef stroganoff around the plate.

He couldn't bring himself to return to Ari's hospital room. Not yet. He stuck his hand in his pocket and fingered the piece of paper that had been jammed under the windshield wiper of Ari's convertible. Enigma's threat was seared on his brain.

> *Time is running out for Bridgette Van Sloan.*
> *Hope you enjoyed your apple pie because it'll be your last slice.*
> *-Enigma*

It wasn't the first sentence that had sent his heart plummeting to the pits of the Underworld. It was the second.

Enigma knew he'd eaten apple pie at Granny's house. There was only one way that was possible. They were being tracked. And watched.

His family needed more than a warning—they needed protection. An FBI safe house, but the only way to get that was to tell the authorities the truth.

Enigma's words echoed in his mind. *"If you alert the authorities, Bridgette Van Sloan will die. Is that clear?"*

To protect his family, to protect Ari, Bridgette would die.

Turning everything over to Updike was the only option. Tell the truth, let the FBI handle it, and step out of the way. Getting fired from DSS would be a small price to pay if it meant keeping Ari and his family safe from a maniac. He wouldn't continue to risk their lives chasing after a phantom and a girl who was probably already dead.

It's a dangerous game, and we're the pawns. This ends now. It's not worth it.

Nick threw his uneaten dinner into the garbage can, then took the elevator to the fourth floor. Ari's voice carried through the open doorway, joined by her aunt's.

He stepped into the room, and the two women looked his direction. Ari gave him a little wave but didn't smile. Her eyes looked brighter than before, and her color had improved, but the random wincing indicated that she was in pain. A lot of pain.

"How long did the doctor say you'll be in the hospital?"

"Too long, if you ask me. I—"

Deputy Secretary Powers interrupted her niece. "They want to monitor her for any signs of infection, and as long as all goes well, and Arizona promises—" she nailed her with her eyes— "to rest and take her antibiotics, she can go home in a day or two."

What would Ari say when he asked her to give up this mad search? She was stubborn and fixated on things like a hawk on a rodent or a frog on a fly.

Enigma was her current quarry.

"Enigma knows where to find my family." He handed Ari the note.

She took it from him and read the chilling words. "What? He was following us?"

"We're being tracked."

"How?" She laid the paper on the bed. "Never mind. It doesn't matter. The best thing we can do for them is to find Enigma and arrest him."

"Didn't you hear me? My family is in danger. You're in danger."

"I heard you."

"We need to tell Updike what's happening. I need to get you and my family into a safe house."

Ari held up her hands. "Whoa. I'm not going anywhere. We still have to rescue Bridgette."

Nick's jaw clenched. His lips pursed. "Bridgette is dead." Or she would be soon.

She flinched. "How can you say that?"

His arm shot out, and he tightened his fingers around her wrist. "I know you don't want it to be true, but Bridgette is dead. If Enigma killed those other women, then he's not someone to mess around with. We need to get you to safety before he takes another shot at you. He might not miss next time."

Ari ripped from his grasp and grimaced. "If you want to give up, that's fine. But I can't. I won't."

"I'm not giving up. I'm accepting reality. We'll never find her in time. We were never supposed to. She's gone." For all they knew, she'd been dead since the first clue had been left in Ari's office. Nick's chest swelled, then his shoulders collapsed. He closed his eyes and rubbed his fingers through his hair, massaging his crown.

"We're never going to figure this out. Don't you see? Enigma is just messing with us. One clue will lead to another that will lead to another. It's a psychotic game."

Enigma had sent them on a wild goose chase, preying on

Ari's need to be in control. If the authorities, with all their intel and manpower, hadn't found Bridgette by now, what made them think they could do it on their own?

"Ari." He perched on the bed and took her hand, caressing her knuckles. "It's over. I'm calling this in. I'm giving the FBI everything we've collected, and I'm arranging for my family to be moved to a safe house. It would make me feel a lot better if you went with them."

Ari's face scrunched. "You can't do that. Bridgette will die. Enigma said so."

"I know. I wish there was another way, but I don't see any alternative. Enigma wants you dead. He almost succeeded. You might not survive another encounter. It's too risky. I can't let you put yourself in harm's way."

"What are you trying to say, Nick?"

"It's over. We're not playing his game anymore."

His cell rang. He wanted to ignore it, to focus on Ari, but something urged him to take the call. He stepped into the hallway, withdrew the device from his pocket, and held it to his ear. "Nick Trueheart."

"Trueheart, this is Special Agent Reid from the FBI. I have some good news for you."

"You found Miss Van Sloan."

A moment of silence, then Reid's throat cleared. "We have not. We're doing everything we can, but that's not why I'm calling. We've been presented with some new evidence regarding your wife's murder. We're reopening the case."

"Wow." He must sound like an idiot, but that's all he could think to say. He swallowed the lump in his throat. "Thanks for the update. Please keep me in the loop."

"Keep you in the loop? I'm offering you the opportunity to help us apprehend your wife's killer."

Lord, is this the answer I've been praying for?

"I'll—I'll let you know. Is Updike available? I need to speak with him."

"Sure. Just let me transfer the call."

The line rang.

"Hello." Updike's voice answered.

"It's Nicholas Trueheart from DSS. Agent Powers is in the hospital. She's been shot."

"Shot! Where? How?"

Nick started at the beginning and explained the whole enchilada from start to finish.

"I'm disappointed in Agent Powers. And you. But we'll make sure your family is safe."

Agent Updike walked Nick through the protection protocols, then hung up.

Nick lowered the phone, his eyes wide, his chest heaving. He stepped back into the room and tucked his phone into his pocket.

"Who was that?" Ari pushed up on her bed. "Have they found Bridgette?"

"Agent Reid. It was about Rachel. They found some new evidence. They're reopening the case."

Ari blinked. "Wow. That's … that's good. So, they'll keep you in the loop?"

He didn't answer.

"They're going to keep you in the loop, right?"

Nick's chest rose and fell. "Ari, they want me on the team."

"Isn't that a conflict of interest?"

His shoulders jerked upward. "I don't know. But I'm not going to say no. This is my chance."

Her jaw dropped. "Your chance? You mean, you're leaving? What about Bridgette?"

He'd already said it was over. There was no need to rehash it again.

"A car is on the way to pick up my parents, grandma, and brother. The officer will explain the situation when he arrives. I'll call my dad and let him know what to expect. Updike says he'll post a twenty-four-hour guard here until you're released, then someone will take you to the safe house until this is all over."

The numbers on the heart monitor climbed higher. A shrill beep started.

Deputy Secretary Powers laid her hand on Ari's shoulder. "Calm down. You're getting too worked up."

A nurse entered the room. "What's going on?" She silenced the alarm. "Your heart rate is too high. Take some deep breaths."

The nurse demonstrated, but Ari ignored her.

"I thought you were my friend. Can't you see how important this is to me?"

Nick clenched his jaw. "Forgive me for caring, but your safety is important to *me*. You can't control everything, no matter how badly you want to. I know you try, but you are not God. Things will happen. Terrible things will happen. And we have to take comfort in the fact that we did our best. That's all we can expect of ourselves. The game is over. At least for me it is."

CHAPTER 28

S o far, the drive from the hospital to her house had been as silent as the very depths of an unexplored cave. Ari faced the window and watched the commercial district fly by. It was beyond her imagination why Aunt Sheila thought this was a good idea. Ari hadn't seen or spoken to Nick since he'd left the hospital after quitting on her, and the tension in the vehicle had the viscosity of wet cement.

She'd put her whole adult life into becoming an FBI agent. She wanted to protect others, to keep them from experiencing lostness, abandonment … the feeling that no one cared about them.

The game wasn't over until she said it was over. Enigma would not win.

But what if Nick was right? What if Bridgette was already dead, and all this was for nothing? Ari refused to believe they'd lost. She was going to find her. Alive. And she would bring her home to her family.

Nick moved the Honda into the turn lane and flipped the

blinker. The orange arrow flashed on the dashboard. "Why didn't you tell me your aunt was my boss?"

His sudden question startled her. That's what bothered him? "I didn't want you to think I got the assignment just because my aunt works for DSS."

"But you lied to me."

She gave him a sidelong glance. "I didn't lie. I just left out that particular detail."

"You didn't trust me with the truth." His fingers squeezed the steering wheel until his knuckles turned white.

"I know. I'm sorry. Can we just forget about it?"

"We were partners, Ari. I don't know if I can just forget about it."

What did it matter now? They never had to see each other again.

Her stomach ached at the thought. He was a nice guy—a good man—even if he worried too much and over-analyzed everything.

Nick shifted beside her. "Updike says he'll meet us at your house and take you to the safe house himself."

It wasn't a question—he expected her to comply with orders. To hide and let the big boys run the show. That was not going to happen. Bridgette had been her assignment. Her responsibility, and Ari would not let her down. She needed to get out of there, and she had to do it before they reached the safe house where she'd be under guard 24/7.

"I need time to pack a bag."

If she made eye contact, he'd know she was up to something.

Nick turned the vehicle onto her street and parallel-parked along the curb. "Updike expected as much."

Unbuckling her seatbelt, she finally ventured a glance at her driver. "I'll be back."

"Want me to go in with you?"

"I'll be fine. I have this." She held up the empty Glock that had been returned when she left the hospital, then shut the car door and forced her body to walk to the front door. Her legs wobbled. Once on the stoop, she straightened her spine, took a deep breath, then put the key in the lock.

She waved at Nick.

He waved back.

Inside the house, she warily scanned her surroundings, then climbed the stairs, gulping down the sense of panic that rose in her throat. Her plan hinged on her ability to do this alone.

Each step sent pins and needles through her gunshot wound. The house was empty and quiet. Her heart thudded against her ribcage. *I can do this.*

The easiest escape would be to exit out the back of the house and climb over the fence, but then what? Abbot Castle hadn't revealed another location—so if the game was still on, where was she supposed to find the next clue?

First, she needed to reload her weapon. Ari opened the closet door in the office, grabbed a bullet magazine, and slid it into the grip until it clicked in place. Turning, she tapped it on the desk, then racked the slide to move a bullet into the chamber.

A new piece of paper had been taped to the desk. Ari sucked in breath as she read the familiar handwriting.

Where giants once roamed, where rocks reach the sky,
In colors of red and white, where ancient echoes lie.
A labyrinth of hoodoos and legends,
of winding gullies and bends
Tucked under the rock in a safe hiding place,
you'll find the last clue to finish this race.
-Enigma

Last clue. Those two words sent her mind and heart whirling. The final clue to Bridgette's location. How long had the note been waiting there? Two days? Three?

And she knew exactly where Enigma wanted her to go.

Rocks of red and white. A labyrinth of hoodoos and gullies.

She'd never heard of a hoodoo associated with anything other than Chroma Cliffs, located about an hour outside of Platte City.

Was there any chance Enigma had kept Bridgette alive despite the delay and even though Nick had told the authorities everything?

She had to try.

Ari raced down the stairs, note in hand. The pain in her side nearly stole her breath. She stopped in the living room, bent over, grimaced, and peeked behind the curtain.

Nick paced the sidewalk beside his car, talking on his phone.

Would he be willing to help her?

"The game is over. At least for me it is."

She had two choices. Show Nick the riddle, but he might insist on giving it to the police and still demand she go to the safe house. Or she could take control and handle this herself. Without his help.

The answer was obvious.

She exited through the exterior door in the kitchen into her xeriscaped yard. In the far corner, she climbed the six-foot wooden fence, hauled her body over the top, then dropped to the ground below. Fire shot through her ribcage.

She grabbed her midsection, closed her eyes, and groaned. As long as she didn't rip open her stitches, she'd be all right. Shaking off a wave of nausea, she ducked between the houses behind hers, pulled her cell phone from her pocket, and dialed.

"Yellow Cab. How may I assist you today?" A female voice came over the line.

Ari glanced to the right and left before crossing the street. "I need a taxi at the Burger Barn on Cotton Street. As soon as possible. Thank you."

CHAPTER 29

Nick glanced at the clock on his phone a second time. Ari was taking too long. Even if she'd gotten distracted, it didn't take twenty minutes to pack a bag. Did it?

He shot off a text.

Nothing.

Strode to the front door and tried the handle.

Locked.

Should have expected that. She wouldn't have wanted someone to follow her inside. What other way was there to get into the house? The garage door opener was with Ari's car at the repair shop. Did the home have a rear exit?

He dialed her number. Voicemail.

His gut twisted. What if something happened to her? What if Enigma had been waiting to strike?

Ari hadn't asked him to check her house, but maybe he should have insisted. Every time before, she'd asked him to make sure her house was safe, but this time she hadn't. Why the sudden surge of bravery?

Unless … she didn't want him to know what she was doing.

She wouldn't *run*, would she?

A black SUV pulled up in front of the house. The driver's door opened, and Matt Updike stepped out. His dark suit looked like it had been slept in. One shoelace had come untied, and his hair was in desperate need of a comb. The senior special agent removed his sunglasses. His mouth twisted in a frown. "Is she ready?"

"I'm just checking on her." Nick's pulse throbbed in his temple. No need to alert the agent just yet. "She went inside to pack her things, but she's not answering her phone."

Updike gave a sharp nod. "I'll wait here."

Nick took the lock picking kit from his trunk and jimmied Ari's front door. He stepped inside and closed the door behind him. The house was eerily silent.

"Ari."

No response.

After clearing the first floor, he took the stairs two at a time, his heart in his throat. "Ari!"

Still no reply. It took only a moment to confirm the house was vacant. No Ari.

Nick bolted through the front door, skidding to a stop at the curb. He bent to catch his breath. "She's gone."

Updike straightened. "What do you mean, gone?"

Nick expanded his lungs. "She's not in there. I think she might have been—"

Updike growled and pulled his phone from inside his coat. He tapped the screen then put the device to his ear. "I should have realized she'd never go into hiding. Stubborn woman." Someone must have answered because his tone changed. "Yeah. Updike. Powers is on the run."

A second later, he lowered the phone. "Come with me."

"She can't have gone far. She doesn't have a car. We'll catch up to her easily."

Updike shook his head. "Nope."

Nick's blood pressure rose. "Why not?"

"She's a trained agent. We won't find her if she doesn't want to be found. Our only chance is if she thinks we're not tracking her. Enigma will be looking for her, too. Didn't you say he was tracking the two of you?"

"We think so. Not sure how, though."

Couldn't be a tracker in the vehicle—they'd used several, including a rental. Cell phones? Had Enigma been alone with Ari's phone? Nick's phone? Could that be how he kept tabs on their every movement?

Nick eyed the electronic device in his hand. "We need to check my phone for a bug."

Updike opened the SUV's driver's door. "Get in. We'll do it back at the office. Put a trace on Powers's phone, too."

Nick headed for the passenger side. "Can you do that without a warrant?"

"She's on the lam. We'll get a warrant."

It was nearly sunset when the taxi driver dropped Ari at the outer edge of Chroma Cliffs National Park.

Ari got out of the car, and when the driver handed her a card reader, she scanned her credit card. "Thanks." She handed the reader back through the window.

"Hey, lady. It'll be dark soon. You got a way out of here? Should I wait?"

A four-mile trail through a gully lay just out of sight. How long would it take to search through every nook and cranny of it? How long did she have? Nick and Matt would be right on her tail. "Give me until dark. If I haven't come back by then, leave without me."

The driver raised his eyebrows. "You sure?" His eyes flickered back and forth. "Little spooky out here all alone."

The Glock pressed into Ari's back. "I'll be fine."

"If you say so." The window rolled up.

Ari headed toward the erosion-worn ridge. She took her

phone from her pocket and turned it off. Now, Updike couldn't trace her, and neither could Enigma.

The possibility hadn't escaped her that Enigma was using her phone to track them.

Ari set off at a quick jog and entered through the eastern side of the cliffs. The walls rose above her head, cradling her in a canyon.

The riddle had clearly stated that the next clue would be found tucked under a rock. Not exactly an obvious hint. The whole thing was nothing but rocks.

"You know what else is under rocks, Enigma? Snakes and spiders." She shivered. Just what she wanted to do today—trespass on the home of a creepy-crawly. Especially one with fangs.

Enigma had marked the castle tower with the odd eagle symbol. Was it too much to hope he might mark the location of the next clue in the same way? It would certainly make it easier to find.

She stepped over a long stick and a whiskey bottle that the high desert winds had blown into the canyon. The sun lowered in the sky, setting the rocks ablaze.

How would she find anything in here? This task teetered on the impossible.

With her back against a hoodoo, she slid down and sat on the dirt floor, knees to her chest, forehead against her kneecaps. It would be pitch-black in a matter of minutes.

A coyote howled in the distance, and Ari's mouth went dry. The desolation of the open prairie pressed around her, stealing her breath. The canyon walls closed in, and oppressive silence sent pulses of dread through her veins.

Sagebrush across the way shivered, shooting goosebumps down Ari's limbs. She yanked out her cell phone, turned it on, and shone the flashlight toward the canyon wall opposite her position.

Two red eyes shimmered in the glow. A kangaroo rat

bounced on two big feet along the rocky soil. A marking on the rock face moved her attention to the canyon wall. Could that be it?

She crawled forward, scaring off the kangaroo rat, then traced the eagle symbol with her fingertip. Just below the symbol, a rocky ledge near the ground jutted outward.

Thank you, Jesus.

She put out her hand then jerked it back. What if a snake lived in there? After retrieving a stick, she returned to the spot, then jabbed the piece of wood underneath the ledge.

A blur of motion struck at her boots, and she jumped back to avoid getting bit.

In the dim light, the triangular head and dark blotches of a prairie rattlesnake twisted at her feet. Its rattle warned her to leave.

Ari gulped, then swung the stick like a golf club, sending the snake sailing through the air. She hoped that wherever it landed, it had sense enough to move along, rather than come back for revenge.

She penetrated the hole with the stick once again. Something crinkled. Scraping carefully, she dragged the stick toward her until it appeared with a plastic bag caught under the tip. She tossed the stick aside and snatched the bag. Her phone light illuminated dark text printed on a jagged piece of paper.

Latitude: N 39° 43.521' Longitude: W 104° 59.712'

A beefy arm tightened around her midsection, and a rough hand clapped over her mouth, cutting off her air supply. Stifling the urge to scream, she jabbed her elbow into her attacker's stomach. He let out a sharp blast of air and doubled forward but did not release his hold.

Her gunshot wound flamed. She steeled herself against the pain, then stomped on his foot as hard as she could, sending spasms surging through her own leg. Of course he would wear steel-toed boots.

Glass smashed, and the tight grip released.

Ari spun around, sweeping the flashlight to take in the scene. The brute from the train station lay unconscious on the ground, and above him, stood her taxi driver, holding the shattered remains of a glass bottle.

"Are you okay?" she asked him.

A surprised look engulfed his face, and he laughed out loud. "I should ask you that." He gave the broken bottle a toss. "Hurry. Before he wakes up."

"Right. Thanks." Ari shook off her fear and followed the driver back to the taxi. "How did you know where to find me?"

He held open the back door. "I followed the giant lunkhead. Just had a hunch he wasn't out for an evening stroll."

She slid inside then took the note from the bag.

Once the driver buckled his seatbelt, she leaned forward and handed him the coordinates. "I need to go to this location."

The driver nodded, took the paper, and entered the directions into his phone. Tires spinning and gravel crunching, he followed the dirt road back to the main highway.

This was the moment she'd been waiting for.

Enigma would finally pay the price for his actions.

CHAPTER 30

1900 Hours

Nick's eyeballs felt like they'd been scratched with sandpaper.

The FBI bullpen smelled of stale coffee, too much aftershave, and Lysol. The fluorescent lights beamed as brightly as if it were ten o'clock in the morning, but beyond the floor-to-ceiling, wall-to-wall, bullet-proof windows, night had fallen.

Perched on the straight-backed metal folding chair, he sipped the tepid coffee in the Styrofoam cup and watched the remaining agents. Most had gone home. He hadn't been given a tour of the office. Instead, Updike had barked strict orders not to touch anything or enter any restricted areas.

Like he didn't know better.

If only Arizona would switch on her phone, he could apologize. They'd only been out of contact for a couple of hours, but it felt like an eternity. He shouldn't have tried to force her into the safe house. This case was of utmost importance to her, and he should have respected that. Her needs should have been priority over his own fears.

Nick scrubbed his palm over his growing five o'clock

shadow. She'd needed him, and he'd let her down. Now, his initial concern for her safety was nothing compared to the knowledge that she was out there alone. And Enigma was still after her.

The door of Updike's office hung open, and his size twelve shoe tapped a rhythm from on top of the desk. The senior special agent seemed not the least bit worried. Why was there no sense of emergency?

Nick carried the empty cup to the trash can, then his gaze swept the room, looking for Ari's workstation. His fingers twitched to get a look around her desk. Would anything in her files help him locate her? He should have just gone looking for her instead of coming to the office. What good was he doing by sitting around, accomplishing nothing?

As he paced the patterned carpet from the coffee station to the restroom doors and back, Ari's strange reaction to the music box that first day took control of his thoughts. Had she seen it before?

While they both recognized the song from the escape room, it was the object itself that had set her off, not just the music, though, that too had certainly seemed like it struck a chord with her. And when the key was turned, and the ballerinas danced to the unfamiliar lullaby, Ari transformed into a cowering, spineless jellyfish, in the same way being alone in the dark affected her.

Nyctophobia, the fear of the dark, was a common phobia in children, but it had been known to persist into adulthood, though usually spurred by traumatic experiences. What trauma had Ari faced?

Her mother died in a mysterious helicopter crash, and she had no knowledge of how her father died. After her mother's death, she'd been uprooted and moved to Platte City to live with her aunt—an aunt she didn't know well at the time. That was a lot of tragedy for a formative teenager to bear, but he couldn't see how that connected to the music box or her fear of the dark?

What else did he know about Arizona Powers other than the fact that she was uber-organized, loved Elvis's music, and wasn't afraid to order takeout from food trucks.

He'd opened *his* heart and let her see the hurt and heartache inside of him. But Ari was sealed up tighter than this facility. How could he get her to trust him? Why did he want her to?

I don't have room in my heart for another woman.

He looked at his empty ring finger and tried to picture his wife.

Ari's face filled his mind instead.

Her round brown eyes twinkled when she teased. Her smile seemed to make the sun beam brighter … She made him want to be a hero. He'd walk over hot coals to keep her safe, and he'd kick himself until the end of time if anything happened to her.

Familiar crackling noises emanated from Updike's office, and a secondary male voice carried over the airwaves.

Nick dashed across the room, shoving furniture out of his way, then stopped in the doorway, his grip crushing the life out of the door jamb.

Updike held a transceiver. "Ready for your report, Agent Moore."

"I just followed Agent Powers to twelve-hundred West Foxglove. Backup requested."

Nick frowned. If they had an agent trailing Ari, that would explain Updike's lack of concern.

Updike glanced at Nick. His poker face revealed nothing. "Request denied. Don't make a move until you have confirmation Enigma is on location."

"Roger that. I'll report in once I have identified the target."

Updike lowered the two-way. His steely eyes met Nick's. "You weren't supposed to hear that."

Nick swallowed the lump in his throat. "You're using Ari for bait."

Updike rose from his chair and locked his gaze on Nick with

an intimidating stare. "Sometimes sacrifices have to be made for the greater good."

Nick narrowed his eyes and faced the agent. "Whose greater good would that be?"

CHAPTER 31

1930 Hours

Ari pounded on the exterior door of the two-and-a-half-story brick house at 1200 West Foxglove. The windows were dark, and it looked like no one was home. "Open up. This is the FBI."

Without her credentials, she couldn't have proved she was a law officer, but maybe she wouldn't have to.

She waited several more seconds, listening for any kind of response, but heard nothing. She knocked once again. "FBI. Open the door."

Still nothing.

Pulling the firearm from her waistband, she aimed it at the lock and fired twice. Wood splintered, metal curled, and the blast echoed in the still neighborhood.

It was bound to draw attention, and probably the cops.

She gave the door a swift kick. It swung open and slammed against the wall, and she entered the house, her weapon raised. "This is Agent Powers from the FBI. Come out with your hands where I can see them."

She waited for the gunshots.

Nothing.

The wood floor creaked beneath her shoes. Her temples twitched, and her pulse throbbed in her throat. Goosebumps tingled her skin. "Hello? Is anyone here?"

Maybe this was a bad idea. At any moment, she could be ambushed.

The streetlights filtered through the open doorway and dirty exterior windows, giving her little visible light to work with. She flipped the electric switch on the wall, but it didn't work. Pulling her cell from her pocket, she tapped the flashlight icon. A steady beam drove away some of the pitch-dark.

A single chair sat dead center in the room on her left, ropes coiled around the legs. A table with three chairs appeared in another room ahead. A gaudy chandelier dangled from the ceiling. Stairs led to a second story.

Someone sniffled.

Ari pivoted right, aiming at the shadowy corner.

An older man with saggy jowls, bushy eyebrows, a receding hairline, and wide, frightened eyes cowered against the wood panel wall. He raised his hands to shield his eyes from the bright light.

She didn't lower the firearm. Or the flashlight. "Who are you? What are you doing here?"

"Kye Warner." His voice trembled. "I live here."

He appeared unarmed, but she couldn't be too careful. "Where's Bridgette?"

"I ... I ..."

"Are you the only person here?"

"Yes." His eyes flickered toward the ceiling.

She didn't want to give Mr. Warner the opportunity to escape, but she needed to sweep the remainder of the house in case he was lying.

"Stay here," she ordered, doubting he would comply, then darted for the stairs, taking them two at a time. Pain sliced through her side with each step. A hallway opened at the top of the stairs with four closed doors.

A third arm would be so useful right now.

She turned off her phone and dropped it into her pocket, momentarily blind until her pupils adjusted to the dim light. She stepped forward and the floor creaked. Grasping the first handle, she threw open the door, and lunged into the room, weapon raised.

An empty bathroom.

"Clear," she shouted out of habit and continued down the hall, her back pressed against the vintage wood paneling. At the next door, she repeated her actions. A vacant bedroom with a closet. She shoved open the sliding door. Also, empty.

An unpleasant smell filled her nostrils.

A familiar smell.

The smell of blood.

Ari pivoted. Dark spots marred the blanket on the bed. Returning her weapon to her pants, she withdrew the phone and turned on the flashlight.

A black leather jacket, folded neatly, rested on the pillow. Bridgette's jacket.

Using the edge of her phone, she flipped the coat open, uncovering large stains on the interior fabric. The stench grew stronger.

Ari raised her head and panted. She clenched her jaw until her teeth hurt. As adrenaline surged through her veins, she seized the jacket and tore down the stairs.

The old man still cowered in the corner.

"Where is she?" She grabbed him by the front of his shirt and dragged him to his feet.

"W-who?"

"Where is Bridgette Van Sloan? I know she was here. What did you do with her?"

"I-I don't know what you're talking about."

"Ambassador Van Sloan's daughter. She was abducted earlier this week. Where is she?" Ari tightened her grip as her temper soared. "Where is she, you miserable little troll? Tell me what you've done with her."

"She-she's dead."

The scene before Nick stopped him in his tracks—Ari held an elderly man pinned against the dining room wall.

Uniformed officers rushed past him like a stampede circumventing a boulder in their path, and Updike shouted over the clamber. "Stand down, Agent Powers."

Nick's tongue loosened. "Ari, it's me. Nick. Let the man go."

She released her grip, and the man slumped to the floor, wheezing.

An officer hauled the man to his feet and clapped handcuffs over his wrists.

Nick stepped aside as the officers led the man out of the house. Silence pounded his eardrums.

Updike nodded his chin at one of the other officers who removed a set of handcuffs from his duty belt. "Special Agent Powers, you are under arrest for assault with a deadly weapon and interfering with a federal investigation." He yanked her arms behind her back, and the handcuffs clapped in place. "You have the right to remain silent. Anything you say can and will …"

Nick shut out the rest of the officer's spiel.

Flashlights illuminated Ari's pale face and blank stare. She hadn't moved. Hadn't responded. Wasn't fighting back.

The officer escorted her toward the exit.

Ari paused beside Nick, meeting his gaze with a look of utter defeat, clutching a bloody jacket to her chest. "She's dead."

His instinct was to ask who, but he held his tongue. The answer was obvious.

Bridgette Van Sloan was dead.

How Ari knew, he wasn't sure. Maybe the old man had told

her, but the despair in her body language was undeniable. "I'm so sorry." Nick touched her arm.

A sob caught in her throat. "I was too late."

He brushed a loose strand of hair from her cheek. "It's not your fault."

The officer propelled Ari out the front door, and they disappeared out of sight. Moments later, a car engine roared, then faded in the distance.

Nick squared off with Updike. "What do you think you're doing?"

Updike's eyebrows shot upward. "Excuse me."

"You weren't getting anywhere without her. She was only trying to help."

Updike stalked across the room, then stopped in front of Nick, hands on his hips, towering over him. "I put her on leave. This wasn't her case."

Nick locked gazes with the special agent. "You can't blame her for caring."

"That's always been her problem." The senior agent pivoted away and barked instructions across the house. Flashlights dimmed as the officers moved to cordon off the crime scene and collect evidence.

Nick crossed his arms. "What do you mean by that?"

Updike spun back with his face nearly submerged in the shadows. "Agent Powers considers it a personal failure if she doesn't find a child alive or if an investigation goes cold. But that's an unavoidable downside to this line of work. She can't save everyone."

"Why does it affect her so profoundly?"

Updike shrugged. "How should I know? I'm not a shrink. But this is the same thing that set her off before."

"Are you referring to her nervous breakdown last summer?"

Updike's arms folded, mirroring Nick's stance. "When we found that senator's kid dead, Powers just lost it. She became obsessed with tracking down his killer. She didn't sleep, and she went days without a proper meal or even a shower. Once she located the perp, she was too drained to see he was unarmed. I ordered her to stand down, but she didn't. He moved his hand, and she shot him. Double tap to the heart. If not for her lawyer getting her an acquittal based on a plea of insanity, she would have gone to prison for manslaughter rather than spending months in a psych hospital. Director Carlton's uncertainty about her stability was on point. She wasn't ready to go back to work. She's unable to separate her emotions from her job. That makes her a liability."

"Don't do this. The Bureau is all she's ever known. Her career means the world to her. Give her another chance."

Updike shook his head. "There's nothing I can do. My hands are tied. Agent Powers is, as of this moment, relieved of duty. She no longer works for the FBI."

CHAPTER 32

The last time Ari had sat on this side of the table was just after her nervous breakdown six months ago, and she didn't like it now any more than she had back then.

Nick's news had rocked her world, but being fired might be the least of her problems once Ambassador Van Sloan learned the truth about his daughter. His threat had been very specific. They could add criminal negligence to the charges of assault and interfering with an investigation.

Had they told him yet?

She kept glancing at the door, expecting his hulking frame to barge into the interview room, spewing profanity and injurious accusations.

An immeasurable amount of grief mixed with her overwhelming regret. If only she had gotten there in time. If she'd called Matt right away, maybe things would have worked out differently.

The door to the interrogation room opened, and Ari lifted her head.

It wasn't the ambassador.

Matt entered, followed by another agent. Reid, or something like that. She'd seen him around the office, but they hadn't worked any cases together.

Matt remained standing, while Reid took the chair across from Ari and slapped a manila folder onto the table. "You did it."

Ari was taken aback. "Did what?"

"You apprehended Enigma," said Reid.

She blinked in shock. How was that old man Enigma? That wasn't what she had expected from him at all. Simpering and cowering in a corner? Shivering and sniffling like a lost child?

Reid opened the folder and slid it across the table. "Warner's fingerprints match the ones found in the SUV abandoned at the river. The blood in the trunk was Miss Van Sloan's. Boots from his closet match the shoe prints on the riverbank. And Warner worked at a pharmaceutical company, so he had access to the syringe that matches the cap you found at the escape room."

Ari glanced over the vague report. "How did he know Bridgette? How did he know she was in the escape room? Did you get a confession?"

Reid folded his arms. "Not yet, but we're working on him."

She raised her head to catch a glimpse of her boss.

Matt had yet to say a word.

Her frustration grew. Something about this didn't make sense. "Did you ask him about the obituaries he mailed to me? What did he say about the deaths of Jayda Roach, Lila Dominguez, Tanya Keller, and Rachel Trueheart?"

Reid waved his hand. "Totally unrelated. Warner used the obituaries merely as couriers for the ciphers. It was all just a game to him."

"Did he say that? Or is it your assumption? What about Tyrrhenea? The journal? The list of mercenaries?"

Was any of this ringing a bell? They had to have seen the connection.

"Doesn't exist." Reid reclined in his chair, folding his hands over his head with a confidence that soured her stomach.

Ari sat straighter. "Excuse me?" Her temper hovered on the verge of boiling.

Reid dropped his hands and leaned forward again. "Tyrrhenea doesn't exist. You won't find it on any map. It was fictional. Made up. All part of the game."

"But—"

Reid stood. "Director Carlton thanks you for assisting us with the capture of Enigma. In exchange, all charges against you have been dropped. You are free to go." He exited the interrogation room.

"Am I still fired?" She aimed her question at her boss.

"Yes." Matt headed for the door.

"Do I get a severance package?"

Matt turned, with an eyebrow raised. "Yes, of course. I'll speak to HR on your behalf. Have a good life, Powers. We'll—" he hesitated— "miss you around here. Take care of yourself."

With that, the door and her career in the FBI closed behind him.

"Why don't you sit down?" Nick patted the couch cushion beside him.

Ari was wearing a hole in his carpet. He'd been surprised to find her standing at his door when he came home from his meeting with Santiago where he'd been told the same thing she had. Kye Warner was Enigma, and everything they'd encountered had simply been part of his twisted game.

"I can't sit." She about-faced and shuffled toward him again. "It couldn't just be part of the game. The obits, the journal, they had to mean something."

Enigma had played them for fools. He'd pulled their strings

and sent them on a snipe hunt for his own amusement. "It was all an elaborate hoax. And we fell for it."

Ari's body deflated, and she perched on the arm of the sofa, covering her face with her hands.

She was obsessed, just like Updike had said.

"Updike told me about ... you know ... what happened with the senator's kid."

She lowered her hands. Her eyes were red, and her cheeks were tear-streaked. She sniffled and arched an eyebrow. "I would have thought you already knew about that. Every news station in the country broadcasted my descent into madness."

Nick shifted, putting his foot on the opposite knee. "He said you care too much and can't separate your emotions from the cases."

She stiffened. "What's wrong with having a little compassion?"

"He made it seem like more than compassion. He said you become obsessed. You don't sleep or meet your basic needs. A thirst for justice consumes you."

Ari looked at the carpet and chewed her lip.

He dropped his leg, stood, and faced her. "Answer me this. Why did you become an FBI agent?"

A simple question. It should be a simple answer.

"I don't want to talk about it." Her eyes closed, and her voice fell. "Why didn't you do something? Why didn't you stop him?" she muttered under her breath.

Was she talking to him or herself? He leaned forward and laid a hand on her knee. "Don't blame yourself. You did the best you could."

Her head snapped upward. Daggers shot from her eyes. "I don't blame myself. I blame God."

He fumbled, taken aback by her accusation. "How is any of this God's fault?"

"He could have stopped all of this." She waved her hand.

He swallowed. "He could have, but He chose not to."

"Why?" she snapped.

"I don't know. I'm not God."

She hopped off the couch and pointed at her sternum. "How can I be expected to trust a being who allows evil men to get away with hurting innocent people?"

He shook his head. "Enigma isn't getting away with anything. He's in jail. He'll go to prison."

She paced, then paused and pivoted to face him. "But Bridgette's dead. A prison sentence doesn't make up for what he did to her. Why would a loving God allow good people to suffer? How is that love?" She met his eyes, daring him to argue with her.

He worked his jaw. He was only a new Christian. His faith was just beginning to grow. He didn't have all the answers.

He shrugged. "I don't know. Only God knows why He allows bad things to happen. He sees what's happening, and I know that He cares. He's still on His throne. I can only see a part of the picture. Someday, maybe, it will all make sense, but until then, that's good enough for me."

"He let your wife die."

He blinked back the tears and sucked in a breath. "He did." It hurt. He wouldn't deny that. Knowing God could have stopped Rachel's death and chose not to … but instead of cursing God, it had drawn Nick to Him.

"And you're okay with that?"

He sighed. "No, of course not. But I—"

Ari hugged her chest. "If I were God, I wouldn't allow suffering. I'd do away with pain and heartbreak and grief."

Nick closed the distance between them and laid a hand on her shoulder. There was so much pain in her big brown eyes. Her skin had paled, making her lips and eyes stand out against the pallor of her complexion.

He laid his other hand against her cheek. "That's the point, Ari. You're not God. You can't control what happens. And while He could, in his infinite wisdom and knowledge of the future,

He doesn't. We don't understand why He does what He does. Maybe we were never meant to. But He's there. He walks beside us. He weeps for us. And He picks up the broken pieces so we can go on. And He promises that someday He will wipe away all tears from our eyes. That's faith."

She moved away, picked up her purse, and slung the strap over her shoulder. "I just want to go home. I've been wearing the same clothes for three days. I need a bubble bath and an iced mocha latte."

He headed for the door. "Let me drive you home."

She shook her head. "I can show myself out. Goodbye, Nick. I doubt we'll see each other again."

The apartment door closed behind her.

He opened the sliding glass, stepped onto the patio, and watched her drive out of the parking lot.

Goodbye, Ari. I hope you find the answers you seek.

He scrubbed his hand over his face, walked to his desk, and dropped into the swivel chair with a heavy sigh. If he looked in a mirror right now, he'd probably see bloodshot eyes and dark shadows.

Enigma had been arrested.

Nick should feel elated, but if what his boss said was true, then Enigma was not Rachel's killer, and Nick was back at square one. Hot tears burned his sinuses. Why was this so hard? All he wanted was justice.

His own words tugged on his heart like an undertow. *We don't understand why He does what He does. Maybe we were never meant to. But He's there. He walks beside us. He weeps for us. And He picks up the broken pieces so we can go on. And He promises that someday He will wipe away all tears from our eyes.*

That's faith.

Nick slogged across the room until he stood face to face with his corkboard and the evidence he'd painstakingly collected over the past two years.

Could he trust God with Rachel's death? Whether he ever

saw justice in this life, could he let it go? Would he let God be God?

Only God knows why. And that's good enough for me.

Whether or not he had a future with Ari, it was time to let the past go.

In his next breath, he ripped the papers from the corkboard. Like ticker tape, the pieces fell to his feet. He stuffed everything into a trash can, then turning from the empty board, he snatched the owl brooch from his desk, then carried it to the bedroom where he pulled a plastic tote from underneath the bed.

After snapping off the lid of the tote, he removed a small wooden box that held his wedding band. He opened it and picked up the ring. The plain metal band felt cool in his hand. He kissed it, then put the ring and the brooch into the box.

Sliding the tote back under his bed, he picked up his cell phone and dialed Special Agent Reid's number.

It rang twice.

"Go for Reid."

"It's Nick Trueheart. I just wanted to let you know that although I appreciate the offer, I can't assist with Rachel's case. I need to let her go."

He paused and took a deep breath. "I am letting her go."

Why did you become an FBI agent? Nick's question had plagued her all the way home.

Ari entered her house, swept for danger, turned on her music, then climbed into the shower. As the warm water coursed over her body, she let her mind travel back to a time she'd worked desperately to forget.

Centennial High School. 10th grade math. Mr. Dexter Rothschild had abused his authority and took advantage of his students' trust.

Her skin crawled at the memory of his hands being where

they shouldn't have been. She'd tried to report her teacher's inappropriate behavior, but the school board had protected him, and the judge had dropped the case.

Three months later, he violated her best friend, and the shame of what had transpired had been too much for Cassandra, and she took her own life.

No kid … no human being should ever have to go through what she did.

It was why she was so meticulous at her job—there would never again not be enough evidence to get a conviction. It was why she obsessively tracked down the bad guys. They must be made to pay for their crimes.

Why didn't God keep him from hurting her? Hurting her friend? How was that just? How could she trust that He wouldn't let other evil men go unpunished?

She shook her head, shut off the faucet, then swept water out of her eyes. When she opened the curtain, she half-expected to see a message in the steamed-up mirror.

Nothing.

She should have been grateful that Enigma was behind bars, but it felt anti-climactic. That blubbering low life didn't mesh with her mental picture of the mastermind who orchestrated Bridgette's abduction and the puzzle hunt that had ensued.

But the evidence fit. Case closed.

She wrapped herself in a towel, then scooped her dirty clothes from the floor. At the laundry hamper, she shook out the garments, then dropped them in one by one, checking her pockets for used tissues first. She'd shed enough tears in the last week to last her a lifetime.

A piece of paper crinkled between her fingers. She withdrew the note then unfolded it.

It wasn't her handwriting. It was …

Enigma's.

A key from your passed will this riddle unlock.

The length of thyme not bound by clock.
Things unforgotten are knot what they seem.
Only felt by the heart or scene in a dream.
-Enigma

She walked in reverse until she perched on the edge of her bed. But the game was over. Why would he leave her another note?

Passed. Thyme. Knot. Scene.

The misspelled words distracted her as she tried to unravel the message. She inserted the correct words into the riddle.

A key from your past will this riddle unlock.
The length of time not bound by clock.
Things unforgotten are not what they seem.
Only felt by the heart or seen in a dream.

Ari closed her eyes and rubbed her aching forehead. Enigma might have tracked her phone or researched her background, but he had no way of knowing what went on inside her head. Or her heart.

She had two options.

Toss the note in the trash and forget Enigma ever existed.

Or she could drive down to the county jail and demand he tell her the truth.

She chose the latter.

CHAPTER 33

Monday, 12 February
1000 Hours

A ri jerked when the buzzer sounded.

The electronic door opened, and she followed the correctional officer to the visiting area of the Centennial County Jail.

The guard opened a second door and led her into a room with a row of partitions facing a glass wall. An old-fashioned telephone was mounted between each divider. He gestured to a plastic chair. "Have a seat. This will take just a minute."

She lowered into the chair as the guard left the room.

Barred windows behind her let in sunlight, reflecting off the plain white walls. She'd never visited anyone in jail before. Usually, once a culprit was arrested, her job was finished.

A door on the other side of the glass opened, and Kye Warner entered, wearing an orange jumpsuit. Another guard stood outside the door as it closed. Kye sat across from Ari and picked up the phone on his side.

She did the same.

"I see you finally found your next clue." His voice was dry and gravelly.

"When did you put it in my pocket?"

"When you so rudely grabbed my shirt." Kye smoothed down the front of his coveralls.

"Sorry about that. I got a little carried away." Ari sighed, then laid the note on the tabletop. "Why did you give me this? The game is over."

He shook his head. "But it's not over. You're still alive."

Goosebumps prickled her skin. "How can you do anything to me now? You're in jail."

His eyes narrowed. "I am. Enigma isn't."

Ari met Kye's stare. "You're not Enigma."

"No. I'm not."

The police had the wrong man.

It didn't make sense. "What reason do I have to continue with Enigma's twisted game? Bridgette's gone."

"Because the game was never about Bridgette Van Sloan. The game is about Enigma." Kye paused. "He wants you to know the truth."

"What truth? What does he want me to know?"

"Finish the game."

"But—"

Kye hung up the phone and stood. His lips moved as he spoke to the guard.

"Wait. No. I don't understand." She banged on the glass, trying to get Kye's attention.

The guard opened the door, and Kye disappeared down a corridor.

Ari turned and rose from her chair as the first guard entered the room.

He gestured toward the door. "It's time to go."

I know. But where do I go from here?

Someone was pounding on his front door again.

Nick sat up on the couch and rubbed his eyes. His copy of *The Vanderbilt Code* dropped to the floor. Sleep clouded his mind.

The knock sounded a second time.

"Coming. I'm coming," he hollered as he pushed himself from the cushion and crossed the apartment. He opened the door to find Ari standing on his welcome mat. "Ari! What are you doing here?"

After their last conversation, he was surprised to see her.

"The police have the wrong guy." She stepped inside.

Nick closed the door. "What do you mean?"

She inhaled, then blew her hair out of her face. "I just came from visiting Kye Warner in jail. He's not Enigma."

His eyebrows shot upward. "You visited Enigma at the jail?"

"Weren't you listening? Kye isn't Enigma."

Nick raked his fingers through his hair. "But Warner's fingerprints were on the SUV. His boots matched the shoe prints found at the river. And he works for a pharmaceutical company, so he had access to the night-night juice."

Ari spun. "I know. I know that's what the evidence said. But Kye told me he's not Enigma. There's someone else."

"And you believe him? Criminals will say anything if they think it'll get them acquitted."

She pulled a piece of paper from her purse. "I found this in my pocket Saturday afternoon. He stuffed it in there just before he was arrested."

Nick took it from her and read the riddle aloud. "A key from your past will this riddle unlock. The length of time not bound by clock. Things unforgotten, are not what they seem. Only felt by the heart or seen in a dream." He raised his head. "It's another clue. But the game is over."

"According to Kye, it's not over. There's more to it." Her eyes scanned the room. "Where's your evidence board?"

He ignored her question. "Why don't you have a seat?" He gestured to the couch. His mind burned rubber, trying to comprehend what was going on here. None of it made any sense.

As Ari sat, he took the swivel chair, pulled it closer, and straddled the seat. "Bridgette is gone. You said so yourself."

"I know. But apparently, the game was never about Bridgette. It was about Enigma. He wants us to know the truth."

"The truth about what?" He emphasized the word *what*. "Why should we continue playing Enigma's game?"

"I don't know. But I think it has something to do with that journal and those women." Ari swallowed. "And because of this."

She sighed, then reached into her purse and pulled out the broken pieces of the wooden music box and laid them on the coffee table.

"The music box?" Nick frowned and scrubbed his beard.

Ari lifted sad eyes to meet his. "Do you remember my reaction when I first saw it? That day when we found the SD card."

"Yes. Of course." How could he forget? That moment had started them on this baffling puzzle hunt in the first place. "You recognized it."

"I recognized it." She stared at the ballerinas as if one of them was going to suddenly get up and attack her.

"I thought so." He furrowed his brows. "From where?"

"My dreams."

He coughed, stood, and moved around the room. "You've seen that music box in your dreams. And it just so happens to play the same song we heard in the escape room just before Enigma or Kye or whoever abducted Bridgette."

How was that even logically possible?

"I know it sounds ludicrous, but—" Ari groaned. "Maybe I should have told you before, but I didn't want you to think I was a total nut."

"Tell me about this dream."

Ari's lips twisted. "I'm in this dark, damp basement. It smells of straw and mildew and ..."—She cleared her throat—"... other things. There's this thin mat in the corner, and I only have one thin blanket. I'm so cold. I feel alone, and there's no way out. The only toy I have is this wooden music box with ballerinas."

She pointed at the table and shifted. "That music box, and I play it over and over to drown out the silence. I've been having these nightmares for as long as I can remember.

"I struggle to lock doors or park in my garage because I'll have no escape. I can barely bring myself to close them. I keep music and the TV on so it's not silent in my house, and I'm ... I'm afraid of the dark."

Nick furrowed his brow and frowned. "Is this a nightmare or did it really happen?"

"I don't know. I've tried looking up the police records and asking questions, but no one seems to know anything about it. Or if they do, they're not saying." She met his gaze. "How could my entire state of mind be built around a nightmare?"

He rolled his neck. "You missed your mother. Maybe your subconscious created this scene in response to your grief. Maybe you only think it happened before her death."

"My shrink said I'm seeing myself in the situations I rescue children from, but the nightmares occurred long before I became a federal agent. Before she died, my mom would hold me and tell me it was just a bad dream, but it felt so real. It still feels real. I—I think it really happened. I think I was kidnapped and held in a basement. I don't know how long I was there ..." Ari's voice cracked. She swallowed. "But I've never forgotten how scared I was."

"If there's no proof—"

"But how do you explain that music box?"

Nick returned to his chair. It was very odd. He couldn't argue with her there. If someone really had kidnapped her, shouldn't there be a police report or a news article about it? "Have you asked your aunt?"

"Years ago."

"What did she say?"

"It's just a dream. Go back to bed." Ari smiled.

Nick chuckled. "You think Enigma might know something about what happened? Maybe he was the kidnapper."

"I don't know for sure. But he used this music box to start the game. Why would he plant it in my house if it wasn't connected?"

It seemed so off-the-wall that there had to be some truth to the whole thing. "How do we track down Enigma?"

"Kye said we have to finish the game. I think this is the key he's speaking of." She touched the key from the broken music box, then turned the paper on the coffee table, stanzas facing him. "These words are misspelled. Passed, thyme, knot, and scene. I replaced them with the correct words, but that didn't change anything. I've tried to rearrange them. I've tried marking out certain letters. Nothing. It still doesn't make sense."

Nick leaned forward and picked up the paper. "Everywhere Enigma has sent us before has been a location. Silver Lake, Wynkoop Station, Abbot Castle, Chroma Cliffs."

"You forgot the library."

"Right." He didn't forget. "This clue should lead us to a location as well."

"But where?"

What if they weren't supposed to change the words? Passed, thyme, knot, scene. Thyme was an herb, knots had to do with ropes, and scenes related to movies, books, and plays. What about the word passed? Where could they find herbs, ropes, and a theater or bookstore all together where they could walk past them? A shopping mall?

Nick spun his chair to face his new computer, then pulled up the map program. It took only a second to find what he was looking for. "Hey, Ari. Look at this."

"What?"

A second later, he felt her brush his arm.

"The Fifteenth Street Mall." He pointed at the 3D image of

the outdoor shopping area. "If you walk past Thyme of Day, Knot Your Boat, and Platte City Theater, look where you end up."

Ari squinted and leaned forward. "The clock tower."

"Yes but look at the store that's underneath the clock tower. Timeless Reflections. Timeless—the length of time not bound by a clock."

"Do you think that's where we need to go?"

"It's worth a try." Nick stood and moved to get his wallet and keys. He'd just gotten his car back from the shop, but he'd have to risk it getting damaged again. For Ari's sake.

He stuffed the essentials in his pocket, then turned for the door, but Ari hadn't moved from her seat on the couch. "Are you okay?" He stepped closer and squatted until he was eye level with her.

She laid her hand on his arm. "Thank you for believing me."

He wasn't sure he did … yet. "You're welcome."

His chest swelled as he inhaled. He reached out and touched her cheek

Her brown eyes flickered with surprise. "And thanks for helping me with this. I honestly expected you to tell me to go to the police."

She needed him to believe in her right now. Needed his help. "The police are convinced they've got the right guy. We have to prove they don't. When we find enough evidence to support your theory, we'll turn it over to them. Until then … let's finish what we started."

Ari smiled and held up her keys. "I'm driving."

CHAPTER 34

C lock hands struck the top of the hour. Hundreds of chirping birds bombarded Ari's eardrums. She mashed her palms over her ear canals to block out the painful screeching.

Timeless Reflections was not one of those glass knickknack stores where customers added wedding dates and such.

Just walls and walls of cuckoo clocks.

She glanced over her shoulder at Nick. He, too, had covered his ears.

"What now?" she shouted over the noise.

Nick held up his finger. When the bird calls stopped, he blinked, shook his head, and wiggled his ear. "There. That's better. You were saying?"

She waved her hand around the room. "What are we looking for?" Nothing in the clue indicated what they were supposed to find.

Nick scanned the room, eyes wide. "Let's split up. Give me a holler if you spot anything promising."

"Got it."

She left Nick's side, moving from the first showroom into a second. Here, the clocks looked older, more handcrafted. Gears ticked. Weights hung beneath the ornately carved facades, each displaying a unique design.

Ari touched a carving of a goat on an Alpine-styled dwelling.

"May I help you?" A nasally voice spoke from behind her.

She whirled to face a short man wearing thick glasses, a silver beard clear down to his shirt buttons, and lederhosen. He carried a house-shaped clock.

"I'm so sorry. I didn't know anyone was here."

The man raised an eyebrow. "It's unusual for a shopkeeper to leave his wares unattended. I was in the back." He thumbed over his shoulder.

A curtain covered an opening in the wall, probably the entrance to a work area or storage room.

Her face warmed. "Did you make all of these?"

"I did. Now, what can I help you with?"

"I'm not really sure." He'd think they were nuts if she tried to explain Enigma's clues. "Do you have any clocks with eagles on them?"

"Eagles?"

Ari nodded. "An eagle wearing a crown, holding an ax and a key in its talons."

The old man squinted. "That would be an unusual carving, don't you think?"

"Yes, of course. Well, thanks anyway."

She'd seen the security cameras when they'd entered the store. It would be impossible for Enigma to have hidden anything inside one or more of the clocks in either showroom.

She turned, then looked back. "Do you take clocks on consignment? Or have any that might have come in for repairs?"

The clockmaker straightened his glasses. "Not recently, no." He paused. "What's your name, young lady?"

"Arizona Powers." She cringed, waiting for his reaction. If he'd seen the news six months ago, he'd know exactly who she was and what she had done.

The old man stroked his beard. "Powers, you say?" A look of recognition sparked in his kind eyes.

"Yes."

"I think I have something for you. Follow me." He disappeared behind the curtain.

Ari hesitated, then followed him into the workroom.

A workbench held a variety of clocks in various states of repair and a row of tiny hammers and screwdrivers. Small buckets contained gears, springs, and chains. The table also held a magnifier like one might see in a jewelry store.

On the opposite side of the room stood two metal shelving units stacked with boxes and clocks. It was here the clockmaker set down the clock he carried and lifted another one. He squinted at a tag dangling from a string taped to the roof.

"Yes, here it is." He spun around and held out the clock. "For one, Arizona Powers."

"I don't quite understand." Ari kept her hands at her side. "How do you know it's for me? Where did it come from?"

The clockmaker smiled and wiggled his nose. "Your name isn't exactly a common one, my dear. As far as where it came from, a man came into the store, oh, a month ago. He asked me to hold on to this until Arizona Powers could pick it up."

"Uh, thank you for keeping it for me." Ari took the clock from him. "Do I owe you anything?"

The clockmaker shook his head. "I'm just happy to see it returned to its rightful owner. Have a good day, Miss Powers."

Ari left the curtained room.

Nick met her at the doorway between the first and second showrooms. "You found a clock."

"Let's go outside."

Nick followed her out of the store, and Ari took a seat on the concrete bench surrounding the fountain in the middle of the plaza.

Bare Aspens sprouted from openings between the decorative tiles on the ground. An airplane roared as it passed overhead. Two ravens fought over a French fry, and shoppers strolled along the storefronts, carrying shopping bags and paper coffee cups.

She ran her fingers over the intricate design. "A man brought this clock into the store a month ago and told the clockmaker to hold it for me."

Nick remained standing, one knee bent with his foot propped on the bench. "Are you serious?"

"As a heart attack."

"Do you think it's our next clue?"

"I don't see how it could be anything but the next clue. I mean, it's too coincidental otherwise." Ari turned the clock upside down and shook it. "How do we get inside this thing?"

"Whoa." Nick stayed her hand. "You don't want to break it. It's at least two hundred years old."

"I'd break it if it meant figuring out the next part of the game faster."

Nick rolled his eyes. "Look here." He touched a crudely burned design on the wood base.

The eagle emblem. "I guess we're on the right track."

Nick held out his hands. "Let me take a look."

Ari relinquished the clock, and he balanced it on his knee. Lips pinched, he turned it this way and that, looking it over carefully. After a minute, he pushed on a slat of the roof.

It moved, and Ari gasped.

He pressed another panel in the opposite direction. As soon as he moved the third, a rod sprung from the side of the clock. "It's a puzzle box."

Ari frowned. "What's a puzzle box?"

He kept working while he answered. "It's a special trick box that uses a series of sliders, gears, and sometimes keys to be opened. I utilized human-sized ones in my shows."

Like the expert he was, he maneuvered the panels and rods. Finally, he gave the clock face a half turn forward, and it popped off in his hands, revealing a keyhole. He traced it with his finger. "Let me have the music box key."

Ari handed it to him.

He laid the clock front on the bench between them, then

inserted the key into the lock. With a twist, it unlocked, and a wooden panel opened. He reached his hand inside the clock.

Ari leaned in with the giddiness of a schoolgirl. "What's in there?"

"Give me a second." He withdrew a curled sepia postcard from the last century, handed it to Ari, then stuck his hand back inside the clock. "There's something else."

Beneath the photo of a brick building with a dome roof surrounded by pine trees were the words, Eagle's Nest Observatory. She flipped the postcard over and read the back aloud.

Among the stars, above the moon,
A constellation sings a tune.
The eagle's eye will point the way
A string of pearls in silence lay.
The celestial equator need not fear.
For three kings reside so near.
The rightmost king is two in one.
An unbreakable bond from sun to sun.
-Enigma

"The eagle's eye must be referring to the telescope at the observatory." Nick dropped his foot to the ground and sat on the concrete bench beside her.

The observatory at the University of Platte City housed a twenty-six-foot-long, twenty-inch refractor lens telescope made of steel, brass, and cast iron. Every Tuesday and Thursday, the observatory held public events where visitors could look at the night sky through the lens, but they were always sold-out months in advance.

Ari groaned. "We're never going to get a ticket."

"No need. The three kings and string of pearls refer to Orion's belt. It resides along the Meridian, the celestial equator.

The rightmost king or star is Mintaka. It's actually two stars that orbit around each other."

Her jaw dropped. "I'm guessing Enigma didn't expect me to have a bona fide genius at my disposal. But how does that help us? It's not like we can just rocket up to the star to look around."

Nick held out a jigsaw puzzle piece he must have removed from inside the clock.

Ari took the puzzle piece and turned it over. A little ink had smeared, but in Enigma's handwriting, the word *Voices* was written on the back of the cardboard.

"Anything else in there?" she asked.

"Just this." Nick handed her a piece of canvas material—a crude drawing of a town. An X marked a spot on the map.

She closed her eyes for a moment. "A treasure map? Are you kidding?"

He pulled out his cell phone and started typing. "Wanna bet there's a town called Mintaka around here?"

While he researched, Ari let her gaze drift, scanning the open-air mall. A boarder skateboarded to the end of the plaza and jumped the stairs that led to the parking lot.

"I always wished I could do that," she whispered, barely audible.

A woman, wearing sunglasses and a headscarf, stood at the corner of the clock tower. Her long silver hair caught the sunlight. The woman from the train station.

Ari got to her feet, pretended to stretch, then moved in her direction.

The woman bolted across the plaza, her high-heeled shoes echoing across the pavestones.

Ari launched after her. Who was this woman, and why was she following them?

The woman cut around the back of the coffee shop.

Ari rounded the corner, but the woman had disappeared. Ari slowed her steps and bent to catch her breath. Her gunshot wound flamed. If she wasn't careful, she'd tear open the stitches.

She turned to head back to where she left Nick, but he was walking in her direction, carrying the clock.

"Who was that?" he asked.

"I don't know, but I saw that same woman at the train station. I'm pretty sure she's following us."

She grimaced. Pain sent a wave of dizziness over her. She closed her eyes and waited for it to pass.

"You okay?"

"I will be in a minute." She exhaled and opened her eyes as the discomfort diminished. "Did you uncover any information about Mintaka?"

Nick shifted the clock to his other arm. "Mintaka was a Russian settlement about two hours west from here. It started with a silver mine, but when the mineral ran out, everyone deserted the area. It's nothing more than a ghost town now."

"Ghost town, huh? I'd rather be there in the daylight, so let's get a move on."

He shot her a mischievous grin. "You're not afraid of ghosts, are you?"

"No. In my experience, it's the live ones you have to watch out for."

Nick chuckled, then gestured for Ari to lead the way back to her car.

Once they arrived at the convertible, she unlocked the doors, then popped the trunk for Nick to place the clock in the back. She dropped onto the driver's seat, slipped the key in the ignition, and gave it a turn.

The starter revved and groaned, then sputtered to a stop.

"What's wrong?" Nick appeared in the open doorway.

She tried again and got the same result. "I think the battery's dead."

Nick raised the hood, then used the prop rod to support the weight. "We'll need a jump. You got cables hidden in this Lilliputian limo?"

"Don't make fun of my car. 'Though she be but little, she is fierce.'" She always felt the Shakespearean quote applied to herself as much as her choice in transportation. "In the trunk."

Nick's brow furrowed. "I didn't see them when I was back there."

"That's odd. It's not like there's a bunch of other junk for them to be buried in." She rounded the bumper and frowned at the lack of jumper cables. "Huh? I thought I had some."

A man walked their direction, carrying a cup of coffee in one hand and a newspaper in the other.

"Excuse me, sir." She waved to get his attention. "Do you have jumper cables we could borrow?"

The man stopped. "Sure. I'll give you a jump, too. Just let me pull my car closer."

Ari sighed in relief. "Thank you so much. We really appreciate it."

The man jogged to a white four-door sedan a few aisles away, climbed inside, then drove around to park in the empty space beside her car.

Ari stood out of the way while Nick and the man worked to attach the jumper cables in the right places. A pine air freshener dangled from the stranger's rearview mirror. A pair of sunglasses and his coffee were set in the center console, and the newspaper lay on the passenger seat open to the front page. The headline caught her attention.

CEO of AegisTech Solutions Arrested for Murder

Raymond Roach, CEO of AegisTech Solutions, was arrested Monday night for the murder of his wife, Jayda Roach. Four years ago, Jayda was killed in her own home. At the time, no suspects were apprehended. In recent weeks, new evidence had come to light that led law enforcement to the conclusion that Roach was murdered by her husband.

Just days before her death, a life insurance policy was taken out under Jayda's name, even though she was unemployed, and the couple had no children. According to Chief Wayland, the murder weapon was discovered in the state park during a recent thunderstorm. Fingerprints were matched to those of Roach, as well as the bullet casing found at the scene of the crime matched the gun markings ...

Reid claimed the obituaries were unrelated to Bridgette's case and were randomly chosen to transport the ciphers. Maybe Enigma didn't kill Jayda. And if he didn't kill Jayda, maybe he didn't kill the others either.

"Nick, you should see this."

No response.

Ari raised her head. "Nick?"

Both cars were still there. Hoods raised. Cables stretched between them.

But both Nick and the other man were gone.

CHAPTER 35

Nick had rarely seen Ari so worked up.

"Where were you?" She practically screamed at him as he approached the car.

"We went to wash our hands." He dropped the hood, and it slammed closed. "I told you, but you seemed distracted by something in Ed's car."

"Ed? Who's Ed?"

"I am," the stranger answered, then dropped his hood, jumper cables in hand. "You're all set, Nick."

"Thanks for your help. We appreciate it."

"No problem. Nice to meet you folks." Ed hopped in his car, shut the door, tossed the cables over the seat, then backed out of the space.

"I'm sorry I got so upset. I thought something had happened to you." Her voice quivered.

Nick stepped close and laid his hand on her shoulder. "Nothing's going to happen to me." He made eye contact. "Now, what were you staring at so intently you didn't hear me tell you where I was going?"

Ari's face contorted, then relaxed. "Oh, the newspaper. They arrested Raymond Roach last night for Jayda's murder."

"So, Reid was right. It wasn't Enigma." Nick slid his hand to Ari's fingers and gave her a tug toward the open driver's door. "If we don't hurry, it's going to be dark before we get to Mintaka."

Ari lowered into the seat but kept her focus on him. "I'm not so sure. My gut tells me it's all connected. The obits, the journal, the emblem. I still think Enigma is getting revenge on the mercenaries."

"The only way we can know for sure is to ask Enigma."

Or talk to Van Sloan. Though, would he really admit to betraying his country and slaughtering innocent people? It would be the end of his career. They wouldn't get anything out of him. Their best bet was to track down Enigma and see what he had to say.

Nick shut Ari's door, then walked around the car. As he buckled his seatbelt, Ari put the MINI Cooper in reverse. She took the ramp to merge onto the main highway westward out of town.

He hadn't been able to get what Ari had told him that morning out of his mind.

She was right about it being odd that her idiosyncrasies could be based on something that never actually happened. Plus, the amount of detail she remembered seemed out of place for a dream, even one that was repeated frequently. She'd said she'd tried to locate evidence to support the theory but came up empty.

The brain was a simple thing to confuse, and false memories were fairly common, especially in cases of traumatic experiences, and they could contain enough details to feel real.

That's most likely what they were—false memories created by the trauma of losing her mother. She'd already lost her dad, and her mother was all she had left. Her death could have been enough to send Ari's young mind into chaotic scrambling to make sense of the tragedy.

Nick pulled out his phone, then typed *Tyrrhenea* into the

search browser. He swallowed as the answer appeared on the screen. "Reid was right."

"About what?" Ari leaned across the console. The vehicle vibrated on the rumble strips as it drifted toward the shoulder.

"Hey." Nick grabbed the wheel and moved the car back into the lane. "Watch what you're doing. I'll explain, but you keep your eyes on the road."

"Sorry." Ari shifted in her seat. "What was Reid right about?"

"Tyrrhenea. It doesn't exist. I can locate a Tyrrhenean Sea, but no Tyrrhenea."

Ari checked her mirrors, then flicked the turn signal and passed a slow-moving vehicle. "What about your dad? Would he know anyone who could help? Maybe we could ask him."

Nick checked his watch. "We can try. They're supposed to be on the road home right now." He dialed the number and put the device on speakerphone.

"Hello," Mom answered.

Wind and road traffic echoed in the background.

"Hey, Mom. It's Nick. Can I speak to Dad?"

There was a moment of silence. "We're at a rest stop in Kansas. He's helping Toby into the restroom." Tears clogged her voice.

"Are you crying? What's wrong?"

She sniffled. "Nothing. It's just … you know, that's the first time you've asked to speak to your dad in seventeen years."

"I know, Mom. I'm not going to wait that long again."

"I'm grateful you all could talk things over." She paused. "Here they come now." Another pause, then she whispered, "It's Nick."

"Hello, son. What do you need?" Dad's voice came through the speaker.

Nick cleared his throat. They may have been able to work some things out, but this still wasn't easy. "Do you remember when we were talking about that eagle emblem? The one you didn't recognize."

"Sure. What about it? Did you figure out what it meant?"

"No, not yet. We did find a military field journal that mentioned a country called Tyrrhenea. But I can't find any information suggesting that it exists. I'm thinking they're somehow connected."

"What was the name again?"

"Tyrrhenea." He spelled it out.

"Never heard of it. I can contact the geography and world history professors from the university and see what they have to say. It might take a day or two before I can get back to you."

"Thanks, Dad. I appreciate your help."

"No problem. That's what Dads are for."

Nick's vision blurred. "Tell Mom and Toby I love them."

They had spent the entire weekend making up for lost time.

"Will do. Love you, son."

"Love you, Dad."

The line died, and Nick lowered his phone to his leg. "Dad said he'll ask some professors at the university about it."

Ari glanced at him. "Are you crying?"

"No." He rubbed his eye and chuckled.

He hadn't told Ari about the chasm between him and his parents. Maybe he should. She'd opened up to him about her nightmares. "Remember when I told you about running away from home to join the circus?"

Her mouth quirked. "I thought you were joking."

"No. I really did. I thought my parents blamed me for Toby's accident."

"Accident? Is that why he's ... you know ..." She shifted uncomfortably.

"Disabled. It's okay to say it. I was thirteen, and Toby was five. He loved to watch me practice my escape tricks. I had a special trunk. Climb inside and it locked, but it had a tiny button on the inside to make the lock release. One day, I left it open, and Toby climbed in. The lid closed, and he didn't know how to get out. We found him several hours later, blue and unresponsive. I always thought my parents blamed me for what happened. I wasted seventeen years thinking they hated me."

"But they don't?"

"No, they don't. But my impulsive decision nearly cost my brother his life."

"You didn't do it on purpose." Ari turned on her blinker and slid into the fast lane to pass another slow-moving car. "You couldn't have known that would happen."

"I could have prevented it, though, if I hadn't been in such a hurry."

Same with Cosco and Rachel. His impulsiveness had resulted in tragedy.

"Speaking of thinking things through." He looked from the dashboard clock to the setting sun. "The sun sets at seventeen thirty. We won't get to Mintaka before dark."

Ari cringed and shifted her weight in her seat.

"Are you okay?" he asked.

"Just uncomfortable. What do you want to do? Turn around and come back tomorrow."

"Yeah, let's do that."

Two miles later, Ari took the exit. At the stop sign, at the top of the ramp, she pointed at a sign for a Bed and Breakfast. "We should just stay there. We're only thirty miles from Mintaka. It'll take us another two hours to get back home."

He worked his jaw. "I'd rather just go home."

Ari turned her head and glared. "And I'd rather not waste four hours driving home and back."

"We don't have clean clothes for tomorrow."

She shrugged. "Wouldn't be the first time I've worn the same clothes for days on end."

"That's disgusting."

"That's life as a field agent."

A work truck pulled up behind them. "Ari, there's a vehicle behind us. We need to move."

She turned on the blinker, checked the road, took a left, crossed the bridge, then pulled onto the shoulder.

The truck passed.

"You're being ridiculous. Why can't we just stay at the B&B?"

He'd have to tell her the truth, or he would never win this argument. "I don't eat food I didn't cook. Unless it comes from a package." Or family.

She covered a cough. "Why?"

"Because." He pinched his lips together. "I just don't."

"What if we stop by a grocery store, pick up some stuff, then get a room at an Air BnB, or one of those hotel suites with a kitchen? You can cook dinner."

"I don't know." He waffled, cracking his neck.

"We can even stop somewhere and get some clean clothes, too. Will that work for you?"

"Fine. That's a suitable compromise."

"Good. I'll drive toward town. You get us a map to the nearest shopping center."

CHAPTER 36

A tantalizing aroma wafted between the adjoining hotel rooms, making Ari's mouth water, and her stomach gurgle. She hadn't dated anyone before who'd known how to cook.

Not that Nick and I are dating. Our relationship is strictly professional.

That wasn't true, either. If it were professional, they would still be calling each other by their last names. So, maybe their relationship *had* moved beyond business to more of a friendship, but that's as far as it was going to go.

As soon as they located Enigma and put him behind bars, they would go their separate ways. Nick back to the DSS. And she to whatever she decided to do now that the FBI wasn't an option. Would they reconsider her employment?

It's all I've ever done. All I've ever known. I don't want to work anywhere else. I love what I do... a rock settled into her gut ... *what I used to do.*

A knock on the door separating their rooms startled her.

"Hey, dinner's ready," Nick's muffled voice carried through the barrier.

"Just a minute." She stood from the bed, viewed her

reflection in the mirror, wiped her nose with a Kleenex, then combed her fingers through her hair.

There was nothing she could do about the red eyes. "Coming."

She entered Nick's suite, and the fragrance of pungent herbs grew stronger.

Soft classical music played from his cell phone. The desk had been pulled from the wall and set with two plates, silverware, napkins, and a single rose in a vase. The same flower decorated her hotel room, but somehow it looked more romantic here.

Romantic? She chided herself for even entertaining the thought.

He pulled out a chair. "Please have a seat, Signorina."

Ari smiled, then sat. Her smile faded as a sharp pain shot through her midsection.

"Hurting?"

She shifted. "Yeah, I took some Tylenol earlier. I'm just waiting for it to kick in."

He gave the chair a push, tucking her legs under the table. He pivoted, then turned back, holding two cans of soda. "Which would you like to drink? We have Coca-Cola or Dr Pepper?" he over-dramatized an Italian accent.

"Coke, please."

"Ah, you have chosen well." Nick popped the pull tab. He grinned, and his eyes twinkled. "Because I wanted the other one."

She couldn't hold back her laughter. "You're a nut."

"Thank you for noticing." He set the second can of soda in front of the other chair, then moved into the kitchenette. A second later, he returned, carrying a skillet filled with pasta and meat sauce.

"We have for you tonight a lovely Spaghetti Bolognese." He scooped a large portion and twirled it onto her plate. "Buon appetito."

He put some on his own plate, returned the pan to the

kitchen, then took his seat at the table. "I'd normally serve this with garlic bread and a Caesar salad, but there isn't an oven or utensils to toss a salad."

He'd dropped the fake accent.

She picked up a fork and moved it through the pasta. "This is fine. Actually, it's more than fine. This is beautiful, and it smells amazing. Where did you learn to cook?"

Nick grinned. "A chef never reveals his secrets."

"That's a magician."

"I'm that, too." He held out his palm. "Would you mind if I said grace?"

Ari's eyes widened. "No. I don't mind."

When she laid her hand in his, his skin felt soft and warm. She closed her eyes and bowed her head. His prayer was simple. But dignified. An ethereal ambiance filled the room, as if the Spirit of God himself had bent down to listen.

A God she used to believe in—before He let her down.

When Nick said amen, and they lifted their heads, Ari wiped away a tear.

"Dig in," he directed and twisted noodles around his fork.

She wrapped the spaghetti around her fork, then put the utensil in her mouth. Flavors of garlic and basil exploded on her tongue. She sighed in delight. "You really are a magician. I've never had anything so delicious."

"You're welcome."

They ate in comfortable silence.

When the plates were scraped clean, Ari reclined and put her hands on her stomach. "Oh, I'm so stuffed. I rarely eat that much all at once."

"I'm glad you enjoyed it." Nick carried the dishes to the sink.

"You cooked. I'll wash."

She rose, but he waved her down. "I've got it."

"Are you sure?"

"I'm sure." He turned on the faucet. Steaming water filled the sink, and soap bubbles rose.

Ari watched as he wiped the porcelain plates and laid them in the dish drainer. A man who cooked was rare. One who washed the dishes was an absolute anomaly.

"This might seem like an odd question, considering how amazing your cooking is, but I'm curious. Why don't you eat out?"

He put the scrubbed silverware into the drying rack, then wiped his wet hands on a towel. "How squeamish are you?"

She patted her gut. "Like iron."

Homicides were ugly. She'd seen a lot of rookies lose their lunch after visiting their first crime scene.

He returned to his chair. "Rachel and I were traveling on tour with the show. We went to this hole-in-the-wall restaurant and both of us got food poisoning. I spent days clutching the porcelain throne. After that, I learned to cook, and we never ate out again."

"Why you and not your wife? Not that there's anything wrong with a man in the kitchen, it's just unexpected."

"She had a thing against raw meat. Loved it cooked. Just couldn't touch it."

Ari's mouth twitched. "If it wasn't for takeout, I'd starve."

"I can teach you how to cook."

"It's not that. I'm not a total loss in the kitchen. I just never have the time."

The air conditioner kicked on, and Ari shivered. "Can you turn up the thermostat? I'm freezing." She rubbed her bare arms.

"No can do." He tossed her his coat. "Put this on."

"Why can't you turn it up? Is it broken?" She put the jacket around her back and her arms through the holes.

"Another time, Rachel and I stopped at a motel in Alabama. It was the only establishment for miles around, and we were exhausted. When we got in the room, we noticed it was freezing cold, so we turned up the thermostat, changed clothes, and went out to dinner. Obviously, this was before the food poisoning.

"When we got back to our room, there were cockroaches

everywhere. In our luggage. In our bed. Rachel screamed so loud; it woke the neighbors. Come to find out, cockroaches like heat, and the motel kept the rooms cold to keep them at bay."

Another Rachel story. "You loved your wife very much."

"I did. She was the light of my life. Her death nearly ended me."

Would he ever be able to move on? Remarry? A guy this perfect shouldn't be single.

"I noticed your evidence board was missing that last time I was at your apartment. I asked you about it, but I guess you didn't hear me."

Nick lowered his eyes and rubbed his forehead. He swallowed, and his Adam's apple bopped. "I heard you." He lifted his gaze. "How could I encourage you to let God bring about justice if I wasn't willing to do the same?"

"What if He never does?"

"He will. Either in this life or the next. I just have to leave it in His hands."

Ari pulled the coat tighter as a sudden chill swept over her skin. "What if you get to Heaven and her killer is there because they asked Jesus to forgive them?"

That thought had always bothered her. Wouldn't that traumatize a victim to see their offender walking the street of gold?

Nick ran his fingers across the tabletop. "Then Jesus's blood covered their sin in the same way it covered mine. What makes my sin any less sinful than theirs? God sees all sin the same. Some sins are not worse than others. He gave His only Son to die for all of it. Whether we're a Hitler or a Bundy or stole a cookie from the cookie jar, we deserve death."

He stood and moved to the nightstand.

The music stopped.

He carried his phone back to his seat. "If I try to quote it, I'll get it wrong." His eyes flickered as he looked at something on the screen. "Here it is in Ezekiel thirty-three, verse eleven. 'Say unto them, As I live, saith the Lord GOD, I have no pleasure in the death of the wicked; but that the wicked turn from his way and live: turn ye, turn ye from your evil ways.'

"In another verse, I think it's in first or second Peter, it says that the Lord is 'not willing that any should perish.' Why should I take pleasure in something that breaks God's heart?"

Ari frowned. "But what about all the verses in Psalms that says God laughs at the wicked or that He's angry with the wicked every day?"

He bounced one shoulder. "I guess there's a difference between being angry with someone and wishing them harm. God laughs because they think they're in charge, that they'll never have to face consequences for their actions, but He knows their day of judgment is coming. Still, that doesn't mean God is happy about it. He would rather they repent and turn to Him than punish them, but His justice demands reparation—one way or another."

"May I see that?" She held out her hand, and Nick placed his phone in it. She looked at the Bible verse on the screen. She'd never heard or seen it before.

For every person who didn't accept Jesus's sacrifice on the cross, His death was in vain. And the life of that wicked one was a life wasted. A life that had refused to be saved.

What if she went on a rescue mission, and the victim refused to let her save them? What if she held out the means of hope, and they refused her help? She'd be devastated. In that moment, would it matter if they were a good person or a bad person?

"There's another verse that came to mind just now," Nick said, pulling her from her thoughts.

"Yeah, what's that?"

"It's in Matthew. It says that God makes his sun to rise on the evil and on the good and sends rain on the just and on the unjust. I don't understand why He works that way, but I know for sure that—"

"God is God, and I'm not," she finished.

241

"Exactly."

Ari laid the phone on the table. "You've given me a lot to think about. Thank you for dinner. I'll see you in the morning."

"Goodnight, Ari." Nick stood. "By the way, you can leave the doors between our rooms open if that'll make you feel more comfortable."

Her vision blurred. "Thank you. I appreciate that."

She left the doors ajar, then climbed into the bed, starting the playlist on her cell phone. Her mind raced. The wound in her side ached from sitting too long.

Maybe she was wrong for taking vengeance on Reece Wayne, but what about all the good things she'd done in her career? All the victims she had rescued. All the lives she had saved. Why did one mistake make her a villain?

He'd deserved to pay for his crimes. What if there hadn't been enough evidence to convict him? What if there'd been a mistrial? What if he'd hurt someone else?

In her own mind she'd done the right thing, but in the eyes of the law, and in the eyes of his friends and family, she was the bad guy. His mother's tears during the television interview were forever seared on Ari's brain. At the time, she'd been stunned to think that anyone could love someone so wicked, but maybe she'd had the wrong perspective all along.

She chose his consequences for him when she took his life into her own hands. What might have happened if she'd allowed God to bring about justice?

That was a thought she could chew on for a long time.

Ari's tiny hands patted the lumpy mattress on the hard concrete floor. Her legs felt wet and sticky. Peeling back the thin blanket, she shivered. Her tummy hurt, and the inside of her neck felt like she'd eaten sand from the sandbox.

She crawled across the floor and sipped water from the ball-shaped bottle. She found the last of the crackers and nibbled on them, making her even thirstier. One drop of water splashed onto her tongue, then nothing.

She shook hard. Why wasn't the water coming out? She laid the bottle in the basket. It was all gone. What would she do when she got thirsty again?

Sadness washed over her, and her eyes grew blurry, making it hard to see. She wiped away the tears and crawled back to the mat, her heart as heavy as the giant panda in her pretty pink bedroom.

Why couldn't she go home? How long did she have to stay in this scary place?

Her eyes and nose stung. Where was Mommy? Why didn't she come? Was Mommy angry with her? She didn't remember making Mommy mad, but maybe she'd been a bad girl, and Mommy wanted her to say sorry.

I'll say sorry, Mommy, just as soon as you come get me.

Sitting on her bottom, with her legs sticking out, she picked up the only toy in the tiny room—a music maker with the pretty ladies on top. She turned the twisty key, and the twinkling sound started playing, feeling like a hug and a tear at the same time. Curling as tiny as possible, Ari closed her eyes and let the sadness steal the air until she drowned in her tears.

CHAPTER 37

U ncontrolled sobs reverberated from the next room.

Nick sprang to his feet, threw on a shirt, grabbed a kitchen knife, and bolted into the adjoining suite. The lamp beside the bed glowed. He scanned the room. No attacker. Only Ari, eyes closed, tossing and turning on the bed, wails emanating from her throat.

"Arizona, wake up."

She woke, arms flailing, tangling the blanket around her legs.

He approached the bed and touched her shoulder. "Shh. You were having a nightmare."

She turned wide eyes on him, her chest heaving. Her hair and skin were soaked. She pushed down on the mattress and scooted upright against the headboard, gulping for air. "I'm sorry. Did I wake you?"

"It's fine." He handed her a Kleenex. "I heard crying and wanted to make sure you were all right."

"I'm okay. Now." She swallowed and used the tissue to mop her skin.

Nick fetched a cup of water from the sink, then brought it to the bed.

Ari gulped it down. Dribbles wet the neckline of her oversized T-shirt. She wiped her lips on the back of her hand, then set the plastic cup on the nightstand.

She picked up the alarm clock. "One-thirty." She closed her eyes, hung her head, and set the clock down. "I've only been asleep for a couple of hours."

"Would it help if you talked about it?"

She opened her eyes. "Talk about what?"

"Your nightmare."

Her shoulders bounced. Her fingers twisted the white sheet into a knot.

"Was it that same one? Where you're locked in the basement?"

Her head moved, just barely. "It's always that one."

Nick scratched at the faint shadow of stubble on his jawline. "How could we go about finding the truth? Is there someone we could ask? Some files we could search?"

"I've already asked. Nobody knows anything. They all tell me it's a dream. That it never happened."

"Would the newspaper archives in DC have any—"

She jerked in agitation, causing a strand of dark chocolate hair to fall in front of her face. "Any articles about it? No. I've already tried that. If it's real, someone did a bang-up job deleting all the evidence and all the records of the event. Maybe they're right. Maybe I am crazy."

Nick sat on the edge of the bed and tucked the flyaway behind her ear. "You're not crazy."

"You thought so when we first met." She met his gaze.

She had him there. "That's because I didn't know you."

"And now?"

His opinion had changed. Drastically. "You're a passionate woman with a big heart."

Her long eyelashes fluttered, and she raised her big, round

gingerbread eyes. They sparkled in the lamplight. Her cheeks beamed a rosy pink. The edge of her alabaster collarbone was visible.

His gaze flickered to her lips. Her tongue ran over them, and his stomach fluttered.

This wasn't the time or place. He wouldn't take advantage of her vulnerable state of mind, plus it wouldn't be right to pursue a romance with anyone else until he was sure he was ready to move on. Besides, Ari might not even be interested in him.

Nick cleared his throat and stood. "I should let you get back to sleep. It's going to be a long day tomorrow." He turned to leave.

Her hand grabbed his. "Please. Stay with me."

"I can't. It wouldn't be proper."

"I trust you."

She might trust him, but he wasn't sure he trusted himself. A week ago, they were strangers. Now, he couldn't help but wonder if they could be more than friends.

His gaze traced her figure hidden beneath the blanket. His skin grew warm, and he tugged at his T-shirt neckband. He might be a Christian, but he was still a man.

Her eyes pleaded with him. "Please. I don't want to be alone."

He raked his fingers through his hair, rounded the bed, spread the bedspread flat, then crawled on top. He sat ramrod straight against the headboard. "Just until you fall asleep."

When she scooted down until her head rested on the pillow, he leaned over and tucked the blanket up around her neck.

Her hand crawled out and took hold of his. Her eyes closed and her breathing grew shallow. A soft snore emanated from her parted lips.

Lips, he still wanted to kiss.

Morning light peeked from behind the heavy curtains. Nick tried to stretch out the kinks in his back from sitting up all night. He'd nodded on and off but hadn't left Ari's side.

Ari moaned, rolled over, and opened her eyes. She gasped, then sat upright. "You're still here."

"I'm still here." He chuckled at her declaration of the obvious.

She blinked. "You didn't have to stay."

"I couldn't leave. You didn't let go of my hand until about an hour ago. By then, my legs were asleep."

Her cheeks pinked, and her eyes lowered to the bedspread. "Sorry," she whispered under her breath.

"At least one of us got a good night's sleep. No more nightmares?"

"No more nightmares."

He slid off the bed. "I'm going to shower and make some coffee. Do you want some?"

"Yes, please." She tossed off the blanket, revealing bare legs from the thighs down.

Nick quickly put his back to her. His neck warmed. "Great. I'll see you in a few minutes." He scurried through the inner doors as fast as his legs would carry him.

Twenty minutes later, coffee percolated in the hotel provided appliance. Nick used the mirror to fix his collar and comb his wet hair with his fingers.

A knock sounded.

He looked behind him, and his pulse picked up speed.

Ari stood in the doorway, wearing a navy turtleneck and jeans. Wet hair hung loosely around her shoulders. "Coffee ready?"

"Uh, yeah." He cleared his throat. "Let me pour you a cup." He lifted the hot carafe, his hands shaking while he poured the steaming liquid into the disposable cups. He returned the coffeepot to the warming pad, then handed one cup to Ari. "You —you look lovely."

"Thank you." Her cheeks flushed as she sipped the black coffee, then arched her eyebrow. "You seem a little jittery this morning."

"It's just that—the jitters," he lied. "Only God knows what today will hold." Which was true, but he couldn't tell her how much her presence affected him.

He bent, scooped up his dirty clothes, then stuffed them into the shopping bag from yesterday's purchases. "Are you ready to go?"

She blinked rapidly, probably surprised by the abrupt change in subject. "Yeah, sure. Just let me grab my stuff, and we can get on the road." She and her coffee disappeared into the other room.

Dear God, help me. I'm falling in love with her, but I don't know if either of us is ready to pursue a relationship beyond friendship.

And with Enigma, hopefully, within their reach, there wasn't much time to find out.

Ari checked the mirrors, left the acceleration lane, and merged onto the highway.

A green road sign confirmed it was only thirty miles to Mintaka.

She glanced at Nick. He'd been acting strange all morning. She hadn't meant to make him uncomfortable by asking him to stay in her room last night, but his presence had brought her a sense of tranquility she hadn't had in a long, long time.

Just having him beside her had driven away the nightmares.

Even if it had been a little awkward.

He'd wanted to kiss her, she could tell. And to be honest, she'd hoped he would. No one had ever made her feel the way Nicholas Trueheart did. He was kind, tender, funny, patient … the list went on and on. He was everything she wanted in a life partner.

But they couldn't be together as long as he pined for his first wife. And just because he put away the murder board wasn't proof he was ready for a new relationship. Not that Ari expected him to forget about Rachel—the woman would always be a part of him—but she didn't want to be compared to her or have him think of her whenever they were together.

He would need to give Ari his whole heart ... or not at all.

His silence was getting to her. "What do you think we'll find in Mintaka?"

Nick startled, then looked her way. "I don't have the slightest idea. What do you want to find?"

"Besides Enigma? Answers."

He narrowed his eyebrows. "Answers to what?"

She waved her hand. "All of it. How it's all connected."

He jerked his chin toward an opening in the highway. "I guess we'll find out soon. That's our exit."

Ari switched lanes. An arrow indicated Mintaka was to the right. She checked for oncoming traffic, then turned onto a winding country road leading to the middle of nowhere.

It took another twenty minutes before the town sign appeared. Rugged and worn, faded white paint announced, Welcome to Mintaka. Elevation 7,403.

She slowed the vehicle as the road changed from pavement to dirt. Snow-peaked mountains surrounded the valley. A scattering of old western buildings lined the main street.

Ari parked, shut off the ignition, and unbuckled her seatbelt. "Got the map?"

Nick held it up, then exited the car. He stretched and took a deep breath, pounding his chest like a gorilla. "Ah! There's nothing like that fresh mountain air."

"You know, you've done that every time we've come out here."

Nick shrugged. "What can I say? I love the mountains. I'd like to have a house out here someday."

Ari gave the town a once over. "I agree, but I kind of wish

Enigma had been a little more efficient with his clues. Last night, we passed the exits for the Abbot Castle and for Silver Lake."

"I guess he's not as organized as you." Nick raised the map and held it out in front of him. "I'm trying to gather my bearings. But I can't tell which way to orient the map. There's no compass rose or legend of any kind."

Ari stepped closer and touched his hand. "Hold it down here where I can get a better look."

He lowered the map to her eye level.

She squinted and compared the rough drawings with the surrounding landscape. None of the buildings on the map were labeled. No symbols to represent geographic features or landmarks. No instructions.

Seemed Enigma had left them completely on their own.

One rendering on the map vaguely matched a funky-shaped tree. She pointed at it. "If that's this tree, then we should face east." She faced the opposite direction and compared the map again. "This looks right. See how this square is shorter than the others?"

She pointed at a building to her right, the only one in town without a false front. "What are we supposed to do when we find this X, anyway? It's not like Enigma left us a key. What are we looking for?"

Nick shrugged, glanced over at the map, and started moving down the street. "I guess we'll know it when we see it."

Seven buildings remained from Mintaka's heyday in the silver rush of the late 1800s. When the mine closed, the Russian immigrants abandoned the town, looking for work elsewhere. What must it have been like during the silver boom? More exciting than the ghost town that lay before them.

A lonely wind blustered through town, kicking up dust.

Nick paused in front of what remained of the Mintaka Saloon

and spit out the granules of sand that had landed in his mouth, then shielded his eyes from the brightness of the sun. He half-expected a cowboy to come strolling through the swinging doors.

He didn't like being exposed like this in the middle of the street. Maybe he'd seen too many spy movies, but he kept picturing a helicopter swooping out of nowhere and gunning them down, or an infrared bead appearing on Ari's forehead from a sniper's laser.

The pain on her face made her discomfort obvious. The gunshot wound bothered her more than she let on.

"Do you enjoy watching westerns?" Ari's voice startled him.

He matched her pace as they continued through town. "No, not really. Why?"

"Just making conversation. I don't do well with silence."

They passed a building with a crooked placard written in Cyrillic script.

"Can you read Russian?" she asked.

"No, sorry." He spoke five languages—Russian was not one of them. "What kind of movies do you like to watch? Romantic Comedies? Dramas? Thrillers?"

"Animated."

He looked at her, eyes wide. "Really? I never would have guessed."

She tucked her hair behind her ear. "It's a relief from the stress of my day job. Pixar's my guilty pleasure."

Her admission brought a smile to his mouth. "Which one is your favorite?"

"UP."

"Why?"

Ari shrugged. "What about you?" She squinted and looked him up and down. "Let me guess. Mystery fan, right?"

"Can't watch mysteries. I solve them all before the end."

"Too bad you can't solve this one." She flushed. "Sorry. I didn't mean that."

"I'm doing my best." He looked down at his shoes shuffling through the dirt. "I love romantic comedies."

Ari covered her laugh. "Really? I never saw that coming. Why?"

"I guess I'm just a hopeless romantic at heart." His phone rang. He tapped the screen and put it to his ear. "Hey, Dad. I'm surprised to hear from you so soon."

Ari continued ahead without him.

The connection wasn't good. Dad's voice crackled. "I'm just eager to share what I learned from the Professor of European History about Tyrrhenea."

Nick's heart picked up speed. "So, it is a real place?"

"In a way. Tyrrhenea doesn't exist. Not anymore. But it was once a sovereign nation in the Mediterranean Sea. Thirty years ago, there was a land dispute between Italy and Tunisia. Both countries thought they should have the right to the island's only natural resource—iron ore. They went to war over it."

"Who won?"

"Italy gained control of the island, claiming it as an Italian province, and renamed it San Michele. The royal family was executed, and the nation faded from history. In fact, it's rumored American mercenaries aided Italy in an attack on the island. I wonder if it has anything to do with that military field journal you found. Isn't this exciting?"

"Yeah, Dad. It's great." He tried to sound elated, but the rumors confirmed the authenticity of the soldier's confession. Ari's dad, Ambassador Van Sloan, his own father-in-law, and three others were all guilty of international crimes.

"I asked the history professor about that emblem you showed me, and it's the former flag of Tyrrhenea, from an old island legend. A North African fisherman was washed ashore during a big storm. An eagle rose from the sea and gave the fisherman an ax and a key to build his kingdom on the island. In exchange, the fisherman made the eagle ruler over the sea and sky around the island. I thought that was fascinating."

"Very neat." His response was flat.

"Son, what's going on? I thought you would be more interested. You asked me to research this, but you sound like I just told you to schedule a root canal."

Nick sighed. "It's Ari."

"The FBI agent? What about her?"

"I'm in love with her." His stomach flipped.

"Why is that a problem?"

"What if I lose her, too?"

CHAPTER 38

A ri held the map aloft to compare it with the two-story building in front of her.

Nick joined her. "I just got off the phone with my dad. Tyrrhenea used to exist." He relayed what his dad had learned from the professor of European History, including the flag and the legend behind it.

"Interesting, but I'm not sure how useful the information is. Other than it confirms the journal entries weren't fiction."

Her pulse pounded. Her adopted dad had been a mercenary and had participated in an unauthorized attack on innocent people. Shame warmed her collar. How could he do such a thing?

Nick kicked a pebble. "What if Enigma immigrated to America from that island? It would prove your theory that this is about revenge on the mercenaries, and it proves Reid wasn't lying when he said Tyrrhenea didn't exist. Because apparently, it doesn't."

What must that have been like? To see your entire world destroyed. If what Nick said was true, it would explain why Enigma was so angry. Who could blame him?

Now she sounded like Nick.

They stepped up on what remained of the boardwalk and entered the decrepit building. A horseshoe, mounted next to the door, had been rubbed shiny by all the fingers that had touched it upon passing through the doorway. A small amount of light filtered through boarded-up windows.

They both pulled out their phones and turned on the flashlights.

The floorboards creaked as they moved into the old general store, and the structure groaned and shuddered. A century's worth of dust had collected on a check-out counter and empty storage shelves. Several cobweb-covered barrels stood in one corner, and more cobwebs clung to the ceiling beams. A single coffee tin and jar of peaches remained on one shelf, while an antique cast iron cash register sat on the counter.

"Now what?" Ari circled the interior, avoiding a hole in the floorboards, and held out her arms.

"Enigma marked the other locations with the eagle emblem." Nick brushed a spiderweb out of his face. "We could start by looking for one of those."

"Okay." She plodded along the walls, running her fingers over the dusty shelves. A loose splinter caught her tender flesh. *Ouch.* A dot of blood appeared, and she popped her finger into her mouth, instantly regretting it when the taste of hundred-year-old dust violated her tongue. She spat, swallowed, grimaced, then wiped her hands on her pants.

A doorway caught her attention. She checked it out.

Empty.

Returning to the main room, she found Nick testing the bottom step to the upper floor. It screeched when he put his weight on it.

"What do you think's up there?" he asked.

"Probably nothing. The storeroom was empty." She gestured over her shoulder as she crossed the room, rounded the counter, and faced the cast iron register. She frowned. "Does this register seem out of place to you?"

Nick lowered his foot to the floor. "What do you mean?"

"Everything else in here is coated in one-hundred-year-old dirt. It's clean."

The eagle emblem had been burned into the wooden counter just off to the side of the till.

On the left side of the machine ran two columns of letter push keys, A, B, D, E, H, and K. Beneath those were the push keys for *charge* and *paid out*. The middle section was made up of two rows of red push keys with dollar amounts marked on them, and on the right side were two columns of black keys marked with cent amounts—1 through 9, then 10 to 90, counted by 10s.

She rubbed her finger on the drawer keyhole. Too bad they didn't have the key. A crank on the side was used to open the drawer or reset the gears, but it was missing.

A subtotal key would make the drawer pop out. But that seemed to be absent as well. She thought back over the clues they'd received along the way and recalled the Dewey Decimal number that had gone nowhere.

"Nick. Can you come here?"

He pushed away from the windowsill and joined her behind the counter. "What's up?"

"What were you looking at?"

"Nothing. I just thought I saw something move outside. How can I help?"

"Do you remember the call sign from the library?"

"Sure. HDE one-two-three, E four-five, A six-seven."

Ari hit the keys in order. HDE 123.45 A 67.

Nothing. Her shoulders slumped. "I thought that would work."

The floorboards overhead groaned.

"Did you hear that?"

"It's probably the ghosts. We are trespassing on their territory."

She rolled her eyes and playfully punched him in the arm. "Let me try something else."

She entered the letters again. Then, instead of punching the numbers separately, she entered them like a dollar amount. There wasn't a hundred-dollar key. She pinched her lips together, then pressed the ten-dollar key ten times, then the twenty-dollar key, the three-dollar key, the A, the sixty, then the seven.

The drawer popped open and bumped her in the stomach. "It worked."

She opened the drawer farther. Inside, lay a compass, a puzzle piece, and a note. Her flashlight illuminated the handwriting she'd come to despise.

Fifty paces to the North.
From here to yon, you must go forth.
Beneath the floor where silver died.
Your final resting place abides.
In the ashes will remain
An explosive ending to our game.
-Enigma

"Beneath the floor where silver died. What does that mean? Do you think we have to go to the silver mine?" Ari asked.

"Abandoned mines are dangerous." Nick folded his arms. "I don't care what secrets it might hold. I refuse to risk your life in a mine collapse."

"It was just a suggestion."

He picked up the puzzle piece—mostly brown with a hint of blue in the corner—and flipped it over. *Truth.* In bold black ink. Just like all the others.

Could they really be that close to learning the truth about everything?

Ari grabbed the compass and the note, then walked outside.

Nick's footfalls sounded on the boardwalk behind her.

Standing in the middle of the street, she used the compass to find true north. "Fifty paces? By whose stride? Yours or mine?"

"That's a good question." Nick looked down at their legs. "Your limbs are a lot shorter than mine."

"How are we to know how long to make each pace?"

Nick scratched his face. "Let's use mine. If Enigma is male, he'll probably have a longer stride. If we're wrong, we'll come back and try again with yours."

"Got it." She handed him the compass.

He counted off as they headed straight north. A crumbling building loomed closer and closer. Fifty paces would likely take them straight through the open doorway. A sign above the entrance displayed another Russian word in large letters.

"Forty-nine. Fifty."

They stood smack in the middle of the old bank building. Iron bars covered the windows. One side held a tall counter, and in the back corner stood a large empty vault, hanging open on its hinges, with the words *National Bank* painted in gold letters on the door.

She blew hair out of her face. "Beneath the floor where silver died. Do you think Enigma's just referring to the fact that the last of Mintaka's silver went through this bank?"

Nick rubbed his chin. "I like that idea better than searching a mine. Check for loose floorboards." He stomped his leg, then moved to another spot in the room.

Ari joined him. She stamped her foot, and a board echoed. "This one." She dropped to the balls of her feet. "How do we get it open?"

Nick crouched and curled his fingertips around the edge of the loose floorboard. Flexing his muscles, he pried the board upward toward him.

It groaned, and he grunted. Suddenly, it sprung loose,

knocking him backward onto his rear, board in hand. "That's how." He laughed and set the broken board aside.

"You're a lot stronger than you look." She reached over and squeezed his bicep.

He raised his eyebrow. "I'm assuming there's supposed to be a compliment in there somewhere."

"Think whatever you want." Ari lay on her stomach and shone her flashlight down into the hole under the floor. The light glinted off a long metal box. She grabbed the slim handle and hauled it out, setting it on the floor. "It's a WWII ammunition box."

"Open it." His voice trembled with apprehension and excitement.

Something didn't feel right. It went against every fiber of her being, but they needed to take a step back and think this through.

Your final resting place.

Why didn't the riddle say *the* final resting place? Why *your*?

Her phone rang. Matt? She hadn't thought he'd ever want to speak to her again.

"Don't open that without me." She swiped the phone screen and stepped out onto the boardwalk. "Hey, I'm surprised to hear from you."

"Yeah, well, I thought you deserved to know."

"Know what?"

"We found Bridgette."

The breath got knocked out of her. "You found Bridgette? Is she okay?" Her heart pounded her ribcage.

Matt cleared his throat. "Maybe I should rephrase that." He paused. "We've located Bridgette's body. She's dead."

"Oh." The truth settled over Ari like the weight of Niagara Falls crashing over her head. She'd clung to the hope that Kye was wrong, that they'd find Bridgette alive—that somehow she'd have escaped or survived. "Where?"

"In a shallow grave in the national park. Jogger found her. Gunshot to the head, execution style."

That jogger wouldn't get that image out of their mind anytime soon.

"Do you think Van Sloan will press charges for criminal negligence against me?"

"I'm not sure. He was pretty distraught when we delivered the news. Kept alternating between screaming profanity and sobbing uncontrollably."

She didn't blame him—she kind of wanted to scream herself. Why did the villains always win?

Across the street, a flash of color caught Ari's eye. "Hey, Matt. I've got to go. Thanks for the update. And if a warrant goes out for my arrest, would you mind giving me a heads up?"

"You plan on running again?"

"No. I just don't want to be blindsided." Ari hung up.

A shadow across the street moved, and she stepped off the boardwalk.

Nick's voice stopped her forward progression. "What do you think is in here? I'm going to open it."

An explosive ending to our game.

Ari spun, hands extended. "No, Nick, wait, don't open that!"

Too late.

Light flashed, and an explosion shook the ground. Heat blasted her skin as she was propelled into the air. A second later, her back impacted the ground, knocking the air out of her lungs. Searing pain swept over her body, like a million fire ants all biting at the same time.

She squinted and tried to lift her head. A pillar of black smoke billowed from what remained of the bank. Pieces of wood littered the surrounding area.

"Nick," she screamed, then coughed. "Nick, where are you?"

Oh, dear God. Help us.

No one knew where they were. Her phone was probably in a thousand tiny pieces. Unbearable agony drained her strength.

She laid her head back against the dirt as hot tears rolled down her cheeks. Bright sunlight radiated overhead.

Her skin begged her to move, but her muscles refused.

Everything grew hazy.

A featureless face blocked the light, and silver strands dangled from the blurry image. "Help is on the way," a soft voice with a thick accent whispered.

With a final breath, Ari slipped into the abyss of unconsciousness.

CHAPTER 39

B *eep ... Beep ... Beep ...*
I'm such a fool. I should have known something like this would happen. I should have weighed the risks rather than rush ahead. I thought I'd learned my lesson.

Beep ... Beep ... Beep ...

"Nick." A deep, familiar voice called him.

Dad? What's he doing here?

Beep ... Beep ... Beep ...

That sound grated on his nerves. Would someone turn it off? Where was it coming from?

Nick blinked and opened his eyes.

White wall with a TV mounted on it. He turned his head to his left— a pastel-patterned curtain. And to his right, a silhouette, backed by a large, brightly lit window.

He squinted. "Dad?"

"Welcome back to the land of the living."

"Dad, I can't hear you." The voice was muffled like he wore earplugs. "Speak louder."

Why did everything hurt? "Where am I?" He tried to

remember, but not much came to mind. Just a flash of light, then darkness.

An icy hand touched his own. "You're in the hospital. A bomb exploded." Dad's voice grew louder. "You've been out like a light for a week."

A week?

"How—how bad is it?" He turned his head, and the room spun. "Where is Ari?" His throat felt like a desert, and his tongue stuck to the roof of his mouth.

"You have a concussion, chemical burns in your airways, lacerations, fractures, and ear trauma. You've already had three surgeries, and another is scheduled for tomorrow morning. The doc says you'll be here for months. It's a miracle you're still alive."

Had Dad purposefully avoided mentioning Ari's condition?

Oh, dear God, please tell me she's still alive.

"Dad, what about Ari? Is she …"

He couldn't bring himself to say the word. If his stupidity had cost her life, he'd never forgive himself.

"It's touch and go, Nick. Like you, she has third-degree burns over a large part of her body. They're keeping her sedated to help with the pain. The blast tore the stitches from her last injury, and a couple of her ribs are broken. The biggest concern—for both of you—is infection."

Nick touched the thick bandage around his head. He closed his eyes and let the tears flow. "I messed up, Dad." His voice caught.

"It happens. You might be a genius, but you're not perfect."

"No, Dad. I really messed up. It's just like all those other times. I made an impulsive decision, and it ended in disaster."

"What other times are you talking about?"

"It's my fault Toby can't play soccer or graduate college. Cosco and Rachel are both dead because of decisions I made. And now, Ari's teetering between life and death because of my actions."

Dad didn't respond, and the only sound in the room was that infernal beeping.

Nick tilted his head backward to catch a glimpse of the heart rate monitor. That jagged line represented his pulse—a clear sign he was still living, but they—his friend and his wife—were not.

"Did you put that bomb in the box?"

Dad's voice startled him. He jerked forward, then grimaced at the sharp pain in his neck. "No." He groaned. What was Dad getting at?

"Did you shut Toby inside that trunk?"

"No."

"What about Rachel? Did you set that fire?"

"It was set for my stunt."

Dad sighed and rubbed his forehead. "But did you know it was going to burn down the theater? Did you hit Rachel over the head and tie her up under the stage?"

"No. Dad, where are you going with all this?"

Dad leaned closer and wrapped both his hands around Nick's. "You are not responsible for what happens on this planet. Not everything is your fault. You make mistakes. I make mistakes. None of us are perfect. We just do the best we can and hope for the best. Bad things will happen to the people you love, but that doesn't make it your fault. You could have done everything right, and Toby still could have gotten hurt. Cosco and Rachel still could have died. Agent Powers could have opened that bomb herself."

Nick closed his eyes. "She warned me not to open it. Somehow, she knew. If only I had waited." If only he could apologize.

"If only. If only. Son, you can count your regrets until the cows come home, but that'll never change the past. Being impetuous isn't always a bad thing. Sometimes opportunities are missed because people wait too long to act. Sometimes an impulsive decision will become the most wonderful thing that ever happened to you. Just look at your mother and me."

Dad and Mom had met in college. They went out on a blind date as a dare. Two weeks later, they were engaged.

"I've lived with that woman for thirty-five years, and I've never once regretted jumping into love with both feet. You can analyze something to death, but the greatest risks often bring about the greatest blessings." Dad patted his hand. "I'm going to get you some water and let the nurse know you're awake. Just think about what I said. Don't let fear of making a mistake keep you from taking a chance. It's better to have tried and failed than to live with regret."

Dad disappeared behind the curtain.

Beep … Beep … Beep …

He'd been given another chance.

A chance to make things right with Ari and tell her how he felt about her. To take a leap of faith and trust God with the outcome. If only he were brave enough to take it.

CHAPTER 40

Thursday, 22 February
0600 Hours

The ghostly melody filtered through her foggy brain. The tune from her nightmares. Louder, then softer, as if someone was playing with the dial on the radio. Pins and needles crawled over her skin.

It sounded so close. So real. As if it were.

Ari's eyes fluttered, then opened. Darkness enveloped her. As her pupils adjusted, a figure formed beside the bed. The phantom vocalized the same sad, lonely tune that had haunted her all her life—the lyrics whispered in a foreign tongue.

But that voice ... soft, mellow... and strangely familiar.

Where had she heard that voice before? It wasn't Aunt Sheila's. Was it the voice of an angel? Was she dead?

Pain coursed over her entire body. No, she was very much alive.

But that voice ... it called to something in the deepest recesses of her heart.

A hazy image formed in Ari's mind. The memory of someone she knew a long time ago. A woman with dark ringlets, a sad smile, and a gentle touch.

Moments passed. The forgotten image faded, slipping away before Ari could fully recall its meaning. Inky tendrils crept across her consciousness and snuffed it out.

———

Ari's eyes flew open. Her chest heaved as she struggled to catch her breath. Something covered her mouth, suffocating her. She grabbed it, tugged, then tossed it aside. She tried to sit up, but her body refused to cooperate.

"Nick!" she shouted, but her voice came out in a whisper. "Nick, where are you?"

The asphyxiation grew stronger.

Aunt Sheila appeared in her field of vision and laid a gentle hand on Ari's shoulder. "It's okay. You're okay. Deep breaths."

Ari struggled to draw a breath. "Where's Nick?"

"He's in a room down the hall." Aunt Sheila leaned down, picked something up, and tried to attach it to Ari's face.

Ari knocked it away. "I don't want that."

"It's your oxygen mask. You need it."

Ari slowed her breathing and allowed her aunt to restore the plastic respirator to its proper place. The last thing she remembered was turning around to see a flash of light from the box Nick opened. Everything that happened after that was a murky collection of nothingness.

"How long have I been here?" The mask muffled her voice, but at least she could breathe.

"Just over a week. Are you in any pain?"

Flames penetrated from her epidermis to the marrow inside her bones. "A little."

"I'll get the nurse." Aunt Sheila turned to leave the room.

Ari grabbed her hand. "I don't want to go back to sleep. I'd rather be in pain than not know what's going on around me."

Aunt Sheila's eyes lifted to something above Ari's bed. "The pain is making your blood pressure rise. You'll have a stroke."

"Please."

"I'm sorry. It's for your own good."

Aunt Sheila's hand slipped from her grasp, and Ari's arm sank to the cool bed sheet as hot tears stung her cheeks. This feeling of total helplessness was one she had never wanted to experience again.

Ari shifted, trying to get the pillow behind her back in a better spot. Two more weeks had passed, and she still hadn't been able to see or talk to Nick, but Aunt Sheila assured her he was healing as well as expected.

The curtains were open, allowing sunshine to warm the chilly room. Get-well cards, flowers, and balloons from her former co-workers at the Bureau—an agency she would never work for again, but at least she knew cared—filled the sterile space with a splash of color. The gesture should have lifted her spirits, but she just wanted to be left alone. To wallow in her misery.

She hadn't been out of bed in three weeks, but they had stopped sedating her. The pain was manageable with the help of legal drugs, and the longer she was awake, the clearer her mind became. Some of her memories returned, opening a myriad of questions.

Someone had been there that day in Mintaka. Ari had seen them just before the explosion. And that person had saved their lives.

She'd asked around, but no one remembered their guardian angel. Who was it? Enigma? But hadn't Enigma also set the bomb?

It made little sense, and Ari's pounding headache prevented her from doing much wool-gathering. Though she had plenty of time for it. Except for visits from nurses, doctors, and Aunt Sheila, her days were spent staring at a blank ceiling or basking in self-pity. The doctors said it would be another three, maybe four weeks, before they could move her to rehab.

She rolled over and turned her face to the wall.

Aunt Sheila assured her she was still beautiful, but Ari knew if she looked in the mirror, she would see differently. Between the burns and the bruises, she could only hope she wasn't permanently disfigured.

"Knock, knock."

The male voice startled her.

"Come in." Those weren't the words she wanted to say, but it was better than being rude. She peeked over her shoulder as the curtain opened.

Nick's dad stepped forward, and the curtain dropped into place behind him. He carried a bouquet of daisies. "Hello, Miss Powers. How are you feeling this morning?"

She arched her eyebrow and frowned.

He chuckled. "Tiring of that question, aren't you?" He set the vase down along with all the others. "They're about to bring your breakfast. Looks delicious."

The corner of Ari's mouth curled. They both knew it was disgusting. "Is Nick surviving the hospital food?"

"He's doing fine now. Went on a hunger strike the first week, but his growling stomach finally convinced him that starving wasn't the answer."

"Have the doctors said when he can be released?"

"I'd say it's going to be another month or more. They're waiting for the skin grafting to take."

"Does he—"

She paused. Should she ask this? Did it matter? "Does he still look like Nick?"

"Yes. Despite everything he's gone through, he still looks like my son. And he's still as ornery as ever. He asks about you every day."

Ari lowered her eyes and tangled her fingers in the top sheet.

"Doctor Trueheart, you met me before the explosion. Do I still look like me?"

"No."

Her heart sank. Tears squeezed out of the corner of her eyes.

He leaned in close and brushed a tear from her cheek. "You, my dear, grow more beautiful with each passing day. By the time they let you out of here, your beauty will rival that of Aphrodite."

She didn't believe in the Greek gods and goddesses, but she appreciated the sentiment. "Thank you, Doctor Trueheart."

"You're welcome, my dear. But it's true. I know things seem hopeless right now, but hope is the very thing that's going to get you out of here. Don't give up. Keep fighting, and you'll feel well again before you know it."

CHAPTER 41

Tuesday, 20 August
1200 Hours

D arkness and silence—her new best friends.

Ari sat on the couch, still in her pajamas, feeding her fear. She wasn't in physical pain anymore, but the mental and emotional loss had taken their toll on her spirit.

All that remained was a broken shell.

Her outer appearance had healed, but her inner being was nothing more than a scrambled mess, like fifty-two Card Pickup —a game she'd never quite understood.

Enigma had slipped their grasp. No one mentioned it, but Ari knew it to be true. Bridgette Van Sloan was dead. Her funeral had been months ago while she and Nick were being treated in the hospital.

Enigma won, and Nick had been right—it was just a game. He'd warned her to let it go, but she was too stubborn. She just had to be in control, and see where that had gotten her. Her desperate search for Enigma had only proven that nothing was under her control. Not really.

Control was nothing more than an illusion. A mirage. A smokescreen. A facade.

A knock sounded on the front door, but she ignored it.

"Arizona. It's Sheila. I know you're in there."

"Go away," Ari hollered back.

The deadbolt unlocked, the handle turned, and the door opened. Aunt Sheila filled the doorway, backed by bright sunlight, wearing a dress suit and pumps. A spicy fragrance wafted from the takeout in her arms. "Not going to happen. I brought lunch."

Ari's stomach growled, and she crossed her arms. "I'm not hungry."

Aunt Sheila closed the door with a pop of her hip, tossed something onto the dining room table, then brought the paper bag to the coffee table and started unloading Styrofoam containers from The Taj Mahal Grill.

"Liar. I heard your stomach from the foyer. You're going to eat. You're going to stop feeling sorry for yourself, shower, dress, and turn on the lights. In fact, I'm going to take care of that right now." She flipped on the light switches, then threw open the curtains.

Light flooded the room.

Ari squinted and held up her palm. "Ow, it's bright out there. Why can't you just leave me alone?"

"Because I love you. And I just spent way too much money on your hospital bills to let you sit here and waste away."

Ari frowned. "It's too soon for jokes." Scar tissue on her arm itched, and she scratched. "Fine. I'll eat, shower, and dress, but I will not stop moping. I have a right to mope as much as I want."

Aunt Sheila shook her head then took a seat on the couch. She opened one of the containers. Meat chunks swam in a pungent reddish-orange sauce, topping a mound of basmati rice. "I think this is the Tikka Masala."

She handed it and a fork to Ari. "I don't know what you have to mope about. You're alive, for goodness' sake." She opened the second container. "This one should be the Murgh Makhani." She stuck her finger in the steaming sauce, then in her mouth for a taste. "Yep, that's it. Naan?"

Ari turned down the charred flatbread. "Enigma escaped. He got away with his crimes. I've got a uniform posted outside my house." She scooped up a bite of rice and raised it to her mouth. "Bridgette is dead."

"If it'll make you feel better, I'll dismiss the bodyguard. It's been six months. I think you're in the clear. You faced off with Enigma and survived. From what you've told me; I don't think you were supposed to. Those other women didn't. God was looking out for you."

"I don't know if God had anything to do with it."

Aunt Sheila's fork dropped into her food. Pieces of rice flew out of the container. "Arizona Elaine Powers, what does God have to do to convince you He cares about what happens to you?"

Ari shrugged.

"He died on the cross for you. You trusted Him as your Savior. Why isn't that enough to believe He loves you? Why isn't that enough to prove He loves the world?"

"But He—you know what, I don't want to talk about it." Ari set her food on the coffee table. "Did you bring in the mail?"

"I tossed it on your table."

Ari stood, winced, then crossed the house to the dining room. She shuffled through the stack of envelopes, not looking for anything in particular, just avoiding the conversation with her aunt. An envelope with a government seal grabbed Ari's attention.

Months ago, she requested a copy of her original birth certificate—the one containing her birth parents' names. She tore open the envelope and skimmed the letter, muttering aloud as she read. "… can't be located … What?"

She jabbed the letter toward her aunt. "It says my original birth certificate can't be found. What does that mean? How hard did they look?" She released the letter into Aunt Sheila's outstretched hand and paced the room. "It has to exist. I was born somewhere, by someone. Why can't they find the original one?"

"I don't know. It should have been filed along with the new one."

"Are you sure I'm adopted?"

Aunt Sheila laid the letter on the coffee table. "I'm positive. Your mother was physically unable to have children of her own."

Ari flopped onto the couch and groaned.

Aunt Sheila reached out and touched Ari's cheek. "Maybe I should have told you sooner about your adoption, but even if I could go back and do things differently, I'm not sure I would. I'm sorry if I hurt you, but I wouldn't change them."

At least her aunt was honest, even if painfully so. "No, I get it. I've made choices that others might not agree with, but I had my reasons for what I did, and I wouldn't change them, even if I could."

Aunt Sheila looked at her for a moment. "Arizona, why didn't you lower your gun when Updike ordered you to? Why did you shoot that man?"

Ari looked down at her hands and picked at her fingernail. It hurt so much to admit what had happened. The entire experience was humiliating. Then to see him leave that courtroom with not even a slap on the wrist. What else was she supposed to conclude but that justice didn't work?

After the case was dismissed, they'd never again talked about what her teacher had done to her all those years ago.

Aunt Sheila continued. "I know you obsessed for weeks trying to locate that missing child, only to find him dead. I remember how devastated you were. How you devoted yourself to tracking down his killer. You did everything right until you had a nervous breakdown and took matters into your own hands."

Ari shook her head. "That has nothing to do with it."

Aunt Sheila frowned. "I don't understand."

"It's because of Mr. Rothschild."

"Dexter Rothschild, your tenth-grade teacher?"

"Who else?" Ari folded her arms.

Aunt Sheila rubbed Ari's leg. "Oh, sweetheart. I'm so sorry. I didn't know that still bothered you."

"Of course, it does. He got away with what he did to me. Then he hurt my best friend. And no one cared. No one even believed me."

"I cared. I believed you."

"Did you? Because from where I stood, you let them throw out the case. You didn't fight to see him punished. I had to plaster posters all over school, warning kids to stay away from him."

Aunt Sheila stood, retrieved a tissue, and handed it to Ari. "And got yourself expelled."

"At least I did something." Ari dabbed her eyes. She hadn't even realized she was crying.

Aunt Sheila returned to her seat on the couch beside Ari. "I did something. First, I enrolled you in a new school. Then, I went to the board of education. I encouraged them to do their own investigation into the accusations, and I put the outcome into their hands and God's. Within six weeks, they had found enough evidence of other unethical practices to justify firing Dexter. In the months following, his wife left him, he lost his house, ended up homeless, and got arrested on charges of grand larceny."

Ari picked up her fork. At this point, even cold curry sounded good. "Then he got what he deserved."

"But that's not where the story ends."

Aunt Sheila's words froze Ari's hand halfway to her mouth. "What do you mean?"

"In prison, Dexter Rothschild met Jesus Christ. When he got out, he made things right with his wife and with Cassandra's family. Now, he's a major advocate in the battle against crimes against children. I allowed God to exact judgment however He saw fit, and now, that man who was once a predator is saving lives every day."

Ari swiveled. Words failed her. "I didn't know."

"I know you didn't." Aunt Sheila took her hands. "Is that why it's so important Enigma pays for what he did to Bridgette? Why you felt the need to take revenge on Reece Wayne?"

"If I don't avenge their victims, no one else will."

"Doesn't the Bible say, 'Vengeance is Mine, I will repay, saith the Lord'? Doesn't He keep His promises?"

Ari swallowed. "I want to believe that."

"It takes faith, trust, and—"

"Pixie dust." Ari shot Aunt Sheila a mischievous grin.

Aunt Sheila rolled her eyes. "At least you're feeling well enough to crack jokes."

Ari sighed and ran her fork through her food. "I needed to find Enigma for other reasons too, not just for justice."

"Why is that? Glutton for punishment?" Aunt Sheila broke off a piece of Naan, dipped it in sauce, and dropped it in her mouth.

Ari's leg ached. She repositioned on the soft cushion. "I want the truth behind Bridgette's senseless death. About my adopted dad and his part in the attack on Tyrrhenea. The truth behind my nightmares."

"Your nightmares?" Aunt Sheila's body tensed. "Why would Enigma know anything about your nightmares?" Her fork hovered mid-air. "What are you talking about?"

Ari rumpled her forehead. "The nightmares I had as a child. I still have them." She explained about the music box left on her desk and the lullaby they heard in the escape room. "It's identical to the one in my nightmares. It ... it feels so real. Like a deep part of my mind remembers being kidnapped as a little kid. But ... that's crazy, right?"

Aunt Sheila was so still, even her lungs seemed to have stopped drawing breath. Ari's own heartbeat was the loudest sound in the room. Aunt Sheila wouldn't look Ari in the face. She pinched her lips together, then drew a shuttering breath.

"You've got sauce on your shirt," she stated plainly, reaching for a paper napkin from the coffee table.

Ari blinked rapidly. "Forget the sauce. Why did you change the subject?"

"Here. Let me get you a clean shirt." Aunt Sheila stood and moved toward the stairs. "I'll put that one in the laundry. We don't want it to stain."

What was happening right now? Why was her aunt being so evasive?

"You're not going anywhere. Sit down," Ari ordered. "What are you not telling me? I want the truth."

Aunt Sheila pivoted slowly. "And you think Enigma can give you the answers?"

"No, I think you can."

Aunt Sheila groaned. "Arizona, there are some things … sometimes the consequence of knowledge is worse than not knowing."

Ari pinned Aunt Sheila with a steely gaze. "Tell. Me. The. Truth."

Silence descended over the living room as Aunt Sheila's hands twisted like soft pretzels.

Ari had never seen the confident woman so erratic. She almost felt bad for pushing.

Almost.

"You can tell me. I'm a big girl. What is it?"

Aunt Sheila wouldn't look at her. "When you came to live with me, you had terrible nightmares. Almost every night."

Ari nodded. "I dream I've been kidnapped and held in a basement."

Aunt Sheila lifted her head and met Ari's gaze. "You were."

Her world turned right side up with a bang.

Ari leaped to her feet. "I knew it. Everyone tried to convince me I was nuts. Mother. The doctors. What happened to all the news coverage? Why are there no police reports?" Questions spilled at rapid fire. Why didn't anyone ever tell her the truth?

Aunt Sheila walked back to the couch and settled on the cushions. "That was all Jamison's idea."

Dad? More lies? "How old was I?"

"Three."

"Do you know who kidnapped me? Were they ever caught?"

Aunt Sheila patted the cushion next to her. "Her name is Esme Aquila. She spent twenty years in prison for child endangerment and kidnapping."

Ari couldn't sit. Every muscle in her body was wound tighter than a spring. "Spent? Where is she now?"

"I don't know. She was released five years ago and disappeared without a trace."

Ari's mind raced. Five years ago. About the same time the first murder took place. Could they be connected? Could Esme Aquila and Enigma be the same person? "Why didn't you ever tell me the truth? Didn't I have a right to know what happened to me?"

"The shrink said it was better for you if we didn't talk about it. That, with time, you would forget and … and making you relive those days … he said you would forget."

Ari dropped onto the couch. "Well, I didn't."

Aunt Sheila blinked. Tears ran down her cheeks. "I realize that now. I never meant to keep secrets from you. I honestly believed it was better for everyone if you could live your life without remembering what had happened. That you would be … happier without the knowledge."

Ari exhaled. Aunt Sheila had her best interest at heart, even if it was beyond frustrating to discover so much of her life had been a lie.

Ari scooted closer and took Aunt Sheila's hands in her own. "Please. Tell me everything you know about Esme Aquila and Jamison Powers."

CHAPTER 42

Nick shut off the TV and leaned back against the couch cushion.

Six months had passed since he'd nearly blown himself and Ari to pieces. He'd lost count of how many times he'd heard the phrase "lucky to be alive."

It wasn't luck. It was God. God had given them both a second chance.

He still hadn't seen Ari in person, but his feelings for her hadn't changed. They'd spoken on the phone, but once he'd been released from the hospital, his time had been consumed with doctor's appointments, therapy sessions, and just trying to get back to normal. From the beginning, the doctors had been optimistic about his recovery—he was young, healthy, and driven.

Maybe he should give Ari a call and see how she was doing. Would she go out with him if he asked?

Dad entered the living room, carrying two chilled glasses of lemonade from the kitchen, handed one to Nick, then took a seat on the couch beside him. "It's over a hundred degrees out there this afternoon. Good thing your air conditioner is working."

The machine kicked on just then, and cool air blasted through the vents.

Condensation on the glass wet Nick's hand. "I talked to Santiago earlier."

"Yeah? What did he say?" Dad sipped his lemonade.

"I can start Monday."

Dad licked his lips and lowered the glass. "Are you sure you're ready to go back to work?"

"Doc cleared me yesterday. That means you can make plans to head home to Mom and Toby."

Dad set the glass on the coffee table. "I sure have missed your mother. I'll look at plane tickets tonight."

Nick frowned. Dad sounded almost … sad.

"It's not that I'm ungrateful. I wouldn't have made it this far without you, but we both know things have got to get back to normal. It's time."

"It is."

Nick leaned over and embraced his father. "Thank you for everything."

"You're welcome, son"—he choked up—"I hope you know how much I love you."

"I do now." Nick released his hold. "I do now."

Dad had taken an indefinite sabbatical from his job at the lab. His presence had done more to aid Nick in his recovery than all the doctors, pills, and exercises combined. They could never make up for lost time, but they'd grown close during this interlude in Nick's life, which was closer than he'd ever thought possible.

Dad shifted, then gulped the lemonade. Doctor Trueheart had never been sentimental. All this emotion was probably making him uncomfortable.

Nick downed half the glass, then set it aside. "Will you still have a job when you get home?"

"They'd be stupid to let me go. I'm smarter than Einstein." Dad cocked a smile.

Nick chuckled. "Humble, too."

"I brought the mail in earlier. Have you sorted through it?"

"No. I'm sure it's all bills." Nick moved to face the pile of white envelopes on his desk. He picked up the stack and tossed them one by one onto the table. "Bill. Bill. Bill." He paused at a blue square envelope. "Not a bill."

"What is it?"

Nick set the others down, then opened it, pulling a fancy invitation from the envelope.

You are cordially invited to the Under the Sea Gala
September 1st, 7 PM
Platte City Aquarium

In memory of Bridgette Van Sloan.
Please join us for an elegant evening of dining, dancing,
and giving back at the annual SeaGuardians Initiative Gala.
Your presence will have a significant impact
on saving our oceans in support of Bridgette's favorite charity.

Please RSVP by August 25th
to ensure your seat at this prestigious event.
Kindly respond online at sea-guardians.org
or contact Kelly Bishop,
Personal Assistant to Ambassador Van Sloan.

Nick shook his head. "I'm not going." He tossed the invitation into the trash can.

"Why?" Dad retrieved it from the metal bin. "It's an honor to be invited to an event like this."

"They probably invited everyone at DSS. I'm no one special. Besides, it doesn't feel right. I let the ambassador down." They still hadn't heard whether Van Sloan was pressing charges for criminal negligence or not.

Nick's phone rang. He snatched it from where it charged on the desk. Ari's name on the caller ID brought a smile to his face. "Hey, it's been a while. How've you been?"

"Can you come over? I need to talk." Her voice sounded strained.

"Of course. I'll be right there."

Nick rapped on the fiery red front door, and a moment later, it opened.

Ari, wearing sweats and a long T-shirt, stole his breath. She'd never looked more beautiful. "Hi." His voice cracked. His neck warmed, and he felt fourteen again.

"Come on in." She stepped back. "Thanks for coming."

"No problem." He crossed the threshold into the living room.

Used coffee mugs and magazines cluttered the coffee table along with crumpled napkins, takeout containers, and pill bottles. Empty water bottles and food crumbs littered the carpet surrounding the sofa.

His feet hitched, and he blinked rapidly. The room smelled of rubbing alcohol, sweaty socks, and curry. He glanced at Ari—she was watching him take in the disarray.

"Sorry, it's such a mess." She ducked her head. "I've sort of struggled with depression since the accident."

Nick nodded. He had, too, but maybe not to this extent. "How are you doing today?"

"Getting there. I think. Can I offer you something to drink? There's soda in the fridge, and I have clean glasses if you just want water."

"I'm fine. Thank you. You said you needed to talk."

"Right." She walked to the dining room, and he followed.

Obviously, she'd taken to eating on the couch because the table was the only piece of furniture as spotless as the last time he'd been in her house. She'd pushed aside the centerpiece and table runner and had laid out drawings and computer printouts on the flat surface. The music box, still in pieces, set off to the left from the rest of the papers.

She sat, crossing one leg over the other. "Do you remember when I told you about my nightmares?"

Nick nodded as he lowered into a straight-back chair. "Of course. What about them?"

"They aren't false memories or figments of my imagination. Someone kidnapped me when I was just a toddler."

"What? Who? How?"

Ari held up a mug shot. The woman had bronze-colored skin and curly brown hair. "Her name is Esme Aquila. When I was three years old, Aunt Sheila got a phone call from my mom in hysterics. Mom had left me playing in the sandbox in the backyard while she ran inside to answer the phone. She was only gone for a couple minutes, but when she returned, I was nowhere to be found.

"Three days later, the police got a tip from a woman who said she heard crying coming from the basement of the house next to hers. They broke the window, lowered an officer inside, and pulled me out. A social worker brought me to the hospital, where I was reunited with my parents. Aunt Sheila said it was about a month later that they learned Esme had been arrested for a minor offense, but the police had found her fingerprints all over that room I was in, and they got a match. She got twenty years for child abduction and child endangerment. When she was released five years ago, she disappeared."

Nick swallowed. So, it was true. This woman had abducted Ari and kept her in a dark, dank basement. No wonder the dreams had seemed so real. No wonder they still haunted her to this day. Who wouldn't be traumatized by such an ordeal?

Ari ran her hands over the papers. "This is everything I can remember about Enigma's game. I printed photos of the locations Enigma sent us, too, as well as rewrote the riddles as best I could. I wish we had the originals, but—"

He'd given them all to the FBI.

Ari continued. "I want to go over everything we remember

about Bridgette's case from before the kidnapping until the explosion that put us in the hospital."

He picked up a printout of the Abbot Castle. "That was a long time ago." Some things were still a little fuzzy.

"I know, but can we at least try? Maybe we missed something that will help us locate Enigma."

"Why would you want to do that? He almost killed us."

Ari's eyes misted. She took a deep breath. "What if Esme is Enigma?"

The doorbell echoed through the house.

Nick lifted his head. "Who's that?"

Ari's brow furrowed. "I'm not expecting anyone. Aunt Sheila left just before you arrived." She laid the computer printout on the table, crossed the room, and opened the front door.

"Nick!" Terror filled her voice.

He catapulted to her side, and his heart stopped.

An unlabeled box sat on the front stoop. The delivery contained no return address. No mailing address either. Someone had just dropped it off, mashed the doorbell, and ran.

Ari pressed her fingers to her lips. "Oh, dear God. What do we do?" She hugged her chest, and her color drained.

A black SUV eased away from the curb just down the street. Tinted windows blocked the view of the driver. No license plate. It hadn't been there when he'd pulled up a few minutes ago.

Nick's stomach knotted. Someone had been watching the house. Maybe waiting for them to meet up again.

The vehicle disappeared around the corner.

Nick clenched his jaw. He knew what they had to do but it wasn't going to be easy. "We have to open it." He squeezed Ari's shoulder.

She trembled beneath his touch. "Nick! We can't. What if it's another bomb?"

"I know." He squatted and eyed the mysterious package. "But we can't spend our entire lives afraid of every box, crate, and package. We have to face it head-on."

Face it head-on. How things had changed. He was learning to let go of his fears. Returning to the man he used to be before Rachel died. *Thank you, Lord.*

"Can we at least be smart about this?" Ari asked.

He looked over his shoulder. "And do what?"

"Call the bomb squad."

CHAPTER 43

Ari held her breath as the X-ray technician rolled the portable machine into place.

The K-9 unit had come up negative for explosives, but she'd begged the commander to look inside the box. A blockade had been set up to keep anyone from driving too close, and the neighbors' homes had been evacuated. A crowd had gathered in the street with the arrival of the bomb squad. Local police kept the onlookers at a safe distance.

Nick squeezed Ari's hand. "You did the right thing."

Ari exhaled. "I sure hope so."

A moment later, the technician signaled to the commander, and he joined her on the porch. Ari couldn't make out what they were saying, but with a nod, the commander turned and approached. "It's a puzzle."

Her mouth dropped open. "A puzzle?"

"What kind of puzzle?" Nick asked.

"The kind you put together on a bad weather day. A jigsaw puzzle."

She blinked and jiggled her head. "A jigsaw puzzle."

"Yep. This note was with it." He handed her a piece of paper, then turned to the crowd. "Everything's clear. You can all go home now. There's no threat. Sorry for the interruption."

The bystanders dispersed, grumbling about the disruption to their schedules and having to stand in the blistering sun, making Ari feel worse than she already did.

"I'm so sorry," she hollered.

The neighbors ignored her.

The bomb squad loaded their van and drove away, leaving her standing in the front yard looking like a total fool.

Nick's hand rested on her shoulder. "You did the right thing."

"Stop saying that." She shrugged him off. "I called the bomb squad over a puzzle."

"And if it had been a bomb?"

"But it wasn't."

Nick grabbed Ari's shoulders and spun her to face him. His expression grew earnest. "But it could have been. There's nothing wrong with slowing down and being sure. You might endure a little embarrassment, but isn't that better than blowing your neighbors sky high and us with them?"

Ari searched his expression. It was so caring. So genuine. Without pretense. She traced the contours of his face from his puppy dog eyes to his stubble-covered square jaw, back up to his lips. Her stomach flipped. She laid her hand on his cheek. "So, you're saying it never hurts to take an extra minute?"

His gaze dropped to her mouth. "Yes. Except in some situations."

Ari's throat went dry. "Like this one?"

Maybe it was just the relief from knowing they weren't in life-threatening danger, but she desperately wanted him to kiss her.

His hands climbed from her shoulders to her face. His fingers tangled in her hair. "Could be."

She lifted her chin until his breath caressed her skin. "I think so."

"Me, too."

His lips met hers, and a bomb went off inside of her, sending shock waves through every fiber of her being.

His kiss was tender yet filled with longing.

The rest of the world slipped away, and just for a moment, there was nothing but the two of them.

Then he released her, and she instantly felt cold, even though it was still over ninety degrees outside.

His thumb caressed her cheek. "What did the note say?"

The note from the mysterious package—she'd forgotten all about it. She raised it to eye level.

Complete the puzzle and all will be revealed.
-Enigma

Nick's eyes twinkled. The corner of his mouth twitched, then his chest vibrated with laughter. "Let's do this."

They were so close. The final pieces were falling into place. The truth was within reach.

Ari dumped the puzzle pieces onto her dining room table. It was a small puzzle—only about one hundred pieces.

Ink marks snagged her attention.

Enigma had left them a message—on the back of the puzzle.

A half hour later, the puzzle was complete—except for five missing pieces. The ones Nick had turned over to the FBI, along with all the other clues.

The puzzle formed a stunning picture of a beautiful coastal shore with the bluest ocean, sandy beach, and a stone tower at the top of a rugged cliff. "Wanna bet that's Tyrrhenea?"

Nick ran his finger over the smooth surface. "I don't bet, but I'll agree with your assessment. Ready to turn it over?"

Ari took in the majestic scene for a moment longer, then nodded.

They'd built the puzzle on top of a cardboard panel, so they could flip it over smoothly. Nick laid a second piece of cardboard on top, then working together, they flipped the whole thing over and set it back on the table. He removed the cover. Still intact, Enigma's bold handwriting vaulted from the plain cardboard background.

> My _____ was stolen from me too soon.
> _____ is too kind of a punishment.
> Once the _____ is exposed, they'll know the depth of my pain.
> And when I've silenced their _____, my _____ will be complete.

"We can't finish it without those pieces." Ari retrieved her cell phone from the sideboard.

"Who are you calling?"

She swiped the screen, pressed the contact, then held the phone to her ear. "My former boss."

Matt answered on the second ring. "Agent Powers." He didn't sound happy to hear from her, but it didn't escape her notice that her number was still in his contact list. Or at the very least, he had it memorized.

"Hey, Matt. I know you're upset with me, but I need a favor."

Silence.

He sighed. "What kind of favor?"

"I need the puzzle pieces Nick gave you when he turned over all the evidence from the Van Sloan case."

"Why?"

She swallowed. She couldn't tell him. "You'll just have to trust me."

"That's the problem, Powers. I don't trust you. Not anymore. You went behind my back and put yourself and others in the line of fire. Your need to be in control almost cost you your life. If everything went well on the security detail for Bridgette, I had planned to speak to Director Carlton on your behalf and get you reassigned to the field, but you had to stick your nose where it didn't belong. You almost got me fired. I can't help you. You're on your own."

The line went dead.

Ari lowered the phone.

"What'd he say?" Nick asked.

"He said we're on our own." She laid the phone on the table. "We'll just have to recreate those pieces ourselves."

It didn't take long to cut the cardboard into the shapes of the missing puzzle pieces and write the final words on them. *Revenge, Death, Daughter, Voices, Truth.*

They fitted them into place, then stepped back to view the completed message.

My daughter was stolen from me too soon.
Death is too kind of a punishment.
Once the truth is exposed, they'll know the depth of my pain.
And when I've silenced their voices, my revenge will be complete.

Ari read the lines, then reread them. "The murders started about the same time Esme was released from prison."

Six women.

Six mercenaries.

Nick furrowed his brow. "If Enigma and Esme are the same person, why didn't she kill you when she had the chance? Why did she risk you being recovered?"

"Maybe she intended to sell me once the heat died down, or maybe she was just going to keep me in that basement forever. Whatever the reason, she's waited twenty years to get her revenge."

Nick picked up the printout of Tanya Keller's obituary. "What about Tanya Keller? It's obvious from the newspaper that she took her own life."

"Unless the suicide conclusion is wrong, and she was killed just like all the others."

Ari's eyes flickered back to Enigma's message. *My daughter was stolen from me too soon.*

My daughter ... stolen ...

An uneasy feeling took root in Ari's stomach, and she

lowered into a chair. "When I was in the hospital, I woke up to hear the tune from my nightmares. Someone was in my room, and she was singing. And the sound ... it was comforting, familiar."

Nick sat. "Who was she?"

Ari shrugged. "I don't know."

He reached out and held her hand. "Is there a possibility your mother didn't die in that helicopter crash?"

Ari shook her head. "It wasn't my mother's voice. Hers was weak, breathy, and she couldn't carry a tune in a bucket. This woman had rich tones, soft, mellow, and strong. And she sang in a foreign tongue. My mom never spoke any other language but English. At least not to me."

"Do you think you could sing or hum the tune you heard?"

"Not very well. I'm a terrible singer, but I think I can eke it out." She'd heard it a thousand times before. Ingrained in her memory as much as the alphabet or the times tables.

Nick released her hand, picked up his phone, and pulled up a website on the Internet browser. "This site can determine any known song just by hearing part of it. Why don't you try? Vocalize into the microphone while I record."

"Okay." Ari leaned close to the phone and hummed the tune.

"Now," Nick tapped the screen. "Let's see if it recognizes the song."

They waited.

The loading icon spun.

One match.

"What is it?" Ari asked.

"*Sottu u Cielu Stellatu*. It's a Tyrrhenian Lullaby."

Her mind whirled. "You don't think—" She stopped. It was too ludicrous to even consider.

"What?" Nick laid his phone down on the table.

Headiness surged over her like a flash flood in a dry canyon.

"Ari," Nick patted her hand. "Do you need to lie down?"

"All this time—" she struggled to form words "—we thought

Enigma was getting revenge on the mercenaries for the death of his daughter. What if ..." Her hands trembled. Adrenaline pulsed.

Nick's brows furrowed. "I don't think I'm following you."

She stood and paced the room. "'For crimes done in times gone by. For every hurt and every lie. Unless you admit the pain you caused, everyone will see your flaws.' What if Enigma isn't taking revenge because her daughter was killed by the mercenaries, but because her daughter was kidnapped by the mercenaries?"—Ari swallowed— "What if Esme is my birth mother, and Jamison Powers stole me from Tyrrhenea? What if she had been rescuing me from my kidnapper, not the other way around?"

Nick's eyes grew to the size of saucers. "That doesn't make sense. If Enigma is your birth mother, why would she shoot at you or try to blow you up?"

Nick was right—that blew a big hole in her theory. Could Esme be so intent on getting revenge, she'd take the life of her own daughter to achieve it?

Who else would want to get back at those six men? Who else knew what they did?

Ari inhaled deeply, then exhaled. "We won't know until we talk to someone who knows the truth."

Nick arched an eyebrow. "Enigma?"

"The remaining mercenaries. Starting with Van Sloan."

Ari reread the last two lines of the message.

Once the truth is exposed, they'll know the depth of my pain.
And when I've silenced their voices, my revenge will be complete.

Ari raised her head and made eye contact with Nick. "Enigma is going to kill the ambassador and those other men. We have to get to them before she does, or the truth dies with them."

CHAPTER 44

Nick banged his phone on the table. "I can't get through."

They'd been trying for an hour to reach Ambassador Van Sloan, but every attempt had been thwarted. It had taken everything he had to keep Ari from bursting into Van Sloan's office and demanding the truth.

There was, of course, the possibility that all of this was more of Enigma's twisted game. All this time—someone else had been pulling the strings. Why think they had stopped now?

Ari paced her living room carpet, waving her hands in the air and muttering to herself. From time to time, Nick caught her frustrated words. He couldn't even fathom coping with the possibility that her adoptive father had kidnapped her from her birth mother, then sent the birth mother to prison for kidnapping when she tried to take back her child.

It was hard enough grappling with the possibility that after two years of searching, he had the name of Rachel's killer—Esme Aquila.

Losing Rachel had been the final nail in the coffin of his plans and dreams, turning him into a risk adverse overthinker with a severe case of analysis paralysis. He'd shut down his emotions, focusing his attention on his career as a risk analyst.

He thought he would feel something—anger or the need for revenge. But he didn't. He'd given all that over to God. People depended on him every day to keep them safe from potential threats, and every day, he did his job. And he did it well. He wasn't always perfect. But he could give his utmost, and leave the outcome to the Lord.

He rubbed his chin. If Van Sloan wouldn't talk to them on the phone, they needed to meet with him in person. If they showed up at his office or home, he'd likely ignore them or call security. How could they get close to him?

The "Under the Sea" Gala.

Nick snagged Ari's arm as she passed. "I have an idea."

"What?" She stopped pacing.

"How would you like to go to a charity event at the Platte City Aquarium? Ambassador Van Sloan is raising money for SeaGuardians, Bridgette's favorite charity organization."

Ari frowned. "I doubt I'm invited."

"But I am. You could be my plus one."

Her eyes widened. "I can get Van Sloan alone and make him confess—"

"Stop." He grabbed her hands. "You're doing it again."

"Doing what?" Her voice took on a defensive tone.

"Taking control. Our focus needs to be on keeping him safe, not interrogating him about the past." He rubbed his thumb over her knuckles. "If we're going to do this, I need you to trust me. There's no guarantee that things will go the way we want, but I need you to follow my lead. We're going to do our best and trust God with the outcome. Can you do that?"

Ari looked down at their hands. "But I want him to confess that he and the other mercenaries aided in the overthrow of Tyrrhenea and kidnapped a child from her homeland."

What if Ambassador Van Sloan denied everything? His only child was already dead. What did he have to lose by lying? What if Esme got to him before they did? She could exact her revenge, and the truth would die with him.

Nick cupped her cheeks. "Can you do that, Arizona? Can you let God be God? No matter what happens."

Let God be God.

Ari's voice quivered. "I'm going to try."

He kissed her on the nose. "That's all I ask."

Matt Updike's face turned the color of a beet, and he shot out of his chair like a rocket. "Absolutely not," he roared. "We'll put another agent on this. Not her. She no longer works for the FBI."

Ari stiffened, and her jaw hardened.

Nick had seen that look before. She wasn't going to back down. He hurried to her defense. "It has to be Arizona. She can do this."

"I agree with Agent Updike." Agent Reid stood. "She's too unstable. If her temper gets out of control, she could blow the whole thing."

Nick flattened his lips. As if blowing the lid on mercenaries hiding within the US Government would be such a bad thing.

Santiago pivoted from the window and shook his head. "Maybe I'm slow, but I'm still trying to wrap my mind around all this. Walk me through it again."

Nick explained. "From what we can figure, thirty years ago, six mercenaries aided Italy in a battle against Tunisia for ownership of Tyrrhenea, an island nation in the Mediterranean Sea. They committed heinous crimes against the Tyrrheneans, including kidnapping an infant.

"According to a journal entry written by one of their own, the mercenaries were Ambassador Van Sloan, Governor Dominguez, General Burgess, Jamison Powers, Private Tyler Keller, and Congressman Reynolds."

That last one brought a knot to his throat. He was actually glad Rachel wasn't here to learn the truth about her father.

Nick continued. "They've kept their actions secret for all these years. They won't surrender willingly."

Santiago flipped up his suit jacket and lowered into his chair. "I see. Why does it have to be Agent Powers again?"

Ari cleared her throat. "We think I'm the infant they abducted from Tyrrhenea."

Silence fell over the room. That had to be hard to admit. She had said little since presenting the theory that Jamison Powers stole her from her birth mother.

Nick waited for the information to sink in, then continued. "We believe Ari's birth mother, Esme Aquila, is Enigma. She's taking revenge against the men who killed her people and stole her child."

At Santiago's arched eyebrows, Nick nodded. "Yes, the same Enigma who threatened the ambassador and murdered Bridgette Van Sloan."

Ari spoke up again. "My family has been connected with the Van Sloans for decades. The ambassador still sends us a Christmas card and a check every year. He must feel at least some guilt. I'm hoping I can get him to admit what happened."

Nick set his coffee cup on the DSS conference table. "Ari will straight up ask him about Tyrrhenea. With any luck, he'll name the mercenaries."

Reid rumpled his forehead, leaned forward, and grasped the back of the chair. "You're referring to that journal and those obituaries, aren't you? I told you, they're unrelated."

Nick stood now. "I respectfully disagree. It's no coincidence."

"But Tanya Keller committed suicide," Reid countered.

Nick nodded. "We're aware of that. But what if that was an incorrect assumption? Did anyone actually find a suicide note? What if Tanya was murdered, too?"

Reid crossed his arms. "We've already arrested Enigma."

Ari shook her head. "Kye Warner is not Enigma. He told me himself."

"There's one hole in your theory," Ari's aunt, Deputy

Secretary Powers, spoke from across the table. "Are you forgetting that Enigma tried to murder you and my niece just a few months ago? If she's Arizona's birth mother, why would she try to kill her? That doesn't make sense."

He hadn't forgotten. How could he? His body bore permanent scars from that day in Mintaka. "I don't have all the answers, other than that she's obviously a mentally disturbed woman. Maybe in her own mind, Ari's dad had to pay, even if it meant sacrificing her own child. She'd tried kidnapping Ari once before and failed. Spent twenty years in prison. That's a long time to plot your revenge."

Santiago leaned back and rubbed his chin. "Seems to me that other than Powers here, Esme's revenge is complete. What's left?"

"We received this message from Enigma just yesterday." Nick slid the paper where they'd written down the riddle from the back of the puzzle. "She won't stop until each of the mercenaries pay for what they did ..."

"... with their own lives." Ari finished.

"And you think Enigma will show up at the gala?" Updike finally returned to his seat with his arms crossed. He picked up the paper coffee cup and took a drink. His Adam's apple bobbed.

Deputy Powers crossed her legs and tugged on the edge of her skirt. "This morning, I received the guest list for the SeaGuardians gala next weekend. Van Sloan, Dominguez, Burgess, and Reynolds will all be in attendance."

His father-in-law would be there. This was the first time he'd heard this. The news felt like a kick to the gut.

Forgive me, Rachel. But he needs to answer for his crimes.

"What about Keller?"

"We couldn't locate him. It's possible he was killed during the attack on Tyrrhenea." Deputy Powers answered. "His military file is marked as MIA."

Keller's diary spoke of his reluctance to take part in the

attack. A lack of confidence could have easily translated into poor judgment and inattention to his surroundings, resulting in his demise. Nick had done his own search for Keller's last known address and had come up empty. No one had filed a death certificate either, which had led Nick to agree with Deputy Powers's conclusion.

Tyler Keller had never returned from the Mediterranean.

Nick continued, "If Esme doesn't show, then we're in the clear. We'll get Van Sloan's confession and make the arrests. But if she does, I'd rather be prepared, wouldn't you?"

Deputy Powers lowered her leg to the floor. "That's why DSS would like to partner with the FBI on this. We need more eyes and ears at the gala."

Updike pinned Ari. "You didn't consider unauthorized involvement a problem six months ago. Seems you and Nick were more than happy to handle everything on your own without alerting the proper authorities. Why now? Why is this time any different?"

Ari tilted her chin and met her former boss's gaze. "You're right. And I'd like to go on record with an apology for my actions. If we had turned in the SD card that first day, maybe Bridgette would have been found alive. Maybe not. We'll never know. Nick and I made some bad decisions, but we acknowledge we were wrong. We also realize we can't do this alone. We have some ideas about how to proceed, but we want your professional guidance and participation."

Updike cupped his chin. "What's the plan?"

Ari turned in Nick's direction. "Nick." She gestured with her hand.

A smile tugged at his lips.

She was learning to yield, and that might be her saving grace in this situation. If she'd come in there trying to strong-arm everyone, they'd never have let her anywhere near the gala, much less participate in the takedown.

"Our thought is to mic Arizona. During the gala, she will get Van Sloan alone and confront him." He unfurled a blueprint of the aquarium. "We'd like agents at the exits here and here." He pointed to the locations on the map. "Much of the aquarium is closed for renovations. If Esme was going to sneak in anywhere, we think it would be this entrance here. Behind the closed-off areas."

Updike leaned forward, setting his knotted hands on the table. "Anything else?"

"We need a dog." Nick rolled up the blueprint. "To sniff out any explosives."

Reid jerked upright. "You think she'll set a bomb?"

Nick shrugged. "It's not beyond possibility. We already know she has knowledge of explosive materials and the guts to use them. I don't think it's too much of a leap to think she might hide a bomb at the gala and detonate it during the event." He cleared his throat. "It's the fastest way to take out her remaining enemies."

"Even with her *daughter* there?" Reid air-quoted the word *daughter*. Obviously, he wasn't convinced. "Though I guess that hasn't stopped her before."

Nick nodded. "Exactly. Plus, Esme is hopefully unaware that Ari is attending the gala. She's coming as my plus one—her name won't be on the guest list."

"Interesting." Updike leaned back, propping one foot on the opposite knee. "I suppose I can allocate two of my agents for this assignment. I'd expect frequent updates."

"You aren't attending the gala?" Ari said.

Updike shifted. "I have a prior commitment."

Nick gave a curt nod of acknowledgment. As long as they had the FBI's cooperation, Updike could fly to the moon for all he cared. He rotated his wristwatch. "Let's meet here on the first at eighteen hundred hours to prep Arizona for her confrontation with Van Sloan. Deputy Powers has arranged for a car to take us to the gala. If the dog could clear the building before the guests arrive, that would be best. We don't want to create unnecessary panic. Van Sloan is scheduled to arrive at nineteen thirty. We'll be in place exactly twenty minutes earlier at nineteen ten."

The nods around the room confirmed their agreement.

Whatever Enigma had planned, they'd be ready.

CHAPTER 45

Sunday, 01 September
1730 Hours

A ri finished blotting her makeup to hide the scar that ran the length of her cheek, then reached to fix a strand of hair falling from her updo. Pain shot through her neck. "Ouch." She winced. Most of her wounds had healed from the explosion, but there was still the occasional ache or twinge.

"Here, let me." Aunt Sheila crossed the bedroom and took the bobby pin from Ari's hand. "You don't have to do this. It's not too late to get someone else."

Ari faced her aunt and took her hand. "Yes, I do, Aunt Sheila. I want the truth."

She could only hope Ambassador Van Sloan would give it to her.

The heavy feeling she'd carried for the past few hours gained weight, making her nauseous. Tonight's mission was two-fold. They not only planned to get a confession and take the former mercenaries into custody, but they also hoped to arrest Enigma for the murders of five women and stop her from taking any more lives. What if Esme was her birth mother? How would Ari feel when they took her away in handcuffs? Would she feel a sense of relief or of loss?

Tingles ran from her fingers to her toes, and a million what-ifs raced through her mind. Her fingers knotted in the silk fabric of her navy ball gown.

Aunt Sheila's hands dropped. She sank to the bed and released a heavy sigh.

Ari twisted to face her aunt. "What's wrong?"

"I'm so sorry, Arizona. Please forgive me for my part in the deception, but it honestly never crossed my mind that my brother might have kidnapped a child from overseas. To be honest, I don't think Ophelia ever knew the truth, either. Adoptions were far less monitored in those days, and we simply took him at his word."

Ari blew out a frustrated breath. "Unfortunately, he's not here to pay for his crimes. But I've paid every night since Esme tried to steal me back from him. I thought there was something wrong with me, that maybe people were right, and I was insane."

Aunt Sheila's eyes misted. "I'd always hoped the nightmares would go away and you would forget all about it. I knew you had paralyzing fears, but I thought telling you about the kidnapping would only make things worse."

Before Ari could respond, the doorbell rang. She pointed over her shoulder. "That'll be Nick."

Aunt Sheila nodded. "Get the door and tell him I'll be ready to leave in two minutes."

They both stood. Aunt Sheila disappeared into the guest bedroom down the hall, and Ari walked downstairs to open the door.

Nick stood on the front stoop wearing a tuxedo, cummerbund, and bowtie. His polished shoes reflected the evening sunlight. He removed his sunglasses like James Bond, then ran his fingers through his slick hair. "Ari, you look stunning."

Heat crept up her neck. Occasions to dress up weren't frequent on her social calendar. Instead, she spent most of her days dressed the same as the men.

The long sheath gown draped around her frame to her calves, while the jewel neckline kept her modest. Teardrop earrings dangled to her jawline.

His gaze traced her figure appreciatively until he reached her feet. He laughed until he coughed. "Hiking boots, really? Don't you think that's going to make you stand out?" He swallowed, and his eyes flickered over her once more. "Not that you're not already going to stand out. You clean up good."

"So do you." Ari stepped onto the porch, clutch purse in hand, and laid a kiss on his cheek. "Aunt Sheila said she'll be ready in just a minute."

Nick offered his arm. "May I escort you to your carriage?"

A long, sleek, black limo waited along the curb.

"Of course." She slipped her hand into the crook of his elbow. "As long as I don't turn into a pumpkin at midnight."

He chuckled. "I'm pretty sure it was the carriage that turned into a pumpkin, not Cinderella."

"That's right. She lost her shoe." Ari lifted her boot. "Which is not likely to happen tonight. Not in these bad boys."

Nick opened the back door of the limousine, and Ari slid across the smooth leather seat.

Aunt Sheila wasn't far behind, pausing long enough to lock the front door. Her stiletto heels clicked on the concrete walk as she approached. Just before entering the vehicle, she opened her purse and pulled out a handkerchief, holding it out to Nick. The corner of her mouth twitched.

"You've got a little something …" She pointed at her cheek.

Nick blushed and snatched the cloth. "Thank you." He wiped off Ari's lipstick, then handed it back. He followed Aunt Sheila inside the limo, then closed the door. "Ready?"

Ari took a deep breath. *As I'll ever be.*

Nick wasn't sure if it was nerves or Ari's striking appearance, but he'd forgotten how to breathe.

As he checked the placement of her microphone once more before they entered the aquarium, he stood close enough to feel her breath on his neck.

"Why don't you try it?"

He inhaled, and the faintest scent of peaches filled his olfactory.

A rosy hue tinted her cheeks. She lifted her face to meet his eyes, flickering like she was trying to read his thoughts. "Come in, Santiago, this is Powers. Can you read me?"

Santiago's voice carried through Nick's earpiece.

"I hear you," Ari replied.

A strand of hair dropped into her face, and he tucked it behind her ear, his fingertips just brushing her soft skin. Second thoughts plagued him like a locust swarm. "I don't think this is such a good idea."

A puzzled expression crossed her face, and she laid her hand on his arm. "Nick, it's fine. We've got this."

"Are you sure? What if we're wrong, Ari?"

Wrong about Van Sloan. Wrong about Esme.

She shrugged. "Too late now."

"I can't lose you. If I think it's too dangerous, I'm going to pull the plug on the whole thing."

He couldn't control what the other agents did, but he could at least remove Ari from harm's way. Enigma would not get off another shot. He'd analyzed the risks of pursuing a relationship with Ari and had found it worth the cost. The pain of losing her would be worse than risking everything to love her. And to love her was to love all of her, even her desperate need to see this thing through.

"Ari, I ..." His lips parted to say what was on his mind.

Santiago interrupted. "Assume your positions."

As soon as it was all over, he would take Ari aside and tell her how he felt. Would she concur? "I'll be beside you the entire time."

He offered his arm and led her up the concrete stairs to the two-story all-glass building, lit up like a Christmas tree. Lights twinkled, shimmering like stars on the surface of the water in the fountains. Tiki torches lined the entrance plaza.

Ari paused at the top of the stairs. "Not the whole time. If this is going to work, I have to get Van Sloan alone."

A doorman opened the ten-foot-tall glass door and tipped his hat. "Welcome."

Nick recognized him as one of Updike's agents. "Thank you."

He laid his hand on Ari's back as she walked through the entryway. In the center of the rotunda stood a life-sized ice sculpture of a dolphin. She gasped softly.

"Have you ever attended an event like this before?"

Ari shook her head, her enthralled gaze taking it all in.

"I guess we'll both feel like a regular fish out of water."

Ari smiled, then rolled her eyes.

He checked his watch. "Most of the guests should begin arriving in about thirty minutes. Until then, I'd like to look around. Get the lay of the land, so to speak."

"Me, too."

After perusing the first floor of the aquarium, which housed the restaurant, ballroom, gift shop, lounge, fun zone, 4D theater, and administrative offices, they paused at the blocked-off stairs leading to the construction zone on the second floor.

"Have you ever visited this aquarium before?" Nick asked.

"Couple of times."

"Favorite exhibit?"

"Shipwreck," she answered without hesitation. "I'm a sucker for sharks."

The 50,000-gallon Shipwreck Exhibit was home to three kinds

of sharks, sawfish, and barracudas, along with a host of other creatures.

Nick shivered. Ari might think sharks were fascinating, but they were not his forte. Something about those eyes ... "Would you ever swim with them?"

"Like in a cage or loose?"

Nick thought. "Loose."

Ari shook her head emphatically. "I'm not that brave. But from inside a dive cage might be kind of cool."

Nick threw back his head and laughed, releasing his tension. It felt good. He hadn't laughed in far too long, and Ari seemed to bring out the best in him.

She tapped his shoulder. "We should head to the ballroom. The other guests will be here soon."

He sobered. For a moment, he'd forgotten why they were here. "I want to check in with the K-9 unit. See if they found anything."

They circled back to the main lobby, where the guests entered after being searched with a metal-detecting wand. Every purse and handbag passed through the hands of the security officers. The men had dressed in formal attire, while the women wore a rainbow of sparkling ballgowns in every shape and size. Diamonds and gems glittered.

A hum of voices grew louder with each passing second.

Nick surveyed the crowd until he spotted the bomb squad commander signaling from the gift shop entrance. "I'll be right back." He whispered in Ari's ear, then made his way over. "What's the report?"

The commander kept a low profile in civilian clothes. "All clear. The dog didn't find any trace of explosives."

"That's a relief."

"What's the plan now? Do you want us to stick around?" The commander checked his watch and rubbed his bulbous nose. "We can do a check every hour."

Nick nodded. "Just stay out of sight as much as possible. We don't want to cause a panic." The guests expected extra security. A bomb squad, on the other hand, would be an unwanted surprise. "Keep me posted."

"Ten-four." The commander slipped out the back through the gift shop, and Nick returned to the lobby.

Ari stood next to the ice sculpture, making conversation with a purple-haired, curvaceous woman wearing a shimmery gold gown.

Nick approached and laid his hand on Ari's shoulder to signal his presence.

Ari looked up and smiled. "Mrs. Gabriel, let me introduce Security Specialist Nick Trueheart from the Diplomatic Security Service."

The woman put out her hand as Ari continued.

"Nick, this is Davida Gabriel. She's the CEO of SeaGuardians Foundation, the nonprofit organization sponsoring the gala."

Nick bent at the waist and laid a kiss on the back of Mrs. Gabriel's hand. "A pleasure to meet you, Mrs. Gabriel."

"A pleasure to meet you, Mr. Trueheart. I hope you came prepared to give generously to our cause. Tonight's gala is in memory of Bridgette Van Sloan. She loved all things oceanic, and SeaGuardians was her favorite charity."

He couldn't picture the selfish, entitled teenager possessing a love of anything but herself, but he kept his mouth shut.

"Poor dear," Mrs. Gabriel continued, laying her hand on her buxom chest. "I was simply horrified to learn of her tragic death. Phooey on those idiot agents who let her be abducted right under their noses. I don't know how they sleep at night knowing that young girl's death was their fault."

Ari cleared her throat.

"Yes, well, I'm sure they did their best. Have a good evening." Nick dipped his chin, then escorted Ari toward the ballroom entrance before Davida Gabriel realized they were the idiotic agents.

"That woman makes my blood boil." Ari hissed, a flush

rising from her collarbone to her ears. Inaudible words spit from her lips. "She wouldn't last one day in law enforcement."

"Don't let her get under your skin. Let's just focus on the task ahead of us."

Passing through the dive lounge, they entered the Nautilus Ballroom together. Round tables with white fabric cloth held seating for 250 guests. Above them, light reflected from beaded chandeliers onto the hand-painted ceiling. A row of square dark gray pillars, painted the same color as the walls, ran the length of the room. The blue and beige carpet pattern gave the space a nautical feel, with a wooden dance floor in the center, cornered with potted ferns.

Each table held five place settings with a name card, three forks, a steak knife, a glass of ice water, a folded cloth napkin, and bread plate. A podium with a microphone stood at the front, and in the back, a glass door led to the observation deck and a romantic view of the city skyline.

Under normal circumstances, he could imagine stealing a few kisses with Ari in such an atmosphere. If things went well, maybe there would be time for that later.

A roaming server offered them a glass of champagne. They both declined then found their seats with a view of the entire room as requested. He held Ari's chair for her, then tucked her legs underneath. The remaining chairs at the table sat empty. He glanced at the name cards but didn't recognize any of them.

"I wasn't expecting to see you here."

A deep voice spoke from behind him.

Nick pivoted to face his father-in-law, Congressman Elliot Reynolds. "Good evening, sir." He held out his hand, but the older gentleman ignored it.

"Why are you here? Not causing trouble, I hope." No hint of a joke underlay his tone—Elliot's expression was unmoved.

"I was invited."

Elliot grunted. "Wouldn't know why after that botched job you and that hack agent did protecting Van Sloan's daughter. I'd think you'd be ashamed to show your face in this company. Or any company."

Nick inhaled. "None of us are perfect. Not even you."

Elliot's eyebrows narrowed. Daggers shot from his darkened pupils. "What would you know about it?"

"Nothing, sir. I just meant in general." He bit his tongue. Retribution would come soon enough. "I hope you enjoy your evening. I've heard they're serving Chesapeake blue crab."

The Marylander would be pleased.

Elliot's expression softened. "Nothing like seafood from the Old Bay."

He gazed down his nose at Ari as if he smelled something foul. "Interesting choice in footwear."

He moved on without another word, and Nick released a sigh of relief.

"Pleasant man." Ari's sarcastic comment reached his ears.

Nick lowered into the chair beside her. "He still blames me for Rachel's death. She was in Vegas on spring break when we met. Instead of returning to Johns Hopkins University for med school, she stayed and became my assistant. He's convinced she would have been a highly acclaimed brain surgeon by now if I hadn't gotten in the way."

"She was training to be a doctor?"

Nick fiddled with his fork and stared at the bread plate. "She hated it. It was at her father's insistence she'd enrolled. It's what we had in common, parents coercing us into being something we weren't."

"What did she want to do?"

"Write."

"Anything I'd recognize?"

He gave Ari a sad smile. "Never finished a manuscript."

"I'm sorry he stirred up painful memories."

"Doesn't matter." If everything went well tonight, they'd see Rachel's killer behind bars, and Elliot Reynolds would face the consequences for his actions relating to Tyrrhenea. "Have you spotted Burgess or Dominguez?"

"Burgess is there at the front table, schmoozing with Mrs. Gabriel, and Dominguez is there,"—she jutted her chin— "on his third glass of champagne. I haven't seen Van Sloan."

"He'll be here." Nick checked his watch. The ambassador was running late. Adrenaline pricked his nerves. The plan hinged on Ari getting a confession.

Without it, everything else fell apart.

CHAPTER 46

A ri straightened her dress and kept an eye on the happenings of the room.

A boisterous laugh boomed from her right. Ambassador Van Sloan entered the ballroom, a brunette on his arm. The twenty-something-year-old woman, too young to be Bridgette's mother, wore a scarlet mermaid gown with a low-cut bodice. Diamonds shimmered at her throat, and her hair brushed her pale bare shoulders in soft, rolling curls.

The crowd rose and welcomed them with a rousing round of applause.

The ambassador accepted the accolades as if he'd won the Golden Globe Award. "Thank you. Thank you, my friends. Please be seated."

Van Sloan led the smirking young woman to a table close to the podium, held the chair for her, then once she'd taken a seat, sat in an adjacent chair.

Mrs. Gabriel moved behind the podium, tapping the microphone to get everyone's attention. "Good evening."

Feedback squealed, and Ari covered her ears until the shrill scream faded.

Davida started again. "Good evening, and welcome to the

annual SeaGuardians charity gala. We've dedicated tonight's event to the memory of Bridgette Van Sloan, the daughter of Ambassador and Juliana Van Sloan. Bridgette's light was snuffed out too soon this past February. Miss Van Sloan was a sophomore at Platte City University, studying to be a marine biologist. Her interests included beach beautification, sailing, and volunteering at the Monterey Bay Aquarium Research Institute on her school breaks."

It seemed Bridgette wasn't as shallow as they'd thought.

Davida continued. "All the proceeds from tonight's donations will go to help combat illegal fishing operations in Southeast Asia. Thank you for listening. Please open your heart and your wallets to this important cause."

Ari glanced around the room and caught Aunt Sheila's gaze.

She nodded.

Ari turned to Nick. "It's time." She stood and wove her way between tables toward the ambassador but froze when he rose to his feet with a champagne glass in hand.

"Friends, tonight, let's raise a glass in memory of my daughter, Bridgette." His hand squeezed his date's shoulder. "We know she's in a better place." He raised his glass. "To Bridgette."

People around the room stood, and glasses were lifted into the air as they echoed his words. "To Bridgette."

Pop! Pop!

Shots rang out, and glass exploded, sending food and liquids flying.

Ears ringing, Ari pulled her weapon and surveyed the crowd. Where were the shots coming from?

Screams filled the room as people jumped up, knocking over their chairs.

More shots were fired, and a bullet struck the column above Ari's head.

General Cal Burgess groaned, grabbed his chest, and

crumpled to the floor. Blood soaked the front of his white dress shirt.

Someone took to the microphone, shouting over the noise. "If everyone will please make their way to the exits in a calm and orderly fashion. The police are being informed of the situation. Thank you."

Ari fought the horde moving toward the emergency exit, losing sight of Ambassador Van Sloan. Jostled and elbowed, she waded like a fish going upstream until she burst from the ballroom into the dive lounge. Stepping aside, her back to the bar, she waited for the mob to clear.

Nick found her, his jacket rumpled and his hair mussed. "Do you see the ambassador?"

Ari put her finger in her ear to block out the noise. "Santiago, do you read me?"

"I hear you, Powers."

"We've got an active shooter situation. Does anyone have eyes on Van Sloan?"

A unanimous resounding negative echoed over the earpiece.

"We need eyes on Van Sloan. Find him." Santiago shouted orders. "Reid. Nixon." He addressed the loans from the FBI. "I want you outside. Trueheart. Powers. Take the inside."

"Got it. We'll report in as soon as we locate him. Over." Nick answered as he and Ari headed for the lobby. "Did you see which way he went?"

"No."

"Let's split up. We'll cover more ground that way. If you need help, just call." He tapped his earpiece. "I'm going to head through the gift shop, restaurant, and fun zone. Be careful."

Ari nodded. "I'll clear the classrooms and the administrative offices."

Nick disappeared into the gift shop, winding his way through displays of stuffed stingrays, T-shirts, and water bottles.

Ari pivoted, then circled back through the dive lounge,

through a coral arch to the education classrooms in the back. She kept her firearm aimed as she checked the dark classrooms, turning the lights on one by one.

"Clear," she shouted instinctively, knowing Nick could hear her on the headset.

At the end of the hall, she braced her back against the wall. She leaned forward, peering into the front room. In the dark, she could make out a couple of chairs and a coffee bar with an espresso machine and a microwave.

After locating the light switch, she turned it on, then cleared the manager's office and the locker rooms. "Nick, can you read me? I'm finished in the back. I'm heading to the exhibit entrance."

"Ten-four. I'm just finishing the fun zone. We'll go upstairs together."

"Roger." Ari took a few steps toward the ticket booths.

Shots echoed from somewhere in the aquarium.

As she raced back to the lobby, she tried to determine in which direction the shots had come from—Nick's or the construction site upstairs.

Another shot rang out, and the dolphin ice sculpture exploded. Shards of ice pelted her skin as Ari dropped to the floor and covered her head. The lobby grew quiet, and she half-rose on her elbow to get a look around. Ice pieces created a minefield across the tile floor. A figure flashed past the top of the non-running escalator, and Ari leaped to her feet and hightailed it after them, taking the stairs two at a time.

"Come in, Powers. Do you need backup?" Santiago's voice came over the speaker.

"Nick and I have things under control for now. If someone could hack into the security cameras and get us a visual, that would be great. How's Burgess?"

"He's stable and in transport to the hospital. I'll get someone on that visual."

"Thanks. Keep me posted. I want to know the minute you have eyes on the inside."

"Ten-four. And be careful. I can't offer you a job with DSS if you get yourself killed."

His words brought a smile to her mouth, and she stumbled and nearly missed the last step. At least she'd have a job when all this was over. If she survived.

She entered the North America exhibit, and the musty smell of fish and algae filled her nostrils. Otters swam in a tank to her right, rainbow trout and other freshwater fish to the left. Under a stone archway, she stepped into the Desert exhibit of bearded dragons, tarantulas, and a flash flood demonstration.

The entrances to the Rainforest and the Coral Lagoon were blocked off and covered with a plastic tarp. Movement, heading under the stone arch toward the Under the Sea exhibit, caught her eye—a familiar flash of silver hair.

Nick's voice came over the earpiece. "Van Sloan ... shot ..." It was hard to hear through the static.

"Nick, you're breaking up."

She entered the underwater tunnel, stepping carefully in the dim light. The tank was designed to make the view into the saltwater easier. Keeping the firearm close to her chest, she edged forward, every muscle tensed. In the tunnel, she was exposed, with nowhere to hide.

Suddenly, the electricity powered down, entombing her in complete darkness.

Her heart seized. Come on. Come on. How long would it take the generator to kick on? Lights along the floor flickered, then lit. A shark swam silently past the glass window of the tank. Its dead stare sent chills running down her spine.

A reflection appeared in the glass, and Ari spun on her heel.

The woman from the train station—the one that had been following her.

"Who are you?"

Without answering, the woman pivoted and lurched out of the tunnel.

Ari gave chase, through a door marked 'Employees Only.'

They raced down a long hallway lined with doors. The woman ducked inside one of the open doorways. Ari followed her into the dark room. Her eyes took a second to adjust to the dim light. One second too long. Something hard slammed into her temple. Her vision blurred, and everything went black.

CHAPTER 47

Darkness had swallowed her. Her head swam. Ari sat up and inched backward until she reached the wall. She squeezed her palms against her aching skull, and her stomach roiled.

Everything came rushing back. The reflection. The woman. The chase. The assault.

How much time had passed? Where was her gun? She patted the smooth floor around her. The firearm wasn't in reach. She touched her ear for her earpiece. Also gone.

She was on her own, cut off from the others. As her eyes adjusted to the dark, shelving units, boxes, and empty fish tanks materialized around her. Adrenaline and fear coursed through Ari's veins, sending shivers through her nerves. The walls closed in. The lack of light pressed in, suffocating her. She wheezed as she struggled to draw air.

A dark figure stood a few feet away, watching her.

"Who are you?"

The figure didn't answer ... or move.

"Who are you?"

"I'm your mother."

It was the same voice as in the hospital. Rich, low, and familiar.

"Please let me go."

No response.

"Please. I'm afraid of the dark, of closed-in spaces. I can't. I can't breathe." Her vision blurred again. Here was her chance to learn the truth, but all she could think about was escaping. Her sinuses stung. "Why are you doing this to me?"

"I am protecting you." Esme's heavy accent held the lilting cadence of her native tongue.

What was she talking about? The woman was insane. Ari had to get out of there.

She lunged to her feet, stumbled, and fell. Pain shot through her hands, knees, and cheek. Rolling over, she sat up and touched her feet. An ankle shackle held them bound. Frustration raised her blood pressure. She scooted on her rear until she faced Esme. "Are you Enigma?"

Esme squatted, her face inches from Ari's with Ari's gun aimed at Ari's chest. Her features were far clearer at this distance. Only a faint resemblance remained from the mug shot taken twenty-five years ago. Time and prison had not been kind to the once-stunning woman.

"I will not let them take you again."

Was that supposed to answer her question?

Ari slowed her breathing. Panic was getting her nowhere. She cleared her throat. "Why all the mystery? Why all the riddles and clues? I'm a grown adult. You could have just shown up at my house and told me who you were."

"I do not know what you are talking about."

"Why did you kidnap Bridgette? Why did you have to kill her?"

Esme flinched. "I did not kill anyone. I would never. You were my child. Jamison Powers stole you from me, from your homeland. I thought I would never see you again." Anger filled Esme's voice.

"I don't understand. If you are my mother, why did you lock me in a basement? Why did you leave me alone with almost no food and water? I was only three years old. All I wanted was to go home."

Esme's head dropped, and her fingers clutched the hem of her T-shirt. "It took three years to get to America and find you. All I wanted was my daughter back. It happened so fast." Her voice cracked.

She cleared her throat. "I watched you, made a plan. That other woman left you alone outside. I saw my chance, and I took it. I hid you in the basement of an abandoned house, then I went to my apartment. I always intended to come back. But someone watched my building. He must have hired someone to follow me. I couldn't leave for fear of leading him to you. I was crazy with worry. Three days passed before they disappeared. When I finally could return to the house, you were gone."

"Why are you doing this to me now?"

Esme raised her head and fixed her eyes on Ari's face. "I am protecting you."

"From whom?"

"From the soldier, Keller."

Ari's breath caught in her throat. "Keller? As in Specialist Tyler Keller?"

"He tried to kill you. I will not let it happen. He will not succeed."

"Did Keller set the bomb at Mintaka?"

"If I had not been there, you would have died."

"Why did you tell me to stay away from Bridgette Van Sloan? I was trying to rescue her."

"I was protecting you. Keller knew you would come for her."

"How do you know that?" Ari asked.

Esme stood. "He remembered me from Tyrrhenea. He knew I was your mother and that I would do anything to keep you safe. That is how he got the music box. I gave it to him. He promised he would not hurt you. He lied."

"Is Keller here tonight?"

"He is going to kill the men who destroyed my country. They deserve to die. But I will not let him hurt you."

Why would he take revenge on them? He was on their side. He was as guilty as they were. Something must have happened during the attack on the island.

Ari struggled against her bonds. "Let me out of here. I have to warn Nick. He could walk into a trap."

"That is not my problem." Esme moved toward the door. "You will be safe here."

The door opened, and a soft light poured into the room.

Ari lunged again but fell short, landing on her face. "Please, let me go."

"Stay safe, my darling," Esme whispered.

The door closed, then locked, shutting Ari alone in the dark. She rolled to her rear, then tucked her face into her knees, circling her legs with her arms.

Lord, if you're there, please help me. I don't know what to do. I can't get out of this on my own. If you really care about me, send someone to help.

And don't let anything happen to Nick.

I love him.

Radio silence.

Nick tried again. "Come in, Ari. Do you copy?"

No response.

"Santiago. Do you copy? Powers has gone silent."

"I hear you. What's the update on the active shooter situation?"

"It's been quiet." Nick moved into the hallway.

Blood drops stained the rough concrete floor. He squatted and touched the wet spots. Definitely fresh.

"Want me to send in SWAT?" Santiago asked.

Nick shook his head, then remembered Santiago couldn't see him. "Not yet. I don't want to risk Ari's safety."

"Van Sloan," Nick shouted. "You're not getting out of here without answering some questions, so you might as well give yourself up."

No answer. Not that he expected one.

He continued down the corridor in the restricted access area. A loud banging caught his attention. He turned a corner and listened again. More banging. Indiscernible shouting. A familiar voice.

"Ari," he called out. "Is that you?"

No response.

He crept down the hall. The sound grew softer. He changed directions. "Arizona, where are you?"

The banging grew louder. His name grew more distinct. "Nick. Help me!"

He stopped at the last door. The noise was loudest here. "Ari. Are you in there?"

"I'm here. Esme's got me trapped in here."

He tried the door handle, but it was locked. Raising his firearm, he shot the deadlock. Metal twisted, and plaster littered the floor. He shoved, and the door opened.

Ari sat in the corner with her feet shackled.

"Nick! Oh, thank God, it's you."

"What happened?" He crouched beside her, scanning for injuries.

"Esme whacked me in the head then hauled me in here and locked the door."

He listened as she told him about her conversation with her birth mother. "Keller's here. *He's* taking revenge on the other mercenaries. I think Keller is Enigma. Not Esme."

Nick furrowed his brow. "Keller?"

"Tyler Keller—the one from the journal. Can you get me out of these?" She jiggled her feet, and the shackle rattled.

He inspected the lock. "Do you have a couple of bobby pins?"

"Sure." She pulled two pins from her falling updo and handed them to him.

He worked them through the tumblers, one at a time. After several seconds, the locking mechanism popped, and the shackle released. He removed the constraints from her legs, then returned the bobby pins.

"Sorry that took so long. I'm a little rusty." He cracked a smile at Ari's wide-eyed expression. "Escape artist, remember?"

"Yeah." Ari stuffed the pins back into her hair. "That was impressive."

He stood and held out his hand.

She grasped it, and he pulled her to her feet.

"Follow me." He paused at the door and held out his firearm. "Here. You should carry this. You're a better shot."

"Thanks. Esme took mine." Ari gripped the weapon.

He peeked around the door frame. "It's clear."

Their footsteps echoed in the empty corridor.

Ari moved to the front, keeping the firearm close to her chest. "Can you ask Santiago if they've hacked the cameras yet? Esme stole my headset."

"Santiago. Do you copy?"

A moment of radio silence.

"Roger." Santiago's voice came through his earpiece.

"What's the status on getting a visual inside the aquarium? Over."

A brief delay.

"We've not been able to establish a visual. The cameras are offline. Over," Santiago answered.

"Roger. Over and out." Nick signed off, then caught up with Ari. "He says the cameras are offline. The only way we're getting a visual is if we can turn them back on."

Pipes overhead groaned. The air conditioner kicked on.

She cautiously approached the doorway into the main

attraction area, then checked for danger. "The offices are on the first floor. Which way to the stairs?"

"Where are we now?" Nick leaned forward to look over her shoulder.

Ari scanned the area. "We've got the snack shack and touch ponds to the right. Shipwreck Exhibit to the left."

He pointed. "Head straight through that archway to the Sunken Treasure Exhibit. Just beyond the shark tank is the Rainforest."

Ari took two steps into the exhibit, then paused midstride. "If I wanted to hide, the construction area is where I'd go." She pivoted to the left and quickened her pace.

Nick lengthened his stride to keep up. "I thought we were going to get the cameras back online."

"No need. We know where they're hiding."

Plastic tarps hanging from the ceiling loomed closer.

He halted. "Ari, we need to think this through. Make a plan."

"I'm not waiting around for them to find me first. If we can't see them, they can't see us either. I'll be careful and won't let them get the jump on me." She lifted the tarp and disappeared inside.

Shouting after her would only alert the hostiles to their location.

The lights were off in this section, but enough spilled through that he could see where he was going. Empty exhibits. Piles of construction materials, buckets of paint, rolls of wiring. A rocky cliff rose toward the ceiling with a drained pond below. The animals had been removed, but some of the plant life remained. Mangrove roots clawed their way out of an empty swamp.

A shadow moved.

"Ari, is that you?" he called.

Where did she go?

He proceeded forward with caution, defenseless. He spotted her through the stone archway dividing the areas. Picking up speed, he joined her, noticing too late her raised arms.

Van Sloan, standing beside the vacant tiger exhibit, pointed a handgun in their direction. A dark blot stained the man's white dress shirt sleeve.

Nick put his hand on Ari's shoulder. If they backed away slowly, they might be able to get out of range before Van Sloan noticed. Nick slid his hand from her shoulder to her hand, then gave a gentle tug as he stepped backward.

"Going somewhere, Trueheart?" A male voice spoke from behind him.

Nick whirled.

A stranger, tall, dark, and in his mid-fifties, held a semi-automatic aimed at Nick's chest.

Van Sloan hadn't been aiming at them.

Nick's stomach knotted. "You must be Keller."

"Nice to finally make your acquaintance. Put the weapon on the floor, Powers, then kick it out of reach."

Ari squatted, laid the Glock on the floor, then straightened as she gave it a sharp kick.

"I've enjoyed our little interlude. But now, it's game over for you and the daughter of Jamison Powers."

CHAPTER 48

"You're Enigma."

As Ari appraised Tyler Keller, a flicker of recognition crossed her mind.

A bone-chilling grin slithered across Keller's face. "I see you've finally connected the dots. Took you long enough."

Ari swallowed. "But why? Why are you doing this?"

Keller's expression hardened as a roar carried from where Van Sloan stood.

He climbed out of the exhibit. "You're Enigma? You sent those threats? You killed my daughter?" His body trembled as he joined them.

"That's close enough." Keller aimed the weapon at Van Sloan. "It's your fault my daughter is dead. I just settled the score."

Van Sloan's jaw dropped. "Tanya took her own life. How is that my fault?"

Keller cocked the rifle. "It's yours and the others—Powers, Reynolds, Dominguez, Burgess. I didn't want any part of that attack on Tyrrhenea, but you all wouldn't let me out of it. You called me a coward, a turncoat. You dragged me into it, then when I got injured, you left me to die. I spent three years in a prison camp in Tunisia. When I finally returned home, I managed to keep what we'd done a secret for decades, but Tanya found my journal. My shame was complete when she walked into that lion's cage and let them maul her to death. You all took my precious daughter from me. I took yours. And now it's your turn to die."

Van Sloan moved closer. His voice grew hard and agitated. "I gave you a job. I welcomed you into my home. And this is how you show your gratitude. You're nothing but a coward, Keller. You always were."

Ari remembered where she'd seen Keller before. The butler at Van Sloan's mansion.

Van Sloan raised his handgun.

Keller shot first.

The blast knocked the ambassador backward to the floor. He swore and clutched his chest. Blood spread through the fabric of his white dress shirt as he curled into a fetal position.

Ari knelt at the ambassador's side.

"What do you think you're doing? Leave him be," Keller commanded.

"Let me stop the bleeding." She grabbed the panels of Van Sloan's shirt and ripped them open. Buttons flew. Blood soaked his undershirt. She shredded that one too, then tore the length from her dress and pressed it to the wound. Van Sloan howled like a banshee.

"It's going to be okay. Help will be here soon." Ari kept her voice steady.

"False promises, Agent Powers?" Keller clicked his tongue. "I thought you were better than that."

Ari lifted her head and glanced over her shoulder. The semi-automatic pointed her direction. She glanced at Nick's Glock about five feet away. Could she get to it? What about Van Sloan's weapon?

Another glance at Keller told her no. He'd shoot her before she could grab either one.

"Get up," Keller demanded.

"That's not helping. Don't antagonize him." Nick looped his arm through hers and helped her to her feet. Van Sloan's blood stained her hands.

Ari stiffened. "It's two against one, Keller. You can't stop us both."

"Actually, it's two against two. And neither of you have a weapon." Andre the Giant stepped from the shadows, holding a second semi-automatic rifle pointed in their direction.

"Who are you?"

"My name is Rene Roscoff."

"Let's go." Keller signaled down the hall with his gun. "I'll take that." He stalked forward, yanked Nick's earpiece out, threw it on the ground, and crushed it under his foot. He circled them, then pointed. "That way, both of you. And no funny business. If you run, I'll put bullet holes in your backs."

Ari pointed to the ambassador. His chest barely moved. "What about him? We can't just leave him here to die."

"Watch me." Keller grabbed her arm and jerked her forward. "Get moving."

Rene led them through the main concourse to the "Employees Only" section of the aquarium.

Rain pattered on the roof. A sand shark cruised past the glass wall. The soundtrack to *Jaws* played in her head.

Every escape plan she came up with ended with at least one of them getting shot—an event she wasn't longing to repeat. A phantom pain rocketed through her side at the thought.

Rene gave the restricted access door a tug, then held it open. "Inside."

Ari stepped forward, nearly tripping over her own feet, and the door closed behind them.

The security lights gave the hallway an eerie glow.

"Where do you think they're taking us?"

"I don't know. But it can't be good." Nick whispered in her ear, entangling his fingers in hers. "Just keep walking."

"I'm so sorry, Nick. I should have listened."

"We'll figure it out. We always do."

"I did exactly what you told me not to do."

"Ari—"

"Stop whispering," Keller ordered.

At the end of a long passageway, a green exit sign glowed above a metal door. Keller opened it, and Nick and Ari passed through into a large, well-lit room with blue painted walls. Pipes ran every which way, and the roar of running water bombarded her ears.

Metal stairs with yellow handrails climbed the side of a concrete wall. An acrylic glass cage with holes like Swiss cheese was visible at the top. A sinking feeling sent waves of nausea through her stomach.

"Up there. Both of you." Keller ordered.

Everything in Ari screamed to rebel, but one look at the barrel pointed at her chest, and she forced her feet to climb. Higher and higher, until her head topped the edge of the wall. 50,000 gallons of water churned at her feet. A blackish dorsal fin sliced the surface tension.

She stepped onto the narrow dock, and Nick joined her. Keller kept back a safe distance, just far enough to prevent them from shoving him overboard or reaching his gun.

He pulled a pair of handcuffs from his back pocket. "Cuff him." He jutted his angled chin toward Nick.

Ari pinched her lips together. "No."

Keller chuckled. "Feisty, aren't you?" He aimed the rifle. "It's your choice. You can handcuff him, or I can shoot him. Either way, he's going in that tank."

If Nick was bleeding, he'd be attacked. If he struggled against the handcuffs, he'd be attacked. Either way, this wasn't going to end well for him.

She tried another approach. "I'm sorry you lost your daughter, but revenge isn't going to bring healing."

Keller took two steps up the ladder. "Handcuff him," he barked.

Ari continued to stall. "Why the game? Why didn't you just shoot me from the beginning?"

"I wanted you to know what Jamison Powers had done before my revenge was complete. You weren't supposed to survive Mintaka."

"What about Esme? You stole me from my birth mother."

Keller scoffed. "That was all Jamison's idea. I tried to talk him out of it, but he insisted. Ophelia was barren. No one would ever miss one infant in all the chaos."

Except for the mother. "You forced her to help you. You used her against her own child."

"The police already know, Keller," Nick shouted over the roar. "We turned your journal over to the FBI."

"You mean this journal?" He held up the leather-bound notebook.

"How did you get that?"

Keller smirked. "An old friend of yours. It's amazing what people will do if you threaten everything they love."

Matt's voice echoed in her memory, *"I have a prior engagement."*

"Did he also agree to stay away from here tonight?" Ari asked.

Keller tossed the diary into the tank. It floated, then as the pages grew wet, sank. A tiger shark's pectoral fin sent it spinning to the bottom. Keller shook the handcuffs, still dangling in his outstretched hand. "Cuff him, Powers."

She took the manacle from him, then faced Nick. "I'm sorry."

"I understand." He held his arms extended, and she clapped the cuffs in place.

She pivoted. "Let me guess. You want me to push him into the tank."

"That would be too easy." Keller gestured. "Get in the cage, Trueheart."

Ari's gaze traced the holes in the acrylic box. Without diving gear, Nick would drown, and with the handcuffs, he'd be unable to escape the cage.

"Get in the cage, or I'll shoot … her." Keller swung the rifle to face Ari again.

Nick held his shackled arms over his head. "I'll do it. I'll do it. Just let me say goodbye."

Keller grunted.

Nick shuffled his feet until he faced her. His eyes grew glassy. "Arizona Powers, I love you." He looped his arms over her neck, pulled her against him, and lowered his face to hers. His warm breath caressed her skin.

Ari stood on her tiptoes, and their lips touched. As he held her in his arms, the kiss deepened, and his fingers dug into her hair, pulling her tighter against his chest.

"Enough," Keller shouted. He leaped onto the platform, grabbed Nick's shoulder, and yanked them apart, nearly knocking Ari off her feet.

She swung her arms to keep balanced.

Keller pointed at the cage. "Let's get this over with."

Nick carefully made his way across the deck. He climbed the ladder, then dropped down inside, taking a seat on the metal bar running the length of the cage.

Tears clouded her vision.

Keller's palm mashed a red button on a control panel.

An alarm sounded. Mechanical gears whirled, moving the cage until it was suspended over the water, then lowered it into the tank. As the first holes sank beneath the surface, water began filling the cage.

She lunged for Keller, but Rene locked his arms around her elbows. She struggled to break free. "Nick!"

Deeper into the tank, the cage sank. Water reached his waist, then his chest.

"I love you, too." Hot tears ran down her cheeks.

Rene released her as she dropped to her knees.

The gears stopped once the cage was completely submerged.

How long could he hold his breath? A minute? Maybe two? Not long enough for her to save him. *Lord, Nick is in Your hands. When You see him, tell him I love him.*

Keller grabbed Ari's arm and hauled her to her feet. "Now, for you."

"What are you going to do to me? Feed me to the sharks as well."

Without responding, Keller pushed her down the stepladder. Rene came behind.

Her feet slogged down the hallway. If the concrete floor were a swamp, a loggerhead turtle would bite her toe. It took everything in her to keep moving. Part of her didn't care if Keller shot her. What did it matter now? Ari sank to the floor, back against the wall, and plopped her head into her hands.

Rene's shoes appeared. "Get up," he ordered.

"What's going on back there?" Keller's voice drifted from farther down the hall.

Rene pulled on her arm. "Get moving." He let go, and she let her arm drop. "She won't move," he shouted at Keller.

Ari lifted her head as Keller's heavy footfalls grew louder.

He jerked the rifle from Rene's hand. "Pick her up, and let's go."

The big man scooped her up and tossed her over his shoulder in a fireman's carry.

She went limp, making herself as heavy as possible. If they were expecting her to put up a fight, she'd do the opposite. The added weight slowed Rene's progress and further irritated Keller.

"Hurry up," Keller bellowed.

"I'm trying. She's heavier than she looks."

"Hey, I've put on a few pounds since the explosion, but that's only because I haven't been able to work out for the past six months. Blame it on Keller. It's his fault." She bounced as Rene shifted her weight. She lowered her voice to a whisper. "Don't take orders from him. Surrender and turn state's evidence on him. He killed Bridgette Van Sloan. He's murdered others, too. Lila Dominguez. Jayda Roach. Rachel Trueheart. There's no need for you to go down with him."

Rene halted and set Ari on her feet.

Keller opened the door to the roof access.

A wild scream exploded from their left. Esme plowed into Keller, sending him sprawling. Both rifles flew from his grip.

The older woman clung to his back.

He body-slammed her over his shoulders.

Leaping to her feet, Esme clawed his face and tried to prevent him from retrieving a weapon. He managed to reach one and used it to shove Esme into the wall.

She slumped to the floor.

Keller turned, breathing heavily, blood seeping from a scratch on his face.

"Run," Esme whispered. "Run." Her eyes closed, and her body went limp.

Ari bolted, cutting left toward the construction zone, flipping the tarp up as she entered. She crouched behind a manufactured boulder, lungs heaving, muscles trembling.

Lord, help me!

CHAPTER 49

Wet footprints left a trail from the shark tank across the concrete floor. Nick's soaked clothes weighed him down and chilled him to the bone. He stuck Ari's bobby pins into his pocket. They'd come in handy before, but this was the first time they'd literally saved his life.

The behind-the-scenes area was a labyrinth of passageways and doors leading into storage rooms or the backs of exhibits. He continued through the maze of white walls, taking a right turn. A green exit sign appeared at the end of the hall. He hastened his steps and covered more ground. Another hall opened to his left.

A large mound on the floor in a puddle of red snagged his attention. Van Sloan had apparently tried to go for help and collapsed here. His eyes were closed, and his chest lay deathly still.

Nick slowed. "Van Sloan?" he shouted. "Can you hear me?" He dropped to his haunches and touched his fingers to Van Sloan's throat. His pulse was thready and weak, but present.

The man needed help.

Now.

Nick tried to lift the ambassador, but the dead weight was too much for him. If he didn't seek medical attention for the ambassador, he wouldn't make it.

Why should I help him?

The ambassador was partly to blame for the entire mess. He was one of the mercenaries that had attacked Tyrrhenea and had stolen Ari from her homeland and birth mother. One of the mercenaries that left Keller to die, fueling his revenge.

Van Sloan deserved to die.

Vengeance is mine, I will repay, saith the Lord. Nick groaned and rose to his feet. *You're right, Lord. You don't take pleasure in the death of the wicked, and neither should I. No matter what he's done.*

He started to pull off his shirt to make Van Sloan a new packing, then stopped. The algae and bacteria in his wet clothes would give the man gangrene. What was already there would have to do for now.

"Hang on, Ambassador. I'll be back as soon as I can."

Nick made his way through the winding corridor into another open area. A sign read "Roof Access" with an arrow pointed to the left. Blood stains streaked down a wall, leading to a small puddle on the tile floor.

A woman lay crumbled in a heap.

Nick crouched and felt for a pulse. Strong. Breathing steadily, but out cold. He pushed from the floor then dashed for the down escalator. Taking the stairs two at a time, he jumped the last few steps then burst through the main entrance of the aquarium.

Blue and red lights flashed in the darkness. Multiple agencies surrounded the building. Uniformed officers kept a crowd of gala guests and spectators at bay.

Santiago appeared. "Trueheart! What's the situation? Where's Powers?"

Nick inhaled. Coughed. "We need medics on the second floor. Two people are down, maybe a third."

Santiago shouted orders into the radio on his shoulder. "How many armed suspects?"

"Two. Tyler Keller and Rene Roscoff, Keller's lackey."

"Tyler Keller?" Santiago's eyes grew wide. "The guy from that journal?"

"The same. He was one of the mercenaries that attacked Tyrrhenea. Apparently, his daughter, Tanya Keller, learned what happened overseas, and in her humiliation, she took her own life. Keller blames the other men. Where's Dominguez and Elliot Reynolds?"

"They're being detained back at headquarters. Why are you soaking wet? What happened in there?"

"Long story. I'll tell you later. Right now, we need to extract the victims, arrest Keller and Rene, and locate Ari."

Santiago laid his hand on Nick's shoulder. "Why don't you take a break? You look strung out. We'll take it from here."

"No can do." He shrugged off his boss's hand. "I'm going back in there."

"Think this through, Trueheart. You're exhausted. It's too risky."

"I don't need to think about it. This is Ari we're talking about. I'd risk my life for her."

Santiago grunted and cracked his neck. "That might be necessary."

"Then so be it."

Ari slowed her breathing.

Keller's footfalls echoed. Closer … closer …

Her muscles twitched. Adrenaline surged. She closed her eyes.

It wasn't her normal *modus operandi* to wait. She had a reputation as someone who rushed in without thinking about the consequences. She'd gotten things done—no doubt about that—but how much more successful could she have been if she'd slowed down, weighed the risks, and made a calculated decision?

"You can't hide forever, Powers. I will find you." Keller's voice sounded louder than before.

She didn't dare peek. Wouldn't give him something to aim at. She needed the element of surprise if she was going to have any chance of getting out of here alive.

Every muscle in her body tensed.

Wait.

Footsteps drummed.

Wait.

Her pulse hammered in her throat.

Wait.

Keller moved into view, firearm extended.

Now!

Ari vaulted from her hiding place, then spun out a roundhouse kick, knocking the weapon from his hands. The gun clattered to the floor and slid out of reach. She lunged for it, but Keller's arm snaked around her middle, flattening her against his body.

She let out a yelp.

Something sharp pressed against her throat.

"Nice try, Powers, but this game is over. And you lose." Keeping one arm around her waist and the other holding the knife to her throat, Keller dragged her through the construction zone.

She struggled. Tried stepping on his foot. Fought to loosen his grip. But nothing worked. The tender flesh beneath the blade stung.

"Do you know how easy it would be to slit your throat? Stop fighting me, or this ends now." He shoved the plastic tarp aside.

"Hands up, Keller. We've got you surrounded." An authoritative voice came from off to the side. SAC Luke Santiago stepped from behind the stone arch, weapon drawn.

Another agent appeared from the other side. Reid.

Keller's arm cinched tighter.

"Ari. We're going to get you out of here." Nick's voice soothed her angst like salve on a wound.

A happy sob released from her throat. "Nick? Nick, is that you?"

The knife dug deeper.

"It's me, Ari. I'm okay." Nick assured her.

She couldn't see him, but he was there. And he was alive.

Tears squeezed from the corners of her eyes. *Thank you, God.* "He has a knife, Nick."

Nick stepped out from behind the jellyfish tank, hands raised. "Let her go, Keller. It's over. We've captured your lackey. You're on your own."

Keller growled. "It's not over until I say it's over."

A sharp twinge zipped through her skin.

"Please," Ari cried. "Please let me go."

"Forget about it. The minute I let you go, those two will blast me full of holes. Put your weapons down."

The agents exchanged glances with Nick.

He gave a curt nod.

Bending, they laid their firearms on the floor.

"Now what?" Santiago asked.

"Arms in the air," Keller ordered.

The agents complied.

"Kick them over here."

Two Glock 19s slid in the direction of Ari and Keller.

"Okay, Keller. What'll it take to get you to let her go?" Nick switched into hostage negotiator mode. Not a position he'd ever taken before. She hoped he knew what he was doing. Her life depended on it.

Edging backward, Keller pulled her along with him. "I want a helicopter out of here. Or she dies."

"Fine. You can have it. Is that it?" Nick asked.

Keller must have nodded because Santiago spoke into his radio. "This is Santiago to base. I need a helicopter for Mr. Keller. Over."

"A helicopter?" A puzzled voice answered.

Santiago never took his eyes off them. "Yes, a helicopter for Mr. Keller. He has a hostage. This is his only demand. Over."

"Roger that. One helicopter on the way."

Santiago addressed her captor. "Okay, Mr. Keller. We have your helicopter coming. We'll take you wherever you want to go. As a sign of good faith, why don't you let Miss Powers go? You have our weapons."

Keller's chest vibrated against her back as a chilling chuckle erupted from his throat. "How dumb do you think I am? You can have her back after I leave."

The knife moved from her neck long enough for him to open the roof access door. "I just haven't decided whether you get her back alive or dead." He tugged her backward into the dark stairwell.

The door closed.

A few more steps and the black sky opened overhead, echoing with the sounds of thunder. Cold rain pelted her skin. The blade pressed harder, forcing her toward the edge of the roof. The brightly lit windows of nearby buildings created a glowing tunnel to the ground below. Vehicle headlights glinted off the wet blacktop.

A wave of dizziness washed over her, and Ari pivoted away from the ledge.

Headlights appeared in the southern sky as the faint whirl of a rotor rose above the city noises. It drew nearer until the blades tossed Ari's hair into her face and wrapped what remained of her dress around her knees.

A rope ladder descended, and Keller released her, reaching for the bottom rung.

A dark figure lunged at Keller, shoving Ari to the side

Ari shrieked and stumbled backward, landing on her rear.

Keller and his attacker struggled, locked in a violent tangle, then disappeared over the edge of the roof. Keller screamed—the sound grew fainter with each passing millisecond.

Stunned, Ari shivered on the concrete slab, her heart racing and her breathing shallow. Once she recovered from her shock, she leaped to her feet and leaned over the wall. *Oh, dear God, please don't let that be Nick.* Neither person was anywhere to be seen. A section of the roof slanted downward from where she stood.

"Help. Help me. Please." A woman's voice carried from somewhere out of sight.

Esme? "Hang on, I'm coming."

Ari climbed over the wall and skidded toward the woman. Wet, slick shingles made it hard to maintain her balance. She eased herself down, inch by inch, until she lay prostrate on the ground, then army crawled across the rough surface. This woman, her birth mother, had saved her. The least she could do was attempt to return the favor.

"Hold on." She reached the edge and peered over the side.

Esme's fingers gripped a wet metal rod holding the aquarium sign. Her face stared upward at Ari. Fear twisted her features.

The rain continued.

Ari's hands slipped. She gasped, closed her eyes, and took a deep breath.

I can do this.

She inched closer, shifted her weight, then reached for Esme's hand, but it was still just beyond her grasp. She scooted forward and tried again. Her body tilted, more off the roof than on.

"Arizona!" Nick's shout startled her, and she nearly lost her balance.

"Hang on, I'm coming down," he said.

"My fingers are slipping. I can't hold on much longer." Esme's panicked cries increased Ari's adrenaline.

"Can you grab my hand?"

"I cannot." Esme tried with her loose hand but wasn't strong enough to pull her body upward. "Please know that I love you, my daughter."

Esme's fingers slipped from the metal pole.

Ari dove off the roof. With one hand, she gripped her

mother's slippery palm. The other hand grabbed the same rod her mother had just released. She struggled to maintain her grip on the slick metal and Esme's wet hand. Beneath them, just off to the left, hung the observation deck.

"Kick your legs. We need some momentum. I think you can land on that lower deck if we time it right."

Esme lifted her head. Tears glistened on her cheeks and in her eyes. "We can try." She kicked her legs and swung back and forth.

Ari's muscles strained. It might work if the movement didn't tear her in two. She winced and moaned, then suddenly, the weight released from Ari's arm. A split second later, metal rattled, and Esme grunted.

Esme dangled from the white railing surrounding the deck. With a groan, she pulled herself up and dropped over the guardrail, hitting the concrete slab with a thud.

Momentary relief flooded Ari's being. But her own predicament hadn't changed. Her fingers cramped. Flames licked her arm muscles from her wrist to her shoulder. The joints strained like any minute they'd release from their sockets.

Nick's head appeared over the edge. "Ari!"

"I can't hold on, Nick."

He reached for her.

She strained and tried to pull up. Too weak. She couldn't do it. Her fingers slipped. Suspended for a second in the air, she grabbed the edge of the sign with her other hand.

Nick groaned as he stretched. "I can't reach you. It's impossible."

Dear God. Give me the strength to hold on.

"Nick," she screamed. "Nick!"

No response from Nick. A blank space remained where his head had been.

A moment later, his face reappeared. "Ari, listen to me."

She pinched her lips closed and sniffled. "I'm listening."

"I know this sounds crazy, but I want you to let go."

"I can't, Nick. I'll fall."

"Do you trust me?"

Lord, I don't understand. Letting go is contrary to everything I believe. It's always been easier to trust myself. To think that if I'm in control, I can keep bad things from happening. But it was all an illusion. I was never in control of anything, was I?

No matter what happened. God was in control of the outcome. Not Ari.

Unbearable pain cramped in her knuckles. She closed her eyes and grimaced. "I trust you, Nick." *I trust you, Lord Jesus.*

"Let go," Nick shouted over the noise of the helicopter.

And she did.

Time fractured.

Nick and the building receded, leaving only the rush of air and the empty space around her.

A sudden jolt stopped her fall, then an arm snaked around her waist, securing her against a rough, wet material.

"I've got you." A deep voice shouted in her ear. "We're going to climb down together."

Her mind struggled to grasp what had happened as cold metal handrails chilled her palms. A firefighter in turnout gear hugged her from the back. Her feet connected with something solid. Stairs.

"We're going to take this one step at a time. Keep your head up and your hands on the rails." The firefighter's voice was calm and reassuring.

She reached the base of the ladder, and another firefighter gave her a hand to the ground. Blue and red strobing lights reflected off the wet asphalt. A paramedic wrapped her in a blanket then rushed her to a waiting ambulance for evaluation.

Through the crowds and chaos surrounding the aquarium, Nick appeared. Soaked clothes clung to his frame. He'd never looked more handsome.

A sob choked her throat, and tears squeezed from her eyes. How did he escape the shark tank? "I thought I'd lost you."

He rushed forward, scooped her into his arms, and kissed her full on the lips. With a gasp, he leaned back, running his thumb over her wet cheek. "Everything's okay. We're okay." He kissed her firmly a second time, then pulled back, squeezing her hands. "I love you, Arizona."

She cupped his chin in her hands and felt the weight of him against her chest. "I love you, too, Nick."

CHAPTER 50

Friday, 22 November
0845 Hours

"Are you kidding me? I'm not doing that." Ari stopped at the coffee bar in the DSS resident office. The man had lost his mind.

"Come on. It'll be fun." Laughter shook Nick so hard he could barely stand up straight.

"But bungee jumping? What happened to the old Nick, the one who was afraid of his own shadow?" Ari chuckled and shook her head. Last week it was rock climbing, and the week before that, it was white water rafting. "I like a good thrill as much as the next person, but this is too much, even for me."

Nick shrugged and poured hot coffee into a Styrofoam cup for himself, then poured one for Ari. "I've embraced my daredevil side again. I'm not going back into performing, but life is too short and unpredictable, so I might as well make the most of it while I can."

"I'm proud of you. I still can't believe you escaped that shark tank by using my bobby pins to unlock your handcuffs. I didn't realize you could hold your breath that long. Four and a half minutes."

"It used to be longer before the explosion. Lucky for me, Keller didn't do his research, or things might have worked out differently."

Nick and Ari picked up their coffee cups from the beverage bar along the wall and carried them to their back-to-back desks in the bullpen.

A bouquet of roses sat on Ari's desk. She set her coffee down on the desk and smelled the flowers.

"Who are they from?" Nick perched on the edge of his chair.

She snatched the envelope from the card holder and opened it, removing the small white rectangular card. "Esme. Mother."

No one had seen hide nor hair of Esme Aquila since the night of the gala. She'd simply disappeared.

"Do you think you'll ever see her again?"

Ari leaned back against her desk, arms behind her. "I don't know, but something tells me she'll be around the next time I need her."

Maybe they'd never have a normal mother-daughter relationship, but Ari was positive Esme was keeping an eye on her from afar.

Ari's inquiry into her birth certificate had opened an investigation into Judge Hawthorne—the corrupt judge who'd pushed her adoption through without the proper paperwork. He was arrested for fraud and awaited sentencing.

Van Sloan waited out his court proceedings at his luxury condominium in Key West, Florida. Ari planned to attend a few of the hearings and provide a character witness. Nick, too. Van Sloan had turned state's evidence on Tyler Keller.

Keller, still in traction after his fall, would be incarcerated in a maximum-security prison without bail once discharged from the hospital, and Reynolds, Burgess, and Dominguez had all been deemed flight risks and were being held in DC until their trials at the international criminal court in The Hague, Netherlands.

Her former boss, Matt Updike, had been charged with aiding

and abetting a criminal. He pled not guilty until the investigator found Keller's fingerprints in Updike's office along with written correspondence threatening Updike's family if he attended the gala or assisted with security that night.

"It all still seems like a dream."

"Which part?" Nick blew across the surface of his coffee, then took a sip. He lowered the cup and licked his upper lip.

"The whole ordeal. Learning I was adopted, that my nightmares were memories. Discovering a group of mercenaries kidnapped me from my homeland." Ari picked up her cup, then crossed her arms. Her vision blurred. "Learning to let go."

A tear dripped, and Nick caught it. He rubbed his finger on his shirt. "Thank you for trusting me."

Ari sniffled and gave him a smile. "You're not the only One I've learned to trust."

He set his coffee cup down, then took her hand in his. "We can't see what lies ahead, but He does. And He's there to catch us when we fall."

"I know that now. You know what else I've realized?"

"What's that?" His thumb rubbed her knuckles.

"The Bible says that the rain falls on the just and the unjust. But God can use that rain to water the flowers—" She caressed the tender petals. "Or He can flood an entire city. Neither of those choices is within our control. Just His. And while I can't control what happens around me, I can control my perspective. At the end of the day, whatever happens … it's in His hands, not mine, and I just have to trust that He knows the reason why."

Nick grabbed her other hand, pulled her close, and feathered a light kiss on her lips. "I'm proud of you."

Heat crawled up her neck. Tucking a loose strand of hair behind her ear, she circled her desk and sat on the rolling chair. "What's on the agenda for today?"

Nick pulled a manila folder from his inbox. "Santiago tossed this over here when you were in your meeting with Deputy

Powers. He wants a security plan in place for Ambassador Beridze's visit to America this next week. She'll be staying at the Grand Palace downtown."

Ari removed her keys, badge, and firearm from the desk drawer, then dropped the weapon into the holster around her shoulders. "Let's go speak with the manager."

Nick chuckled. "Slow down. I've arranged a video call with him at ten thirty. Then, we can schedule a time that works for all of us for a tour of their security measures. After that, we can write up a list of suggested changes or additions."

She dropped into her chair with a loud groan. "That'll take too long."

"That's what our job entails."

She groaned again and banged her forehead on the desk.

"What's wrong? I thought you enjoyed working with me."

Ari raised her head. "I do. It's just ..."

"You miss chasing down the bad guys."

Nick had read her mind. "Exactly. I'm thankful for this job, but I miss being a field agent. I know it bothers you, but I don't mind getting shot at occasionally. I need the excitement. High-stress situations. I thrive on them."

"I understand. I think you're crazy, but I understand."

"That's why I've spoken to my aunt about being reassigned to the special agents' team. She said she would speak with the Secretary of State about a transfer."

"Oh, wow. You're leaving?"

Ari nodded. "Being a DSS special agent would give me the opportunity to see the world. Hong Kong. United Kingdom. South Africa. Venezuela. I've never traveled out of the country before. I wasn't made to sit behind a desk. Can you see that?" She paused. "I'll miss you."

"You've got to do what you feel is best for you. But if that's what you want, I want you to go. I'll be waiting right here when you come home."

One Year Later

Arms full, Ari entered her townhouse through the garage door, kicking off her shoes and releasing a heavy sigh. This last mission had been a long one. But it had been successful, and now, all she could think about was a hot bath, a hot cup of coffee, and Nick.

They'd phoned and messaged as much as possible, but it wasn't the same as being together in person. To feel his arms around her and his lips on hers.

She touched her cheek as warmth heated her skin. Their date couldn't come soon enough.

Humming, she set the mail and her groceries on the dining room table, sorted through three months' worth of ads and bills, then brought the junk into the kitchen and dropped it into the garbage can under the sink.

A note taped on the fridge door caught her attention.

She crossed the room, snatched the paper, and scanned the familiar handwriting.

I'm a terrible poet and can never make a rhyme.
But if you'll bear with me, we'll have a marvelous time.
Get back in your car and drive to Aspen Park.
Follow the signs. Take a walk in the dark.
—Nick

She grabbed her keys and purse off the table, then paused in the mudroom long enough to put her shoes back on before running out to the car, starting the ignition, and driving across town to Aspen Park.

Twenty minutes later, she pulled into the empty lot and parked in a marked space. Before she turned off the headlights, she caught sight of a handmade arrow pointing down the hiking trail.

She climbed out of the car, locked the door, then followed the sign. Leaves and gravel crunched beneath her boots. A chilly wind blustered through the branches and sent goosebumps running down her arms.

A faint light glowed across the field, coming from the gazebo, and Ari picked up her pace. A dark form rose from a sitting position.

She broke into a run, dashed up the steps, and jumped into Nick's arms, kissing him soundly. As he held her, she longed to remain in his arms forever. When his embrace loosened and he set her feet on the wooden floorboards, she leaned back and brushed a tear from his cheek.

A round table sported a tablecloth, a single rose in a glass vase, and a takeout container from Bao House.

"Nick, what is all this?"

Soft music flowed from his cell phone on the corner of the table.

He cupped his arm around her waist and pulled out a chair. "Your seat, mademoiselle."

"Thank you." Ari sank into the chair, setting her purse on the wooden planks at her feet.

Nick knelt, pulled a small velvet ring box from his pocket, and took her hand.

She gasped.

"Since we first met, I have learned that some risks are worth taking, especially where you are concerned. I am ready to risk my heart, to take a leap of faith, if you'll have me. I love you, Arizona Elaine Powers. Will you marry me?"

Ari jumped into his arms and kissed him. He was comforting, strong, and everything she wanted in a life partner. Her fears had lost their power over her, and the nightmares had stopped. The puzzle within her heart had been solved. All the confusion, all the turmoil—gone. She knew exactly who she was, and who she wanted to be.

His wife.

"Yes."

Marriage was the greatest mystery ever, and they would spend a lifetime working to solve it. Together.

THE END

AUTHOR'S NOTE

Thank you so much for choosing *The Puzzle Within* for your next read. This book has been "in progress" for about four years from when I first conceptualized the idea of turning an escape game into a book. I'm thrilled to partner with Scrivenings Press LLC to finally see this story come to life.

It is my prayer that you will enjoy and be blessed by my new romantic suspense novel. I've designed this book to be "an escape room in a novel." It can be savored just how it's written, or if you'd like an extra challenge, you can work through the puzzles yourself and see if you get the same solution Nick and Ari do.

THE GAME MASTERS SERIES

When solving puzzles becomes a matter of life and death ...

In the mind of these villains, riddles and puzzles are more than just games—they're deadly challenges that force participants to confront their pasts, their fears, and their faith. As secrets are unearthed and cryptic codes come to light, each story reveals a hidden darkness lurking just beneath the surface.

Book One—*The Puzzle Within*: FBI agent Arizona Powers and DSS analyst Nick Trueheart are drawn into a treacherous race against time when a diplomatic protection assignment spirals into a deadly escape room challenge. To save an ambassador's daughter—and themselves—they must unlock the hidden secrets buried within their own hearts.

Book Two—*The Escape Game*: When puzzle shop owner Demi Kayne cracks the code her father left behind before he vanished twenty years ago, it leads her to a secluded mansion—and into a deadly trap. Teaming up with Liam Shepherd, a missionary searching for his missing sister, they must navigate a maze of twisted puzzles and buried secrets. But the sinister mastermind who designed the game is always one step ahead… and escaping may cost more than their lives. Coming in May 2026.

Book Three—*The Missing Piece*: Passionate activist Ginny Clarke never imagined her best friend's disappearance would be linked to a decade-long hunt for the infamous serial killer, Cipher. Forced to work alongside homicide detective Freddie Hood, Ginny must unravel Cipher's cryptic messages before she becomes his next victim. As the stakes rise, they both learn that the missing piece in solving the case might just be their own faith. Coming in May 2027.

ACKNOWLEDGMENTS

Thank you to the Lord Jesus Christ. It is only because of His grace that I have stories worth sharing. Thank you for giving me the gift of storytelling.

Thank you to my husband, Daniel, for his support in my dream and all the time, effort, and finances, he's put into making my dream a reality. We make a great team, and I love that about us.

Thank you to my daughter, Lydia. Your enthusiasm for my writing makes me smile. I love that you are following in my footsteps.

Thank you to my beta readers and launch team members. I couldn't do it without you!

Thank you to my editor, Erin Howard. Because of you, The Puzzle Within shines!

Thank you to all my friends and family who have encouraged me along the way.

Thank you to Hannah Linder of Hannah Linder Designs for the beautiful front cover.

Thank you to the judges of the 2024 "GetPubbed" contest for choosing The Puzzle Within as the grand prize winner and giving me this opportunity.

Thank you to Scrivenings Press, Linda Fulkerson, and the authors of SP, for opening your hearts, making me feel welcome, and coming alongside me in this endeavor.

Thank you to Mary Alford, Patricia Bradley, and Joanna

Davidson Politano for your endorsement and support of this book. You are dear friends.

ABOUT THE AUTHOR

Gina Holder is an American hybrid author known for her Christian romantic suspense novels and cozy mysteries. She published her debut novel, *Whither Shall I Go*, in 2017, marking the beginning of her writing career. Her works often weave themes of faith, redemption, and forgiveness, aiming to inspire readers with uplifting messages rooted in Biblical principles.

Holder was raised in a family that fostered her love for books from a young age, which eventually led her to pursue a career in writing. She began writing short stories as a child and crafted her first novel by the age of twelve. Her dedication to her craft is evident as she continuously seeks to grow as an author.

Living in Wyoming with her husband and daughter, Holder

balances her writing career with her role as a stay-at-home mom and an active member of her church community. When she's not writing, she enjoys activities like playing the piano, singing for worship services, cooking for her family, and indulging in Hallmark mysteries.

Holder's novels reflect her passion for creating flawed characters who find redemption through faith. Her stories resonate with readers who appreciate suspenseful plots combined with Christian values. As an author, she is motivated by her desire to bring glory to God through her writing, often incorporating personal experiences and spiritual lessons into her work.

Holder is also an active member of the Christian readers' and writers' community and is involved through her social media and blog, where she shares insights, interviews, and book reviews.

YOU MAY ALSO LIKE …

Failed Protocol by Cindy Bonds

Olivia Lloyd has left the U.K. to work in Texas as head of security for a tech firm. Her training in the British Army had given her a chance to get into the SAS—Special Air Service. But she washed out, with the help of her uncle and his contacts. Now, she was here at her uncle's request—miserable and lonely after running away from her last life-altering loss.

Kenton Matthews' Recon days are over as he now works as a detective in Dallas, offering assessments for security when high-value targets come to town. But a request from an old friend has his heart pounding, as the threat to the large tech firm holds more than just a breach of security.

Kenton is determined to battle the failed mission from long ago and will do everything he can to protect Olivia from facing the same torturous man her uncle did. But can Olivia trust the one man her uncle deems more than worthy?

Get your copy here:

https://scrivenings.link/failedprotocol

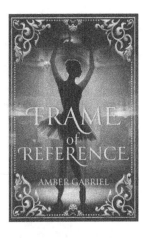

Frame of Reference by Amber Gabriel

One down, two to go.

The prima ballerina with the Grand Kyiv Ballet, Iryna is excited for her American tour—and the chance to reconnect with the brown-eyed American she hasn't seen since childhood. Her trip is just beginning when tragedy strikes, resulting in a close friend's mysterious death and a fear that she might be next.

Rick Carter wasn't looking to fall in love, but the moment he laid eyes on his sister's childhood friend all grown up, he fell hard. Their courtship, however, is haunted by unsettling threats and near-misses. Is someone hunting him and Iryna? And if so why?

As their newfound love deepens, so does the danger surrounding them. To survive they'll need all their wits but also their faith.

Get your copy here:

https://scrivenings.link/frameofreference

Stay up-to-date on your favorite books and authors with our free e-newsletters.

ScriveningsPress.com